400ᵀᴴ ANNIVERSARY

Keeping History Alive…

Your purchase makes a difference, as a portion of the proceeds will be donated to The Leiden American Pilgrim Museum (Leiden, the Netherlands). Contributions will also be offered to the locations where this book is sold, such as the Rijksmuseum (Amsterdam, the Netherlands), the Pieterskerk (Leiden, the Netherlands) and Plimoth Patuxet (Plymouth, Massachusetts, USA).

Praise for *Before the Mayflower*

J.L. Rose pulls her readers into the secretive community of 17th century English Separatism, telling a story as vivid and vibrant as the magnificent Dutch paintings from the period. She follows an obscure group of religious dissenters as they move briefly from England to Holland before voyaging to America, and forever changing world history as they do. Rose has brought to life a fascinating history, woven rich in details and high drama as only a master storyteller can.

Desiree Mobed, Executive Director
Alden House Historic Site, Massachusetts, United States of America

Before the Mayflower reads as a movie. It visualizes details of the past and gives good insight into life at the time, and explains why people fled England and risked their lives to venture to the Netherlands and America. That freedom of religion is still not tolerated in many parts of the world makes this history real and relevant. The book also gives a strong voice to women and the importance of their roles, bringing them to life as essential figures as opposed to silent bystanders.

Marcella van Zanten, Expert Museum Guide
Rijksmuseum, Amsterdam, the Netherlands

J.L. Rose has written a wonderfully immersive story, fluently and convincingly uniting the origin story of the Pilgrims with a tale of family, love and destiny. Her narrative and language really bring to life a distant period in history, in a way that is both richly detailed and genuinely heartfelt. Seeing 17th century Leiden through the Pilgrims' eyes was both a new, enriching experience and what is called in Dutch *een feest der herkenning* (a feast of recognition).

Ward Hoskens, Curator and Conservator
Pieterskerk, Leiden, the Netherlands

Before the Mayflower is not only a moving story on the Pilgrims in England and The Netherlands before they embarked on their most important journey to the New World, but is also interesting because of the vivid and accurate descriptions of several locations in the vicinity of the dwellings of the Pilgrims in the University town of Leiden. The Pieterskerk, the Botanical Garden and the Anatomy Theater of the university really come to life in this novel by J.L. Rose. The visitor unknown to the city of Leiden may use Before the Mayflower as a guide to follow into the footsteps of the Pilgrims during their 11-year stay in the city.

Drs. Kasper van Ommen,
External Relations/Scaliger Institute, University Library Leiden

Before the Mayflower

the

Mayflower

A Novel by J. L. Rose

(1587 – 1620)

For my twins

Published by Choir Alley Press

Before the Mayflower: A Novel / Rose, J. L.
Choir Alley Press
ISBN: 978-0-692-19737-0
400th Anniversary Reprint, November 2020
Copyright © Jennifer Sinsigalli, 2018

Cover: *Winter Landscape with Skaters,* c. 1608, Hendrick Avercamp,
Rijksmuseum, Amsterdam, the Netherlands
Cover Design: Julia Blake

Printed in the United States of America

PUBLISHER'S NOTE

This is a work of fiction. Names, characters, places, and incidents are either products of the author's imagination or are used fictitiously. Any resemblance to actual events or locales or persons, living or dead, is entirely coincidental.

For information regarding bulk ordering, please phone: +1-508-243-3659

www.beforethemayflower.com

✠ Choir Alley Press ✠

Table of Contents

Maps, images, and illustrations precede each chapter.

Introduction

Arriving at the decision to cross the Atlantic Ocean on the ship *Mayflower* in 1620, is a story all its own, filled with risk and romance. The thirty-three years preceding the voyage are revealed in *Before the Mayflower*, a novel highlighting the path of those English aboard the ship who spent more than a decade prior in Leyden, the Netherlands.

This group, including surnames like Brewster, Bradford, Carver, and Winslow, originated in England, separated from the King's Church, and found refuge in Leyden until the *Mayflower* voyage in 1620. There are names of those who might not be as familiar, but are no less important. Names like Robinson and Brewer are significant, but they never made the crossing.

In reading the book, remember that England during this time period was Protestant, the Church of England operating under the authority of the Queen (Elizabeth 1 until 1603, then King James). To separate from the Church of England was a crime punishable by death. Those who wanted reform, or purification, are known to us now as Puritans.

Although some who made their way aboard the *Mayflower* desired reform and had Puritan leanings, the group featured in this book are those that separated from the King's Church, fleeing to the Netherlands prior to the New World. One should realize there were some aboard the *Mayflower* who had no issue with the Church of England at all, and were risking their lives to journey to the New World strictly for the opportunity to own land.

Woven into this history is the critical role of the printing press, and how it served this group. Where history is not proven, fictional characters play a part, abiding by the customs of the late sixteenth and early seventeenth centuries, but fictional nonetheless.

In the last pages of the book, the reader can find the list of characters, separated into their categories of "Fact" and "Fiction," along with a glossary highlighting period dialect and wardrobe definitions. Those interested in a further exploration of this history can refer to my list of sources and suggested reading, while for the travel-seekers, I offer the path and list of many of the places I visited in researching and writing this novel.

Dedication

This novel is dedicated to the people who created the history and constructed the core of the story you are about to live. The objective in writing this book is to examine and clarify the journey of these people in the thirty-three years leading up to, and resulting in, their decision to board a ship to the New World. My hope is that many popular misconceptions are erased, with the truth revealed.

I am also dedicating this novel to the memory of my mother, Rose, who passed away in February of 2007, at the age of sixty. Even while suffering from pancreatic cancer, she enjoyed hearing the first few pages of what I had written, the day before her passing. I will never forget her asking, "When do the love interests come into the book?" Many times, I thought about giving up on the project, but recalling that memory of her sitting up in bed that day, eager to hear more, motivated me to press on. Lastly, the book serves as a symbol to my twins, to remind them to generate dreams, follow them, and never quit.

Acknowledgements

My deepest gratitude goes out to my family, who supported me throughout the decade and a half required to craft this work. I am indebted to my husband, Eric, who encouraged me to continue and travel for my research, to England and the Netherlands, and then aided in the care of our twins so I could work as an interpreter in the seventeenth-century English Village at Plimoth Patuxet (formerly Plimoth Plantation).

My research in Leiden revolved around time spent with Dr. Jeremy Bangs, Director of the Leiden American Pilgrim Museum. His museum contains actual items from the period, and when visiting, you are standing in one of the oldest homes in central Leiden. He tolerated my many visits over the last fifteen years, generous in sharing information from his years of research. Also while in Leiden, I was fortunate to meet Ms. Geeske Kruseman through her work at the Weaver's House Museum in Leiden. For the last six years, she has been an unmatched resource regarding wardrobe in the seventeenth century, as well as foodways, art history, language, and many other cultural aspects of the era.

My former colleagues at Plimoth Patuxet have been indispensable, including Alex Cervenak (lead peer editor), Kathy Rudder, Scott Atwood, Rita Hutchinson, Doug and Julia Blake, Paulette Holbrook, Erin Gillet, Kelley Araujo, Kathleen Wall, John Kemp, Malka Benjamin, Chris Messier, Vicki Oman, Dawn Butkowsky, Grace Bello, Sasha Benov, Sydney Tierney, and Kim Crowley. I am thankful to Ben Emery for hiring me, offering me the chance to experience life in the seventeenth century, as a first-person interpreter.

Bringing the 2020 edition to life could not have occurred without the diligence and creativity infused by Emily DeMeritt and graphic artist Julia Blake. Ms. DeMeritt's efforts on the 400-year anniversary edition extended to the editing, procurement of images and the technical support for the forthcoming audiobook, while Ms. Blake provided ingenious maps, customized visuals, and the final formatting for this enhanced version.

Lastly, I am grateful for the family and friends who maintained their interest in the project. My grandmothers asked me about this novel every time they spoke to me, and they did read the first half of the book, but have passed on. For my father, and family and friends who remain to support me, thank you for the years of encouragement and believing in me. At last, you can hold in your hands the result of years of passionate effort. Now I invite you to step into the sixteenth and seventeenth centuries, to learn and live this critical piece of English, Dutch, and American history.

BEFORE THE MAYFLOWER: THE MAP

Edinburgh

GREAT NORTH ROAD

Scrooby

Hull

Humber River

Grimsby

England

The River Trent

Boston

Cambridge

The Netherlands

Dartmouth

The River Thames

London

Amsterdam

Plymouth

Southampton

Kent

Leyden

Delfshaven

Part One

ADAPTED FROM 17TH CENTURY MAP OF LONDON BY WENCESCLAS HOLLAR AND OTHERS, 1688,
PUBLIC DOMAIN

The Tower of London was home to many notable figures, including Queen Elizabeth I, before she took the throne in 1558. Although it is not documented that Secretary of State Davison was held as prisoner in the Salt Tower (shown above), it is plausible, and would have been one of the more "comfortable" locations on the Tower grounds.

Chapter One

To the Tower

February 17, 1587
Early morning, Greenwich Palace, Greenwich, England

The first light of dawn mingled with the fog, and together they danced atop the Thames, beckoning the oarsmen to join them. William Brewster shivered as he cautiously descended the snow-covered steps, unable to decipher the words made by the muffled voices on the jetty below. Even at such a slow and careful pace, the watermen could hear the clatter of his coins, and that alone resolved their debate about the danger of the fog.

William bade the men good morning through chattering teeth and requested transport to the north side of the Thames, just southeast of the Tower walls.

"With the heavy fog and opposing tide, the fare will cost you a shilling," grunted the veteran operator without looking up or slowing his work with the ropes.

William nodded as he boarded the rocking wherry, numbed by the biting wind and coldness of the damp but cushioned seat. The small two-oared craft awaited the arrival of one more early-morning passenger before heading westward and up to London Bridge.

William's senses were stifled throughout the voyage, the cold silence broken only by oars stabbing the river's surface and choppy, murky waters slapping at the little boat. Even the random holes reluctantly granted by the thick fog offered only glimpses of the few boats daring to share the Thames at such an early hour. Chilled to his core despite numerous layers of linen and wool, William was ready to reach land, regain his senses, and begin his walk to the Tower of London.

Snow drifted off the banks and blanketed the frozen London streets with a light, white dust. With swift steps, William shattered the quiet and ice that sealed the cracks in the jetty steps. He could smell the start of the day as the wind delivered the baker's scent from more than one hundred paces away. Perhaps on his return he would enjoy a short rest and small meal from there.

Even though William Brewster worked and lived in the Queen's Court, his appearance and attire were unassuming. Frigid temperatures coupled with a lengthy return trip on the Thames dictated a selection of only the warmest combination of layers his wardrobe could afford. In a nearly futile attempt to keep his feet dry and warm in his leather shoes, he covered them with not one, but two pairs of blue knit woolen stockings. Over his linen shirt he placed his indigo-dyed wool doublet, connecting the hooks to the corresponding eyes on his heavy coal-colored woolen breeches. Woolen garters were strung through loops at the bottom of each of the breeches' legs, marrying the material just below the knee to the stockings. Over the doublet lay his only frieze coat, a weighty garment made of the thickest, most durable wool, woad-dyed to a deep shade of darker blue. Because of the extended exposure to the elements, he added his grayish-brown cloak as a final measure of protection. Completing his arsenal of attire was a brown woolen Monmouth cap.

His bright-blue eyes sparkled like polished sapphires against his soft, pale skin– a face that was perfectly framed by his thick chestnut hair and medium-length brown beard. Brewster cast a distinguished look without striking features. Perhaps it was that he was as balanced in appearance as he was in behavior. A man of twenty years, he was careful in every manner, from managing the details of his clerical court work, to the state of his clothing. William extended his discreet nature and respectable treatment to all he encountered.

It was a fallacy that all men who worked in the court of Queen Elizabeth I were driven mad with ambition. Brewster was a well-learned, intelligent young man filled with integrity, allowing people to trust him. And these were the very characteristics that awarded him the position of clerk to the Queen's highly regarded secretary and recently appointed Privy Council member, Sir William Davison.

As Brewster reached the top of the jetty steps, he was conscious to walk with his head high, even though his heart sank with sadness and drowned in the irony at hand. The Tower grounds, now home to Secretary Davison, stood magnificently before him. Only ten days prior, the secretary was in the company of the Queen, counseling and carrying out her commands. The imposing stone Tower walls had held as its prisoner countless influential men and women over the years. Some lost their heads; others lost many years of freedom. And some were released to achieve even greater power, such as the current Queen of England, Elizabeth, formerly the Protestant Princess Elizabeth, imprisoned by her Catholic half-sister "Bloody" Queen Mary Tudor, thirty-three years before.

Sixteen days earlier, February 1, 1587...

At this time, a different Catholic Queen Mary, this one of Scotland and a cousin to Queen Elizabeth I, had been plotting to assassinate Elizabeth for many years. In the previous summer, Queen Mary proved with her own pen that the threats were dangerously real. An intercepted letter decoded in Mary's hand showed her approval of assassination plans. At the conclusion of her investigation and trial in the fall of 1586, not a soul in England was surprised when the guilty verdict was declared. Queen Mary must be punished by death to save Elizabeth and England.

On the morning of February 1, 1587, after months of agonizing delay, Secretary Davison recited a silent prayer of thanks as he watched Queen Elizabeth sign the order for the execution of her cousin, Mary Queen of Scots.

"God's teeth, Davison. Obtain the Great Seal for this document at once, so I can put an end to this wretched nightmare," announced the Queen with more than a hint of annoyance.

"Of course, Your Majesty," replied Davison, who began gathering his things so he could obtain the Queen's official closure of the document, securing the contents with her image and title molded in wax.

"Oh, Davison, my goodness, there is no need to run off. We have other business to discuss. In fact, the Great Seal can wait until the afternoon," stammered a shaken Queen.

"Yes, Your Majesty, as you wish," responded Davison, who immediately resumed his place at her working table.

Davison was somewhat shocked then, when the following morning the Queen's messenger knocked frantically on the door of his London home, asking with fear in his eyes if the warrant had received the Great Seal.

"Well, of course, as this was the precise order from the Queen herself," answered a defensive Davison.

As he hurried back to Greenwich Palace, Davison felt his stomach churn as the blood drained from his aging face. His years of court experience and history with this Queen warned him of his precarious position. Over the last months, Queen Elizabeth had been especially tortured by the problem of punishing the Queen of Scots. For many years the dangerous and plotting cousin had been held prisoner in rural England, and was deemed not more than a nuisance by Elizabeth. But now, with the proof of Mary's consent to a very real assassination plot, her conviction and death sentence forced Elizabeth to abandon her avoidance and execute the punishment. And simply put, Elizabeth did not want to be held accountable for the death of her cousin, a queen herself.

Elizabeth paced wildly in her chambers, so much so that her ladies were unable to dress her. "There has to be a better way," she muttered repeatedly to herself, and turned to look out onto the intricate gardens and resume her horrible habit of nail biting. She could just make out the lines of her secretary's concerned face as the morning fog swirled in his wake. She almost pitied Davison as he rushed to her private rooms to request a meeting she already demanded.

Her fidgeting stopped long enough for her Maids of Honour to dress her in a rich black velvet gown, the front adorned with three streaming strips of rubies, diamonds, and pearls. Of the three panels, an identical pair of decorative guards were linked beautifully by the complementary middle row, on top of which lay three strands of pearls, each descending at a different length, the middle one bearing a large heart-shaped ruby. Her magnificently patterned white linen sleeves, embroidered with black patterns of acorns, leaves, and roses, lay safely beneath protective strips of fine cobweb silk, they themselves attached to hanging black velvet sleeves and decorated with a series of gold jewels. One of her Maids was having difficulty securing the wide lace-trimmed ruff around the neck of the already agitated Queen.

"Ladies, I cannot be troubled with delay. You know how I despise sitting for these wretched portraits," she huffed.

Last to be secured was a wig styled in four rows of red curls, topped with a modest crown of linked rubies, a large teardrop pearl dangling from the middle of the elegant headpiece.

Davison's instincts were naturally on target, so he was particularly unsettled about this matter of business. He likened it to a game of chess, where here the best he could hope for was a stalemate. The only lawful way to carry out the death sentence of Queen Mary of Scotland was by order of Queen Elizabeth. Everyone from a Privy Council member in London to a farmer in Nottinghamshire knew this. Why then, was Davison saddled with the impossible task of removing this responsibility from the Queen, and finding, as Elizabeth insisted, "another way?"

The guards stepped back and allowed Davison into the waiting area of the Queen's chamber, where his anticipated arrival was acknowledged by one of her many ladies. He would have been surprised had the Queen been ready to receive him. He envisioned her standing by the window, in between her pacing of course, and looking out onto the knot gardens while she nervously bit at the nails she had already chewed away. As he walked through the fog-filled maze, he had made a point not to look up towards her quarters, feeling her fiery eyes cast upon him. He detested this feeling of discomfort, brought on by a situation lacking his control.

The carved wooden door to the Queen's private rooms opened silently, and Davison was ushered inside. He found Her Majesty dressed magnificently, likely sitting for an artist later that morning– a long and uncomfortable task he knew the Queen despised. Still, she sat there stubbornly and awkwardly, pretending to study a document so intently that she never raised her eyes to greet him.

"It is with great displeasure that I learned the execution warrant, in much haste I might add, has received the Great Seal," she stated sternly, never moving her glistening eyes away from the paper. "Davison, do you dare... I mean, care to confirm this?"

"Your Majesty, in accordance with your wishes and in your and the country's best interest, I had the Great Seal placed yesterday evening," answered Davison calmly.

The Queen, with eyes averted, rose as quickly from her crimson velvet-backed chair as her elaborate gown would allow, and turned to face the window. With an increased volume and intensity in her voice, she began rifling off her concerns.

"Do you fail to comprehend the immense burden that you place on me by carrying the entire weight of this execution? Have I not done enough by signing the warrant? Do you not see the dangerous implications of one Queen executing another? Such a precedent would put my own life in jeopardy. Can you not, with all of your diplomatic experience, find a proper solution to this problem? Her jailers are capable of expediting the act. Simply request they carry out the execution immediately, without possession of the warrant."

Davison looked with pity at the back of the Queen's exquisite gown, knowing that whatever he might think to say would not satisfy her.

"Your Majesty, her jailers are law-abiding men who would never, in plain terms, murder the Queen of Scots. The signed warrant is a necessary part of the process. It is the law we must abide by, and therefore it is the law, and not you, that bears the full responsibility of this execution. Be certain that the people of England, and even those on the Continent, understand that you are acting in accordance with the law and as the great ruler you are, who protects herself and her people."

Davison hoped she would turn and face him, but instead, he was forced to continue looking at the back of her gown.

"Yes, Davison, it is clear to me what you say, and I do want this business carried out," she stated with irritation. "I am quite tired and will need a rest before continuing our other business. Please, be on your way."

Their eyes failed to connect that morning, and as Secretary Davison exited the Queen's apartments, his unsettledness turned to fear.

With his mind whirling, Davison ventured to his own quarters to ponder his strategy. The rooms were deserted, except for the presence of his diligent clerk, William Brewster. Davison was too tormented by the present crisis to spend time explaining it to young Brewster, so he hurriedly wished the clerk good morning and shut the door to his private rooms. The secretary was appalled by the Queen's behavior. One certainty was that as the primary representative managing the execution of Mary Queen of Scots, he was at risk of bearing the Queen's emotional wrath, and worse. He recognized the necessity of conferring with his peers, to receive guidance and disperse some of this suffocating responsibility. After slowly consuming a half pint of beer, he sought out Lord Burghley, the Queen's principal advisor.

Secretary Davison nodded to the guard of Lord Burghley's quarters, entering the outer room in haste. He had always been impressed with Burghley's taste in fine art, and slipped away from his obsession with the execution warrant to indulge in the beauty of the artwork in his midst. He marveled at the brightness of some of the blues, yellows, and vibrant reds in the painting above him.

"Ah yes, that must be from Italy, that one," he whispered to himself.

"Of course, Cousin, that is a most valuable piece painted by Titian, a gift to our Lord Burghley from the Queen herself. Certainly, you know how she showers her close advisors with love and gifts," an unexpected voice quipped. It was the Earl of Leicester, Robert Dudley, who had exited Lord Burghley's private room undetected. "Secretary Davison, you look a complete mess," continued Dudley. "Are you ill again?"

"I am sick on a multitude of levels, all over this execution of Queen Mary. After months of delay, the warrant is finally signed and Sealed, and still the Queen desires to revisit the subject and demand that I, as she states, 'find another way.' Both you and I know that should I find another way to rid this country of the Queen of Scots, such an unlawful act would lead me straight to my own execution. Cousin, by all accounts, you are closer to the Queen than all of her councilors combined, so I beseech you, how shall this poor servant proceed?"

Lord Burghley appeared in the doorway and looked with pity at the pleading Davison.

"Secretary, I am afraid neither the Earl of Leicester nor anyone else in this kingdom can help you in this case," said Burghley with sympathy. "The facts are clear, and it is very well-known amongst the councilors that although our Queen understands the need for Queen Mary of Scotland to be put to death, she in no way intends to bear the full responsibility of this execution. It is clear also that the jailers of Queen Mary at Fotheringay have no intention of 'expediting' the execution, as Queen Elizabeth would surely prefer."

He continued, "All Privy Council members present in the Queen's Court tomorrow will meet here, and together we will agree on a path forward. Sir Walsingham is still confined ill at his London home, but he can manage a signature. Speaking of ill, Secretary Davison, you look deathly. Is your palsy acting up again?" inquired Burghley, who looked terrible himself.

Before Davison could respond, Burghley was reminded of his own sickly state, a sharp pain darting up his leg, causing him to wince as he turned to hobble back into his private rooms.

"The gout is bad today, I expect," said Davison, as he too, turned to go.

"Secretary Davison, my friend, our humours are afflicted in some fashion, whether it be physical or mental, or both. It is what we are committed to."

And with that, Lord Burghley closed his door, and Dudley and Davison departed.

The following day happened just as Burghley had promised. The

Privy Council met, and in an overwhelming fashion, they agreed the warrant for Queen Mary's execution should be sent at once to her jailers at Fotheringay Castle. As the Queen's principal advisors, they characterized this immediate action as imperative. And so, the warrant was sent.

For the next four days, Davison continued his regular duties, serving his Queen. Without fail, after tending to various matters, Elizabeth would unleash her imbalanced emotions, railing with rage on the subject of the execution. Secretary Davison would be pelted with these words for the last time on Tuesday, the seventh of February.

The following morning, Mary Queen of Scots met her fate, and with the swing of that axe, Secretary Davison's career at court was at the same time severed. In the days that followed, Queen Elizabeth expressed her deep displeasure with her advisors who, "executed an order that she never commanded or intended to be carried out." Since Davison was suffering from palsy at his London home, Lord Burghley bore the brunt of her fury. It was only when the Queen announced that Davison would be sent to the Tower that the aching and burning from the gout ceased, as Burghley went numb in disbelief.

Only Davison's palsy kept him from the Tower, and that delay lasted only a few days. On the fourteenth of February, just a week after his last meeting with the Queen, a devastated Secretary Davison was escorted to his new London home.

This unjust turn of events convinced Davison's clerk, William Brewster, that he no longer desired a career in the Queen's Court. Secretary Davison served the Queen with loyalty and honor, and his reward was imprisonment in the Tower. And it was still to be decided whether he would face the ultimate punishment of death. Brewster struggled to comprehend the complexities of life and a career at court. The constant competition for the Queen's favor was an unrelenting and lawless battle. Duplicitous behavior driving the actions around him made him uneasy. The pure approach taken by Secretary Davison was a course that Brewster respected, so with his mentor wrongly accused and incarcerated, Brewster refused to commit his life to the Queen's Court.

Returning to February 17, 1587...

The White Tower, an eerily beautiful stone structure, loomed ominously before him. William never had a reason to be this close to the formidable fortress grounds, and he peered up in awe at the layers of walls and towers erected over centuries. He wondered aloud about Secretary Davison's location and then remembered the papers he carried with him, along with the instructions to approach the grounds by the little-known back entrance, called the Iron Gate. The numbness settling into his toes urged him to quicken his distracted pace to a brisk walk, and this increase in momentum crunched the ice with enough force to alert the Yeoman Warder of William's approach.

"Good morrow. My name is William Brewster, clerk to Secretary Davison," stated Brewster while bowing and doffing his cap.

"Papers," said the guard as he held out his hand, and watched Brewster closely as he dipped into his satchel for the documents.

Still watching the visitor out of the corner of his eye, he unlocked the door to the gateway that allowed them into the space between the outer and inner walls, and towards the Warder's post. Brewster silently reminded himself to appear more official, as opposed to looking around and admiring the tiers of white stone and arched gateways defining the fortress' inner walls.

"Yes," the Warder began. "Sign here, and I shall escort you to Secretary Davison. The secretary resides on the top level of the Salt Tower. I will allow you a visit of half of an hour, and remain just outside the door of the secretary's cell. If you do not require the allotted time, simply knock on the door, and I will lead you out."

Brewster nodded, and the two entered the gate of the inner wall. Once in the main fortress area, they turned right, climbed a limestone staircase, then followed the top of the inner wall to the wooden door at the middle level of the Salt Tower.

Brewster looked to his left during the ascent and marveled at the majestic structures within the Tower compound, the White Tower staring back in a menacing way. Brewster only had a few seconds in their short walk along the top of the wall to capture the Salt Tower's architectural pattern, but could see it consisted of two rectangular stone portions on the left and center, and a curved, cylindrical section sitting on the right, closest to the Thames. One cluster of windows sat in the center of the tower, just above the entrance they were approaching. The other identical window grouping lay just to the right of this door, in the turret segment of the limestone tower. A few smaller windows, some of them merely slits in the stone, could be seen in the tallest rectangular segment on the left, and also in the turret. Brewster wondered what kind of view Davison might have from his cell and looked up at the Gothic arch, its frame holding twin rectangular windows with rounded tops, with a third, round window nestled above them.

After inserting and turning his iron key, the Warder pushed the door open and motioned for Brewster to enter. This empty cell merely allowed access to another wooden door, which opened to a narrow spiral stone staircase leading to Davison's cell above them. "The secretary is on the top level of the tower, not a bad location at all," said the Warder as they approached the stairs. After a short climb, he banged impatiently on the door. "Secretary, it is Warder Thorpe. You have a visitor, a clerk from the palace. His name is Brewer. Are you in a proper state to receive him?"

Brewster could hear his mentor rise quickly from his chair, as the wooden legs scraped loudly against the old planked floor. "Yes, Warder Thorpe. Please allow him in."

As Warder Thorpe pulled back the door, the light that spilled out from the cell and tumbled down the dark stairwell surprised the young clerk. The small, east-facing windows served well in allowing the sun to illuminate Davison's sizeable and strangely comfortable quarters. A massive fireplace pushed a wealth of warmth into the room, much of it working to escape with the light past the door and down the steps. There were suitable, even beautiful, floor and wall coverings, surprisingly rich in blue, green, and red colors, and an elegantly carved oak desk and chair opposite the secretary's sleeping area. By far the most impressive aspect of the space was the hearth, built up of white stone, like the surrounding walls. Dark wooden floors and three structural wooden beams supported the wattle-and-daub construction of the ceiling. Even without viewing other cells on the grounds, Brewster recognized that only a higher-status prisoner would be granted placement here.

"Good morning, William," said Secretary Davison as Brewster entered, removing his hat and bowing to the secretary. "Pray, recover yourself. I do say, it is a comfort to see a familiar face. I trust your early-morning journey went without incident?"

"Yes, Sir William, no trouble in any respect getting to you," replied the clerk.

In spite of the welcoming smile on his master's face, dark circles beneath his eyes and a dull solemnity to his gaze revealed the reality of his situation. In greeting Davison, Brewster had smiled in return, relieved to see his fallen master. Both clearly recognized the truth; a highly esteemed official, diplomat and Privy Council member, stationed now as a prisoner on the upper level of the Salt Tower, existed each day not knowing if this one might be his last.

He easily read Brewster's thoughts. "How sad and tragic the reality is, that the higher you rise at court and the more trusted a servant you become, the more likely you are to be a target and to fall even farther than from whence you came. This punishment of body and mind and, even worse, of character, is devastating. Beyond even the present and future career implications, I am now shackled by the most primitive fear of all, the possibility of execution," said Davison as he leaned against the writing desk, holding his tired head in trembling hands, as if he would start sobbing at any moment. Instead, he looked up with urgency, looking revived and almost possessed as he grabbed Brewster by the arm.

"William, you know that I think of you as a son, and have treated you as such. I have done my best over the years to train and guide you. I therefore request that you do not take my current imprisonment as a reason to abandon a career at court. You and I are part of a select and small group of servants of God and the Queen, that truly, with the Lord's direction, have her and the people of England as their priority. Even if the loyalty is not returned, as in this case, it does not mean we should stray from our commitments. My current state is the product of the emotional tide of the Queen. And as emotions evolve, they change, and I have every confidence that Her Majesty will soon rethink this decision and I will be freed, and possibly restored to my former place at court." He inhaled deeply before looking in Brewster's direction.

Brewster took his blue eyes off the worn wooden floor and locked them steadily upon his master. "Master Secretary, it is only possible for me to be honest with you, as I have been from the moment we met at Scrooby Manor. In the time I have been in your service, I have learned a great deal, and I believe I have grown and matured immensely. There is a fundamental principle that I strive to follow, which is to be faithful to my God, my self, and the people I serve. I fear we have a conflict here, since I am now convinced that a career for me at court is more than doubtful. I came to serve you because I believe in what you represent: honesty, propriety, and loyalty to the Queen. To see treatment bestowed upon you of this nature is illogical and unforgivable. I would be going against all my inner principles if I promised to spend my future years in the Queen's Court."

Brewster watched Davison flinch in receiving the words. The dark circles beneath his eyes appeared to sink and deepen with disappointment.

"That being said," continued Brewster, "I would be going against my ideology by abandoning you in your time of need. For this reason, you must continue to rely on me as your loyal servant, throughout this unjust and ridiculous punishment."

Davison's expression swirled with relief and concern as he rushed to bring his index finger to his lips; Brewster's last words could have easily landed him a room of his own behind Tower walls. Davison kept his finger to his lips as his eyes moved to the door that had silently shifted from closed to slightly ajar. Brewster nodded and gathered his belongings.

The visit was short but meaningful, and as Brewster prepared to depart, Davison awkwardly thrust an ink-scribbled paper into Brewster's right hand. Brewster emptied the contents into his brown satchel, so that the paper joined the coins in the cover of darkness. He cleared his throat loudly so the Warder would be alerted to his departure, tucking the leather bag safely beneath his cloak.

"I shall return in one week's time, Secretary Davison, unless you should require me sooner."

Davison nodded in agreement at the timing and turned towards his writing desk, as if he were in a hurry to get back to his work, as opposed to resuming his indefinite, lonely confinement. Expecting to find an anxious guard with his ear pressed against the door, Brewster laughed quietly when he laid his eyes upon a dozing Warder Thorpe.

"Warder Thorpe, I have finished my visit and am ready to be led out," said Brewster as he gently nudged the napping guard. The Warder awoke at once and stood to attention, startled and embarrassed at being jarred from a forbidden rest. They walked in silence, retracing their steps until they reached the Warder's post, where Brewster again provided his signature before being escorted to the outer wall of the Iron Gate exit.

The armed outer guard looked downriver, grunting as Brewster walked past. Brewster proceeded to make leg in deference, as that was in his nature, and in this case he knew they would likely meet again. He tucked his bearded chin inside his cloak, hoping to stay warm enough until he could find an inn or ordinary to eat something and rest. And he also needed to think about what he had promised Secretary Davison.

He followed the scent to the baker's door and ventured into the neighboring ordinary. Originally, he had intended to purchase his bread directly from the baker and lunch on that as he traveled back to the palace. But now he was desperate to remove that curious scrap of paper from his satchel. The other patrons taking their morning meal paid no attention to young Brewster. He was the only solitary customer, and oddly, instead of standing out, it seemed his brown beard and worn frieze coat blended in with the muted wall coverings and faded cushions of the place. The serving woman noticed him and delivered a pint of beer, along with a trencher of bread, cheese, and salted beef. Brewster normally had only a small bit of bread and beer upon breaking his fast. But this day was different, and as he bit into the cheese, he reached into his satchel and retrieved Davison's paper.

Even though the letters were slightly smudged, they were legible enough for Brewster to see that he would be making another stop prior to returning to Greenwich Palace. As he swallowed the last of his beer, he placed his coins on the table, then departed for the now-populated London streets. He braced himself against the wind and cold, as his walk to Fleet Street would take him nearly a quarter of an hour.

Although the icy wind stung Brewster's exposed skin, he was fortunate to have the cold surround him, lessening the attack on his nostrils as he walked to Fleet Street. The bookshops and printing operations lining the street crossed the Fleet River, serving as an open sewer for the refuse of butchers and leather tanners as it flowed south into the Thames. His love of books filled him with excitement as he walked briskly down Fleet Street, breathing in the odors with a proud indifference.

A former student of Cambridge, Brewster could read, write, and speak both Latin and Greek fluently. He had taken to learning languages easily and had a passion for reading many things, most importantly, the word of God. Brewster viewed the task of obtaining books for his Secretary Davison as a reward instead of a chore. The sounds of the printing presses invigorated Brewster as he made his way down Fleet Street. At the corner of Fetter Lane and Fleet Street, he nodded politely at the apprentice who had stepped outside to adjust the sign hanging above the shop entrance. He wiped ink-stained fingers on his blackened apron before straightening the sign. Brewster smiled at the young man's futile attempt to keep his white sign white; the rectangular wooden piece stating the name Biblio was already speckled with black fingerprints. It dangled almost as an afterthought beneath a bigger, well-established sign depicting a brown bear. Brewster slowed his pace to a stop and decided to turn around. He liked the way the bear appeared on the sign, looking scholarly in his carved profile. With the addition of the little sign below, Brewster could hear the bear growl, "Biblio," but in a beckoning way, instead of a threatening one. He appreciated the additional sign, simply the word "book" in Greek. More importantly, he judged in those few seconds that this passionate printer was worth taking a chance on. He expected that doing business with him would buy him, at the very least, the books on Davison's list.

17th century Dutch tile depicting a stone mason, procured from Antérieur Antiquaariat in Leiden, the Netherlands, located next to the Leiden American Pilgrim Museum.

Tiles from this period would often depict an occupation, a game being played, or a religious or military scene. Images of landscapes, animals and floral designs were also popular, the colors dominated by white, blue, yellow, green, and orange. They would be positioned around the hearth, as well as at the base of a wall.

Chapter Two

The Printer

Nicholas Okes was born in 1564 to a skilled stonemason named Robert Okes, and his wife, Catherine, in the village of Brook, located in the southeast quadrant of Kent. Considered an accomplished artist with his ability to lay and shape stone, Robert aspired to train his only son in the trade. That Nicholas would master masonry was so anticipated, most in the village already considered him part of the trade.

Throughout his youth, he assisted his father on Thursday, when he was not attending school. The boy excelled in grammar school, learning Latin and Greek, surpassing his peers in virtually every area of their studies. His aptitude was unmistakably superior, as recognized by his frustrated bench mates and motivating grammar school teacher, who encouraged Nicholas to pursue a scholarship at Cambridge, where he had matriculated.

To the teacher's dismay, when Nicholas turned fourteen, he left his place in the classroom to work alongside his father. He went from reading and writing to hauling dirt and stone, learning how to chisel and shape the rock into perfect pieces for a wall or well, or whatever masterpiece his father was commissioned to create.

It was about twelve months later, while they were building a wall, when Robert found his son balancing on a pile of fieldstone, a chisel in one hand and a mallet in the other, lashing the air recklessly. Gnashing his teeth in anger, he flung his mallet and chisel viciously at the stone, burying his head in his blistered hands. Both father and son recognized the source of the frustration, but until now had failed to speak of it– that Nicholas lacked the skill to become a master mason.

"Father, I hate that I am failing you in this way. I can see in my mind's eye the designs of our work so perfectly, but when it comes to shaping and placing the stone, I struggle miserably. How can it be that the son of a mason is incapable of building with stone?" He retrieved his discarded tools and placed them in the wagon, tears rolling down through the dirt on his face.

As his father sat next to his defeated son, he surprised Nicholas with a smile.

"Son, don't you know what we have discovered over these months working together? Your talents go beyond moving dirt and chiseling rock. You have the ability to plan the projects, design the walls and even buildings. Do not be troubled by the hard labor, and concentrate on the planning. Let me worry about the execution." Nicholas lifted his head and looked up at his father with an even bigger smile, allowing the concern to shed from his face.

"You are right, Father. Together, we can conquer any challenge," he murmured in amazement. They agreed then, that the last year was not without reward. Regardless of his inability to physically fit the stone, Nicholas unearthed an ability to engineer the stone structures, having become adept at planning his father's projects.

As Robert acknowledged his son's skill to design ingenious stone structures, he determined it would be wiser to invest in formal training and education rather than utilize Nicholas's talents as an immediate resource. With his love of books and learning, Nicholas was quite agreeable to this strategy. At the age of fifteen, Nicholas left Kent for Cambridge, where he received a scholarship to study Language, Philosophy, and Religion.

1580, Cambridge University...

After only fourteen exhilarating months, the excitement of Cambridge would be interrupted, as Nicholas was summoned home. The messenger from Kent arrived just after dawn and notified a college official of the need for Nicholas to depart at once. He scrambled to gather a few things and make arrangements for a hired horse so he could return with the messenger. As he readied his horse, the envoy ambled towards him and with a soft, calm voice told Nicholas about the accident.

His father had been badly wounded by the trade he loved, his skull crushed by a fieldstone dropped into a well he was constructing. Nicholas found it difficult to get his words out, feeling as if he were choking on them.

"Is he able to talk?" he uttered in a whisper.

"When I left Brook only hours after the accident, he was resting peacefully with your mother and some of your neighbors by his side. Your mother had boiled in honey the leaves of agrimony, making a warm plaster for the wound," stated the messenger. "Nicholas, he has not been conscious since the accident," which by his tone implied they would be fortunate to return before his passing. "Your neighbor, Master Burton, hired my services and provided adequate funds for our quick return, meaning we can sprint along the Royal Post route with only one overnight stop. With good weather and fresh horses, we shall reach your father in less than two days."

Nicholas wiped a tear away before it could completely escape his eye.

When he arrived home to a house filled with neighbors and met his mother's gaze, her eyes and the tears she could not contain confirmed his father's death.

His parents' landlord, Master Burton, put his arm around him, draping him with comforting contact and consoling words.

"Nicholas, you can be proud. Your father was a good and very gifted man who lived honestly and faithfully."

Nicholas could only nod in agreement as he looked towards the closed door of the bedchamber, where his father's lifeless body was being washed and wound in a linen burial shroud.

Nicholas's heart pulsed in pain as he dared to look across the dark wooden table in the direction of his mother, where she sat and stared blankly at the bread and beer placed before her. Her straw-colored hair, always tucked under her linen coif, hung like a tattered curtain, only partially hiding her tear-soaked cheeks and bloodshot but beautiful gray eyes. Nicholas knew that she was not hungry now, nor would she be in the days to come.

Upon his father's death, Nicholas assumed the role of provider for his mother. He grieved only briefly for the loss of his scholarly life, as it was an impossibility to return to Cambridge. He would have to send for his belongings and withdraw from the College. As he watched his mother breathe heavily, he knew the end of his academic journey was insignificant now. He rose from his wobbly stool and covered his mother's shoulders with his arms, attempting to ease her suffering.

Master Burton took Nicholas aside later that evening, to explain the funeral details in place for the following morning. "The sexton has prepared the grave, and Goodman Hollis will ring the bell at the appointed times. The minister will meet us at the churchyard stile at eight of the clock and say the prayers by the side of the grave, unless the weather forces us into the church. We have already secured the bier from St. Mary, so that come morning, we will proceed to the church. My servants and Master Sutton's servants will carry your father, with you, your mother, and the other neighbors and friends following."

Feeling overwhelmed, an appreciative Nicholas thanked his father's landlord for assisting his mother and him with the unavoidable details that are companions to death.

Early-morning rain pelting the thatched roof stirred Nicholas from his broken slumber. Lightning struck at nearby trees, and the accompanying thunder roared down with anger on the little town of Brook. He washed quickly and waited for Master Burton, assuming that due to the violent weather the sermon would take place inside the church. Arriving promptly and drenched by the downpour, Master Burton entered out of breath, and carrying a soaked pall.

"I did my best to keep this dry, but this weather will not yield," he gasped to Nicholas as he held up the dripping mortuary cloth. "The servants who will carry the bier are not far behind, and I have already spoken with the minister, and it is agreed that we shall have a short sermon inside the church, where your father can rest in the church coffin before we battle the weather for the burial."

As they proceeded in haste to the church of St. Mary, Nicholas did not say or hear much of anything. He felt his mother's body tremble as he helped support her, with one arm wrapped around her and the other reaching down to clasp her lifeless hand. The sound of the bell broke through the silence and rain, beckoning the group as they marched in sorrow to the church. Greeted at the stile by the minister, they filed in, passing through the churchyard and into the church.

The sermon was brief in accordance with custom in the Church of England, and after a few words from the minister, the pallbearers rose to carry Goodman Okes to his final resting spot. Nicholas wanted to honor his father, as did Master Burton, along with two of his father's longtime workers and one well-known mason from Canterbury. The men gathered around the bier and awaited the minister's signal.

Goodwife Okes was having difficulty standing, so she decided to stay seated in her pew until her husband had been moved from the church to the gravesite. She could not even manage to watch her husband be carried from the church, and after his exit, she was unable to stand. Since she was seated at one end of the pew, her neighbors were forced to exit on the other side rather than try to fit by her. Paralyzed, she looked up at them with embarrassment as they returned empathetic gazes.

She felt as if she were drowning in a raging sea, with her inability to command her body to stand and move out into the churchyard. Her vision blurred as she dipped beneath the surface, her emotions pushing her under. She swayed between consciousness and darkness, struggling to find her son and signal for her rescue. He had insisted on being a pallbearer and was now carrying his father out to where his grave lay open, collecting the rain.

Catherine was frantically silent as her body slumped forward, her head slamming into the top of the oak pew. The ungodly sound echoed off the church walls, to be followed seconds later by the terrifying noise of her body and head colliding with the brown-tiled floor. Nicholas and the other pallbearers stopped abruptly, as they were about to step down into the churchyard. He abandoned the bier and rushed to help his ailing mother.

Barely conscious, Catherine was not certain whether the vision of her son kneeling over her was imagined or real.

"Mother, Mother, I am here. It is safe. Be calm," pleaded her panicked son.

She did not know it, but she smiled at him before her last breath passed through her lips. Nicholas gasped when her chest failed to rise again, sensing in that instant her peaceful soul had slipped away.

He knelt by her cooling forehead and pressed his own chilled lips to her skin, willing life back into her.

"You cannot leave me now," he whispered, choking on the fear that pooled in his throat.

As the men around him gently pulled him away from his dead mother, Nicholas went numb, jolted by the horrifying reality that he would bury both his parents that day. Outside the church, the lightning flashed and the thunder pounded the air, drowning out the sound of a young man weeping. Nicholas Okes shuddered in disbelief, in denial that in a matter of two days, he was without his parents and alone.

The storm passed in the time it took to wash and wind Goodwife Okes in her burial shroud. Rays from the sun streamed into the old Norman-built church of St. Mary, soaking the brown floor tiles. Nicholas chose to wait in the church as they prepared his mother's body and gravesite. He sat quietly in a pew, sitting so still he resembled a corpse himself. The gravedigger's tools pounded in a steady rhythm that was strangely soothing to him. At least his parents would be laid to rest together, alongside one another. There was some comfort in that, even though he was sure their souls had reunited the moment his mother stopped breathing.

Master Burton was by Nicholas's side the remainder of the day, in an unobtrusive, respectful way. They spoke infrequently, mainly to discuss the particulars of the day's proceedings and about the small feast to be held afterwards at Master Burton's home. His servants would serve ale, bread, some cheese, and a small amount of meat. There would only be a few sweets, as the specialty baker had limited offerings on such short notice.

"Nothing lavish of course, as your parents would not want that," he said softly.

"But Master Burton, even a small gathering is something I am unable to afford," responded Nicholas, with concern in his voice. He was so devastated he could barely stand, much less worry about how he would pay for his parents' funeral feast.

"Oh, Nicholas, this meal is something that your neighbors and fellow parishioners are providing, as it is the least we can do for your parents and for you. Please, do not fret over finances, and allow yourself the time to grieve. You can stay at your home if you like, but it would please both Mistress Burton and me if you would stay with us for a time."

Nicholas looked back at Master Burton and nodded, seeing through him, as opposed to realizing the concern showing in his benevolent brown eyes. The peal of the church bell startled Nicholas, announcing the entrance of his mother into the churchyard. Having nothing else to say to Master Burton, he turned away silently and made his way out of the church to meet his mother and father, wrapped in linen shrouds and awaiting a covering of fresh earth.

After the ceremony and funeral meal, Nicholas thanked Master Burton for his guidance and generosity, and politely declined his offer to remain with the Burton family. Still dazed by the day's events, Nicholas stumbled towards his parents' small cottage, which looked large to him now. Upon opening the wooden door, he was overtaken by the smell of rosemary, which the servants had used in winding his parents in their linen burial shrouds. They had spread some of the unused herb on the earthen floor to improve the air in the home; instead, Nicholas was smothered by the haunting scent, choking as he breathed in this constant reminder that his parents were gone and he was alone. The rosemary would drive him to madness if he remained, so he collected his clean linen shirts and stockings and humbly returned to the Burton home.

The Burtons were not surprised when they saw the lone figure approaching. Their door stood open upon his arrival, and as he entered, one of the servants took his clothing and showed him to his room on the floor above. It was not until supper that Nicholas exchanged words with his host.

"Master Burton, I am most grateful for your hospitality, which I promise I will not abuse or prolong. My intention is to take a short time to devise a path forward, and I will be on my way."

"Nicholas," said Master Burton gently, "there is no reason for you to make any decisions in haste. Take all the time you require. Our lands here are fertile and plentiful, so you have the option of learning the farming trade. Also, your academic skill would certainly benefit our children as they enter the later forms in grammar school."

Nicholas digested the words as he swallowed his ale, and while he nodded back, he knew that he would not be able to remain in Brook. Although the Burtons were loyal people, his aspirations did not include farming or tutoring, and most significantly, this place reeked of death to him now. After a few moments, Nicholas summoned his courage, turning to Master Burton.

"Would it be possible for you to assist me in recovering my belongings from Cambridge? I long for my books and other personal items, as you might expect."

It was clear to everyone at the table that this request indicated Nicholas's decision to withdraw from Cambridge.

Nicholas, detecting an awkward silence, swallowed hard and shattered it by saying, "I apologize if you are disappointed in my decision to leave University, but I am simply unable to resume my studies. If I am able to retain my scholarship, then perhaps I will return at some later time."

Without a sound, Mistress Burton rose from the bench and wrapped her warm, motherly arms around the proud but somber young man. He closed his eyes to shut out the tears and enjoy every bit of the loving embrace.

Less than a fortnight later, after a long day on the Burton farm, Nicholas was sitting by the hearth, warming his tired muscles and reading about ancient Greece. His belongings from Cambridge had arrived that afternoon and sat piled in a corner of his room, looking as if they would topple over at any moment. He had hurriedly unpacked the trunk, hungry to find the book and page he had been forced to abandon weeks before. The books brought him happiness and comfort. He was whisked away to other worlds as he read- worlds that were new, exciting, and safe. After reading by the light of the fire, Nicholas began looking beyond the words of the books, studying the pages, print, and even the bindings and covers. The fascination with the books' construction overcame him, and in that moment, he became startled as he recognized a way to meld his love of creating things with his passion for books. Could it be that he was to enter the world of printing?

It took every bit of restraint not to wake the rest of the house with this exciting news. For the first time since he departed Cambridge, Nicholas was happy to be alive. Infused with energy by this newly discovered direction, he struggled to quiet his racing mind. He shook his head in disbelief that he hadn't come to this conclusion sooner. What could be a more perfect trade than this one– driving the pulse of academia and pumping knowledge into the world with bound pages of beautiful creations, enduring as masterpieces for centuries to come? He could only manage brief periods of sleep as he looked out his window, begging the sun to rise so he could speak with Master Burton. Nicholas was certain Master Burton would encourage this idea, as he too possessed a love for books. As dawn crept over the horizon, Nicholas repacked his trunk, washed quickly, and returned to the ground floor to wait for Master Burton.

"Printing is certainly a tantalizing trade for an inquisitive academic, but I must warn you, it is highly regulated and controlled. Between the Stationers' Company you will apprentice into, and the overriding censorship power of Her Majesty and her advisors, it will be virtually impossible to exert any real originality into your work, not to mention obtain any measurable wealth in the process," offered a thoughtful Master Burton. He stroked his white beard and pondered Nicholas's revelation. "I believe you are a capable young man, and one that has a dream to follow. There is the chance that your mind is rattled in the wake of your suffering, but I believe in your instincts and character. If printing is the trade you desire to master, then pack your things, and we shall arrange for transport to London. To Fetter Lane, to be exact. I should be able to produce a plan in a matter of hours."

And so as the family gathered for their dinner, Master Burton reviewed the details of Nicholas's departure and quest to find the printer in London that would mold him into a master of the trade.

"As long as you are ready, you can leave on the morrow at dawn. I have hired a cart to take you to the river, where you will catch the long ferry into London. Depending on the timing of the tide and the mood of the Thames, you will likely have to disembark at London Bridge and hire a wherry to take you to the North Bank of the city, where you will make your final river stop at a jetty near to Fleet Street. Even though you will be very close to your destination, the residence of my dear friend Master Matthew Sumner, you will have to hire a cart to deliver your trunk there. Take this letter with you, and be certain you deliver it only to Master Sumner, who will not only have a place for you to eat and sleep, but will ensure that you sign on with the right printer. He runs an inn near the corner of Fetter Lane and Fleet Street called The Grey Stork Inn, and will have you work for your room and board until you are settled at a print shop. I have assured him in the letter that you are a reliable worker, so once you spend a few days together, he will have additional confidence recommending your services to the neighboring printers on Fleet Street."

Nicholas listened intently, looking at Master Burton with respect for his efficiency and influence.

"As for the matter of money, your father's cottage and few acres of land were leased from me by contract, and with his death, the contract expired. If you wanted to stay in Brook, I would facilitate the terms accordingly, but since it is clear you have other intentions, I propose that I lease the cottage and land to a new leaseholder and sell whatever items of value remain, sending you four-fifths of the money from these transactions. I know that your mother had a good spinning wheel, and your father had many valuable tools in excellent condition. I will be pleased to provide you with enough money in advance for you to make your journey and settle in London. I have requested that Master Sumner send me updates on your progress and of your needs. Remember that my old friend can be trusted with anything, which is why I am sending you to him, as you will be safe and in capable hands."

Nicholas tried to contain his enthusiasm, but he could not stop the smile from overtaking his face. "Master Burton, this is more than I could ever expect. I will be forever grateful to you, regardless of the fate that awaits me," exclaimed an elated Nicholas, nearly out of breath with excitement. "I shall spend some time today looking through my parents' things to see what I can use and what I shall keep for memory's sake. Let's move forward with a departure at dawn."

And with that, Nicholas and Mistress Burton, who offered to aid him in his painful project of sorting and sifting through memories, walked slowly together to the Okes's quiet cottage.

Back to February 17, 1587, The Sign of The Brown Bear,
at the corner of Fetter Lane and Fleet Street, London

Nearly eight years later, twenty-three-year-old Nicholas Okes tore himself away from the printing press to unlock the front shop door a little early on that chilly February morning. Intent on increasing sales and not just getting by in his new role as interim shop manager, Nicholas felt compelled to open before his competition. Master Sayer lay bedridden a floor above him, his broken bones mending after a collision with a reckless cart driver. With his left leg wrapped in a plaster of egg whites and wheat flour and bound to an even board, it would be weeks before he was up, running a press.

Master Printer Thomas Sayer's signing on of Nicholas Okes, which he had done partially as a favor to his friend Master Sumner, ultimately turned into a stroke of genius. A young apprentice without parents and a widowed Master without heirs proved a brilliant combination. The Master committed to teaching and the apprentice to learning, both

driven by the passion to put words into print. Nicholas's fluency in
Latin and Greek found use in proof reading and correcting the growing
number of translations his Master gained patents to print.

Bound as an apprentice for eight years, the commitment transcend-
ed the contract on paper, becoming a lifelong connection. This type of
relationship was surely not typical. In Thomas Sayer's long tenure as
Master Printer, many apprentices came and went, some quitting early;
others learned the trade and moved on elsewhere. He was fortunate to
have trained one other loyal apprentice in the past, a man named Daniel Greene, who ran the second Sayer press over in St. Paul's churchyard. Along with journeyman printer George Turner, Daniel manned
the press and sold books from the stall facing the churchyard, at the
sign of The Black Bear.

Some knew the Fetter Lane location simply as The Bear, but Master Sayer preferred to differentiate his two shops based on the types of
books they contained. The Brown Bear on Fetter Lane catered to the
academic, specializing in Greek and Latin translations, covering mainly
Theology and the study of Law and Medicine. The Black Bear, being
one in a row of bookshops in St. Paul's churchyard, had to satisfy a
wide variety of public interests, showcasing popular broadsides, plays,
and pamphlets. During his apprenticeship, Nicholas spent time selling
at this location, which served well in preparing him to take over the
Fetter Lane location following Master Sayer's accident.

Nicholas had noticed William Brewster while he was still a block away.
As he finished organizing one of the shelves and turned to walk back to
the press, he caught a glimpse of the lone figure out of the corner of his
front window. Nicholas shielded his eyes from the sun and could see
the man was probably close to his age, and dressed in a manner placing him somewhere in the middle class. It was clear by how he looked
around at the surroundings that he was new to these streets.

He hurried outside to straighten the white store sign in order to
draw attention. The passerby nodded politely, and Nicholas sighed

with disappointment as he looked up hopelessly at the new white sign he had somehow decorated with even more black fingerprints.

As he turned to reenter his shop, his movement was interrupted by a voice asking, "My good man, can I presume you speak Greek?" as the stranger pointed to the sign hanging above them.

Startled, Nicholas took a few seconds to remember he had added the small white board bearing the name Biblio, the Greek word for book, to Master Sayer's old sign of The Brown Bear.

Embarrassed by his own delay, the printer stammered the word, "utique," in Latin, meaning, yes, he did. They both laughed at this silly mistake and made their introductions, with Nicholas warmly welcoming his prospective customer into the shop.

William appreciated the coziness of the small shop, savoring the chance to be surrounded by endless pages, some ready to be sold, others waiting to be selected and bound.

"Please, feel free to look through any item that stirs your interest," said Nicholas, answering the question that William was about to ask.

Before departing the ordinary, William had decided to memorize the short list of books requested by Secretary Davison. He recognized the need to keep Davison's privacy guarded and threw the secretary's written words into the hearth where he lunched on the bread and cheese. It was especially necessary in this case, as two of the four books would be deemed inappropriate, discussing reformed views that were unpopular with the Church of England and the Queen. After scanning the shelves, William noticed row upon row of unbound printed sheets awaiting an owner and opportunity to be converted into a finished book. The bound religious titles on display were all of the conventional sort, and not what he was looking for. Sensing that his visitor was not finding what he was seeking, Nicholas made the risky decision of offering a view of his more unusual collections, which he warned were not as neatly arranged and sat in the small back room in the shadow of the press.

More than anything, William was most intrigued by the press itself. He nearly stumbled into the back room, as he was fixated on the impressive combination of oak and metal, and not the uneven boards below his feet. His fascination with the press muffled the sound of Nicholas's voice, and almost a minute had passed before William realized Nicholas was talking to him. He turned apologetically towards the printer to request he repeat his question. Their eyes locked, and William could clearly read the distress his silence had created.

"Oh, my friend, I do apologize for ignoring your question. Please be assured that I am here only for books and not to search your inventories or question you regarding any unapproved titles. My stillness was brought on by the beauty and power of the printing press. I am in awe of what you are able to create with what could be perceived as a ruinous weapon. I understand that your business demands the intellect and skill of a clever diplomat to stay intact, both financially and physically," stated Brewster with sincerity. "I am here to purchase four books, which I will write down the titles and authors for you, and if you do not have them on hand, I will return in time to collect them. Please give me an approximation of their cost, and I will pay you half of the amount now, and the remainder once I receive all of the books."

Overwhelmed with relief and filled with the excitement of new business, Nicholas gestured William towards his writing slate, so he could compose the list. Of the four books, Nicholas located two of them immediately, as they happened to cover the benign subjects of Italian art and Dutch map making. They were used books, bound, and in reasonably good condition. After reviewing Master Sayer's register of stock, Nicholas determined the other titles, two considerably controversial religious writings, would have to be retrieved by William the following week. They settled on the amount owed, and with an exchange of money and books, William left the sign of The Brown Bear.

Nicholas watched his customer walk down Fleet Street, back the way he came, until he escaped from view out of the front store window. He chuckled softly and shook his head as he reflected on this curious visitor and his list, which was written with skilled penmanship and in Greek. He sensed in the few minutes of their transaction that his newest customer was an honest man. He expected that doing business with him would bring him, at the very least, the sale of four books.

ADAPTED FROM 17TH CENTURY MAP OF LONDON BY WENCESCLAS HOLLAR AND OTHERS, 1688,
PUBLIC DOMAIN

The sign of The Brown Bear (corner of Fleet Street and Fetter Lane) and The Black Bear (stall in St. Paul's Churchyard), were owned by printer Thomas Sayer. His dedicated (former) apprentice, Master Printer Nicholas Okes, took over the shops following the death of Master Printer Sayer. The invention of the printing press in the 15th century is one of the most revolutionary events in history. The role of the printer and the printing press have a direct link and influence on many of those who journeyed across the Atlantic.

Chapter Three

Westward Ho, Back to Biblio
(the Sign of The Brown Bear)

Five Days Later, February 22, 1587
Late morning, Greenwich Palace, England

Weaving through the garden's elaborate maze, she masked her nervousness by pretending to admire the iced topiary as she hurriedly circumnavigated the massive, frozen fountain before her. So caught up in her charade, she nearly collided with two men talking just beyond the other side of the circular fountain.

"I do apologize. Please forgive my intrusion," said the young maid, who curtsied as she spoke, and in one motion, continued walking before either man could respond.

Adding embarrassment to her range of emotions, Rose Brewer casually but deliberately made her way through the gardens, under the stone arches and past the gatekeeper to the path leading to the jetty steps and the long ferry waiting to take her up to London.

"Westward ho, room for two passengers here!" shouted the oarsman as he worked the ropes, turning his head only slightly towards the jetty steps.

Rose reached the boat just a little short of breath, and with a calm smile paid her fare and stepped aboard. The final passenger, who made his way onto the ferry without any time to spare, moved cautiously to the remaining empty seat, as the rocking ferry had been pushed away from the jetty and out onto the Thames.

"I am sorry about interrupting your conversation in the garden. I was so caught up in winter's effect on the fountain, and in making my way down to the ferry, that I did not see you."

William Brewster turned to his right to locate the source of these words and saw the young maid who had briefly delayed the conversation between him and his friend, Queen's Post carrier Henry Mercer, just moments before by the central garden fountain.

"Do not fret. The incident was fortuitous, as without your sudden reminder, I would have missed this ferry," said William with a gentle smile.

"And," he continued, "in truth, we had finished our discussion and were parting ways, as my friend was due at the stables over a quarter of an hour ago."

Appreciating his efforts to assuage her uneasiness, she smiled in his direction and made her introduction.

"It is with great pleasure, Rose Brewer, that I finally make your acquaintance," exclaimed William. "You see, I am William Brewster, clerk to Secretary Davison, and due to the closeness of our surnames, people are forever confusing you as my sister."

Rose shifted in her seat and adjusted her hat so she could turn more towards William.

"So you are the brother the other Maids of Honour insist I have here at court? How fitting that we meet by happenstance in the middle of the Thames," said Rose, doing her best to suppress her laughter.

"This is ironic," replied William, "since it was my understanding that the Queen does not allow her Maids out of her sight. How is it that you are here alone on the long ferry to London?"

With a sudden downward shift of her eyes, she told him that her trip was of the clandestine sort. "I am not quite sure how it happened, but I managed to get separated from my escort," she said with a very serious expression, and then winked to confirm Brewster's suspicion. "I have a variety of errands, some for the court, and some of a more personal nature. So what beckons you to London, William Brewster?"

"My destination is that of Fleet Street, to retrieve some books I purchased. Since you shed… I mean, lost your escort, I would be happy to assist you in your travels; the streets of London are not without their expert cutpurses and thieves."

She pondered for only a moment before agreeing that it would be wiser to carry out her journey with company rather than encourage trouble and the criminals in the crowds. Rose had her own list of books she was seeking as a favor to her father, who resided in the west part of Kent, so she already intended to make a trip to the book stalls outside St. Paul's, and on to the Fleet Street bookstores if necessary.

The conversation quieted so that William could locate the letter his friend delivered to him by the central garden fountain. It was a luxury, having a trusted friend employed in the service of the Queen's Royal Post, especially one that was willing to bend the rules by exchanging personal letters, something strictly forbidden for those sworn into the Royal Post. Only official government communications were to be handled by Her Majesty's carriers.

Reflecting Back Ten Years Prior, to the Winter of 1577…

The Great North Road, connecting London and Scotland, and cutting through the village of Scrooby, home of the Brewster family, had been pounded both north and south by the hooves of Henry Mercer's horses for the last ten years. The friendship between a Brewster lad ten years of age and a Royal Post carrier named Henry Mercer began late one winter afternoon in 1577, outside the stables adjacent to Scrooby Manor, where William listened for the post carrier's bugle, awaiting the delayed arrival of the day's final rider. The blizzard had slowed Henry's progress, and the cold, wet and weary carrier was relieved to see the boy, who embodied shelter and a warm meal. They worked in quiet unison, removing the drenched saddle and brushing the clumped snow from the horse's coat and mane before feeding and readying him for the night.

Master William Brewster Sr. sometimes stayed up to converse with the carriers, but on this night, he took to bed a little early, leaving the responsibilities of the postmaster to his young but capable son.

Henry and William ate and drank by the light of the dying fire and conversed late into the night, Henry having an eager audience in a boy hungry to learn about the world beyond Scrooby Manor. For the next three years, prior to leaving for Cambridge, William looked out for his friend, Henry Mercer, ready to supply him with a fresh horse, a bite to eat, or a cup of ale. Most of all, he cherished the time to talk and the chance to hear the amazing stories Henry collected up and down the Great North Road.

Returning to February 22, 1587…

William removed his gloves so he could carefully break the wax seal of the letter. The shaky penmanship on the outside of the envelope declared his father's decline in health, something that saddened but did not surprise him. He expected the pages inside were an attempt to dispel the truth, a father vying to depict an image of strength and independence to the very end, so that his son might pursue his own dreams. He could not have known that William remained in London for the sake of loyalty to his fallen master, with no desire to continue his career at court. His eyes stared blankly out across the Thames, clouded by visions of his failing father struggling to keep pace with his receiving and bailiff duties at Scrooby Manor, not to mention the daily demands of an important postal route stop. As London Bridge inched towards them, William carefully returned the letter to the pocket of his breeches and prepared to disembark.

They walked together without words, making the journey to Fleet Street even shorter with their brisk pace. Rose would have preferred a slower gait due to her long and numerous clothing layers and cold, damp leather shoes. Instead, she smiled politely at her unexpected escort as he opened the shop door marked by the signs of The Brown Bear and Biblio, gesturing for her to enter.

Nicholas Okes emerged from the press room just as the door opened, and froze when Rose crossed the threshold. He stood speechless and motionless, in awe of her raw beauty. Unlike most of her maiden counterparts, Rose embodied femininity and attractiveness without completely conforming to the stringent standards of the day's ideal woman. She loved her black hair and soft brown eyes, and did just enough to whiten her complexion. But on this morning, even the most severe whitening agents would not have been enough to hide the redness that erupted in her cheeks upon meeting the gaze of the stationer standing before her. William recognized after a few silent seconds that the two strangers required assistance with an introduction, since both were seemingly paralyzed by a higher power.

"Good day, Nicholas. I have returned for my books and, by good fortune, am accompanied by one of the Queen's Maids of Honour, Rose Brewer, who also has a need for certain printed materials," stated William plainly, pretending not to notice the obvious interest between them.

With his trance broken, Nicholas welcomed them into the store and immediately tended to Rose, asking her about the particulars of her needs. As William had done a few days before, Rose wrote her list of books on Nicholas's slate board.

So entranced by Rose Brewer was Nicholas Okes that he did not hear William request to revisit the printing press in the back room. Nicholas heard a faint voice and turned towards it, responding with a nod, so William went happily to see the press while he waited. He marveled at the beautiful wood and press paraphernalia surrounding him, such as the variety of metal type and balls of ink, wondering aloud how the press might operate. His eyes followed the path of the large wooden frame while his fingertips unconsciously traced the raised metal pattern of an intricate title page design, stealing from its edges remnants of drying ink.

The last bookshop he explored, just two years prior, did not have its own press. Far from the streets of London, sitting on the Breestraat, the main street in Leyden, the Netherlands, Master Thomas Basson set type, but at the time, printed elsewhere. During his recent travels to the Netherlands with Secretary Davison, William had ventured into this bookshop and found much more than a bookseller. A native Englishman,

Master Basson was fluent also in Latin, French, German, and Dutch, and entertained his eager customer with a brief education on the printing trade there. William maintained his fascination with books and printing following that unlikely foreign experience, which he recalled often, and certainly here, as he stood surrounded by books and in the presence of a press. As William repeatedly rubbed his ink-stained fingertips against his woolen frieze coat, the London bookseller interrupted this reminiscing, apologizing profusely for the lengthy delay.

"I am so sorry for your wait," stammered the rattled printer. "I regret to tell you I have here but one of the two remaining books you requested. The last item has been difficult to locate, but I have been promised a copy from one of the sellers in St. Paul's churchyard, which I will procure today. The titles Rose seeks require a trip to the stalls at St. Paul's as well, so I plan to accompany her and assist in her errands, then escort her back to the palace, along with your book. As you know, it is not wise to venture alone in the London streets."

William smiled as he counted his coins, sensing the excitement in Nicholas's voice. "Here is the balance of payment for the books. I trust Rose and my book will return safely to Greenwich Palace this afternoon. I also expect I will have regular needs for printed materials, and am hopeful you can continue to be a reliable source," stated William in a more serious tone.

Printer Nicholas Okes escorted Rose Brewer and the final book for William Brewster back to the palace without incident. And so it continued to happen this way each fortnight for more than three months, with William leaving Secretary Davison and the Salt Tower and making his way over to the sign of The Brown Bear, picking up the chalk and writing out his list, and Nicholas, after a few days, delivering the books to court. Infused in the routine were the complimentary lessons in type setting and printing provided by Nicholas to William at The Brown Bear, along with the happenstance meetings in the palace gardens that occurred between Nicholas and Rose upon nearly each book delivery.

As the weather finally warmed, the court readied for its annual summer progress. The London palaces would have a chance to air out, or sweeten, as the Queen and her entourage toured the English countryside. Brewster remained in the hot, crowded capital, relocating his living quarters to that of his Master's empty London home. With the Queen's Court on progress, William spent even more time at the sign of The Brown Bear, learning so much about the trade and the press that his abilities offered assistance with some of the printing jobs. With his Maid of Honour away on progress, a lovesick Nicholas desperately required and most certainly appreciated the company.

The months passed by, and by mid-January of the following year, 1588, prisoner Davison had been granted access to two of the three Salt Tower levels. Perhaps indicative of his high court status, or merely a sign that the diplomat was to be a longer-term inhabitant of the Tower, William Brewster unknowingly climbed this set of stone spiral Salt Tower steps for the last time.

His fallen master had suffered a bout of accelerated ageing over the last eleven months, but even so, he always appeared calm and balanced to his dedicated clerk. Davison smiled as William entered with his customary sack of books, and started speaking as William stacked the bound pages on the corner of the large wooden desk.

"The Earl of Leicester paid me a visit yesterday, and during our conversation, he mentioned he is in need of a loyal assistant. Your solid reputation brought your name into our discussion, and Leicester inquired about you entering into his service until my future is better known. Such experience would open endless opportunities for a career at court. Leicester will await my response before approaching you, so you do have a choice in the matter."

Before Davison even finished his sentence, Brewster knew he could never work for anyone else at court, regardless of their status or reputation with the Queen.

"Sir, I am most honored to be considered by the Earl as capable of serving him, but please understand my loyalty is with you, and not with the court. After you deem my service complete, I will return to Scrooby Manor and my family, and determine what opportunities exist there. As you know, I am deeply grateful for your guidance and instruction over the years, but it has become clear in the events of late that my future lies outside the realm of our court."

Secretary Davison only presented the option because he promised Leicester he would, knowing in advance that Brewster would respectfully decline at once.

"Your answer in no way surprises me, since over the months I realized you have remained in London out of loyalty to our working and personal relationship. You are an honorable man, and I am hopeful we can work together again. Advise George Cranmer that he will assume your duties of visitation and errands. I bid you a quick and safe journey up the North Road. May God bless you, young Brewster. You have served me well."

Brewster bowed deeply. They embraced, like two men who knew they would never meet again, firmly and with intense emotion, but managing not to hold on too long.

Obediently, William began the preparations for his departure at once, starting with farewells to his loyal London friends. After leaving the Tower and his secretary for the last time, William took his regular route over to the sign of The Brown Bear and greeted Nicholas as usual, but failed to pick up the chalk and write out his list.

"Oh, my good friend, I knew this day would come, but I hoped and prayed it would not be now," whispered a saddened Nicholas, who turned away quickly to gather some scattered papers and collect his racing thoughts.

"Believe me, Nicholas, I too will miss our exchange of words and books, not to mention your gracious instruction in the art of printing, but as we discussed many times, my future lies outside the complex world of this court. Do not fear that this is the end of our friendship, as I am certain Henry Mercer of the Royal Post will find his way here. You can find me up the Great North Road in Scrooby, aiding my father with his responsibilities at the Manor House. Perhaps I will take over his position should his health decline further. The Manor and its grounds are a sight to behold, suddenly interrupting miles of green and flat farmlands, appearing extravagant to most traveling the road. Regardless of its size and ownership by the Archbishop, the place provides the warmth of a smaller, humble home. We will always have room for you and your loved ones.

"As for Secretary Davison's reading requirements, expect to meet my colleague, George Cranmer. I will instruct him how we discreetly manage these needs. Your courtship with Rose Brewer should not be compromised either, but do remember our Queen and the court will likely be on progress and away from London most of the summer anyway."

"William, you need not remind me, as I am haunted by this unavoidable reality. Never fall in love with someone outside your place in society, or even worse, in the service of the Queen. Getting to see my precious Rose must be more difficult than your gaining access to Secretary Davison in the Tower," exclaimed Nicholas with exasperation.

William smiled and nodded back in agreement. "Sometimes, love is not a matter of choosing, and I am certain you will find your way together."

William paused before putting into words his last meaningful thoughts. "Nicholas, please accept my gratitude for your diligence and quiet manner in procuring the controversial religious works and sermons I requested, as I realize this can be a dangerous pursuit, especially with the heightened pressures surrounding Catholics and extreme Protestant stances. I have learned a great deal over these months, as expected from the variety of books themselves, but most valuable to me are the lessons learned of your trade. How tragic it is to be so tightly controlled by the rules created at court and then governed by your Stationers' Company. I do admire your integrity and loyalty to the Company and Master Sayer, and above all your persistence in achieving your dream," finished William, with a steady, genuine gaze.

Nicholas immediately and emotionally echoed William's sentiments as the good friends embraced.

As William stepped out onto Fetter Lane, he turned to face Nicholas once more and, while walking backwards, uttered the parting words, "This is not farewell but simply goodbye for now. May God guide you, until we meet again."

Nicholas nodded, his throat clogged with sadness. Standing silently in the doorway, he watched his friend walk down Fleet Street, back the way he came.

THE DEATH OF ELIZABETH I, QUEEN OF ENGLAND,1828, PAUL DELAROCHE,
MUSÉE DU LOUVRE, PARIS, FRANCE

The end of an era— Queen Elizabeth I ruled England for forty-five years, taking the throne at the age of twenty-five. A Protestant leader, she was married not to a man, but to her country, referred to by some as the 'Virgin Queen'. Many seeking religious reform hoped that her successor would promote such change, but when King James I of Scotland took the throne, his priority was to preserve his authority, and enforced conformity with the rules of the Church of England.

Chapter Four

A Change of Reign

15 years later, May 24, 1603
London, England

She closed her eyes and slowly lowered her head, barely touching his soft newborn head with her lips, and breathed in as much air as she could. Mistress Rose Okes inhaled the scent of her infant son, born two months earlier, on the same day her beloved Queen left the earthly world. Rose would never trouble her husband Nicholas or her other young children with her fears, but it deeply disturbed her that the birth of her son Robert matched the day of the Queen's death.

Queen Elizabeth, unlike Rose's mother, stayed supportive and loyal to Rose, even when she married "beneath her status" against the wishes of her shamed parents. Unlike many of the other Maids of Honor, who chose to marry covertly in the hope of escaping Elizabeth's wrath, Rose spoke directly to the Queen about her love for printer Nicholas Okes and their desire to marry. In contrast to some of her counterparts, a marriage to a printer could never threaten the throne. Regardless, a lifelong commitment was expected from her closest Maids. For Rose Brewer, the key to obtaining the Queen's blessing was honesty and the ultimate loyalty- remaining in Her service even after marriage.

Nicholas and Rose married in June of 1591, after courting for four years following their chance introduction on Fleet Street. They lived apart even after marriage, until the birth of their first daughter. When Elizabeth was born in the fall of 1595, the Queen bestowed her blessing upon her loyal Maid and infant daughter, granting the gift of freedom to leave court.

Nicholas had purchased the property on Foster Lane in the spring of 1595, from the widow of a fellow master printer. The sign of The Rose marked the shop, a place he had eyed shortly after meeting the Rose he would marry. Since taking ownership, Nicholas had invested in a more impressive sign, still bearing a rose, of course, but now a brighter, richly carved and red-painted flower welcomed customers into the shop. The building, sandwiched between a baker and a brewer, was by no means extravagant, but at the same time not without its adequate space. Nicholas recognized the place needed to contain his shop and press, as well as inventory. Most importantly, he desired suitable accommodation for his bride and their future family. There would also need to be room for an apprentice and compositor and possibly even servants, and the location at the sign of The Rose provided just that.

For Rose Brewer, a woman born into the gentry class, educated as such and then serving as a maid to the Queen, moving into the sign of The Rose would be a drastic change. But for this Rose, the change was welcome and inviting, as she traded a world filled with pageantry and political games for a life dedicated as a housewife to a loving man. The elaborate palaces, sophisticated apparel, and exquisite meals were happily exchanged for a more physically demanding, but overall simpler existence. She had her memories from her childhood in Kent and from the Queen's Court, and that would be enough.

Returning to May 24, 1603…

Not long after sunrise, her newborn son, Robert, had started to squirm. She held him, watching him closely to see if he would settle back to sleep or if he needed her milk. The voices coming from the ground floor below had become even louder, and she presumed this indicated the arrival of her cousin, Master Thomas Brewer. Pleased as always to see her close relative, Rose, in this instance, was irritated not only by the commotion, but by the decision that had been made for her and the children to leave London and travel north, accompanied by Thomas and his retinue of servants.

"It is the wise thing to do," assured her nearly panicked husband. She pleaded with Nicholas to remain in the city with him for the summer, but he was convinced this wave of the plague would be devastating, and he wouldn't allow his wife and children to be counted among its victims. Between caring for her two daughters, eight-year-old Elizabeth, Rose, aged five, and a newborn son, this mother had no energy to spare in debating with her husband on the matter. Of their two servants, Katherine would make the trip north, and Margaret would stay behind at the sign of The Rose with Master Okes and his apprentice, Thomas Corneforth.

Katherine knocked lightly on the door, careful not to disturb Mistress Okes and her infant. She entered quietly and, with a nod, indicated the carts and coach were being loaded, confirming this by closing the lid of a wooden trunk filled with clothing and linens. Rose decided to remain in the privacy of her room until she was summoned for the departure. She trusted Katherine to ready her girls and finish packing for the journey. Rose clung to her son even closer and savored the moment of sitting silently in the comfort of her own chair; the exhausting journey would be desperately long and physically taxing.

The rhythm of her husband's footsteps on the stairs announced their departure. As Nicholas entered with a forced smile, Rose reached for him to embrace her and their son.

"Nicholas, I do not want to live like this forever, constantly running from the present to preserve the days ahead. We should stay together at all times and let life unfold as God has planned," said Rose in a whisper but with great emotion.

"My dear Rose, if you stay in London, the plague will likely capture at least one of our children and probably you as well in caring for them. Anyone with the means to leave London, who wants to survive the summer, will go. I only wish I could make the trip with you, but the press must run, especially with King James now taking the throne, as I have numerous requests to print sermons and broadsides speculating on reform of the King's Church. This change of reign could alter how we are allowed to worship, and even relax the policies within the Stationers' Company. It is an exciting and hopeful time, and certainly, our press could help propel this wave of change. It is critical that our family remain intact to enjoy these new freedoms and reap the benefits associated with them."

Rose almost pitied his enthusiasm, and did not want to insult or disrespect him by disagreeing. She had been by the Queen's side for over ten years, and anyone who experienced life at court understood the struggle of obtaining power and then maintaining it over time. The talk in London was that this Presbyterian King of Scotland could lead the path of religious reform, and the more extreme Protestants, patiently awaiting this change for years, welcomed him to the throne. In Rose's mind, the new King would simply follow where his predecessor left off, and maintain the church hierarchy that would, in turn, preserve his power.

"Oh, husband, I hope for us all that your vision holds true, but in the meanspace, I am faced with a long journey up to Scrooby Manor, which I am dreading. I must gather all my strength to convince the children otherwise, as they are little mirrors to my mood. Come, let us forget the things we cannot control, and spend our last moments in prayer."

Together, they huddled in silence and hope, and prayed.

Thomas Brewer made numerous valiant attempts, but he could not manage to hide the smile on his face. He sat across from his cousin, Mistress Okes, as the coach jolted its reluctant riders out of London. He knew she was putting on a good show for the sake of her children, and that the last thing she wanted to be doing was making a journey up the Great North Road with her infant son and two small girls.

"Cousin, the journey will be as tolerable as possible, as young Hugh Mercer of the Royal Post is a bit ahead of us, and he will alert the post stops of our arrival. We should have no issues in securing proper accommodation or meals at the better inns along the way. Everything we can control is in order. Just pray the weather cooperates, as heavy rains and muddy roads could be our biggest obstacle."

Rose rolled her eyes and shook her head in disgust. She was irritated on a number of levels, and her well-intentioned but far less experienced younger cousin was not making the situation any better for her.

"Thank you, Thomas, for all of the travel insights. I spent ten years traveling with the Queen on summer-long progresses. A trip up to Scrooby Manor is nothing but a short jaunt to me. What I don't appreciate is being told to leave my home and drag my children with me, without any real discussion," stated Rose, doing her best not to appear upset.

"But Cousin, it is primarily because of the children that you are making the trip. The plague will ravage London. What loving mother and wife would keep her children in a hot, filthy, plague-infested city if she had the chance to escape to a manor in the country? You will be welcomed warmly by old friends, who have children of similar ages. I exchanged letters with William Brewster only weeks ago, and even he suggested you leave London to stay in Scrooby. This is not a game. This is about the life of your children, not about debating a point or having control." Thomas leaned forward in dismay and drew back the curtain to alter his view and calm his emotions.

Thomas's comments stung, and Rose shifted uncomfortably as they bumped along the road. She knew he was right, at least about getting the children out of London. Not having a part in making decisions was inherent to her gender and role as a housewife. She should have been wise enough to accept that. In the weeks after the birth of Robert, her emotions were unusually erratic, and she was still consumed by the disturbing fact that her son shared his date of birth with that of the Queen's death. Perhaps time would assist her in overcoming what she hoped was an unfortunate coincidence and not an ominous mark of things to come.

Her two daughters were attempting to stick their heads and arms out the small coach window, pretending to wave to the invisible onlookers as if they were the queen on progress.

"I am the oldest, so I should be the queen," announced young Elizabeth with conviction.

"Well, the Queen is gone now, so there is no queen. I should get a place in the window, as Princess Rose."

"I am older, so I get the window space, and that's that," responded Elizabeth in a frustrated tone.

The two girls resumed their quest for sole possession of the window space, now physically jockeying for position. Rose sighed as she watched her daughters. She was counting the minutes before the two would get bored with this game and start arguing about who could get out of the rickety coach and ride pillion saddle with one of the servants.

Thomas attempted to read a sermon Nicholas had loaned him earlier that day, which had been left anonymously at the door of the shop. Many original manuscripts found their way to the printer's door, most of them never having a chance to be set in type, at least not legally. Within the legal process, there would need to be two separate readings, one by the appointed clergyman, and then one by someone within the Stationers' Company before a license would be granted. This painstaking process might take many years, and, worse yet, result in rejection of a license altogether. So it was not uncommon for a work to be left mysteriously at a print shop, or a printer to take the risk of printing without a license.

Rose watched her cousin as he struggled to keep the pages still, the coach jarring them as the wheels fought against the deep ruts in the road. The other challenge he had was the sloppy pen of the author; most original copies existed in a generally shabby state. His hat rested on the seat beside him, revealing his curly black hair. Although he combed it back neatly, the rough journey loosened a number of longer locks out of place. The rebellious curls danced along, drawing attention to his pale-green eyes and long dark lashes. Rose marveled at her young cousin's appearance, as not only was he always handsomely dressed, but the color of his eyes seemed to alter according to the season. There were times when she could have sworn his eyes were nearly blue, and the next time she would see him they would look green again. It was a very strange but appealing feature, and Thomas Brewer most certainly had no trouble in attracting interest from the opposite gender.

A man of twenty-five years, of the gentry class, having earned a degree from Oxford and some years of study at Gray's Inn in London, Thomas Brewer was desirable on many levels. The Brewer family owned acres of land rich in Fuller's Earth, a vital component in wool cloth finishing. This grand estate would be sought after by just about any woman in England. He was taller than most men, but Thomas's most definable qualities were the invisible traits of honesty and humility. An entrepreneurial spirit coupled with unusually accurate instincts in merchant trading also drew the attention of young women. But Thomas never sought women aggressively. He relied on the Lord and believed firmly that God would lead him to his bride.

"Cousin," whispered Rose, trying to get Thomas's attention without waking her son. Thomas looked up from the sermon he was reading.

"You are right. We must get the children out of London. I apologize for my ugly behavior and want you to know I do appreciate your assistance and accompaniment to Scrooby Manor. My head seems to swim these days, and it pains me to be without my husband," murmured Rose as her quiet voice trailed off.

"Do not worry, Cousin. Your apology is accepted, as we are family and in this together," he said tenderly. "It truly is a pity that your parents chose to cast you off simply because Master Okes does not hail from gentry stock. If our family had any sense at all, you and the children would be on a much shorter journey south to Kent. But let's forget the ignorance of others and see the good fortune that lies ahead in Scrooby with the Brewsters. Once we arrive at the manor, I will stay a day or two to ensure you are settled, and then I will continue over to Gainsborough to conduct business there. I will stay with the Hickman family and won't be far in the event you require me."

"What dealings do you have in Gainsborough?" inquired Rose, relieved to have a fresh start.

"The primary business has to do with Fuller's Earth, of course, coming from our lands in Kent. The cloth makers insist our Fuller's Earth is the finest in all of England, and that with it, they can pound out most of the impurities in the wool. Not only do I seek to expand trade throughout Nottinghamshire, but I am looking for contacts to assist me with distributing and trading in the Netherlands and elsewhere in Europe. In addition, I have begun investigating a more exotic material called cochineal. This intriguing gem is the secret to producing the brightest red dyes in the world. It is so obscure that no one even knows precisely what it is or exactly where it comes from, other than the general area of New Spain in the Americas. I believe my wool contacts can connect me with some men in the dyeing arena, so cochineal may be a worthwhile pursuit."

Although Rose listened intently, her son began to stir and whimper, requesting their talk of business be resumed farther up the road, as the infant required his mother's milk. The timing worked well, with the young girls desiring a break too, so Thomas called to the driver to pull off when possible.

The coach driver sighed with relief at the order since his perch at the reins bordered on punishment. Each and every time he drove the draught team and pulled the coach, he wondered at how such an uncomfortable, tortuous design could have been engineered. He was convinced that the inventor's wife had run off with a cart driver.

Up ahead, he viewed a level, open field with woodlands less than a quarter mile from the road. In just a few minutes the party was at rest, including the team of six horses pulling the coach, and three additional horses for the four servants, with Katherine riding pillion saddle. The flat, open field would make it difficult for preying highwaymen to pounce, since the woodland cover stood far enough in the distance. And the children would have room to run and stretch their legs, and nibble on the bread, salted meats and dried fruit and nuts packed by

Katherine. They all savored a cup of beer, knowing the stop must be brief, as daylight would not wait for them, and the welcoming sign of The White Hart Inn lay twenty long miles north.

The old Norman-built ivory spire of St. Wilfrid's peeked over the horizon, welcoming the tired group to the small town of Scrooby, following nearly four days of bone-jarring travel. Not long after, the horses, servants, and passengers noticed a span of limestone wall about three and a half feet in height lining the west side of the road. This wall connected to an iron gate marking the entrance to the church grounds, and a path on their left that curved up a grassy hill, leading to a south-facing covered entryway. Some turned to look up the small hill and view the church's east side.

Sturdy blocks of magnesium limestone withstanding centuries proved the little Gothic-style church a well-built structure. Some of the travelers noticed battlements running along the tops of the east and south edges of the roofline, as well as on the base of the tower supporting the octagonal spire. Crocketed pinnacles rose from the four chamfered corners of that same tower, adding an eye-catching detail to the small parish church. The clusters of windows, mostly in square limestone frames, contained three long rectangular glass panels with rounded tops. A group of four slim east-facing windows sat within an elaborate arched border, with intricate stone pattern carvings below. Directly above these altar windows, atop the battlement, stood a beautiful cross carved from Roche Abbey limestone.

Rose pulled back the wagon's window curtain, knowing they must be a stone's throw from the manor house now, and could just make out an obstructed outline of the vast estate through the thick rows of chestnut trees lining the Great North Road.

A few paces farther, the two young girls peered wide-eyed out the coach window at the impressive scene before them. After many rolling miles of landscape, speckled with sheep and small, scattered cottages, the extensive manor grounds of the Archbishop of York appeared almost magical. Outbuildings including stables, a large wooden-and-bricked barn, brewery, and stone dovecote, were a sight to behold. Perimeter walls constructed of limestone bricks separated the manor lands from the road, and after another eighth of a mile, the cart driver maneuvered his team to the right and followed the path of the Great North Road to the east, leading to the iron gates of the main entrance. Although the gates stood open, a manor guard stepped out from his bricked gatehouse to meet the visitors. He recorded the names of everyone in the party and returned the heavy, leather-bound book to its desk before gesturing the travelers forward.

The path forked one way to the kitchen, brewery, and bakery, and the other towards the stables. Either direction led to its own bridge spanning the semicircular moat running in front of the main house, which ended on the north side of the property, adjacent to the River Ryton. The coach driver chose the path to the right, only because this path brought them closer to the scent of cooking food and brewing beer. The three horses ridden by the servants went to the left, toward the stables, for the same reason.

Casting her gaze upon the main house and grounds of Scrooby Manor stirred Rose's memories from her days with the Queen on summer progress. During her last four years of service, Rose dreaded the trips out of London, as that put her even farther from Nicholas. The faint, nagging feeling in the pit of her stomach seemed to swell bigger as she scanned the grounds before her, reviving that same emptiness of being separated from her husband.

Signs of tiredness showed on the face of the main house, its age revealed by sagging timbers and a grayish hue to what should have been a bright white exterior. The timber-framed structure, supported and covered in parts by brick, stood proudly, but neglect told its story, rendering it a shadow of its spectacular past.

A bird flying north would describe the shape of the manor house as a letter *E* flipped backwards, with the top and bottom pieces representing two wings and levels of habitation, with connected towers situated on each of their ends. The rooms positioned south and west provided accommodation for travelers, visitors, and some of the kitchen staff, where the living spaces sitting north and west made more permanent homes for the Brewster and Jackson families, along with some of the servants who called Scrooby Manor home. The middle part of the *E* boasted one level with an extraordinarily high ceiling, affording space for the Great Hall and a small chapel, the stone-framed windows facing east.

Connected by a brick corridor to the northern wall of the main house, the Great Kitchen, a bakery, and brewery lay to the northeast, closer to the River Ryton and the mill. These grounds, as a stop on the route of the Royal Post, required two stables. One smaller stable stood to the left of the main entrance gate, right off the Great North Road. Here, a carrier could get a brief rest, perhaps a bit of food and drink, and for certain a fresh horse. A larger stable lay to the north and west of the main house and held other animals, such as cows and sheep. Chickens and goats penned nearer the kitchens afforded easier access to eggs and milk and, eventually, their meat flesh.

Rose counted eight bricked chimneys and guessed there were two sizeable roof openings to accommodate larger fires in the Great Hall and Great Kitchen. Such extensive grounds functioned like a small village and provided habitation for multiple families, servants, visitors, and travelers.

Now, even Thomas felt the strain of travel and eagerly opened the stubborn coach door before his cart driver could do it for him. Before the door opened fully, a panting Jonathan Brewster popped into view, out of breath with excitement, having run from the path by the stables up to the manor to announce their arrival to his mother, Mary, and sprinted back once more to greet Master Brewer and the Okes family.

"Ah, you must be young Jonathan," said Thomas as he smiled, gazing down at the boy.

"Yes," replied Jonathan as he removed his cap, bowing deeply in greeting Master Brewer. "While Father is inside, finishing some business, Mother has arranged any comfort you might desire. There is a meal ready for you, but if you would rather wash up and rest prior, the maids are warming water. Our friend Hugh Mercer of the Queen's Post alerted us to your progress." Ten-year-old Jonathan, who worked to regain a regular rate of breath, beamed with pride as he played the role of host to these special guests his father had told him so much about.

The Okes girls giggled at the sight of the handsome fair-haired boy. To Elizabeth, only two years younger than ten-year-old Jonathan, he seemed nearly old enough to be a young man. His golden hair glistened in the bright sunlight as his sky-blue eyes shone beautifully back at them. Elizabeth crept shyly behind her mother, who was attempting to straighten her coif and hat and smooth her clothes, all while baby Robert shrieked in discomfort. Rose Okes craned her neck back towards the stables to see if Katherine was on her way. There was no sign of her, so she gathered her tired family and followed Jonathan towards the stone steps of Scrooby Manor's main entrance.

Inside the manor house, Mistress Brewster knelt on the floor so she could soothe her frightened daughter, and at the same time get a better look at her bleeding lip. An active three-year-old, Patience Brewster had been racing up and down the hall's widest wooden spiral staircase when her good fortune escaped her. She tripped during one of her many ascents, cutting her lower lip when it slammed into the edge of the top step. The injured child whimpered as she burrowed into her mother's loving arms.

"Little one, you were fortunate. It is just a small bump which will heal up in a few days," promised Mary in a gentle, reassuring voice.

"But, Mother… blood," exclaimed Patience in a quivering voice.

"That's what lips do when you bang them– they are red, remember? Trust me, darling. You will be back to your hippity-hop and clippity-clop before you know it." She was so consumed in caring for her daughter she did not hear her guests entering the main house. She stayed at the level of her daughter's eyes, stroking her light-brown curls until her little girl returned a smile, puffy lip and all. Only then was Mary able to rise to her feet and recognize the bustling activity going on around her.

Rose entered in time to see the scene between Mistress Brewster and Patience, and by this observation, realized she shared a key trait with her gracious hostess. Motherhood, a role granted to the majority of childbearing-age women, did not imply equality among mothers. The mothers offering endless unconditional love were surprisingly rare, regardless of wealth or class. Detecting that genuine love in Mary, Rose was immediately drawn to her.

Mary stood up, still with a hand on her daughter, and smiled warmly at Rose. "Welcome to Scrooby Manor, your home now, away from London."

The two women embraced, sensing the possibility of a long friendship.

"We are grateful for your hospitality and safe harbor from the plague. Some predict this summer to be one of the worst yet," said Rose a little nervously, envisioning her husband working his press back in London. Exhausted and wanting to feed Robert, she cared to exchange pleasantries but also wanted to wash up and begin settling in.

The wife of a postmaster and bailiff for more than a decade, Mistress Brewster understood travelers and their needs. The manor staff could also read visitors, and in moments two maidservants appeared by the banister.

"Yes, well, Anne and Catherine, my most reliable maids, will be assisting you during your time here."

Both women smiled and curtsied to Mistress Okes.

"I'll have Jonathan fetch your belongings," continued Mary. "Do you have a chest with you?"

"Actually, we have two, one for my family and one belonging to my cousin, Master Brewer. I believe Master Brewer plans to stay here a night or two before moving on to Gainsborough," answered Rose.

"Of course," said Mistress Brewster. "Now, allow us to aid you in unloading your things and assist you in tending to the children."

By now, Patience and young Rose had noticed one another and cautiously peered out from the safety of their mothers' petticoats. Finally, Rose began to giggle, and this was invitation enough for Patience to respond with a smile of her own.

"Would you like to hear a riddle?" asked Patience.

"Yes. Yes, I would," answered Rose.

"What is it that has two hookers, two lookers, a snooker, four stiff standards, four dilly danders and a flip-flop?" challenged Patience.

"Oh, I know this one. It is a cow, is it not?" asked Rose excitedly.

"It is! Excellent good," exclaimed Patience with great contentment.

Elizabeth's large brown eyes darted from floor to ceiling, then up and over Mistress Brewster's shoulder, stealing a glimpse of the cavernous Great Hall. This enormous area of the manor house could accommodate meals for hundreds, as well as meetings involving larger numbers of people. Covering the whitewashed daub walls were large but faded textile tapestries. That the manor had fallen into a measure of disrepair failed detection by this eight-year-old child. Growing up in the crowded London streets, she had never before seen such size and scale in a residence, at least not from the inside. Elizabeth watched with both curiosity and concern as bodies rushed to and fro, across the floor of the Great Hall and back, ushering travelers and a post carrier here and there. The overwhelmed expression on the little girl's face prompted a hug from her mother.

"This is a special time that you shall always remember. We are safe here. I promise," said Mistress Okes with a reassuring smile.

"You may follow me, Mistress," said Anne gently. Rose's arms ached as she held Robert close and followed the maidservant down the long hallway planked with dark wood. At the end of the corridor, Anne unlocked an arched wooden door, allowing Elizabeth and her sister up the stairwell before her. Catherine followed the group and secured the door prior to her own ascent.

"Master Brewster requested that you and your family take comfort on the first floor of our North Tower. You will have space enough for the two girls and the baby. Your servants will reside in the adjacent quarters, and Master Brewer on the floor above you. I will start a fire and bring some warm water for washing. I can bring an extra kettle for the girls and help them while you care for your son," suggested Anne.

Rose smiled and nodded, and with that, Anne and Catherine curtsied and hurried off. Before the maidservants had even departed, Elizabeth and Rose moved a wooden stool up to the large bed they eyed as a big, soft playground. Made of two feather-filled mattresses and covered in bleached white linen sheets, the bedstead included a bolster and three pillows, topped with a red-dyed wool thrum blanket. This bed boasted an ornately carved wooden headboard and four posts supporting a majestic silk canopy, reflecting brilliant shades of blue.

Their mother was too involved with caring for their infant brother to notice and order them off the bed. They jumped for a while and then off the bed and up into the arched and bricked well of a window overlooking the grounds. As they made their way off the bricks, they scanned the room's ample space, noticing a dark-brown wooden door that differed from the one they entered by. Careful not to alert their mother, the girls quietly pushed the door open enough so they could peek into the space beyond. To their amazement and delight, an enchanting white stone spiral staircase stared back at them. Their view abruptly vanished as their mother firmly shut the door.

"Girls, must I remind you that we are guests of the Brewsters? We have just arrived, and within the hour, you choose to wander around without regard? There could very well be other guests here you might trouble, or worse yet, you could easily take a tumble down a narrow staircase like that. Elizabeth, I expect I can trust you to understand our place here, and guide your sister. Your father has known Master Brewster for many years, and this friendship is allowing us to be away from London and the worst of the plague. Please try to respect our circumstance and, most importantly, the Brewster family."

Both girls looked down and meekly turned back toward the bed they had been using as a play area. Each girl looked to the other for comfort after the scolding, with Elizabeth hoisting Rose up onto the bed in silence. The chill in the air prompted Elizabeth to stoke the fire, seeking additional warmth as they awaited the arrival of their belongings. Rose had quieted her son as he fed contentedly in his mother's tired arms. The chair in the left corner of the chamber proved a pleasant spot. She closed her eyes and whispered her thanks to the Lord for their safe arrival and gracious hosts. With hands clasped, the girls repeated the words.

And by now Master Brewer had been announced to Master Brewster just outside the Great Hall, where the two removed their hats and bowed. This was likely the third or fourth meeting between the men, as Thomas's trade of Fuller's Earth sent him up the Great North Road from Kent through Scrooby at least once per year. They had known of each other for over a decade before their recent personal encounters, with the Okes family as the common link.

"Smooth journey, I trust," quipped William.

"Yes, in that we were not ransacked by highwaymen or thrown from the coach into a swelling river," remarked Thomas. "The road is a muddy mess in spots, with massive ruts in others."

"Yes, of course. Always an adventure, I am sure," responded an empathetic William. "And my apologies for keeping you waiting, especially after your long journey. An unexpected visit from a close friend making his way to London detained me. His coach and horses are being readied for their departure, so please allow my staff to escort you and your belongings to your chamber. Once you are refreshed, have Samuel show you to the gardens, where we can enjoy a cup of beer amidst the beauty of the grounds."

"Shall I bring my lute and serenade you?" asked a mysterious voice, whose source hid behind the panel separating the great room from the kitchen's serving area.

Thomas turned in surprise at the vaguely familiar voice, and there, walking quickly towards him with the widest of smiles, was Master John Carver. John had been a mentor and close friend to Thomas when studying Law at Grey's Inn in London, where the men occupied neighboring habitations.

"Good graces, Master Carver, have more than three years passed since we last met?" inquired Thomas as the men embraced.

"Thereabouts, Master Brewer," answered John as he looked reverently to the sky. "Thanks be to God that our paths have crossed here at Scrooby Manor. I am glad to see you looking well, and trust such is the case?"

"Yes, and I can see you, too, have been blessed with your health, and perhaps good fortune in your merchant ventures, by the looks of your silk doublet. Master Brewster mentioned you are close to making your departure for London. Is there any chance you might reconsider and delay your journey by a day?"

"We have accommodation for you, Master Carver, and your travel party. I was unaware of your connection to Master Brewer. Please, remain at least for the night," requested William. "We cannot ignore our good Lord and this occasion for company and dialogue. There is much to discuss, especially as our new Scottish King establishes himself in England."

"Enough said," responded Carver. "It will be the most memorable part of my trip, to spend an evening in discourse with you most honorable men. Let me inform my party, who no doubt will be delighted to have a reprieve from traveling this afternoon."

Before long, the men reconvened in the gardens, where they reveled in the aroma of spring's powerful scents pouring from the many rose varieties and lilacs– a perfect backdrop to the free-flowing conversation they rarely shared and so deeply cherished. From sheep to fulling, and from Queen Elizabeth to King James, they covered just about every topic they cared about. Above all, they speculated about the future of the Protestant Anglican Church, and prayed together that, finally, the time had come for the church to be reformed and rid of all things connected with the old Catholic faith, especially popish idolatry, and ways not specified by the word of the Lord.

As the sun began its descent, the men prayed for the new King, that he might make the changes so much of the country yearned for, and that they themselves had been awaiting patiently, as long as memory would serve.

Back within the manor, young Rose and Elizabeth happily accepted Jonathan Brewster's invitation to tour the grounds. Their mother remained with her infant son and savored the peace and quiet. Cradling Robert in her rocking arms, she walked from window to window, there being six in this hexagonal chamber. Out of the last window she caught a glimpse of the expansive manor gardens. She could make out three male figures walking toward the manor, easily identifying Master Brewster and her cousin, Master Brewer. She did not recognize the other man, who appeared about the same age as Master Brewer, dressed in clothes a wealthy merchant or member of the gentry class would wear. His fern-green silk doublet danced with the rays of the sun, reflecting the unique shade of green and shimmer of the rich fabric. His breeches were made of something other than silk, perhaps a blend of wool and linen. They carried a deeper green color, while silk garters matched the lighter green doublet. His hat had a brim of around six inches, adorned with a stylish hatband copying the silk of the doublet. Peeking out from the edges of the hat shone striking strands of reddish-blond hair. Rose could not make out the color of the man's eyes, but she assumed from his fair complexion and the unique color of his hair, they were likely some shade of blue or green. As the three men walked the Scrooby Manor gardens, clearly enjoying each other's company and conversation, she could comfortably insert her husband amongst the circle of friends below her.

Such a gift rarely presented itself to a man running a press and shop in London. Rose worried that Nicholas would work so long and hard that God would take him before he realized his dreams, namely the one of having a home outside of London. They had spent many evenings by the fire, exploring that vision. Now, since Robert's birth, Nicholas aspired someday to design a home built of stone. Convinced that young Robert had inherited his grandfather's talents in masonry, the printer often daydreamed of the day the two would create a home for Nicholas and Rose to live out their last years.

Rose never contributed much. She listened mostly, trying not to reveal her frustration with his preoccupation with far-off dreams, rather than living in and enjoying the moment. She respected a need for planning, but in a world with such extreme uncertainty, with sickness lurking around every corner, the future seemed secondary. Furthermore, life on Earth was dictated and already decided by God's plan, and they both believed that.

The one thing they remained completely connected in was their passionate faith and how they worshipped the Lord. Together, they prayed and worked to serve Him in the right way, according to His written word in the New Testament, as doing anything less could lead to a dreadful eternity. Both believed eternal life and happiness lay beyond their time on Earth. The State religion posed a challenge to families like the Okes and Brewsters, in that the Anglican policies incorporated what these families defined as popish idolatry and superstitious rituals. The use of the *Book of Common Prayer*, rules imposed related to baptism, and other requirements directed at clergy attire were some of the areas questioned by those seeking reform or separation from the Church of England.

Anyone with hope for reform relied on this change of reign for purification. Even through Queen Elizabeth's rule, most seeking reform made some effort to abide by the law and attend services as dictated by the crown. But still, many clung to the truth and sought out worship in other places with a congregation that shared a more intimate covenant and unity. The congregations of their choosing were the true churches, the proper way to worship the Lord while on Earth, prior to their possible departure to eternal salvation.

As Rose continued to peer down on the men and gardens below, she contemplated the irony of the reformist talk likely being spoken on the grounds of Scrooby Manor, owned by an Archbishop. She shifted her eyes from the window and gazed down at her son, nestled as if in a cloud, deep in the folds of the soft linens she held close to her chest.

With a frantic entrance into the tower quarters, Elizabeth shattered the solitude.

"Mother, I have lost Rose," revealed Elizabeth, trembling as she wiped the streaming tears from her cheeks. Even though a knot clenched within her stomach, Rose knew better than to panic. All the years in the service of the Queen on progress made her familiar with sprawling estates and manor homes, and she expected young Rose had allowed her curiosity to lure her to some enchanting nook.

"Elizabeth, please, calm yourself, child. Surely, Rose is close by and unharmed. Where is Jonathan? Was he not taking you both around the manor estate?"

Elizabeth's cheeks grew redder with each word her mother spoke.

"He is looking for Rose. We were playing seek-and-hide, and Jonathan and I ended up in the same place, and after a long while, Rose never came for us. We searched for her for what seemed like ages. We even left the main house and checked the bakery and kitchen area, for fear Rose might have happened upon the cooking hearths."

Before her mother had an opportunity to react, someone knocked lightly on the door. Rose opened it with urgency to find Mary Brewster and a second teary-eyed daughter, this one even more frightened and desperate for her mother's embrace.

"Mistress Okes, I am so sorry to disturb you, but I trust you are pleased to have young Rose back in your sights?"

An embarrassed Jonathan appeared from behind his mother. "Mistress Okes, I do apologize for my careless behavior. I can assure you, it will not happen again."

The mothers exchanged a look of relief. "I believe we are in for an exciting summer, Mistress Okes," said Mistress Brewster, with a veiled smile.

"Most certainly. Motherhood has extinguished any possibility of calm and tranquility for me. With the magical backdrop of the manor, the places and ways to find mischief... I mean, excitement, are limitless," agreed Rose.

"Indeed, indeed. Let this be a lesson to you children. You escaped today with a dose of shame and embarrassment but are physically unharmed. Remember, the Okeses have traveled here as a safe haven and refuge from the plague. Amidst the manor's endless offerings of adventure, there are at times unsuspecting dangers, either from strangers passing through, or more natural threats like flowing waters of the River Ryton or a horse running wild from the stables. Let us enjoy this gift of coming together, and refrain from foolish behavior. Be wise in your choices, and above all, listen to Mistress Okes, me, and the maids, and we shall be in for a most wondrous summer. Please ready yourselves for supper in our private dining rooms. Anne and your Katherine will be along to assist you and the children down."

ROYAL POST-HORSE ROUTES

GRAPHIC BY JULIA BLAKE

William Brewster had a direct connection with the post, as from 1590 and into the 17th century, he managed the postmaster duties while living at Scrooby Manor, a residence owned by the Archbishop of York. Post carrier Hugh Mercer, a key fictional character, plays a critical role in conveying communication throughout the novel.

Chapter Five

The Letters
January 1604 - August 1607

Letter from printer Nicholas Okes to William Brewster
January 20, 1604, London

To my dearest friend, W. B.,
Without it being officially confirmed, but from a source I most definitely trust, the result of the words exchanged at Hampton Court will be less than pleasing to you. I am nearly in tears now, with my hand trembling and hope for reform shattered. I can only assume that you, like most of us, held high expectations for the King to listen and react in kind to the arguments for reform to the State religion. Who could have imagined that the King of Scotland, a country of the Presbyterian faith, would agree to such a conference, only to laugh in the faces of loyal, conservative supporters? The attempt to hasten change has given the new King a chance to publicly respond to reformists' requests, and so he has done such, and tragically the most memorable utterance now being repeated is King James's words of "No bishop, no king."

I do believe some minor changes have been agreed to, and will write again with those details. But I imagine you might have those particulars before me even, between the King's Post carriers and other higher-ranking persons passing through Scrooby Manor.

Brother, how can it be that we have waited so patiently, all these years under the Queen, God rest her soul, believing the future might hold reform? Oh, my heart is breaking. I can say no more in this moment.

Your loving friend,
N. O.

London, January 20
Anno: 1604

Letter from William Brewster to Nicholas Okes
April 10, 1604, Scrooby Manor

To Master Okes,

Your letter came safely to my hands before the close of January, but only now am I in a proper state to write you of my knowledge and thoughts on the matters pertaining to the conference at Hampton Court.

I must admit, my first reaction mirrored that as described in your letter: first sadness, then anger, followed by despair. But I have cautioned myself against such thoughts, and seek direction from the Lord through prayer and reading Scripture. Instead of carrying concern about how things might change, or how they may never change in reforming the Church of England in the manner of a true church, I look now to draw strength from the Lord and His plan. I am working tirelessly to bring competent preachers to Scrooby and the surrounding parishes, as only God knows how far the threat of attacking and punishing nonconformity will be taken.

I have heard from multiple visitors in various positions that King James intends to follow through on his now-infamous statement, "They will conform, or I will harry them out of the land, or worse." I cannot imagine that so early in his reign he would feign such a fierce threat, but I still retain faith in my Lord that this end shall not befall us.

God, His Providence, will answer our questions and calm our fears. I do pray daily that our families can remain in this great land, even with Satan using King James as an instrument of evil, in his attack on the true church.

Before I close, I must inform you that Masters Carver and Brewer have passed through Scrooby, staying here with their groups for nearly a fortnight. You may know already that the two gentlemen plan to embark on some business jointly, with Master Carver intending to move his residence nearer to the Brewer estate in Boxley, Kent. Without having the details, I believe the idea is to take a portion of this business to the Low Countries, with Brewer's supply of Fuller's Earth, and Carver's role in the trade of cloth. What may be of the most interest to you is our talk concerning printing, and the idea of printing religious materials overseas, then discreetly returning them to England. Do not be surprised if this topic surfaces the next time Master Brewer visits London. He made mention of some old type you may be storing in your cellar that could be put to use. Of course, I respect your position within the Stationers' Company and your responsibility to support and keep your family safe.

The months ahead will reveal the extent to which conformity is enforced and nonconformity punished. As far from London as we are here in Scrooby, we are still no safe haven. Instead, we may end up running like foxes, dashing through the brambles and scrambling in the race for our lives.

May the Lord be our guide.

Your loving friend,

W. B.

Scrooby Manor, April 10
Anno: 1604

The following year, a letter from John Carver to William Brewster
April 1, 1605, Okes residence, London

Dear Master Brewster,

I would expect that by the time young Hugh Mercer of the Post reaches you at Scrooby Manor, my travels from the Okeses' home in London to my new residence in Norwich should be complete. In the last months it became clear my business required I be nearer to Norwich more often than either London, Canterbury, or by Maidstone, where the Brewer estate lies. I have found that in Norwich the skill for weaving cloth is abundant, due to the arrival of the Protestant Flemish and those from the Low Countries fleeing religious persecution at the hands of the Catholic Spanish on the mainland.

Even more significant is that God has called me to a congregation. I have been attending services with a French-speaking Walloon congregation, meeting at the church of St. Peter Hungate, and in this group have met a woman I intend to make my wife. Her name is Marie de Lannoy, and her family comes from France, not far from the Staple town of Calais. Some of her family remains in France, and she speaks of wanting to return to the mainland. We will have to see how far King James takes this order for conformity.

Within this parish church of St. Peter, I have met a most remarkable man, Master John Robinson. With certainty, I expect you to know of him, as he hails from your region and is a widely respected theologian. Within the last years he has been assistant pastor at St. Andrew's Church here in Norwich, but for how much longer, I know not. His following is substantial, and for good reason, as God has bestowed great gifts upon him.

Is it true that the godly preacher Richard Clyfton was deprived of his position a month ago? If this pressure increases and the impact is too severe on such loyal servants, perhaps the time to make the mainland home is nearer than we would have imagined.

In terms of business, it is clear that Master Brewer seeks to expand his ventures beyond England. Certainly the demand for Fuller's Earth exists overseas. We may have trouble with that, as the export of this material is banned currently. Master Brewer has discussed spending time in the Low Countries– Amsterdam in particular. He also talks often of his desire to invest in the printing of religious works. Master Okes does have a set of type lying idle in his stores that he could part with. His main concern is that, somehow, when the books are published, the type reveals his identity. He explained we would want to incorporate different plates from a variety of sources to confuse those who might take interest. But this topic is best discussed in person.

Master and Mistress Okes send their blessings and regards. Their children send the warmest of greetings to yours. Mistress Okes in particular is missing your wife. She intends to send her a letter in the coming months. You will hear from me again as well.

Your loving friend,

J. C.

London, April 1
Anno: 1605

Letter from William Brewster to John Carver
May 21, 1605, Scrooby Manor

To my loving friend,
My heart filled with joy upon reading your words about the Walloon congregation and the woman you are courting. How glorious that the Lord has guided you to Norwich and you are able to realize merchant activities while expanding your religious and personal commitments.

Our friend Master Brewer made his way through Scrooby this past week. As you know, he is up in the North now to meet with some of the wool and cloth producers, meetings you no doubt assisted in arranging. He stayed only two nights here in Scrooby, but in that time, he mentioned more than once your courtship with Marie de Lannoy and that you are close to marrying. May the Lord bless you and your new wife.

Our own state here is uncertain with regards to the restrictions of our parish services. What is unbelievable to me is that in this demand for conformity, the existence of competent preachers is so lacking. For years, I have spent countless hours attempting to draw gifted members of the clergy to this area. The King has sent agents inquiring why Sabbath services are not attended each Sunday at St. Wilfrid's, our local parish. I've explained many times it is because the preachers are forced to travel to different parishes in the area, so there are not services occurring at St. Wilfrid's every Sabbath. How is it that they are unaware of this, and require me to inform them?

The greatest irony is that we do gather here at Scrooby Manor, a home to the Archbishop of York, meeting as a true church, as God wants. The risks being extreme, how the next months unfold with respect to the pressure to conform, shall reveal our prescribed path.

In the meanspace, Master Brewer reminded me of his desire to print materials overseas. I certainly appreciate his vision, but fear the timing could be precarious. I did suggest he wait another year, as by then it may be clear whether we should be planning to remove to the Low Countries or some other tolerant place. In his opinion, the odds are against us and our days in England numbered. I do admit, far back in my mind, it stirs with the idea we may need to separate from the King's Church and flee. For now, both Mistress Brewster and I are resolved to remain here as long as possible. Still, we are not frightened by the possibility of our lives altering, should we be forced eastward across the water.

In peace and hope,
W. B.

Scrooby Manor, May 21
Anno: 1605

Letter from Rose Okes to Mary Brewster
December 15, 1605, London

My loving friend,

My thoughts and prayers are with you and your family daily, and I am missing each and every one of you. It seems as if decades have passed since our blessed summer together, just more than two years ago.

The mood here in London, since the failed November attack on the King's life, is filled with fear and dread. As I am sure you have heard, they have placed the blame on a group led by Guy Fawkes. The whole incident has incited those pursuing and demanding conformity; Archbishop Bancroft is a man possessed, out to suppress Catholics and the reformed Protestant alike.

Constraints on the printers are heightened as well. My poor husband grows weary with his work. The time to have material reviewed by the Company's governing bodies and approved for printing has more than doubled. Fortunately, Master Okes is one of the patented printers for Cambridge University and their book requirements. I would think that otherwise, we might have difficulty supporting ourselves. Even if the business deteriorates further, my good husband has already declared he will never leave England. His dream of creating a home built of stone for us remains intact, now more than ever with the birth of Robert. And I, as any good housewife would, will support him to the end.

You can inform Master Brewster that the type Master Brewer has been inquiring about has been carefully packed and is available for transport. I am not sure whether my cousin, Master Brewer, will stop here before his next trip north, but in any case, it is very interesting to me that my husband is now willing to part with the type. It is my belief he is tired of being shackled in this profession, especially now with King James attempting to regulate just about every aspect of our lives.

Please tell me, how are Jonathan and Patience? My Elizabeth and Rose speak of them often, missing them like cousins. I do pray we can be together again. I miss you dearly, good Mistress. What a gift it was to grow our friendship that summer. I long for a friend here I can trust and confide in. Our church, at least our true church, meets privately, so we cannot spend much time chatting before or after our services, which is truly a pity. As far as our local parish church, we go as law dictates.

Praise the Lord that we may exchange these letters safely, in the hands of Hugh Mercer. I pray for his safety, and fear at times we endanger his reputation within the King's Post. There is the reality that this luxury to communicate might someday vanish. I suppose though, as with anything dear to our hearts, there will always be a way.

Your loving sister,

R. O.

London, December 15
Anno: 1605

Into the following year, a letter from Mary Brewster to Rose Okes
April 28, 1606, Scrooby Manor

My dearest friend,
You have been in my thoughts more than ever, as spring slowly enters
to green our landscape and stir the gardens from their winter slumber,
with buds now visible on most of the bluebells, rose bushes, and lilacs.

Even with nature surrounding us with vivid signs of life, the hope
for a future in these lands lessens by the day. Many leaders in the local parishes have been deprived of their positions or excommunicated
altogether. Some have abandoned efforts to resist the government's requirements of conformity and have surrendered their ideals and recited
the State's Oath to Conform.

Those that refuse remain under severe scrutiny, including my husband, and many of his circle residing in Gainsborough. It is clear that
many from the congregation under Minister John Smyth will attempt
a departure from these lands very soon. To think that our group in
Scrooby might be next is frightening, but surely not unlikely. The pressure mounts daily, as just this past Sabbath, two men from the Courts
at York passed through Scrooby and spent many hours waiting here at
the manor to speak with, or should I say, interrogate my husband. As
it happened that Sunday, we were worshipping with the godly Pastor
Richard Clyfton in Babworth. The courts still fail to comprehend that
we are absent from St. Wilfrid's only when no preacher attends there.
So in truth, to obey the law, we must travel the more than five miles
south to Babworth for partaking in the required Sabbath services.

Master Brewster expects conditions here to deteriorate further,
as just more than a week ago, Tobias Matthew was named Archbishop of York, following the death of Dr. Matthew Hutton. The new
Archbishop is infamous for pursuing those he would call recusants,

and is rumored to be seeking out those wanting separation from the Church, and any others not willing to conform to the Church of England's requirements.

We hear the predictions out of London are that the plague should not be so strong this summer. If you learn otherwise, please come straight away to Scrooby. We will be here for certain through the summer months, and it would please me greatly if you were to visit us during this time.

Oh, Mistress Okes, I do miss you dearly. Of course, I never trouble my husband with my fears, but so much has changed since the Queen's death, and in such a drastically different way than we all expected. To think, in just three years since her passing, we would be forced out of our homeland? Almost even more disturbing is that we are not allowed to go freely either; I am unsure how it will all transpire, but would not be surprised if we make a move in less than a year's time. How else can we go on here, being threatened should we worship as the Lord hath instructed? We know no choice but to live as God wants, according to Scripture and as a true church, rather than suffer eternally in the depths of damnation.

You may already know that Master Carver is to be married this fall to Marie de Lannoy of the Walloon congregation within St. Peter Hungate, the union being overseen by the godly Pastor John Robinson. Perhaps you and Master Okes will venture down to Norwich to witness their union and partake in the festivities. Master Carver passed through Scrooby with your cousin, Thomas Brewer, earlier this month, and Master Carver indicated he and his future wife intend to visit her family in France prior to settling in a southern province in the Netherlands. Her family has prosperous contacts in the cloth trade, with a rich and talented history in weaving from France and the Low Countries. This should work well for Master Carver, with his merchant ventures in wool and cloth. Perhaps it won't be long for Master Brewer to make the move from England as well, although he did not indicate as such during the visit.

I do hope in whatever God's plan reveals, I will see you and your family again. You, Master Okes, and the children all hold a permanent spot in my daily prayers. May God bless us all.

Your loving friend,

M. B.

Scrooby Manor, April 28
Anno: 1606

A year later, a letter from Thomas Brewer to William Brewster
March 14, 1607, Okes Residence (Sign of The Rose), London

To my loving friend,

I warn you in advance of the brevity of this letter. As I write from the desk of Master Printer Okes, Hugh Mercer of the Royal Post is taking a short rest while he awaits the completion of my rapid writing.

We thank God Master Carver is now married, and he and his wife have made their way to the Continent. Master Carver expects to remain with her family for some time, and then decide whether to settle in France or in the southern part of the Netherlands. For the moment, I will manage some of his merchant activities, as he intends to coordinate my exportation of Fuller's Earth in addition to his existing cloth ventures.

Something else you should know is that the printing type offered by Master Okes has made its way overseas as well. It remains unclear when or where the type will resurface, but to be sure, it will be used. Perhaps even I will follow these metal pieces across the sea, settling near to Master Carver and spreading the word of our Lord. The flood of this January, no doubt you have heard about it, raged like no other in the southwest part of our country, drowning more than two thousand helpless souls. In so deadly a fashion, our Lord's wrath flowed with fury down the ungodly path our King dares to lead us. The worst may lie in the months ahead, as the banter in London predicts a virulence of the plague like none before it.

Whether you remain in these lands is uncertain, I know. Please remember that at all costs, those of us that share in the true faith must remain close, even while we are being hunted here, or when sea separates us.

In trust,
T. B.

London, March 14
Anno: 1607

Letter from William Brewster to Thomas Brewer
August 23, 1607, Scrooby Manor

To my loving and Christian friend,

I write tonight with a shaking hand. It has become clear that there is no other way than to flee to the Continent. Even I, who understands the gravity of our plight, clung to that last improbable hope that we might remain in England. It is certain now that our departure is not only inevitable, but unmistakably imminent. I tremble inside, with my wife merely months removed from giving birth, our future teetering on the brink of what seems certain doom. How could those who follow the truth and light of God be destined for plight and mistreatment?

Good fortune did arrive by way of Hugh Mercer of the Royal Post, in the form of a subtle but clear warning that he passed authorities traveling north from London, pulling a prison cart with their company. I, as you did with your last letter, write hurriedly as carrier Mercer takes his rest. How terrifying that my wife and newly born child must be forced to endure the perils of travel, unauthorized no less, when they should be kept in the shelter and warmth of this manor house?

Strangely, as these words take shape on the paper, I am finding a great deal of comfort in reading them again. There is an element of peace in all of this, for as treacherous as it is to leave England, it really is the only way. My conscience remains undaunted and confident, as I know that this is no choice, but a path carved out by our Lord.

The gifted Master Robinson, who witnessed the marriage of Master Carver, has moved his family near to Scrooby, and has committed to accompanying our group across the North Sea to the Netherlands. I believe you have read, if not heard directly, his sermons, and know the power of his person. Thanks be to God we have such a gifted teacher and leader in our midst.

As you would expect, our plan is to make our way to the Low Countries and seek at least temporary shelter with the members of the former Gainsborough congregation or the Ancient Brethren. Not even knowing at the moment how we will achieve that end, I cannot say for how long we will remain in Amsterdam.

I apologize at this abrupt ending, but there is some commotion in the Great Hall I must see to. Pray it is not the authorities with a prison cart in tow. I will do everything in my power to keep you informed.

With faith in our Lord,

W. B.

Scrooby Manor, August 23
Anno: 1607

Many from the town of Boston, England sympathized with those attempting to flee England in search of religious refuge. Some trying to leave the country illegally, without permission or a pass for ports, were locked in the Guildhall prison cells.

Chapter Six

No Pass for Ports

Spring 1608, London
The Sign of The Rose (Okes Residence)

The muddy, deep-rutted roads would surely send Royal Post carrier Hugh Mercer into immediate retirement by way of injury, if not an untimely demise. A dirt-coated face and uniform indicated a wet and sloppy journey, but that could not keep the postal rider from traveling as fast as he and his horse could ride into London.

After exchanging letters at the Tower of London, he headed west towards Foster Lane, and the Okeses' sign of The Rose. In this unusual instance, he did not possess any personal letters for Master Printer Okes, but only verbal hearsay passed along by his carrier counterparts.

Mistress Okes stood by the front shop windows, seeking out the bright sunlight on this frosty spring morning. She noticed a man leading a horse begin to slow his pace as they approached the shop, their misty exhalations colliding as the rider secured the lead rope to the metal post outside.

Mercer's mud-covered uniform disguised him as she peered through the window, so his presence before her in the front doorway surprised Rose, if not frightened her at this early hour. The luxury of sending and receiving the written word through a trusted source was not a small thing, and for certain the Okeses appreciated Hugh Mercer and the risks he and his father, Henry, had been assuming for more than thirty years. Since he was a messenger of written and verbal information, his presence might mean the delivery of devastating news as well as anything of a more hopeful sort.

"Good day, Mistress Okes," whispered Mercer, a little short of breath. "I do regret I have only minutes to spare. The roads are slower than ever with the mud and flooding waterways, so I have fallen desperately behind on my route. Please inform Master Okes I learned from a trusted source that Master Brewster, his family, and some of their group have failed to make their departure from this land. It is being said some of the men from the congregation are across and safely in Amsterdam, but the whereabouts of the others is not entirely known. Some are in the hands of the authorities. Others have been released, and their locations remain unknown. That being said, let it be no surprise if some such visitors pass by your sign in need of shelter on their way farther eastward on the Thames. Keep your eyes and ears open in the coming days and weeks."

Rose gasped as Hugh Mercer finished his words, her head spinning with questions to which there were no answers. "May I offer you a cup of beer or something to lunch on before you go on your way?"

"If it would not trouble you, good Mistress, I will have a small cup and take some bread for my travels."

"Katherine, please bring some bread and beer," called Mistress Okes.

The maidservant promptly tended to Hugh Mercer, and moments later, he rejoined his equine partner and tackled the messy London streets.

By now, the children's curiosity led them down to the shop's ground floor, and they rushed to the window just in time to see the young post rider set off. Apprentice John Reynoldes and Master Okes entered about the same time, and by viewing his wife's creased forehead, the master printer knew something was amiss. After Rose discreetly conveyed the information to her husband, Nicholas requested his apprentice afford them some privacy and then gathered his family around the hearth. With hands clasped, they prayed for the safety of their friends and the chance to help them with their escape. Even Robert, with only five years to him, realized something might be wrong.

Looking to the heavens, Master Okes spoke in a soft voice, "We pray to our Lord for the safe passage of our dear friends, the Brewsters, and their company, whether it be to rest here or continue directly over the sea. Please keep them free from restraint, allowing them to reach a haven, unmolested. Amen."

"Amen," responded the Okes family wholeheartedly, and in unison.

A month passed before Mary Brewster and her three children landed at the sign of The Rose. The reunion showed signs of joy, but only after Mistress Brewster, Jonathan, Patience, and the infant, Fear, were safely conveyed to their temporary quarters located behind the room housing the press. This area of the Okeses' residence was a secret inventory space for materials to be hidden from the inspector's eyes. Over the past weeks, Nicholas and his apprentice had relocated these titles to the depths of the cellar, and worked to restore the hearth to a proper working condition.

The underground respite lasted just under a fortnight. An appointed meeting place and time with Master Brewster and young William Bradford downriver in Kent prevented any adjustment to that duration. If circumstances were different, Mary and Rose would have elected to spend another summer together. But both women accepted the Brewsters' stop at the sign of The Rose as the result of their predicament, and nothing they might extend.

For those few days, the cloud of uncertainty and fear lifted a little for the Brewsters. Surely there were moments of uneasiness, like the time when the Stationers' inspectors made an unannounced visit to Printer Okes's shop. The inconspicuous wooden door to the left of the Brewsters' hearth popped open easily enough for the refugees to take cover in the brewer's adjacent stores. Master Okes had acquired some extra space from neighbor Goodman Samuel Horn, a brewer and respectable man sharing a decade-long friendship with the Okes family.

Mary and Rose looked forward to the sun setting, when the children were captivated by dreams, and the women could sit together and share all the things from the half decade before. Rose stoked the coals, ensuring Mary and her infant were comfortable before sitting down again. Mary smiled at her friend, appreciating the moment of being warm and safe, and in each other's company.

"Oh, Rose, what a privilege it is to be here together tonight. For more than seven months, our family and congregation have lived desperately, on the run from the law, not knowing which day might be our last," said Mary softly.

"What happened after you left Scrooby Manor last fall? How did your group get to Boston undetected, and what went amiss there?" asked Rose, in amazement that her friend and youngest daughter were sitting before her.

"We would have left sooner than last September, but decided Fear needed more time in Scrooby to gain strength before setting off. With less than twelve months to her life, she is a miracle having survived the cold, long journey to Boston. We traveled afoot along a route our men deemed inconspicuous, and spent two long nights sleeping on damp and frigid marshy ground. I had prayed to the Lord for Fear's safe passage, but thought it more likely that she would be taken and kept in God's Kingdom rather than tolerate such conditions, being in this world only a number of months. But the Lord granted us more time, and Fear survived the trek to Boston and then the unexpected extended stay there, with our leading men imprisoned in Boston's Guildhall cells."

Mary sighed and shook her head before retelling the events of the previous fall. "We had selected the bustling port of Boston, as between the sheer number of ships and the diversity of people passing through, we thought our chances strong of going unnoticed. That was until the sideways English captain with whom we made arrangements for the crossing took a great deal of our money, then arrived late to the meeting point. Many thought he had simply taken our money and left port. To our relief, we eventually heard ripples of water running against the bow. Moments later the crew began to load our belongings as we boarded the ship. Then chaos ensued, and without warning, the crew turned vile. With no regard for any of our people, especially the women, they roughly took as they pleased. Not long after, the authorities arrived and escorted our entire group off the ship and back into town, where they paraded us to the Town Hall as if we were the Devil's doers.

"What a sight we must have been that night. Though in truth, in time, it came to be known that many in the town sympathized with our suffering and did offer comforts and sustenance. But for our leaders, like my husband, William, there was no real respite from the confines of a miserable prison cell, where he remained for weeks before being removed and imprisoned in Lincoln Castle.

"When our men were eventually freed, we had no homes to return to. That we were free as a congregation was enough, as we journeyed back to the lands near to Nottinghamshire to find a temporary respite and create our next plan of departure to Holland. Never utter a word to a soul, but the blessed Hickmans at Gainsborough Hall in Lincolnshire took many of us in during this last incredibly cold winter, at their great risk and expense. Their situation on the River Trent afforded a hidden pathway to the water, with an underground tunnel from the manor house to the river, covering us when we slipped away the first night of April.

"In this, our second attempt to flee England, using the waterways to reach our means of departure across the sea seemed more prudent, but still, we encountered difficulties. All the women and children had traveled in barks downriver to the meeting point, arriving a bit early. Over time, we found ourselves run aground with the tide of the Humber River traveling out to sea. In the meanspace, some of the men started boarding the vessel of our commissioned Dutch ship. At nearly the same time, armed men, some on horses, were spotted running in our direction. The anxious Master of the ship ordered the anchor be raised at once, and before our horrified eyes, the ship drifted away, taking some of our men and leaving all the women and children behind."

Rose gasped at the terrifying story, imagining herself and her own children in such a situation. "What an unimaginable sequence of events! You must have felt completely helpless watching the ship sail off," Rose said with empathy. "And I can hardly bear to think how the children fared, especially those who understood the meaning of the ship fading into the distance with their fathers aboard."

"I will never forget the vision and sounds of the younger children screaming in confusion as they watched the ship and their fathers sail away. For me it was devastating, even with my husband being one of the few men who stayed behind to assist us. Through these months though, we have come to know that God's plan happens, and instead of lamenting these trials, we embrace our journey. Even with the great inconvenience it caused, we still believe our direction is correct and that whatever occurs, the Lord hath set our path. God tries most those he loves most," stated Mary calmly, with conviction.

Rose sat listening, in complete captivation.

"In short time it became clear that the authorities had nowhere to put so many women and children, as the decision to flee England was not, in the eyes of the law, ours, but our husbands'. We were hurried from one justice to another, over time becoming a burden to the constables. Eventually, our freedom was restored, and in less than a month's time, we had the familiar problem of finding transportation and shelter. Oh, how grateful I am, Rose, to be able to tell this story, enjoying your company in the comfort and warmth of your home."

Rose wrapped her arms around her friend and the sleeping baby.

"I am thankful we are here to be of help to you and the children, as you were to us years ago. We will pray for your safe passage down the Thames to meet your husband, and eventually across the sea to Amsterdam. What are your thoughts of residing in that foreign, bustling city, and do you have any idea of what the conditions are like for those of the congregation who have settled thus far?"

Mary smiled as she adjusted the wool blanket around Fear, gently smoothing the folds across the baby's chest. "Before this unexpected stop in the heart of London, I often wondered what London would be like. Living in Nottinghamshire and Scrooby Manor, providing hospitality to so many traveling the Great North Road and hearing their stories, I thought I had an idea of what to expect. It is still overwhelming to me, the idea of living in a city. My whole life, I have known only brilliant green rolling fields and a great expanse of land, fresh air, and space. I have not spent much time on the streets here, but just in getting to your sign of The Rose, the density of people is difficult to comprehend. The senses are so challenged to process everything at once. I think the foul smells are the most intense, then the sights, followed by the sounds. It is so foreign to me, even here in London, so I imagine it will be a greater challenge in Amsterdam, a place where the language and customs are far different from our own."

Mary continued, "I will say there is some measure of comfort hearing the stories my husband shares about his time in the Netherlands, whilst he served as clerk to Master Davison in our beloved Queen's service, now more than twenty years ago. Who knows what remains intact two decades later, and to be truthful, Master Brewster spoke most fondly of a city called Leyden, not Amsterdam proper. As I am sure you know, Master John Carver and his wife now reside in the Low Countries, living in L'Escluse, a southern place in the Netherlands. Master Carver's wife has a sister named Marguerite living in Leyden, along with a young nephew named Phillipe, the son of her deceased brother, Master Jean de Lannoy.

"And I believe your cousin, Master Brewer, has traveled to and from Amsterdam at least twice since the Queen's death, with his trade of Fuller's Earth, and involvement in book publishing, making use of the type that your husband sent across with Master Carver a handful of years ago. Beyond these connections in this foreign land, we are hopeful of some support from the Ancient Brethren in finding housing and options for employment. This is a much larger congregation of English who separated from the Church of England, seeking refuge in Amsterdam more than a decade ago."

"Oh yes, I believe my husband has received requests to publish materials authored by one of the group's leaders, Pastor Francis Johnson. The risk to print the material was far too great, as this writing would never gain approval by either the Stationers' Company or the King's reviewers, and the printing of it considered treasonous. Master Okes remarked on the group's controversial existence, both within themselves as a congregation, and their reputation in the eyes of the Dutch government. Are your intentions to become one with this group?" asked Rose in a concerned tone.

Mary sighed softly as she looked down at Fear. "You are correct in that this group of more than three hundred is plagued by a past marred with controversy and scandal. Such a complicated history is foreign to our small congregation, which numbers one hundred, if not less now. More important than our size, the guiding principle of a united, gathered congregation bound by a covenant, could very well fail to meld with the turbulence of the Ancient Brethren."

"Mayhaps once you arrive there you will find things to be different than you have learned thus far. The nature of the group could change greatly with the addition of your congregation," offered Rose.

Mary nodded in consideration. "Mayhaps the presence of Pastor John Robinson, the brilliant and profoundly godly man he is, along with Pastors Smyth and Clyfton, will alter their direction. My husband has mentioned only briefly, and without detail, that he and Master Robinson have been discussing another plan should we require that. As I spoke of before, he is most fond of the fair city of Leyden, where an impressive university resides, as well as a growing cloth industry. As we both know, God's plan will guide us, and for now, our congregation lies splintered and separated by a sea. It will be by His grace that we reunite even in Amsterdam."

The resolve of Mary allayed some of Rose's fears about her friend's life in hiding. The Brewsters' ultimate salvation was a path predetermined by God, a fate that wouldn't be revealed until they left this Earth. What worried Rose was her friend's immediate circumstance. Until her friends were safely outside the borders of their mother country, prison or torture might befall them.

And as the two women sat amidst the warmth of the fire, Rose pondered her own future, and whether remaining in London and not separating from the King's Church would lead to eternal damnation. Events from the year before clearly revealed God's displeasure with King James and his people, punishing them with a devastating flood in January, the wrath of the plague, and a terrible drought. In the fall, frightening flames streaked across the night skies, an omen of more terrible things to come. She shuddered as the thought of everlasting torture jarred her soul. Nicholas and Rose had discussed many times the idea of fleeing to the Continent, but the printer held fast to his belief that worshipping covertly in a separated, covenanted congregation was adequate, meaning that Nicholas would remain a Master Printer within the Stationers' Company and the Okes family would stay in England.

The two mothers exchanged loving looks of understanding, and glancing down, holding Fear fast to her chest, Mary joined Rose in prayer as the fire dulled to rest.

As much as the mothers cherished the quiet of night, so did the children who were feigning sleep in the Brewsters' makeshift quarters. Both Elizabeth, now aged thirteen, and Rose, a decade old, giggled as Jonathan excited the fire enough so they could all read the numbers to the game the brewer next door had loaned them. Shut the Box, a favorite of Jonathan's, mixed strategy and addition skills with mostly luck, and as luck would have it, he hadn't lost a game the entire evening. His undefeated ways added evidence to Rose's belief that this young man could do no wrong. Rose's admiration for Jonathan had begun half a decade before, when he rushed to greet their carriage as it rolled onto the grounds of Scrooby Manor. Merely a five-year-old then, Rose still held that memory in place, and now the young girl peered across the righted wooden barrel, enchanted by the Brewsters' eldest child.

"Are you frightened by the journey ahead?" asked Elizabeth. Both Jonathan and Patience immediately shook their heads.

"For us to stay here in England would be far more terrifying. Do you know that the authorities have been pursuing our father for more than a year now? But they lack evidence to keep him imprisoned. Our congregation worships as directed by the New Testament, and the Church of England forbids our gatherings. Not worshipping God in the right way carries with it a punishment that follows us beyond this earth. Our parents have explained that the dangers we face here in

England, or possibly even in Holland, are nothing compared to that."

Neither of the Okes girls responded, although both were thinking the same thing. What would happen to them beyond this life? Like the Brewsters, the Okes family met covertly with a congregation outside of the Church of England, but they also obeyed the King's laws and attended the local parish church. Elizabeth and Rose had heard their parents talking in heated whispers about this very subject, and understood their father would not leave the Stationers' Company or England. Rose tried not to think about such frightening things and instead rested her gaze on something, or in this case, someone more enjoyable to wonder about.

Their candle flickered, reminding them they had time for just one more game of Shut the Box. The dice danced in Jonathan's clasped, shaking hands, and with a smile he gave his turn to Rose, knowing how happy that would make her. And he could not have been more right. Her green eyes shone with more light than the candle, and blushing cheeks showed that in her mind, she had won already. In the end, Jonathan finished the game victorious again, but that gesture would make a lasting mark on young Rose.

Finally, it was time to truly shut the wooden box containing the numbered tiles and dice. They said a bedtime prayer before placing their tired heads on the welcoming feather-filled pillows. Jonathan pulled the wool blankets up and over the younger children, checked that the fire cover was in place, and then slipped under the linen sheets of his own bed. His thoughts were of his father now, as he wondered if he, too, was enjoying the start to a peaceful night's sleep. Jonathan longed to be back in his company and reunited as a family so they could embark on the crossing to the Netherlands. With his eyes closed, he imagined the sights and sounds of Amsterdam. Never before had he been off of English soil. From travelers on the Great North Road, he had learned that Amsterdam teemed with people from all corners of the world, as well as exotic items arriving from the world's farthest reaches. He planted himself amongst it all, finding the sights and sounds exciting. A new everything, from language to land, Jonathan was ready to make the journey east.

BEFORE THE MAYFLOWER: THE MAP

Edinburgh

GREAT NORTH ROAD

Scrooby

Hull

Humber River

Grimsby

England

The River Trent

Boston

Cambridge

The Netherlands

Dartmouth

The River Thames

London

Amsterdam

Plymouth

Southampton

Kent

Leyden

Delfshaven

Part Two

CITY of LEYDEN · LANDMARKS

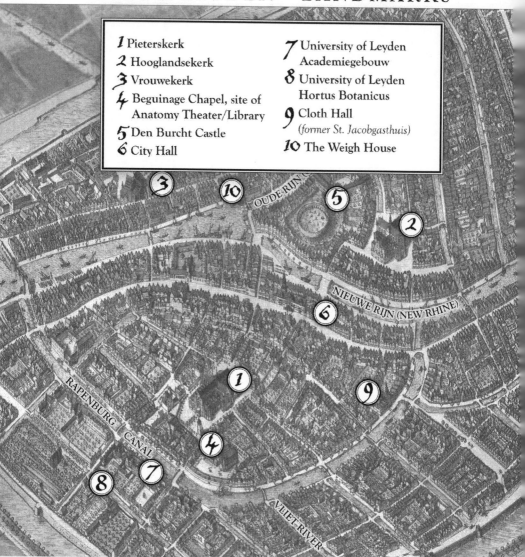

1 Pieterskerk
2 Hooglandsekerk
3 Vrouwekerk
4 Beguinage Chapel, site of Anatomy Theater/Library
5 Den Burcht Castle
6 City Hall
7 University of Leyden Academiegebouw
8 University of Leyden Hortus Botanicus
9 Cloth Hall (former St. Jacobgasthuis)
10 The Weigh House

MAP OF LEYDEN DATED 1600, PIETER BAST, LEIDEN MUNICIPAL ARCHIVES, THE NETHERLANDS

The city of Leiden, then as now, is a brilliant and very walkable city. The landmarks that William Brewster used to navigate the city, like the Pieterskerk, Town Hall, and Hooglandsekerk stand today, aiding the individual in their travel. In the early 17th century, the city teemed with diversity, from immigrants seeking religious refuge and work in the textile trades, to academics attracted to the University, one of the finest in the world. The weekly markets, held on Wednesdays and Saturdays, lined the New Rhine and extended from the Weigh House upstream, past the Corn Bridge to the Steenschur. What was ordinarily available every week in Leyden rivaled what other towns saw only in their annual fairs, according to Jan Orlers, the Leyden historian, author of Beschrijvinge der Stad Leyden, *in 1614.*

Chapter Seven

Removal from Amsterdam to Leyden

A year later, May 1, 1609, the Netherlands

Fear Brewster's small leather shoe floated remarkably well on the waters of the Rokin River. Patience gasped at the sight of the tiny bobbing shoe and closed her fingers a little tighter around the wrist of her active two-year-old sister, Fear. Jonathan, who stood a few paces away, stifled his amusement so that his mother would not be alerted to the swimming shoe.

Their mother had enough to contend with, now more than eight months into her pregnancy and managing their move from Amsterdam to Leyden, Holland's second-largest city, twenty-five miles to the southwest. Their father, Master Brewster, although only a few yards away, was busy helping other families of the congregation. So Jonathan quietly approached one of the ship's workers and in broken Dutch requested assistance as he gestured to the floating leather. Using a wooden pole, the sailor quickly corralled the baby's shoe. Jonathan squeezed the brown leather at the toe end of the small bootie, and once the dripping stopped, he managed to fold it down and fit it into the linen pocket of his brown breeches.

The congregation had hired four of the small boats moored on the Rokin, a southern continuation of the Amstel River, to take them as far as the dam and toll house at the Overtoom, on Amsterdam's south side. Skippers of these smaller boats dealt with passing under low bridges, requiring their vessels to have hinged masts. Twice during the voyage the hinged masts were lowered, much to the delight of all the children on board.

Patience watched the tiled roofs pass by, many adorned with empty stork's nests. She wondered where the birds might be off to and when they would return, reflecting on her own transiency. Windmill arms whirled in a mesmerizing fashion, spinning ideas in young Patience's mind of what Leyden would be like. The nine-year-old had confided only in her brother, Jonathan, about her fear of living in Amsterdam. Residing in Amsterdam less than nine months, Patience disliked the confinement of their living quarters, and her lack of freedom to go and do as she pleased. Her mother sternly warned her to show gratitude for the shelter offered by the Ancient Brethren, and cautioned of the dangers of a child roaming a city, especially a foreign one. She despised the feeling that she was a stranger in a strange land. What a drastic contrast to life at Scrooby Manor, where both interior space and land was plentiful and free to explore, and the air fresh and clean.

Their father, the congregation's Ruling Elder, made a number of trips to Leyden arranging the groups' removal there. The final decision to leave Amsterdam was made in late December of the year before. This was merely four months after the last of the Scrooby congregation arrived in Amsterdam in August of 1608, following the group's unexpected split off the coast between Grimsby and Hull, during their second attempt to flee England.

Life in Amsterdam seemed temporary from the start, with many of the Scrooby families taken in graciously by members of the Ancient Brethren. Some from Scrooby stayed in smaller houses, while others lived in the newly constructed meeting house. Completed the year before, the new building accommodated a large group of English reformists, with the Ancient Brethren numbering more than three hundred. Maybe the greater size of this congregation added to the complexity of maintaining cohesion and unification amongst its leaders and members. Having lived in Amsterdam for more than a decade, dissension strained the

Ancient Brethren within, while rumors tainted their reputation among skeptical outsiders.

When the reformed congregation from the Scrooby area landed with this larger congregation in Amsterdam in the summer of 1608, they found themselves in the eye of that storm of dissension. A decade prior, Ancient Brethren Pastor Francis Johnson had controversially excommunicated his brother, and even more incredibly, his father. Then a deacon named Daniel Studley faced accusations of a most vile nature, including the molestation of his stepdaughter and abuse of his wife. But the history between the two men ran deep. In the past, they were together imprisoned in London and then banished from England to form a colony in Canada. The two ultimately escaped and fled across the ocean to Amsterdam in 1593. Both men remained in the Ancient Brethren, as present leaders of the group.

Another pastor of the Ancient Brethren was Henry Ainsworth, who both Master Brewster and Pastor Robinson knew from England, sharing a deep respect for this learned man. With such a turbulent history, even with Ainsworth's positive presence, a propensity towards unrest did not align with the vision of the Scrooby congregation.

Pastor John Smyth of Gainsborough, who fled England with his congregation and arrived in Amsterdam in 1607, entered into a different world altogether. Smyth, who was well known by the Scrooby group, embarked on his own path, a new journey involving extreme requirements. In Smyth's congregation, pastors had to read from the Bible in Greek or Hebrew, and possess the ability to translate to the people. Such extensive skills were also expected of the teachers and deacons. In addition, Smyth refused financial support from outside of the congregation, a potentially crippling principle. Most significant to him was the sacrament of baptism, where Smyth offered rebaptism or anabaptism, believing it to be the only means of achieving salvation.

Between Pastor Smyth's extremist rebirth and the currents of unrest rippling through the Ancient Brethren, Pastor John Robinson and Master Brewster recognized the dangers of remaining in Amsterdam. Another justification for removal was the lack of regular employment.

Guilds restricted membership to those who were city citizens, having lived in Amsterdam and worked in that trade for a year and a day. So the newcomers faced the challenge of finding a consistent means of earning a living. Even the daily, low-wage jobs, such as that of a brick carrier, were hard to come by. Poverty hovered low and close, an unrelenting menace rapidly gaining ground.

The pastors originating from the Scrooby-Gainsborough area included John Smyth, Richard Clyfton, and John Robinson, who performed the teaching duties in Clyfton's congregation. Of the three, only Master Robinson was aboard the small vessel bound for Leyden. The congregation numbered close to one hundred, venturing to Leyden with written permission to settle within the town walls. On February 12, 1609, Leyden Town Secretary Jan van Hout officially accepted Pastor Robinson and Master Brewster's written request for permission to settle in Leyden. William had made the acquaintance of Secretary van Hout during a visit to Leyden more than two decades earlier, while in the service of Secretary Davison.

Leyden welcomed immigrants, especially when their skilled hands contributed to a resurgent cloth trade. Late in the previous century, the town suffered devastating losses at the hands of the Catholic Spanish. In October of 1574, the siege culminated in the relief of the tortured, crippled city. Every proud citizen of Leyden could tell you what happened on the third day of that month, when the strength of the city rose above the enemy, with heroes flooding the canals and rivers, filling starving mouths with loaves of bread and salted herring. A year later, William of Orange awarded the city with the University, building in Leyden one of the finest institutions in all of Europe.

With Leyden a vibrant city brimming with academic fervor and theological debate, and bubbling with a mixture of foreign inhabitants, Masters Robinson and Brewster believed a relocation there essential in maintaining the unity of the covenanted congregation. And to be geographically distanced from the Ancient Brethren might allow the Scrooby reformists to retain an independent and more pure identity.

Returning to the Removal to Leyden…

Little Fear squealed with delight as the curious white-and-grey gulls circled the tollhouse, swooping down suddenly and screeching in search of scraps. With Fear's damp bootie now replaced, Patience walked slowly behind her toddling sister, grabbing hold of the child's leading strings as they wobbled together toward the plank to disembark. The *Cager* and the *Damloper*, two twelve-ton boats hired by her father, waited a little farther down, alongside the dock. The wooden boats bobbed up and down at their jetties, as if nodding in readiness to carry the group to Leyden.

They would travel south and west across the Haarlem Lake, continue on into the Leyden Lake, and squeeze out onto the Zijl River. On this size boat, the people remained on the top deck, using storage chests as seats, while some belongings rode in the small space below the deck. Aside from a few gulls flying by, there was little more to see than the lake's rippling water and fields interrupted infrequently by thatched roofs and some brick-fronted gables. Occasionally, if you timed your gaze just right, you might spot a church spire. Skipper Adryaen Gerrits was careful to sail across the middle of the lake, as the shallow, sandy shores often victimized careless crafts. Traffic hardly existed along this route; at most, one or two fishing boats could be seen in the distance. The children became a little bored before long, realizing this part of the journey revealed only a flat, repeated landscape pattern coupled with a regular, stiff wind.

The Leyden Lake narrowed suddenly and pushed the two small ships south onto the Zijl River. As they flowed from the Zijl River into the waters of the Old Rhine River, Leyden's impressive landmarks pierced the horizon, marking the direction of the newcomers' next home. The congregation would be navigating the town based on their proximity to structures like the magnificent Town Hall, located on the central Breestraat. A short walk from that building stood each of the three large medieval churches known as the Pieterskerk, the Hoogland-sekerk, and the Vrouwekerk, all landmarks that would aid the newly arrived congregation in finding their way.

Reflecting back months prior, in preparation of the removal to Leyden....

For Masters Brewster and Robinson, the shapes on the horizon were familiar. After three trips made to manage housing arrangements, Leyden had started to feel like home even before the actual move. They enjoyed an invaluable acquaintance in Leyden Secretary Jan van Hout, who introduced Masters Brewster and Robinson to Jean de Lalaing, a principal agent dealing in renting properties to immigrants and larger groups.

Another meaningful figure from the recent past factored into the support of the Scrooby congregation's move. Through fortuitous communication channels similar to those established in England, some being in the cloth trade, others in the printing circle, their dear friend, Master John Carver, learned of the group's arrival in Amsterdam and subsequent intention to remove to Leyden. Traveling to Amsterdam in December for business dealings related to raw wool, cloth, and Fuller's Earth, Master Carver sought out his close friends.

Fluent now in both French and Dutch, it was Master Carver who penned the Scrooby congregation's letter requesting permission to settle in the city of Leyden. With his knowledge of Leyden's developing cloth trade and the city's active recruitment of skilled immigrants, Master Carver fully expected a positive response from city officials. Master Carver, his wife, and their servant Hendrijcke, left their home in L'Escluse, in the southern part of the Low Countries near Belgium, and travelled north to Leyden, arriving in early February, less than three months before Master Brewster and the congregation. Members of his wife's family, like her sister Marguerite, as well as her sister-in-love Marie, and seven-year-old nephew, Phillipe, already lived in Leyden and were members of the Walloon church there.

During their second visit to Leyden, Master Brewster and Pastor Robinson stayed for the better part of a week with the Carvers, making additional contacts and progress in securing rental properties for the congregation. Some of the men they met were also from the city's large Walloon Church, worshipping in the Vrouwekerk.

By the time the group moved as a unit in May of 1609, Masters Brewster and Robinson had grown accustomed to Leyden's landmarks. Gazing at the highest spires of the towering slate-roofed Hooglandse-kerk, admiring the skillfully scrolled gables adorning the Town Hall's white stone façade, and hearing the pulsing sounds of the pipe organ leaking from the leaded glass of the Pieterskerk, were common elements experienced while in the city. And only a few paces from the Carvers' home on the Nieuwe Street, heading northeast, stood the castle called the Burcht, a round brick fortification set atop a man-made hill– the only hill to be found in the city. Directly across the street from the Carvers' home rose the magnificent Hooglandsekerk, also called by some the Church of St. Pancras.

Staying on the second level of the Carvers' home, Master Brewster pushed open the shutters, revealing a remarkable view. Peering up at the stone turrets and spires, William watched the sun blast through the east-facing church windows as light exploded through the inside of the church. He called over to Pastor Robinson to join him at the window. A small flock of birds landed on one of the church's turret tops, hopping along as if performing for the onlookers. The doves eventually landed on a stone ridge below one of the cylindrical turrets. To the right of the landing where the birds had settled, Brewster noticed a curious magenta-painted rounded-top door. Very near to this door, the birds delivered brown sticks and yellow strands of hay, working at building their nests while cooing a peaceful chorus.

"Our flock has much in common with those birds, as they move and rebuild," said Master Robinson with a thoughtful gaze. "It is critical we lead them well, and prepare suitably for the removal to Leyden, so that our group can live here in unity and with a fair start. I am grateful to have Master Carver supporting our efforts. With whom has he arranged meetings for today?" Master Robinson turned away from the open window, escaping the crisp February air to gain warmth from the hearth.

"There are three gentlemen expected this afternoon. Master Jan Janz. Orlers, the nephew of Secretary van Hout, who is an absolute wealth of knowledge. And then Master Jean de Lalaing, whom we met previously, along with a man called van Thorenvliet, who also owns a number of properties in the city center," responded Brewster, carefully securing the shutters into a closed position.

Even with the shutters in place, the church bells could be heard clearly, marking the arrival of their guests. And breaking through the sound of the bells came a voice in English, coated with a French accent, calling Master Brewster and Pastor Robinson down to the ground floor. The Carvers' servant, Hendrijcke, stood on the tips of her toes, on the edge of a narrow spiral staircase step. Barely revealing her white linen coif and big blue eyes, she beckoned the men down with a humble smile. Together they descended, intent on developing their plans for removal to Leyden, and finding their flock nests for settling.

Returning to the journey of removing to Leyden, May 1, 1609…

As the *Cager* continued westward, the buildings and churches creating Leyden's landscape grew taller. Patience watched with wide eyes as their boat passed through a double drawbridge and was allowed to pass through the Zijlspoort, one of the city's protective gates. After only a few moments on the canal of the Oude Rijn, Patience noticed many statues of lions, some standing independently, and others carved into stone archways. She also saw many pairs of red, crossed keys. The repetition of the lions and keys was enough to make her wonder about their significance. Red and white clearly belonged together in this city, with rectangular doors and shutters commonly painted in a pattern with two triangles of red standing vertically and tip to tip, combined with white triangles positioned horizontally, their tips also touching.

She noted the differences between the brick houses lining the canals, but was too young to make the distinction between the function of a house based on its size and configuration. For instance, a smaller weaver's house with space for the loom in the front room and living quarters in the back, as compared to a larger home using the front space as a work room and a shop, as a hat maker might have, with living quarters in the back or above. Patience was able to differentiate a stepped gable from one that scrolled upwards, and admire the different colors of shutters, as that was something she enjoyed doing even in Amsterdam. Seeing something familiar put Patience a little more at ease, and she tried to take pleasure in the last part of the journey.

Patience peered down at Fear sleeping peacefully in the warm folds of her petticoat, hoping her sister would remain asleep until they reached Leyden. Then Patience looked up, noticing something far more concerning. Her mother sat a few feet away, atop their oak chest, with a most distressed expression. Nearly doubled over, Mary Brewster clutched at her pregnant, rigid belly, praying softly for the child inside her. She felt cramping periodically and, being a mother of three, recognized the intense periodic pulses as signs that labour could be near. The baby was not expected for a month or more, so Mary cringed at the thought of her unborn baby suffering.

Patience decided that the overbearing musty odor of water-soaked wood along with the anxiety of making yet another move was the culprit, and nothing more. That once they walked off the ship and on solid ground, her mother would be relieved. The churning of the young girl's stomach continued as she realized her mother was in more than temporary discomfort. Patience had once heard the comparison of the womb to a rough sea, in which the child floats for the space of nine months, the labour of delivery being the only port, but full of dangerous rocks. As they themselves floated along the rivers and lakes to Leyden, Patience acknowledged the bitter irony. Even at nine years of age, she was aware of the perils of childbirth and the possibility of losing her mother in the process.

Patience dreaded waking her sister, but without a choice, spoke to

Fear in a soft tone. "Fear, Fear, we are here. It is time to wake up. Fear, please wake up," pleaded Patience as she watched her mother rise cautiously from the chest, almost afraid to stand up.

Patience propped up her half-sleeping sister and made her way over to her mother, reaching out to hold her hand. Mary smiled down at her daughter attempting reassurance, but Patience was not fooled.

The congregation negotiated their way around ropes and off the main deck, then down the wooden steps onto a stone quay. They stepped forward believing this was God's plan, and where they were meant to be. The city proved vibrant that Friday afternoon, the first day of May, 1609. Leyden exploded with exuberance real to a city beginning a period of peace, with a twelve-year truce now officially in place, and a textile trade blossoming with the highly experienced hands of the immigrants seeking a religious haven. The celebrating city, in acknowledgement of diverse traditions, placed a May Pole in the Breestraat, or Broad Street, outside of the Town Hall for the large number of foreigners and English soldiers stationed there. For the Scrooby congregation, although the pagan symbolism of the May Pole was not to their liking, the aroma of the alluring, exotic market scents were welcoming enough.

The group disembarked outside the Weigh House, where the Old and New Rhine converged. A stone platform jutting out into the Stille Rijn, where the rivers merged, held the city crane and a small structure housing the lift equipment. Wagons pulled up periodically to the Weigh House's side doors, offloading and weighing items destined for the markets on the massive scales within. Bustling activity naturally gathered here, so the English congregation merely added more bodies to an already-busy space. Frightened sheep and calves called from across the confluence, confined and soon to make their last voyage from a cage at the Friday market to the nearby slaughterhouse.

The Mermaid Inn offered an array of meat, fish, bread, cheese, beer, and wine, as well as being an ideal waiting place for those arriving in Leyden by boat. Inside The Mermaid, Masters Carver and Jean de Lalaing occupied a prime corner that allowed a view of the docks outside the Weigh House. It was a bit blurry due to the leaded glass, but adequate enough to make out the nature of the activity beyond the window. Master Carver squinted to improve his view of the boats and people beyond, deciding it was best they finish their beer and join the scene outside.

Masters Brewster and Robinson landed upon the cobblestones, scanning past unfamiliar faces in search of Masters Carver and de Lalaing. Weaving through the crowd, Master Brewster spotted Master Carver's unique violet velvet cap, worn that day for the purpose of easy recognition. Master Brewster had selected his moss-colored breeches and doublet, and black hat adorned with a scarlet hatband for the same purpose. The four men found each other quickly, removed their hats, bowing deeply and embracing in the anticipation and excitement of the congregation's new beginning in Leyden.

The plan crafted by the men involved Master Jean de Lalaing escorting Pastor Robinson, his family, and the other families to the Green Close. This rental property included a large main house surrounded by twelve smaller houses enclosing a courtyard space. Sitting across the alley from the Pieterskerk and down the alley from one of the main University buildings and picturesque Rapenburg canal, the Green Close was a convenient location within the city.

Master Carver's role, with assistance from Master Brewster, was to deliver the remaining families to the surrounding inns where rental accommodations had been secured. Inns like The Dover, also serving as a brewery, The Mermaid, and The Fighting Lion offered temporary lodgings for a number of the families. Nineteen-year-old William Bradford would lodge with Master and Mistress Carver and their servant Hendrijcke.

As the rest of the congregation shuffled off the ship, Bridget Robinson, the minister's wife, recognized Mistress Brewster's discomfort and looks of concern, so she sought out Jonathan Brewster to locate the congregation's midwife, Sarah Willet. Mistress Robinson corralled her four-year-old son, John, and two-year-old daughter, Bridget, and maneuvered past people to reach Mary, who had walked off the ship on her own but sat quietly on another family's wooden chest. Typically, Mary would be taking charge of at least her own family, if not directing others who required guidance.

Bridget wrapped her arm around her friend's shoulders. "What is it, Mary? Are you not feeling well from the dankness and motion of the water, or is it something else?" asked her worried friend.

Before Mary could respond, the midwife arrived and knelt by the side of the storage chest. "Mistress Brewster, are you in constant pain, or feeling the sharp discomfort of labor?"

"I believe the pangs could be the start of labor, Goodwife Willet, mayhaps brought on by the jostling of the journey. I realize the trip was not so long and arduous, but I am not one for the water," said Mary with a confused look.

"Take some slow, deep breaths. I will have Jonathan fetch you a cup of beer from the inn on the corner. In it I will add sage, to help closeth the matrix. I believe I am staying tonight at The Dover, nearby, so I will accompany you to your home and we can have a better look, and see if you are shedding any blood or showing signs of the baby coming early."

As Jonathan hurried off in search of a cup of beer, William Brewster had turned his attention to view the congregation gathered in front of the Weigh House, and noticed his usually very active wife seated upon a chest, Bridget Robinson's arm around her, as Mary spoke with the midwife.

"John, give me a moment to look to my wife, as I fear something is not right with her," William said hurriedly to Master Carver, before dashing in the direction of his wife.

"Oh dear, please Lord, keep my wife and the baby safe," whispered William as he ran towards her.

Master de Lalaing and those going to the Green Close followed the Nieuwe Rijn south. After about fifty paces, they turned right up the Maarsmakersteeg, then made a left on the Breestraat. They headed right onto the Pieterskerk Choorsteeg, but not before catching a glimpse of the impressive Town Hall façade standing triumphantly to their left on the Breestraat. Activity surged through this area of the main street, with markets, and the May Pole erected for those immigrants who might appreciate its presence.

Crossing the Breestraat proved challenging, and de Lalaing muttered words of frustration under his breath, not about the numerous bodies around him, but his decision to take this route. He should have known better, especially on a day when the city celebrated a long-awaited time of truce with the Spanish. The hired carts pushing their belongings behind them forced the uncertain newcomers forward and down the Pieterskerk Choorsteeg, crossing over the Langebrug, and pressing on until they felt the towering presence of the Pieterskerk. The street ended where the Pieterskerk stood, with a turn to the left on the Pieterskerkhof leading them to the Kloksteeg and the Green Close.

The Brewster family's walk would be slightly shorter, down a narrow alley directly off of the Pieterskerk Choorsteeg, just a few paces before the church. Master Brewster spoke in broken Dutch to a man with carts for hire. With great care, he aided his ailing wife into the cart, with Patience helping Fear up so she could nestle in next to her mother. Jonathan and Patience walked on either side of the cart, while the other was filled with their belongings. Master Brewster paused behind the carts, lifted his palms and eyes to the sky, and prayed.

NIGHT BURIAL, ADRIAEN VAN DE VENNE, CA. 1630, ILLUSTRATING A POEM BY
JACOB CATS, LEIDEN AMERICAN PILGRIM MUSEUM, THE NETHERLANDS

*A night burial would not be typical, but as depicted here, they did
occur. The heavy, thick stone slabs served as grave markers, as well
as the floor of the church. If you visit the Pieterskerk or Hooglandsekerk today, you can admire such stones- some of the wealthy had
portraits or other images carved in them, as well as words.*

Chapter Eight

Visit to the Verger

A month later, June 18, 1609, Leyden, the Netherlands

When William Brewster exited his Leyden home and turned left, he could reach the Pieterskerk Choorsteeg in just a handful of steps. A right turn and a few more steps led to the base of the eastern wall of the Pieterskerk, the first bricks placed nearly five hundred years before. If he followed the church's perimeter on the southern side and continued onto the Kloksteeg, he would pass Master Robinson's home on the left. This distance required a walk of less than a minute. Not much farther along on the right, at the corner of the Kloksteeg and Rapenburg Canal, stood the sign of The Music Book. The owners of this busy print shop, Englishman Thomas Basson and his son, Govert, had been known to Brewster since his initial visit to Leyden in 1585 with Secretary Davison.

A left turn at the end of the Kloksteeg would put him on the Rapenburg, traveling south along one of the most lovely canals in Leyden. Lined with linden trees and stately homes, this stretch of canal was argued by Leyden citizens to be the most beautiful in all of Holland. Glancing to the right would allow Brewster a view of the Academiegebouw, formerly a convent, and now one of the University's main buildings. Behind this building grew the world-famous botanical gardens, not visible from across the canal, but its whereabouts known to him.

Should he continue south past the Beguinage Chapel, another former Catholic building used by the University, he would eventually reach the Cloth Hall. One of four weavers' guildhalls in Leyden, this building once served as a hospice for medieval pilgrims traveling to Spain. Now the guildhall declared the importance of Leyden's chief industry, adorned with an ornate copper spire.

Directly across from this guildhall and over a bridge sat the public square known as the Yarn Market, a place where weavers and market-goers could visit on Wednesdays to purchase Leyden-spun yarn. Watching over this yarn market space, a bell tower rang out to the city with authority, announcing the official start and end of each workday.

On this Thursday, the eighteenth day of June 1609, William had no business either at the Bassons' bookshop or at the Cloth Hall. He departed his house before the workday bell rang out, after checking on his wife, who was gaining strength in body now but struggling in her mind, coping with the loss of their child.

He selected his blue suit of clothing, comprised of a doublet, breeches, and knit stockings, all matching in their sky-blue shade of indigo-dyed fustian, save for the orange stockings. William turned left instead of right at the end of his little alley and walked briskly down the Pieterskerk Choorsteeg, at a pace greater than even he expected while carrying the weight of his loss.

He continued in the direction of the Breestraat on his way towards the Hooglandsekerk and a meeting with the verger, the man responsible for maintaining the church and scheduling such things as grave diggings. Upon making a right onto the Breestraat, the workday bell on the Steenschur clanged out as he passed the intricately carved front of the Town Hall. A white stone angel leaning on a sculpted hourglass on the staircase of the Town Hall's main entrance seemed to smirk as William walked past. The symbols of a fleeting temporal existence were never far from sight or mind, and William hardly needed a statue to be reminded of that.

Maybe, on his return home, he would purchase a cut of meat or a duck for that day's dinner. Jonathan could go to the market, but Master Brewster would rather his son stay by his mother's side, especially on this day. Once they had settled in a bit more and the burial was behind them, William would see about taking on a maidservant. At the moment, Jonathan and Patience willingly increased their household responsibilities. Even though they failed to understand the depth of their mother's suffering, they recognized her detachment and desired to bring her back.

William passed a white archway on his right, adorned with a ram's head and Leyden's red lions standing strong, holding a white shield bearing the city's crossed red keys. Through this entranceway, people could find the Penshal, a daily option for less expensive cuts of meat, such as tripe or chicken. After passing both the Penshal and Town Hall, William turned to the left and continued over the Corn Bridge on his way to the Torensteeg.

The Hooglandsekerk erupted powerfully through the cobblestones, but seeing it prompted a feeling of ambivalence in William. The spires he had admired in February from Master Carver's home looked different this morning, but William could not determine why. All he knew was that if the verger agreed, his child would be laid to rest that evening under the slate slabs within that place of worship. He made his way onto the Torensteeg with his head down, intentionally ignoring the imposing church standing before him. The baker's door opened as he neared the end of the alley, the scent of bread unfolding in the wake of his sorrowful steps.

William passed the entrance to the priest's home, where the verger would be, rounded the corner and made his way to the right down the Nieuwe Street, towards Master Carver's home. John Carver's command of the Dutch language was superior between the two Englishmen, so he had agreed to accompany William in making the burial arrangements.

Hendrickje opened the door before William could even knock. She had been reviving the fire and arranging turves of peat when she noticed his presence outside the front ground-floor window.

"Good day, Master Brewster," said the shy maidservant as she curtsied and bowed her head. "Master Carver will be out shortly. Please, come inside."

Together they walked down the narrow hallway and turned left into the main front room, where William chose to stand instead of sit, peering up and out the windows, gazing at the Hooglandsekerk.

"Dear brother, good day, William. I take it you have just arrived?" asked Master Carver with a look of sympathy.

"Yes, friend," said William as the men embraced. "I am most grateful to have your company for this unfortunate meeting. The Lord called this child to His Kingdom, and we must accept that with grace. My wife believes this as well, but having the child grow inside her, then working tirelessly to keep the little one alive– the loss is different for her on levels we cannot know as men. We are most thankful that Mistress Brewster remains with us, unlike so many mothers who share in the child's fate."

"I can only imagine the pain of her experience. My wife does worry about Mary, and has been praying for her ever since your arrival here. The Lord has His plan, and at times like these, handling such a happening is admittedly difficult. It is a great deal to contend with, moving your home once more, and then losing a child," Carver said with empathy. "Will it be the two of us meeting the verger, or will your landlord, Master van Thorenvliet, be present also?"

"The godly man, Master van Thorenvliet, has provided a letter stating his wishes in offering a place in his family's burial space. Pastor Robinson and Master Orlers witnessed the discussion and the signing of the letter, and I have it here, safely tucked inside my doublet."

The brilliance of the rising sun illuminated the room, and as the two men silently admired the radiant blue sky from the front windows, young William Bradford stepped softly towards them.

"Good day Master Brewster," said Bradford, reverently doffing his hat and bowing before meeting his eyes.

"Good morrow, son," said Master Brewster. "It warms my heart to see you this day. Join us in prayer before we take leave for our meeting with the verger."

The three men stood in a half-circle, positioned so they could all look out and up at the rich blue sky. Almost as if the air were swirling in a vat of indigo, the sky took on the appearance of water, as if one could travel these seas on the way to heaven. They peered deep into this paradise, with palms raised, looking up toward the Lord, praying for the Brewster child to be laid to rest in the earth under the church standing before them. The little soul, they all knew, had reached their Maker the day before.

William Bradford was like a son to Master Brewster, and to Master Carver for that matter. A very young Bradford lost his parents early on, so he spent much of his youth passed around from one relative to another. He was often sick as a child, and Bradford's family believed that his generally ill, weak state would offer a shortened time on Earth. But in defiance of all the predictions he battled through each setback, and in time settled in with a wealthy uncle named Robert, the richest yeoman farmer in Austerfield, a town near to Scrooby.

Around the age of twelve, William attended a church service in Scrooby, meeting Master Brewster for the first time, marveling at the approach to worship. From that young age he felt a connection with this reformed congregation, finding a family in sharing their covenant. Direction for this congregation came from the Scriptures, not the bishop or any remnant of papal authority. Bradford enjoyed walking the nearly four miles south to Scrooby, knowing upon his arrival he would be surrounded by the godly men guiding him in his relationship with the Lord.

Over the years, the journey built his strength of body as well as mind, as during the walk back to Austerfield he pondered the Scriptures and Master Brewster's post-sermon teachings. In Bradford's mind, the Church of England's base and beggarly ceremonies were unlawful. While walking he reminded himself of this, believing that whoever saw the evil of these things, and felt in their hearts a heavenly zeal for His truth must shake off this yoke of antichristian bondage, and as the Lord's free people, join themselves by a covenant of the Lord into a church estate, in the fellowship of the gospel, to walk in all his ways, made known, or to be known unto them, according to their best endeavors, whatsoever it should cost them, the Lord assisting them. By the age of seventeen, prior to the first attempt to flee England for the Netherlands, Bradford made his confession of faith, committing to the group as a covenanted member.

Although he was not jailed in the cells of Boston in that first failed effort to escape England in the fall of 1607, he worked diligently to aid the women and children, displaying the skills of a blossoming leader. During the second, partially successful attempt at fleeing English soil in 1608, Bradford was one of the few men left behind. He might have been fortunate in this case, as those on the Dutch ship received quite an introduction to maritime travel. The normally uneventful, brief trip across the North Sea typically took two days. Severe storms hijacked the vessel, and after two weeks, the battered ship limped into Amsterdam's harbor.

For Bradford, his duty in assisting the displaced women and children, distraught at the sight of their husbands and fathers sailing away, was riddled with difficulty. But even considering his young age, William's calm and kind ways endeared the women and children to him. They remained strong in his presence, knowing that he was guided by men like Pastor Robinson and Master Brewster, and could be relied upon.

Back in the home of Master Carver…

Master Brewster looked over at him now, casting a gaze as a father would at a son. In looking at Bradford's attire, Brewster knew that the young man selected his clothing carefully that morning, in the event the men requested he come along to the meeting with the verger. Before William had left England, his uncle provided him with a lead-colored suit fashioned with pewter buttons, the material being a mix of linen and wool, and lined with linen. His breeches puffed out slightly at the thigh and extended down just below the knee. William favored these breeches with two leather-lined pockets, allowing him to carry less in the pocket hanging from the leather garter around his waist. The deeply dyed blue hatband looked rich against the light-grey, felted wool hat. Bradford owned a cloak that same color, for days colder than this one.

Master Brewster appreciated his readiness but expected the meeting would include only himself and Master Carver. "Son, if it would not cause you too much trouble, could you make time this morning to tend to Mistress Brewster and the children for me? I believe a visit from you would brighten the spirits of all, and perhaps you could venture out on any errands my Mistress might require," suggested Brewster.

"Why, of course. I am here to do whatever would benefit you and your family. I will set out with you and Master Carver and make my way over to your home, planning to spend the day there, or at least until you return."

"Many thanks to you, William. Take these coins and purchase meat flesh for a pottage, and plan to eat dinner with us. The vendors inside the Town Hall will be open for business by now. Please be certain Mistress Brewster works minimally around the house. She will protest and assure you of her health, but without her knowing it, lessen her work. Between the aid from you and the support of Jonathan and Patience, she should have little to busy herself with," stressed Master Brewster.

"Of course, Master Brewster. Please, do not trouble your thoughts with happenings at your household this day. You have other more important matters to manage," said Bradford.

The bell of the neighboring Hooglandsekerk marking half of the hour silenced their talk, and with its sound the three men departed the Carver residence. It would only take them a few steps to round the corner onto the Torensteeg, with Masters Brewster and Carver seeking the verger's door, and William continuing on to the Brewster residence.

William Bradford walked the cobblestones with great pride. His direction that day, and beyond, was clear as a dedicated member of the congregation. This reformed group was both his family and church. Pale skinned and fair-haired, Bradford's most noticeable feature was his eye color. The intensity of blue coming from his eyes compensated for the lack of pigment in his skin and the light tone of his thin, straw-colored hair. Or maybe it was because of these lackluster features that the contrast with his cerulean eyes was so pronounced.

His grey suit of clothing, particularly his doublet, tugged at his growing body. A gift from his uncle two years before, the clothing had initially hung quite loose. Of course the intention was that the young man would obtain many years from these pieces, continuing to fill them out. His uncle recognized it might take many years before his young nephew would earn enough money to replace the clothing.

He was fortunate to be residing with Master Carver, as under his roof he received shelter as well as direction from an experienced merchant. Obtaining work in Leyden as a young, untrained Englishman would likely land him a role in the vast textile industry, a trade he knew little about. He was at least familiar with sheep, shearing, and the selling of raw wool, having grown up on a farm near to Scrooby Manor. Lodging with Master Carver afforded him opportunities to learn about dealing with finished cloth as well, and additionally he had access to many contacts from within the Walloon Church, connected to many areas of Leyden's growing textile trade.

Young Bradford had aspirations of thriving in this city. With the congregation at last settling together in one place, William believed the days ahead offered promise. He dreamed of becoming a citizen and purchasing a home of his own, for his future bride and business. Who that woman might be was in God's hands, a happening planned by the Lord, just as in the predestined nature of the congregation's formation.

The sun glistened off the slow current of the Nieuwe Rhine, as it streamed down from the eastern sky, warming William's back. He crossed via the Corn Bridge, his leather shoes conforming to the square cobbled stones as he approached the back side of the Town Hall. He rounded the corner onto the Breestraat and entered the doorway to the right of the main front staircase, where the better cuts of meat could be purchased.

William walked from counter to counter, scanning the options. He had accompanied Hendrijcke on several errands and had an idea of how to bargain for a quality product. The vendors could tell Bradford was not a Dutchman, but that was not uncommon in a city filled with immigrants.

"*Goedemorgen*," said William to the butcher that Hendrijcke typically sought out. "I care to purchase a cut of beef to feed a family of six, with two of the six being younger. If it would not trouble you to cut it for a pottage, I would be most grateful. My Mistress is in recovery, Goodman."

The vendor recognized young Bradford, as any good vendor's memory recalled those that revisited. "Good morning," responded the butcher with a smile, seeing the prospect of a loyal customer.

"*Wat en zoudde dat vleesch kosten?*" asked Bradford.

"Since it is early and not so busy, I will make the cuts without an additional charge. I expect I will see you again, friend," said the butcher as he began cutting.

"I would think so, but the answer lies in the taste of the meal," said Bradford with a smile.

"Ahh, young man, but I am not able to tend the hearth as well," retorted the good-natured butcher while he wrapped the beef. He exchanged money for meat flesh, and William made his way to the Brewster family.

Masters Brewster and Carver walked the few paces to the verger's door and pulled on the ring attached to a bell inside. It took more than a few moments for the verger to unlock and open his wooden door. He opened it slowly and looked out quizzically, as if he had forgotten he would be receiving visitors that morning. Both Brewster and Carver removed their hats as they bowed to the elder man, with Master Carver making their introduction in Dutch. The verger retained his confusion, so Brewster dug into his doublet and produced the letter written by Master van Thorenvliet, indicating permission to use his family grave for the Brewster infant. As the aged churchman read the words his face softened, as he regained familiarity with the request, and began nodding in recognition as he finished the letter.

"The burial can take place this coming Saturday, the twentieth day of June, in the evening– unfortunately, not before then."

Brewster was hoping for an earlier time, even that day, but did not want to appear disrespectful, so he accepted the time with gratitude.

"We are in no need of special accommodations," he assured the verger. "Admittance into the church and the gravesite will be enough. I expect our pastor and my wife and I will be present that evening, in addition to our son we are burying."

"I will meet you at the entrance of the southern transept at five of the clock of that evening. The stone covering Master van Thorenvliet's family grave will be set aside for the burial and replaced once you lay your child within," stated the verger.

"Yes, of course. Thank you, my good man, for your assistance," responded Master Carver.

The verger turned away as he nodded and gestured for them to go. The meeting took no more than a handful of minutes, and by the time the two men returned to the cobbled streets the verger had plunged his damp quill deep into the well. He returned it to the paper patiently waiting on the slanted wooden desk, basking in the light penetrating the window.

VANITAS STILL LIFE WITH THE SPINARIO, 1628, PIETER CLAESZ,
RIJKSMUSEUM, AMSTERDAM, THE NETHERLANDS

Skulls, bones, and snuffed-out candles often appear in vanitas still lifes, which were designed to convey moralizing messages about the passage of time and the ephemerality of life, with death as the ultimate certainty. Here Claesz presents the study materials of an educated painter: books, drawings, armor, musical instruments and a plaster cast of the Spinario, a famous antique sculpture of a boy extracting a thorn from his foot. On the table is a timepiece and an empty roemer glass, reminding the viewer that life is fleeting, and mortality an eventuality.

Chapter Nine

Death Escapes No One

Saturday, June 20, 1609
Leyden, the Netherlands

"Goodman Jepson, this was not necessary," said Master Brewster a little uneasily, as the congregation member entered the Brewster residence. The carpenter had taken it upon himself to construct a simple wooden coffin for his Elder's infant, due to be placed in Master van Thorenvliet's family grave later that day.

"Master Brewster, it is a simple expression of my love for you and Mistress Brewster. If you are not comfortable using it tonight, I will take it away at once. In no way would I want to upset you or your Mistress," explained William Jepson with deep sincerity.

Master Brewster looked towards the staircase where his wife had recently ascended, and wondered aloud about her preference. "Well, I hadn't thought about the use of a coffin, as my wife intended to carry our son to the Hooglandsekerk, wound in his burial shroud. I think she would have worries of offending you, Goodman Jepson, should we not accept the coffin. But to be truthful, I think she would rather continue as planned, staying connected with him as long as possible. So with much gratitude for your effort and kindness, I will ask that you take it away before the good Mistress returns."

"Of course, Master Brewster," said Jepson with understanding. "And to be sure, there is no offense taken. Sadly, the little coffin will be used by another of our congregation before long. Thanks be to God that Mistress Brewster was spared her own life. So many times the Lord must take both." Goodman Jepson shook his head as he turned to go. "I'll be on my way, as if I had never come. You will be in my prayers this evening."

"Many thanks, Goodman Jepson. I will not forget you in remembering us. Peace be with you as you venture home. God by you."

Master Brewster closed the home's wooden door as his wife appeared at the base of the stairs, with just enough time to mask the visitor's presence. "Husband, I have explained to the children about the burial this evening, and Jonathan will look after the girls while we are gone. We shouldn't be gone overly long, so I promised them we would be back to say our bedtime prayers."

"Yes, Mary, the burial itself will take very little time. Pastor Robinson intends to be with us, and after the burial Master Carver invited us to share in prayer and company."

"I would be most grateful to spend time with the Carvers. How is Mistress Carver faring, being with child? Am I right in thinking she is quite far along?"

"From what I know, she is doing well enough. I know her size is preventing her from moving around a great deal, or even getting out to the market. Hendrijcke and young Bradford are handling all of the household duties. Master Carver is of course busy with his merchant ventures, so I see him mostly in the evening and during our time of worship at the home of Master Robinson. Mistress Carver attended worship this past Sunday while you were recovering, and all appeared as expected, outside of her quiet nature. But that shyness could be due to language more than anything. I know she usually speaks to Master Carver in French."

"I am glad to have the chance to visit this evening, and get to know more about her and her family here in Leyden and France. It will also do much good for me to celebrate the new life she and John are awaiting, rather than wallow in the sadness of our loss," remarked Mistress Brewster.

"I am nearly ready to leave. Just allow me some time to comb my hair and change my hatband. I haven't worn this blue petticoat and waistcoat since we moved from Amsterdam, and when I was searching for the linen shroud for the burial, I found this pretty blue-and-yellow hatband hiding between two pillowbeers."

Earlier that afternoon, Mistress Brewster had the good fortune of Goodwife Willet's presence, with the midwife assisting in washing the baby with rosewater. Mistress Brewster had taken one of their finer linen sheets, smoothing it carefully, as if her son were still alive and to be swaddled in the cloth. In fact, Mary refused to complete the winding process and cover her infant's face. She had placed her lifeless child gently in the privacy of her bedstead, with the curtains drawn, silently asking her children to avoid that space.

Master Brewster retied the crimson-colored silk ribbons around the top of his black knit stockings, and checked that his silver doublet buttons remained secure. He set to brushing his finer black hat, its crown equal in height to that of the width of the brim. Sitting on the three-legged stool by the fire, he checked the state of his shoes. Not satisfied, he found a cleaning brush and removed a bit of dried mud where the leather upper met the sole. With a linen cloth, he worked some mink oil into the chestnut-brown leather, reviving the richness of the tanned hide. At least his clothes were in a state of readiness. How was a parent ever ready to bury their child?

Once Mistress Brewster replaced her coif and positioned her hat, now adorned with a beautifully twisted band of yellow- and-blue silk, she tucked away strands of hair that escaped the linen head covering. She straightened and smoothed her dark-blue apron with a sigh, then checked that her keys hung securely from her girdle, safely beneath the apron. Mary turned to see her husband replacing a linen cloth, and reached to open the bed curtains and gather her son.

They did believe the child lived on in God's Kingdom, and for that they were grateful, and for Mistress Brewster to remain longer in this world was a gift as well.

Mary could not have known that once the child was laid to rest in the van Thorenvliet grave, she would experience some relief. Before now, she had been fortunate in avoiding the tragedy of losing a child. Of course, she had witnessed the death of an infant through other members of the congregation, but like anything else, an experience had to be lived before it was truly understood.

"Husband, please come to the bedstead, so we might pray together," asked Mistress Brewster tenderly, with a tightness gripping her throat.

William turned away from the fire and directed a loving look at his wife. As he peered past her, through the parted curtains, his gaze passed by the beauty of the gold-and-brown-patterned cloth bedstead panels, in search of his shrouded son.

The Brewster infant's skin was pale, but not quite as white as his bleached linen shroud, and with some of his brown hair exposed, appeared as if he were sleeping innocently. Of course this boy was innocent. Barely a few hours of breaths had passed his lips before his last soft exhalation, his soul traveling into the Lord's land. His parents looked up to the heavens as they prayed for the peace of their lost child's soul. They were not bitter or angry. They both accepted this was God's plan. William closed his warm hand around his wife's frigid, trembling fingers. Understanding the depth of her sorrow, he turned her towards him and wrapped both arms around her, hugging her close, desiring to fill the deep void with love.

As she wept quietly, she took rapid, shallow breaths, trying desperately to stop. Then she inhaled a deep, courageous breath and ended the hug. Smiling at her husband, she declared, "I am ready to leave for the church."

Standing tall in front of the little square mirror hanging on the wall between the bedstead and the hearth, she wiped warm tears off her damp cheeks with cold hands. The couple finished the winding of the linen shroud, with Mary first knotting the linen by his feet before tying the other end above his head.

Master Brewster owned a beautiful black cape, given to him by Secretary Davison while in his service as a clerk. The richly dyed garment was lined with silk, also dyed many times to achieve a deep black. In this most treasured article of clothing they wrapped the infant once more, as a cover while carrying him the short distance to the Hooglandsekerk.

"God by you, children," called Mistress Brewster up the staircase.

Jonathan had been careful all afternoon about offering his mother privacy, while at the same time protecting his younger sisters from a reality they need not experience fully.

"We will return before you take to your beds. Jonathan, please be mindful of the fire. You can have the relics of the cabbage pottage once we leave. It is ready for you and the girls, along with a round of bread I have left on the table. I am sorry for the lateness of the supper, but I know you understand. Your father and I will eat something at the home of Master Carver, should we be hungry."

Jonathan made his way halfway down the stairs to acknowledge his mother's request. "Yes, Mother," he responded softly. "I will tend to the fire and have supper with the girls once you leave. Do not worry. All will be well here. Go on to the church. Is it not nearly five of the clock?"

Mary hugged her son the best she could on such a narrow stairwell before returning to the ground floor.

Mary exchanged her indoor open-heeled slippers for her blue-dyed leather latchet shoes. The light-blue color of the shoes played nicely with the colors of her hatband, petticoat, and even the deep blue of her apron. From her leather girdle hung a red wool pocket drawn shut, a pair of iron keys, and a knife tucked snugly in an intricately embroidered sheath. William had his set of keys hanging from his girdle, so Mary removed hers, returning them to the bottom shelf on the back wall of the bedstead.

Master Brewster tenderly lifted his wrapped son from the bedstead and placed him in his wife's waiting arms. Mary held her son close to her chest, just as she would if the infant were alive. William opened the door for his wife and son, and silently, that part of the Brewster family made their way towards the Hooglandsekerk's southern transept.

They walked at a moderate pace. Although Mary dreaded the finality of placing her son in a grave, it would allow a path forward, something she needed desperately. For those passing them on the street, the

Brewsters' scene was not an unfamiliar sight. Perhaps the time of day for interment was a little late, but seeing an infant carried in a burial shroud or coffin was a regular happening.

The setting sun passed its last rays of light through the buildings and onto the Nieuwe Rhine, reflecting off the river down to their left as they crossed the Corn Bridge, where grain had been sold that day. Most vendors selling at Leyden's sprawling Saturday markets had either packed up and departed, or were busy doing so. Over the bridge, they passed a man still looking to sell more of his pottery. They walked past without interest and followed the little alley that connected to the Nieuwe Street. To the left, vendors selling secondhand clothing were loading their carts.

As they made a turn to the right onto the Nieuwe Street and in the direction of the southern transept of the Hooglandsekerk, there stood Masters Robinson and Carver. The pair immediately walked towards the Brewsters, their heads bowed in sadness.

"Please, Mistress, there is no need to remove your hat. Hold your child close," said their pastor. The men embraced without words. In continued silence, the pastor and four of his flock entered the Hooglandsekerk through one of the massive red arched doors that the verger had left slightly ajar, anticipating their arrival.

Bells from the church rang out to mark the hour, and as they admired the beauty of the burning candles, soaking in the serenity, the verger entered by way of a smaller arched, yellow-painted door behind them. He grumbled something to himself and knocked the dirt off his hands by rubbing them together, then wiped the rest onto his brown apron. Master Carver, knowing Dutch quite well, could decipher that the verger was annoyed at having to trek up into the depths of the attic and wind the clock.

The verger did not know their level of fluency in Dutch, and at this time of day, lacked the patience to find out. For their purpose, gestures would be enough, so he motioned them towards the open van Thorenvliet grave, where the thick grey stone had been lifted and slid aside. As the Brewsters, Master Carver, and Pastor Robinson moved to its edge, the group took comfort in knowing the Lord held the child safe in His keeping. Mary's strength increased in her pastor's presence, and as she knelt to place her son into the open grave, William shadowed her in case she required his aid. Once she regained a standing position, two men working for the verger suddenly appeared from behind one of the church's thick supporting pillars. After resting their lanterns by the grave's opening, they started the process of replacing the heavy stone, as if everyone had already left. In truth, they were in the way of their labor, so with the infant having been interred, the mourners turned to exit the church. The verger followed them out, preparing to close and lock the large transept doors for the evening. Master Brewster thanked the verger once again for his assistance, placing a stuiver in the tired man's hand.

Mistress Brewster drew in a deep breath of the evening's cooling air and mustered the strength to regroup on the handful of cobblestone steps they walked from the church to the Carvers' home. Upon exhaling, much of the burdensome pain floated out and away. Mary recognized the need to be supportive for Mistress Carver in the late stages of her pregnancy. The poor woman had already dealt with the loss of a child in her life. Just a year before, a Carver child had come into the world three months too soon, lost even before birth.

Mary Brewster knew Marie Carver mainly through the words of others, either spoken or in the letters delivered to Scrooby Manor by post carrier Hugh Mercer. Only a month before had the two women actually met, with Leyden serving as a new home for both. At least for Mistress Carver, the large French-speaking Walloon congregation in this city provided a familiarity in worship and connection to her birthplace in France. She preferred speaking French when possible, even with an impressive command of English, having sought religious refuge in England for a number of years. Growing a relationship with Mistress Brewster meant conversing in English, something Mistress Carver gladly accommodated, as she found the prospect of friendship most delightful.

Since their move from Amsterdam to Leyden, Mistress Brewster had been forced into, quite literally, a mode of survival. Settling into a new household with three children while attempting to keep her un-born child alive left her little unaccounted time. With the child buried and her own body healing, she walked over to the Carvers' home feeling a flutter of promise in moving on, and getting to meet Mistress Carver again.

Both Mistress Carver and Hendrijcke stood at the ground-floor window, looking out in anticipation of receiving the Brewsters and Master Robinson. William Bradford, the home's other regular inhabitant, was away tending to business in Amsterdam.

John Carver walked ahead of his guests and smiled through the front window's wavy glass at his wife and servant as he approached the entrance to his home. He pushed the door open gently and stood to one side, while gesturing his friends inside. The narrow hallway, about three feet wide, opened up to the left into a front room that Master Carver used for business mostly pertaining to the cloth trade. He maintained a hand in the trade of Fuller's Earth with Thomas Brewer, who traveled to the Netherlands from time to time. On this evening, the room served as a gathering space for his pastor and friends, offering comfort in their loss.

Hendrijcke slipped away into the kitchen, built a step higher than the ground floor and towards the back of the house. Earlier in the day, she had visited the sugar-baker to obtain a variety of sweet treats, some containing figs, and nearly all of them coated decadently with crystal-line sugar. She also purchased bread, cheese, and two large spice cakes and set out pewter cups. Typically, this gathering would have occurred before the burial of the child, but the Brewsters cared not to risk the appointed time with the verger.

Upon entering the Carvers' front room, Mistress Brewster was grateful to see her friend so round and seemingly well. "Good evening, Mistress Carver. We are pleased to be in your company this evening, and appreciate you welcoming us into your home," she said in a most genuine voice, as she removed her hat and curtsied.

Mistress Carver recovered her hat and smiled at her visitors. "Thank you for visiting in your hour of grieving. I expect your children are eagerly awaiting your return, so stay as little or as long as you like. Please, come inside to share some food and drink," she requested, desiring to sit herself.

So the women found themselves in the kitchen, while the men remained conversing quietly in the front room.

What the women could not hear was the concern that Master Carver conveyed about the state of his wife and unborn child.

"You know that I am a sensible man and not one to worry, but I fear for my wife and child. My Mistress has been in varying degrees of discomfort for the last week, and I've summoned the midwife more than once, but she left each time without explanation or assurance. With the history of one child lost before birth, the thought of another little life in jeopardy weighs on me. More than that, the vision of my wife in danger haunts me day and night. Her own mother died just after childbirth, shortly after delivering my Mistress," whispered Master Carver.

"John, you do not need me to tell you that the Lord has carved His plan already. There is nothing to do but keep your love for Marie strong and undaunted by fear. Be by her side for this and what lies beyond, trusting that His plan is the right one," said Pastor Robinson calmly and laden with kindness and belief in his words.

Masters Brewster and Carver nodded solemnly in agreement.

Mistress Brewster enjoyed her fig pastry as she listened to her friend speak English coated beautifully in a French accent. As Mistress Carver spoke, she adjusted her coif more than once and shifted uncomfortably in her chair. She dared not ask Mistress Brewster if what she was feeling was typical, as her friend had just buried a child minutes earlier, and frankly, Mistress Carver was afraid to hear her response. Since the loss of her own child the year before, she had spent this pregnancy in a state of constant fear, bordering on perpetual panic. Even though she knew this was not aiding her or the child, her ways of coping failed her miserably, leaving her terrified.

Mistress Brewster sensed her friend's apprehension, and at one point thought she witnessed her grimace, as if experiencing a twinge of pain. "Bearing children can be an overwhelming experience," she said softly to her friend. "Are you feeling well, Marie?"

Mistress Carver shifted to the edge of her chair carefully, leaning towards Mistress Brewster. Tears welled in her tired brown eyes. "Mary, I am not so well. I am consumed in mind and body over the life of this child, and must admit, I even fear for myself. In the last week I have had pain where the baby lies, and noticed blood on my smock– not as much as with a monthly course, but more than the midwife expects to see. I do feel the baby move, thank the Lord, but not as often as before." Mistress Carver looked down, and the tears dropped and rolled into the folds of her red apron.

"Let's pray, Mistress, for this baby and for your own well-being. We know it lies with God, His plan." The two women turned their palms up and gazed to the heavens, as Hendrijcke swiftly made her way to her Mistress's side. The three women prayed silently as the fire crackled ominously, as if mocking their belief and hope that both baby and mother would remain healthy, and in this world.

Even before Mistress Carver gasped and clutched at her swollen belly, Mistress Brewster sensed something was not right, although she never imagined it could be this wrong. Both Hendrijcke and Mistress Brewster lunged forward, moving desperately to catch Mistress Carver's falling body so they could lower her safely to the stone floor. Mary knelt on the cold floor and held one of Mistress Carver's hands while keeping her friend's head off the stone with her other hand.

"Oh dear. Hendrijcke, please inform the men and ask Master Brewster to summon midwife Willet straight away," directed a shaken Mistress Brewster.

In a matter of seconds, Master Carver exploded up into the kitchen and dove onto the floor. He held his wife's empty hand and assisted Mistress Brewster in keeping her head raised off the kitchen floor.

"Hendrijcke, please bring me a pillow, a linen cloth, and a bowl of cold water," requested Mary in a clear and calm voice.

Hendrijcke rushed away for the items, moving but feeling numb in the process. Her head spun at the thought of her Mistress losing her child, and even worse, the idea that she might lose her Mistress at the same time.

Master Carver's words seemed stolen by shock. Watching his wife's lifeless body, with his child inside, he wondered if either one would remain in this world. It was then that they noticed the blood seeping through Mistress Carver's linen smock, coloring her red petticoat an even deeper red. The more red that appeared, the whiter Master Carver's complexion became.

By then, Hendrijcke returned with the pillow, cloth, water and a red earthenware vessel. With a handle on one side and a rounded base shaped for fitting in a cupped hand, the little vessel could be tipped forward, and a narrow, elongated spout delivered liquid to a person in need. Mistress Brewster began wiping Mistress Carver's forehead gently with the cooled cloth, hoping to revive her without a startle.

"Hendrijcke, please bring more cloths. Our Mistress is bleeding considerably," said Mistress Brewster in a calm voice.

Master Carver knelt by his wife's side, still sick with the uncertainty looming over them, but lovingly stroking Mistress Carver's cold cheek with the side of his hand. He began to speak quietly, whispering reassuring words into her ear. He was not certain whether she could hear him, but he had to assume so, and needed her to know she was not alone.

A small stream of water from the linen towel that Mistress Brewster used to wipe Mistress Carver's forehead trickled along the outline of her nose and down across her lips. Her eyes began to flutter, and then opened for a moment.

"Mistress Carver, please awaken. Look at us, talk to us," begged Mistress Brewster. "Midwife Willet should be on her way. Please talk to us," implored Mary.

Mistress Carver opened her eyes then, and was able to keep them open and speak. "What is happening?" she asked in French, as she attempted to sit up.

"Lie down, my love," requested Master Carver in a soft and caring voice. "The time of labour and travail has arrived, our baby likely to be born this evening. The midwife has been summoned. Once Master Brewster and Pastor Robinson return, we will move you to the comfort of the bedstead."

Mistress Carver swallowed nervously. Terrifying thoughts raced through her mind about what was to happen next. Her fingers trembled, and sweat replaced the water applied to her forehead. Just then, she felt the building sensation of a tightening within, a feeling she had experienced in her last pregnancy, when her baby came much too early. Her eyes darted frantically around the room, scanning and assessing the distance to her bedstead, where she yearned to be. She had no idea the bleeding had begun, so when she shifted her position in an attempt to sit up again, the sight of her stained clothing made her gasp.

"Marie, please do not be afraid. You are going to be all right, as will the baby," said Master Carver, in a voice that sounded as if he was reassuring himself as much as his wife, in the midst of the overflow of blood. At that moment they heard the footsteps of Master Brewster and Pastor Robinson, hopefully returning with midwife Willet. Thankfully, she made her way into the kitchen first, entering with confidence and a command craved by all. Goodwife Willet came in carrying an arsenal of items, such as her birthing stool, sharpened knife, sponge, and oil of lilies and almonds.

"Hendrijcke, please ready the bedstead with more sheets, cloths, and pillows. I will need two large bowls, one with warm water, and one empty. I also desire the oil of lilies to be warmed," instructed the midwife as she removed a ring from her finger, her nails adequately trimmed. She continued, "Masters Carver and Brewster, prepare to carry Mistress Carver into the bedstead, once Hendrijcke is ready."

Within minutes the bedstead transformed into a birthing chamber. Hendrijcke stood close by, ready for the midwife's next command, as the men delivered Marie Carver into the bed space. Master Robinson and Mistress Brewster drew near so the group could pray. Master Robinson led them with a powerful sense of grace and directness that made everyone calmer, and certain that what was to happen next was as the Lord intended, whether it meant earthly life or death. After the prayer, the men, including Master Carver, exited the area near the bedstead, returning to the front room. He thought it best that his wife be aided by the women, but wanted to stay close, just in case.

Mistress Brewster intended to stay as long as her friend required her presence. Mary might leave in a bit to summon other women from the congregation, depending how the night progressed. Mistress Carver also had de Lannoy family members in Leyden, along with some friends in the town's Walloon congregation whom she might desire be present.

The pains were becoming more frequent and deepening in intensity, so much so that Mistress Carver began to cry softly in the travails of labor.

"It is time, Mistress. It is time to push, when I say so," declared the midwife. Goodwife Willet watched Mistress Carver closely and, sensing when it was time, urged her to action. As scared as she was, Mistress Carver converted her fear into forceful pushing, working to get her infant out and safely into the world. The exhausting effort continued for more than an hour before the newborn appeared, gathered by midwife Willet in the folds of fresh linen. She rubbed the boy vigorously within the cloth, hoping to obtain a response from him that included movement of the limbs and that loud, strong cry indicating the lungs were at work. The midwife wanted the bluish-grey coloring of the infant's flesh to transform into pink, proving the heart's strength.

Marie held her breath and prayed that God's plan would keep this child alive. "He is doing well enough," announced the midwife. "We need to hear a loud cry to be certain though."

Just then, the little soul responded with a shrill wail, letting his presence be known. And for the first time in weeks, Mistress Carver found her lips relaxing enough to curve into a smile, as she exhaled the longest sigh of relief. A large part of her job was finished, and her son was here.

Pink, healthy hues filled the boy's flesh, and Master Carver entered to meet his son and comfort his wife. He arrived to see the cord cut and navel string tied. Goody Willet washed away the blood and birthing fluids, then swaddled the boy in strips of cloth before placing him in the folds of his father's arms. Savoring this moment, he passed his gaze from his newly born son to the woman he loved and from whom their creation the Lord delivered. He kissed her forehead, letting his lips linger, as he squeezed her hand and laid their child in her tired but waiting arms. The visit did not last terribly long, as he wanted his wife to rest.

Hendrijcke moved into the kitchen to warm the oil of acorns and almonds and ready the burnt wine, brewing with hot spices. Goodwife Willet remained by Mistress Carver, digging in the pockets of her petticoat in search of a salve, the one that would quell bleeding. Of the two clay pots she extracted from her linen pockets, she chose the salve made with the juice of houseleeks, to suppress the bleeding.

Women dominated the activities surrounding birth, and for the next few days, they would be coming and going, bringing spice cake and ingredients for a caudle, such as wine, milk, and eggs. Hendrijcke ground rose and lily petals, saturating them in oil, infusing the air with fresh scents. Encapsulating the childbed in a mixture of warmth and darkness was critical. An extra basket of peat sat next to the hearth, Hendrijcke recognizing cold as an enemy of her Mistress and the newly born boy. The windows would also stay covered and shut until Mistress Carver commanded otherwise.

In the following fortnight, the newborn responded well to the world. He drank his milk easily, accepting his nourishment as well as the sights and sounds of his surroundings. Mistress Carver progressed in her recovery from labor, walking about freely and tending to her son with the aid of Hendrijcke and assistance from friends and family. Finally, it seemed, the Carvers could begin to enjoy the new life flourishing before them.

Days later, Mistress Carver checked on her son in the early- morning hours, surprised he had not awakened her first, and rocked his cradle gently. She knelt down on the cold stone floor, squinting through the darkness while peering into the cradle, hardly able to see a thing. So she brushed her baby's cheek with the back of her hand, and with it feeling unusually cool, panic pulsed through her veins. And this was with good reason, as the boy had ceased breathing and was already gone from this world.

It took less than a week for Mistress Carver to follow her son. Master Carver believed his wife died from a broken heart, that seeing a second lifeless child before her was more than she could bear, and without choice, her mind and body surrendered.

In less than three weeks from the night of the Brewster burial, the Carvers had buried their son, and Mistress Carver lay lifeless and cold. His fears of death had come to life, and John Carver could do no more than manage the pain as Pastor Robinson and the members of his congregation and those of the Walloon community surrounded him. Mistress Carver's sister-in-love and nephew, Phillipe, also living in Leyden, visited to raise the fallen man's spirits. Even with a strong faith in the Lord and all the human kindness around him, a good man could only take so much tragedy before he broke himself. A journey south to his wife's homeland would force him out of his stupor of sadness and away from Leyden for a time.

"William, would you be able to mind the house in my absence?" inquired Master Carver of young Bradford. "It was my Mistress's wish that she be buried in her place of birth, so I must leave at once. Although Mistress Carver has been washed with rosewater and wound with added sprigs of rosemary, time and temperature urge us to move quickly. Hendrijcke will accompany me on this trip, with her return to Leyden uncertain. I have some trade there I need to look after, so I entrust you to manage things here, including some of my pending agreements. I should be back before the year's end."

"Most certainly, Master Carver. I am honored that you charge me with such responsibilities," responded William, standing tall. Hendrijcke stood quietly behind Master Carver and nodded as if understanding the plan, without hearing the words or looking up. The distraught servant did her best to hide the tears, even pulling her felted wool brim lower than normal and repeatedly wiping her blotchy, salt-stained cheeks.

Mistress Carver was laid to rest within hours of reaching L'Escluse. She had to be, as time and heat are not kind companions to decaying flesh. If it had not been for her specific request for burial in L'Escluse, Master Carver would have buried his beloved in Leyden within a day or two of her death. Her family had no warning of her passing, so Master Carver's arrival was received with justifiable concern. When his eyes met theirs, words were not needed to explain his wife's absence. Master Carver's heavy heart was visible to family and strangers alike, and in a matter of hours, his Mistress was buried beneath the de Lannoy slab in the Walloon church.

John Carver continued grieving, eventually tending to some matters of business as he prepared for his next journey. He stayed in L'Escluse until February of the next year, principally out of respect for his wife's family. The additional time also ensured his contracts would be secure for another year.

That death escapes no one is life's unavoidable reality. The reminders lurked around every corner of the city, from Leyden University's Anatomy Theatre, a place where the public could view human dissections, to a Hooglandsekerk window bearing a stone-carved flying skull with wings, one from a bird and one from a bat, surrounded by bones and a scythe. Sounds from the Pieterskerk's powerful organ wailing for a funeral penetrated the air, and just outside the western city gates, a criminal's head impaled on a wooden stake encouraged citizens to abide by the rules. The visual, audible, and at times odiferous symbols of a temporal, fleeting existence were omnipresent.

Leyden's painters routinely captured the symbolism of this brief mortality, featuring skulls, timepieces, remnants of drink and feast, along with books and instruments. For merchants and others reaping the benefits of the booming international trade, there would be the need for a gentle reminder that all things material would be acquired in vain, that nothing and no one outlasted death. And that death does not discriminate was also clear. Higher levels of education, political status, prominent religious positions, or even financial standing could not keep death away forever.

For the Carver infant, with his father successful as a merchant in the wool and cloth trades, his life would have been moderately comfortable, as would have the life of the Brewster boy, laid to rest weeks earlier. He too came into the world the son of educated parents, and in his case with a father spending years at court as well as managing an Archbishop's Manor and Royal Post stop, the boy had an able mentor. Above all, the Carvers and Brewsters remained steadfast in their religious beliefs, seeking to worship in a way most consistent with Scripture. The desire to honor this covenant had forced their departure from England and led them to this city. And even with the soundest and most godly foundations, death stole both lives before they could ever really begin.

A little more than three months after the deaths of the Carver infant and his mother, the Pieterskerk's organ played long and loudly for the large funeral procession of one of the University's leading professors. The pipes of the organ, mounted high up on the west wall, pumped sound through the bricks, leaking music out onto the churchyard, trickling onto the cobblestones of the Kloksteeg. The powerful instrument created sound that crept across the alley, easily reaching the ears of the inhabitants of Pastor Robinson's Green Close.

John Robinson contemplated attending the funeral of Theology Professor Jacobus Arminius, but decided it most appropriate to remember him privately in his home. Regardless of their differences in religious philosophies, he recognized the loss of a pious, godly man and academic. He, with many in the city, mourned the loss of a dedicated professor and servant of the Dutch Reformed Church.

It was widely known that Arminius disagreed with Pastor Robinson's strong conviction that the power of excommunication and election of pastors and elders should be decided by the people of the church, as opposed to church officials. And unlike Master Robinson and his congregation, being strict followers of the doctrine of John Calvin and predestination, Arminius thought that outlook too harsh. Arminius believed while on Earth, man's choices could impact the chance for salvation, a view in absolute opposition to Calvin, and his follower, John Robinson. This gap in religious philosophy was immaterial as far as recognizing the loss of Arminius's mortal life. As much as they respected the professor's earthly existence, Pastor Robinson and his flock would remain absent from both the ceremony in the University's Great Auditorium and the funeral in the Pieterskerk.

Less than two months later, the organ played again, this time even louder, calling out to honor and celebrate the life of one of Leyden's greatest servants of the people, Secretary Jan van Hout. The late secretary's nephew, Master van Orlers, offered four funeral tickets to Master Brewster. The men were neighbors, and in the past six months had developed a friendship. For Master Brewster, Secretary van Hout symbolized loyalty and longevity, traits that reminded him of his former master, Secretary Davison. More than two decades since their initial meeting, Secretary van Hout remembered Master Brewster earlier that year in 1609, granting Pastor Robinson's congregation permission to settle in Leyden.

Pastor Robinson, Master Brewster, his son, Jonathan, and William Bradford comprised part of the silent throng shuffling their way through the southern entrance of the Pieterskerk, eager to escape the rapidly falling, thick flakes of snow.

As the mourners crossed the grey stone slabs of the Pieterskerk floor, they walked with memories of a man who accomplished so much. Secretary Jan van Hout lived more than six decades, known for diplomatic heroics and brilliant poetic prose. Possessing the foresight to receive the skilled hands of religious refugees, he welcomed foreigners capable of resuscitating a struggling textile industry. During the siege of Leyden in 1574, Secretary van Hout stood strong as a leader, refusing any terms the Spanish offered.

The archiving of records of betrothals and recording the buying and selling of homes was attributed to this great leader. He displayed talents in literary theory, poetry and plays, while having a role in the city's printing industry. Along with his developing a system of support for orphans and the elderly, Secretary van Hout's distinctive years of service held a unique place within the city government and University of Leyden, garnering respect from all reaches of Leyden's diverse population.

As the last of those honoring the secretary inched their way into the crowded church, the large wooden doors closed, pushing the already huddled pack closer together. Master Brewster peered around the heads in the rows in front of him, attempting to view the brilliant secretary one last time. From where he stood, he could barely see the richness of the late secretary's black doublet. A black cape made from either silk or velvet covered his shoulders, and beyond that, Master Brewster could make out little more.

Memory served well enough for William to imagine the serene expression on the secretary's noble face. His short white beard would be neatly trimmed, his white ruff collar bleached the brightest white, positioned perfectly, just as it had been more than two decades before, when Master Brewster attended a meeting at The Fighting Lion Inn. Young Brewster stood at a distance while Secretaries van Hout and Davison discussed the cooperative efforts of the two Protestant countries in deflecting the aggressive intentions of Catholic Spain. What struck Brewster then, as it did now, was the calm demeanor that Secretary van Hout conveyed so consistently. His diplomatic and inventive nature led to cooperation with those in the government, and nourished the evolution of the University and its international educational role.

Even in the dead of winter, when it was nearly impossible to keep a large indoor space warm, the love for Secretary van Hout more than filled the cavernous church. Pastor Robinson looked up, his palms facing up as he prayed silently for a man he did not know well, but held a deep respect for. Jonathan Brewster, a young man of only sixteen years, and William Bradford, just three years older, soaked up the impressive scene. Jonathan gazed up at the whitewashed columns supporting arches between them, and bricked areas above. The highest section of these walls included four panels of windows within an arched, bricked frame. Even though Jonathan and his congregation would not worship here, he could still appreciate the size and scale of such a building, and the materials and years it took to create it. With the church teeming with people, including government dignitaries, University officials and professors, and notables from the Dutch Reformed Church, the great secretary's life was celebrated with the dignity he deserved.

After the official Dutch Reformed Service, the church erupted in song, producing sweet and soothing harmony with their psalms. Three beautifully crafted eulogies followed, one being expertly delivered by Secretary van Hout's nephew, Master van Orlers. Leyden's city musicians, joined by twenty trumpet players from The Hague, breathed life into their instruments. Through their notes to the heavens, they requested their servant enter in peace. Jonathan Brewster closed his blue eyes and allowed the sounds to swallow him. Even though his own congregation would not carry out a funeral with formal prayers or music, he could respect this experience. The pipe organs flooded the air, belting out the sound of a city wailing in sorrow. Master Brewster passed a thoughtful glance over to Pastor Robinson. With the loss of Secretary van Hout, how would Leyden fare? Would their newly arrived congregation retain permission to remain in the city?

HET PLOTEN EN KAMMEN, 1594-1596, ISAAC CLAESZ VAN SWANENBURG,
LAKENHAL MUSEUM, LEIDEN, THE NETHERLANDS

Part of a series of paintings from Swanenburg, this painting is illustrating how wool is prepared for spinning, for the production of say (cloth). Looking counter-clockwise, the operations depicted are- in the left background, cleaning the raw fiber (washing, beating, drying); in the left foreground, a little boy carrying a basket of wool to the combers in the front-center, where the combs are warmed in the heating pot sitting to the right of the standing comber. An apprentice brings beer from behind, looking directly in the viewer's eyes. Two men in the right fore-ground are taking wool from the skins of the butchered sheep; the one on the left is pulling out the wool by hand (plucking) and the other is cutting it off with shears (shearing). Behind them, in the background on the right, the washed, dried, mat-ted wool fibers are being whipped with long, thin switches, which frees the fibers for further processing. Farther back, the opened clots are being sprinkled with fat (in this case melted butter), to lubricate the fibers for combing. The actual order in which these things were done was plucking or shearing the wool, washing, switch-ing, combing, then washing again. The translation of the title of this painting is 'Combing and Plucking'.

Chapter Ten

Wool and Books

The following year, February – March 1610
From Leyden to England

Hendrijcke never did return to Leyden. With Master Carver's permission, she elected to stay in L'Escluse with the de Lannoy family. He understood her need to remain there, with her being from that place and loyal to his wife's family. In truth, he was in need of time on his own.

Successful in his merchant ventures in the wool and cloth trades, Master Carver wanted not for money. What he sought had nothing to do with increasing his financial wealth. He longed for answers to questions about the path his life had taken up until now, and what direction he was meant to go. It was not that he took pity on himself with the loss of his family, but those events left him pondering his greater purpose in this world.

Predestination dictated the future; as a follower of Calvin, he believed that. Was the tragedy he endured a test of his faith? He decided it was not, but instead a test of his individual strength, offering a chance to reflect on his larger role within the congregation. Perhaps his path called upon him to play a more active part in supporting Pastor Robinson and Master Brewster in their work in Leyden. Why then, in this time of transition for the congregation, would he decide to abandon the group and return to England?

Even he was not entirely certain of the answer. There was a part of him that wanted to escape the memories on the mainland, and even though England was the country he fled to avoid religious persecution, it was not by choice. It was still his homeland, where many of his family and close friends resided. One of his objectives in traveling to England was to locate Master Brewer, so they might discuss a plan for printing, and his own intentions for removing to the mainland. There was the matter of business in England, where a good portion of his deals originated, and existing contacts could be strengthened and new opportunities explored. His timing coincided with the spring sheep shearing, so Master Carver planned to purchase additional quantities of raw wool for export.

Before crossing the sea to England, Master Carver first travelled up the waterways back to Leyden to obtain some belongings and confer with Pastor Robinson and Master Brewster about the congregation's direction. He needed to confirm that William Bradford was caring for his rented home on the Nieuwe Street, along with overseeing the business contracts and updating the ledger books he left behind. One responsibility involved reselling finished cloth, with a large bolt being purchased at Master Carver's expense and then portioned out and sold by William at higher prices.

Upon entering Leyden by way of the Vliet River, Master Carver disembarked at the icy steps leading to the street level of the Rapenburg Canal, in front of the former Beginhof Chapel. He had been wanting to go into that building ever since he moved to Leyden the year before, as it was no longer a Catholic church but a University building housing the library, as well as an extraordinary Theatre of Anatomy. A visit here would be for another time, as John watched the skipper's men transfer his trunk from their ship onto the little scow tied behind them. He had paid a fare that included the delivery of his belongings to his doorstep, and followed his trunk onto the scow, pleased to be in the final phase of this cold journey, or at least this part of his travels. This would be but a pause before continuing on to England.

The distance for the scow to travel on the Rapenburg to the part of the Nieuwe Rhine nearest to Master Carver's home was not far. They reached the destination in a few minutes, with the men working the scow hoisting the trunk up the steps near the Corn Bridge. Since he had provided the location of his house and tipped them in advance, the men walked urgently ahead to Master Carver's home. They dropped the trunk inside the hallway and scurried back to their little boat before John made his way inside.

"Good day, William," called Master Carver as he walked down the hallway and into the front room. There was no sign of young Bradford. The fireplace lay idle and barely warm, with the cover bell still in place. He returned to the streets in the hope of finding either Master Brewster or Pastor Robinson, or ideally both together. As he crossed over the Corn Bridge, the bells of the Town Hall rang announcing two of the clock, and he pondered whose home he should try first.

It took only a partial knock on the door before nine-year-old Patience Brewster answered and looked with surprise at seeing Master Carver before her.

"Oh, Master Carver, what a lovely surprise," exclaimed Patience while curtsying. "We did not know when you would be back to Leyden. Father will be overjoyed at your return. Please come in and let me bring him to you," announced the exuberant young girl.

"Father, Father, if you can believe me, it is Master Carver here in our home! Please come down," said Patience, calling up the staircase. Instead, it was Jonathan Brewster who bounded down the steps, eager to see the unexpected visitor.

"Good day, Jonathan. You look to be faring well. May I presume things are progressing for you here in Leyden?"

"We are doing our best to find our way, Master Carver, for our family and as a congregation. My father has many connections now to the University. Some are professors, but we have many students coming to our home to learn English. For now, his teaching of English is supporting our family. And with help from members of the congregation, I am meeting many people and starting to learn Dutch. I have also been learning about the ribbon trade. How are you faring? Have you returned to Leyden to stay?"

"I am faring well in that I have my health and am blessed to be back here in the company of your family and the congregation. I spent several months settling accounts in L'Escluse and removing most of my possessions from there. I did not want to leave too soon after the burial of Mistress Carver. For now, my plan entails a brief stop here on my way to England. I do expect I will return here to Leyden for the longer term. My intention in traveling to England is to seek out Master Brewer, as well as my family. I also have business throughout England I can look after."

"John, is that truly you before us?" queried a jubilant Master Brewster. "I had not been informed of your return to Leyden. Should I assume you arrived today then?"

"Yes, William, I stepped off the frigid canal only moments ago. My trunk remains in the hallway of my home, not even unlocked. I called out seeking William Bradford, and when I heard nothing, I set off in search of you, thinking he might be here as well."

"Young Bradford is not here. He actually was here earlier this day. You might find him at the home of Pastor Robinson. Are you back indefinitely, or stopping here on the way to somewhere else?"

"I will keep renting my home here, assuming William is managing things well enough, and do plan on returning to settle. I expect to depart in a fortnight for England and seek out Master Brewer, then travel north to find family and look to my business there. Master Brewer and I had worked extensively in growing our network of trade in Fuller's Earth, and I want to see if that remains intact. I plan to visit family and also spend time with the Hickmans in Gainsborough, as a substantial piece of business is connected to them. Our financial success is essential in supporting the congregation's needs, in addition to whatever publishing efforts we decide to pursue."

"I see. I expect that to be a prudent plan. And to ease any concerns, William has been managing your home and business dealings quite well. Any time he is uncertain of something, he speaks with Master Robinson or me. I am not aware of an instance where he has acted rashly. I have been to your home many times since you left in July, and found it in an orderly state. That is significant, seeing that there is no maid or housewife managing the daily tasks. Do you intend to rent out any portion of the home in your absence? I have been teaching English to many University students, and some might have a need for rental quarters."

"That could be a simple means of acquiring additional income. Yes, if it would not trouble you, please assist William should any opportunities arise. I trust you would be careful in the process. We would not want someone living there that could cause us problems."

"Yes, yes, of course, John."

"Father, if it would not trouble you, please tell Master Carver of your work with the Basson printers, at the sign of The Music Book," requested Jonathan excitedly.

"Ah yes, the Bassons. Later this month I will start checking their books for errors, prior to printing. Mostly they are works in Latin and Greek, and largely for the University. It is not clear how much work they will have for me, but I am eager to read the books and have a place in their busy shop. I expect the experience will increase my knowledge of the trade, and expand our connections within the University. My hope is that both aspects will aid our congregation."

"Yes, of course. Any knowledge and contacts gained in the printing trade would be of interest, especially to Master Brewer. As you know, he has invested in publications printed by Giles Thorp in Amsterdam, using the type I carried over from Printer Okes in London. I believe he intends to invest further in the book trade, in purchasing publications banned in England and distributing them there, as well as funding printing here."

"Do you know of Master Brewer's whereabouts? I am assuming he is back somewhere in England, perhaps even at his estate?"

"I do not know of his precise location, although I am predicting somewhere in England. I think if he were back here on the mainland, you would have known of this. Since the time we were all together in Amsterdam more than a year ago, his intention was to return to England to pursue the hand of a lady named Anna Offley. It could even be that they are married by now."

Master Carver continued, "My time in Leyden will be brief, as this is a stop on my way back to England. I have business matters and family to seek out. I am not sure if I have lost any family members since my departure more than two years ago."

"Yes, of course. That is always a risk in leaving family behind. The possibility that when and if you return, they will not be among the living. Have you visited yet with Pastor Robinson?"

"No, I came directly to you, Master Brewster. Would you care to accompany me to the Green Close?"

"But of course. Let us make our way over at once, as our pastor will be delighted by your return. He will also be interested in your plans to travel to England, as you will be near enough to his family and able to look in on them. Let us depart for the Green Close at once."

After spending nearly three weeks in Leyden, visiting with Master Robinson's congregation and de Lannoy family members and friends of the Walloon church, Master Carver booked passage on the *Dolphin* to Dover, England. Upon docking, his plan was to travel west by wagon to Maidstone, in Kent, to the Brewer Estate, hoping to find his close friend Thomas Brewer. This would be a gamble, as Master Brewer had considerable business throughout the English countryside, especially in the northern parts, and the odds were greater he would be absent. In either case, Master Carver knew he would be welcome there, and could stay as long as he liked.

After reaching English soil, John spent two days traveling by wagon before approaching the impressive estate. He learned upon entering the grounds that he would find his friend inside. Elated at knowing that in minutes they would be reunited, he shook off the weighty months of sorrow and bounded up the stone steps to the main house. The reaction of Master Brewer was fantastic upon learning of his friend's unexpected arrival. The two men ran like children to one other, locking in a most meaningful embrace.

"Surprised does not capture the moment," exclaimed Master Brewer, with the widest of smiles. Even his eyes were smiling. "What a blessing that you are here. It must be nearly a year and one half since we traveled from your home in L'Escluse north to Amsterdam together, in the autumn of 1608. Thanks be to God you are before me, and in good health. What brings you to Maidstone? I pray only trade and nothing more," said Master Brewer with a tone of concern.

"My dear friend, I have journeyed here as you would expect, as directed by our Lord. I stand here before you to work out how I, or we, might support the poor English congregation in Leyden in a bigger way," explained John. "Mistress Carver resides now in the safe keeping of our Lord, along with our two children. She and my youngest son were taken last July, within Leyden's city walls. It was a cruel experience in that the pregnancy had its difficulties, and truthfully, I thought the child would be lost upon birth. But he fought and appeared instead to be well. So our expectations shifted to thinking we were in a safer place, and our baby was strong– until one morning my Mistress awoke to the chilling reality of a cold baby. Oh, Master Brewer, it was too much for her to bear, to see yet another infant gone from this world. How can a mother endure a recurrence of this kind? I miss her each day, without question, but the Lord wills me forward.

"I hear whispers, Master Brewer, voices telling me of a greater plan. And that is why I am here. To understand the path the Lord has laid for us, and how we can make a more significant impact, together."

"Oh, John, I am so sorry for your losses, and pray you can carry on under the burden of that sorrow. I am most grateful that the Lord led you here. Over the months, I have pondered our direction, regarding whether to stay here or venture to the Continent–"

At that moment, Mistress Anna Brewer entered the main hall, eager to have her husband make her introduction. Master Brewer turned and stood a little straighter as he watched his bride enter the room, walking towards them.

"John, may I introduce you to my loving wife, Anna Brewer? Mistress Brewer and I were married this past November in London," said Master Brewer as he reached to hold his wife's outstretched hand.

"It is an honor, Mistress, to make your acquaintance," stated Master Carver earnestly as he removed his hat and bowed deeply. "This is a most welcome surprise. I had no idea whether Master Brewer would be here, and I am blessed to find not only him, but his lovely wife as well."

"Your timing is wondrous good, as I am just days away from departing to London, stopping there on my way to Gainsborough," said Master Brewer. "Please, let us relive old times and join me in the journey. I am traveling up to London to visit my cousin, Mistress Okes, along with Master Printer Okes and the children. We have news of God's blessing, of an unborn child between us," revealed Master Brewer quietly, raising his hands and eyes upward, as he prayed silently.

"How wonderful, my friend, to be bestowed with such a gift so soon in your marriage," exclaimed Master Carver. "I would be honored to accompany you in your travels to London and beyond, into the northern parts of the country. Will you be traveling as well, good Mistress, or shall you remain behind in the safety and comfort of these beautiful grounds?"

Mistress Brewer smiled as she shook her head and gently rubbed her barely swollen belly, indicating she and the unborn child would not take to the wet and slippery roads.

"As much as I would like to remain in the company of my husband, the risks of travel are enough to keep me here. And to be honest, after contending with some of the unpleasant aspects of growing up in London, I dare not return to a place I scarcely miss. Being with child, I would not want to expose myself to the crowds of London, not knowing how deadly the plague will be this spring and summer. Of course, I will miss visiting my family and telling them of our happy news, but Thomas will stop at the home of my parents and share our excitement. Hopefully my father is in London, as his business takes him on occasion to Istanbul and other parts of the Eastern Mediterranean."

"Yes," continued Master Brewer, "Master Robert Offley, the father of my mistress, is a leading merchant and shareholder within the Levant Company, which I am sure you have heard of."

Master Carver thought for a moment, and nodded slowly. "Yes. Yes, I am aware of the Levant Company, but my knowledge is lacking in the details of the group. I do recall this company was a charter from the Queen, God rest her soul, perhaps in the early 1580s?"

"To be exact, 1581. I have been learning quite a bit from my wife about the intricacies of her father's business. The Levant Company is a joint-stock company, with English merchants based mainly in London financing transactions in the different Ottoman ports along the Eastern Mediterranean coast, such as Aleppo and Izmir. English traders, or factors as they are known, might spend up to twenty years living in this region, remaining generally solitary, rarely integrating into the culture of the Levant. What is interesting is that for that sacrifice of living away from England, the factors do not fare nearly as well financially as the dragomen, or local translators. A dragoman holds the key to the treasure, as he knows the mixed Italian trade language, the lingua franca as they call it, so he is the link with the local merchants of the area. This communication and cultural advantage equates to great wealth for some of these men."

"So what are the main items involved in trade? I am guessing silk and perhaps Turkey carpets."

"The main item leaving England is woolen broadcloth, and in trade the Levant Company is shipping back cotton yarn, dried fruits such as figs, apricots, and raisins, in addition to raw silk and carpets. There is also some trade for materials used in dyeing or processing cloth."

"It sounds quite intriguing, with the international flavor of the trade. Has Master Offley approached you about entering this business?" asked Master Carver.

Master Brewer nodded as he looked across at his Mistress, who returned a shy smile. "I think initially, when Master Offley learned of my education and foothold in the Fuller's Earth trade, he expected me to participate in his business. After many thoughtful discussions, I realized the Lord's plan for me is about more than merchant trading, whether it be Fuller's Earth or other items. My success in trade motivates me so that I, like you, might support a bigger purpose."

Master Carver stood speechless as he listened, realizing that may-haps Master Brewer and he had arrived at the same conclusion, the Lord bringing them together. Masters Carver and Brewer recognized their bond was created and predetermined by the Lord. Both men believed that plan involved spreading the Lord's word in the form of printed material, which was precisely why Master Carver carried the type from Master Printer Okes over to the mainland and delivered it to Giles Thorp, an English printer in Amsterdam. As it happened, Masters Brewer and Brewster were present in Amsterdam during that exchange.

"Oh, John, before we go any further with this most important dialogue, let us bring you in properly and get you settled into a room. Do forgive me."

Mistress Brewer instructed one of the male servants to escort Master Carver to his quarters, and the friends agreed to reconvene in the garden before enjoying their evening meal.

Reflecting back to the Fall of 1608…

John took the weight off his feet as he settled back into the rust-colored, velvet-cushioned chair, sitting somewhat stunned, looking straight ahead but noticing nothing of his surroundings. He sat pondering the span of time since his last meeting with Master Brewer and reflected back nearly eighteen months, to the fall of 1608, when they had travelled together from L'Escluse up to Amsterdam, to conduct business in Fuller's Earth. The bigger purpose of that mission was to locate their dear friends Master Brewster and Pastor John Robinson, who were thought to have turned up in Amsterdam, settling in amongst the Ancient Brethren. Thanks be to God, a reunion of the men did occur, in the home of teacher and printer Master Jean de Lecluse, and what a blessing it was.

The little group reconnected with many years separating their last union, and the timing could not have been more fortuitous, for Master Brewster and Pastor Robinson had begun discussing the possibility of leading their congregation away from the turmoil of the Ancient Brethren. They were considering a move to another place, such as Leyden. Master Carver, having been to Leyden, thought about the beneficial aspects of settling there, such as access to the University and the growing textile trade. He decided a move there could be sensible even for him and his wife.

Master Brewer, on the other hand, had plans to return to England within that month. His business at the Brewer Estate was not in a state to be abandoned, and more significantly, he had begun courting a young woman named Anna Offley, with whom he desired a deeper connection. Upon his return to England, his intention was to ask her father permission to marry, and a sudden move to the Continent would most definitely stifle the maturing relationship.

Before the evening came to a close, one more individual came calling at the home of Master de Lecluse. He was a member of the Ancient Brethren, a printer by the name of Master Giles Thorp. He had come for the type being stored there, the very type quietly offered by Master Printer Okes in London, and carried to the mainland by Master Carver.

"Please, be sure to mix this type with plates from your current stores, so as to mask the identity of the type's original owner. He is a dear friend who intends to remain in our mother country as part of the Stationers' Company, monitored very closely by the Crown," warned Master Brewer.

"Yes, without question," responded Printer Thorp, nodding with complete understanding. "That is the strategy with many of my publications, so do not trouble yourself with such concerns. Keep in mind that many founts and ornaments are cast in metal from a master woodcut, so letters and ornaments appearing to have unique breaks are not so. In fact, they are in the hands of multiple printers throughout Holland and Europe, which works in our favor when desiring to remain anonymous. Do you intend to leave the type with me indefinitely, or do you have other plans for it?" inquired Printer Thorp.

"That is a question I do not have a precise answer to. We shall see how this effort develops, but expect to have ongoing use of the type. My level of investment and involvement in printing is uncertain," answered Master Brewer. "I do have intentions of backing publications, especially those that expose the abuses of the bishops and other atrocities within the Church of England. I also seek to put words into print that will spread the message of the New Testament. I will be returning to England within the month and have no immediate plans to travel back to the Continent."

"Is it acceptable, Master Brewer, if I use the type in other works, other than those you support? For instance, in the next weeks, I will begin setting the type for a publication by our godly Minister Ainsworth, to be printed in the coming year."

"Of course, Master Thorp. By offering you this type, I trust you and your judgment. Use it at your discretion to spread our message," encouraged Master Brewer.

Printer Thorp nodded again, thanked the group, and prepared to carry the large wooden box containing the metal type directly to his shop, located a few blocks away. His apprentice waiting in the street took hold of one end of the weighty cargo, and slowly, the men made their way down the darkening street.

Returning to the Spring of 1610...

A light knock at his guest room door delivered Master Carver from the fall of 1608 back to the spring of 1610. Mildly startled, he rose from the chair to answer the sound made by the male servant on the other side of the door.

"I am sorry to disturb you, Master Carver," said the servant. "Master Brewer wishes to know if there is anything in particular you desire for your supper."

Master Carver smiled with affection at the nervous young servant. "Please, tell my good friend that I only require his company, and that of his lovely wife, and nothing more. Any food and drink will be but a pleasant addition."

"Yes, Master Carver, I will pass along that message. Would you care for warm water for washing?" inquired Richard.

"Please. I would greatly appreciate the chance to refresh my weary, over-travelled flesh."

"I will return with the warm water and some linens, with your trunk forthcoming. If you should require anything in addition, please inform me. I am here to assist you during your stay."

"Many thanks, my good man," said Master Carver. "I will not be in need of much, and to my knowledge we are to set off in less than a week's time. So outside of food and drink, I might ask only to have my linens laundered and wool brushed. Also, my shoes could stand a cleaning and oiling should you have the time," mentioned Master Carver, as he leaned down to untie the leather cord and free his tired feet from the muddied leather shoes.

"But of course, Master Carver. Your trunk contents will be laundered or brushed immediately, and again prior to your departure. I will see to it myself. Continue to rest, and I shall return with warmed water, a brass basin, lye soap, and fresh linens," promised Richard as he carefully retrieved the shoes to be cleaned, then backed out of the room, timidly closing the door.

Less than a quarter of an hour later, Richard returned with all the promised items, including Master Carver's cleaned shoes. Two additional servants passed through the room's threshold and rested the oak chest on the floor beneath one of the large windows.

"Wonderful. Thank you, Richard," said John as he nodded in gratitude to the two other nameless servants.

"Indeed, Master Carver. Master and Mistress Brewer await your presence in the gardens found on the west side of the estate. My Master did stress that you take your time in recovering before joining them," conveyed Richard.

"Let your good Master know I will be along shortly, as my finding him here has increased my spirits tenfold, so that a need for rest is minimal. I will wash up and change my clothing before meeting them in the garden. Would you mind returning in a farthing of an hour, to aid me as I dress?"

"Of course. I will take my leave now. Once you have unlocked your trunk, please set aside the clothing to be laundered, and I will remove those items whilst you have your supper."

"Thank you, Richard."

And with that, the servant left John Carver's guest quarters, granting him the privacy to change his linen shirt and knit stockings, wash his hands and face, and review the thoughts he cared to share with the Brewers.

Master Carver unbuttoned his doublet in a meditative manner, carefully pushing the rounded pewter buttons through their partnered holes. Grateful to remove the weighty garment, he laid it on the shimmering green bedcovering of his massive four-post bed. Then off came the matching breeches, having been unhooked from the doublet, and the silk garters untied just below the knee. He peeled the moist linen stockings from his tired feet and placed the pair on the floor as the start of the dirty pile he promised Richard. Shifting the contents of his clothing within the trunk, further distancing the clean from the less-than-fresh items, he moved those things requiring laundering on top of the pair of dirt-laden linen stockings. Exchanging a crisp white shirt was an integral part of the process, and John was grateful to remove the limp, dingy shirt he had worn for two consecutive days and add it to the soiled heap.

The water in the brass basin was not hot, but warm enough to soothe the skin and remove the undesirable elements from his face and hands. First he tended to the needs of his face, dipping one of the linen cloths into the water and wiping the fresh fibers across the top of the little white bar of lye, then over his brow, cheeks, and chin. He splashed his face with warm water from his cupped hands, then dabbed his face dry. Next he rubbed into his hands a bit of the soap and washed away the toil of the travel, smiling at the thought of spending time with one of his dearest friends.

John pulled out one of his favorite suits of clothing. The color of the blue was not terribly dark, but wouldn't be considered a light blue either; it was a medium blue bearing a richness and deepness declaring a successful man fit inside.

He walked over to the corner of the room, away from the large windows overlooking the gardens, so he could stand before the mirror as he fastened the beautiful silver doublet buttons. He would wait for Richard's return to join the breeches to the upper garment. Deep within the trunk he located his orange-colored stockings and blue silk garters.

"Master Carver, may I enter?" inquired Richard.

"Yes. Yes, please do. I require your aid with these points, and with the ruff as well."

With his suit secured and starched ruff in place, Richard again took his leave. Master Carver sorted through his trunk's top compartment and located the comb that would revive his hair. After combing his hair, he replaced his dark-gray hat, then tied the leather cord on his polished shoes, eager to depart for the gardens.

Master Carver walked quickly across the long stretch of hallway and rapidly descended the wooden staircase. He crossed the cavernous space of the Great Hall and found his exit adjacent to the kitchen quarters.

As he made his way to his friends, their backs to him and gazes in the direction of the setting spring sun, he wondered about the Leyden congregation he had left behind, and when he might return to them. He had an intriguing thought come into his mind; perhaps someday, Master Brewer and his wife might make their home in Leyden as well. The idea was pleasing to him, even if unlikely. As he approached the couple, they turned in unison to greet him with welcoming smiles, gesturing for John to sit on one of the wooden benches across from them.

Master Brewer inquired at once about the Leyden congregation, and in particular Pastor Robinson and Master Brewster.

"When I left the congregation in Leyden less than a fortnight ago, the leaders and members appeared settled with housing. Many are still seeking regular employment as opposed to accepting daily work. William Bradford resides in my home there and will continue to, as I extended the rental agreement for another year. I desired the option of returning and did not care to trouble members of the congregation by requiring accommodations elsewhere. This way William can continue running the household, as well as mind the business I left behind," explained Master Carver.

"By what means is Master Brewster generating his income in Leyden?" inquired Master Brewer.

"Much of his earnings come from teaching English to University students. Just before my departure, Master Brewster had taken employment with the English printers by the name of Basson. Master Thomas Basson and his son Govert run a print shop at the corner of the Kloksteeg and Rapenburg, down the alley from Pastor Robinson's home, and just across the canal from one of the large University buildings. Their shop at the sign of The Music Book prints many books for the University. Master Brewster will be reading through works written in Latin and Greek, checking them for errors," replied Master Carver.

Master Brewer nodded knowingly. "Yes, I am familiar with the name. I believe the printer Thomas Basson spent some time in Cologne prior to moving to Leyden. He is a curious man, and from what I know he prints very little in English, in spite of his English origin," responded Master Brewer thoughtfully. "I expect though, that to succeed in the business, you print in the languages that are in demand, especially in light of the connection with the University. That is exceptional news regarding Master Brewster, as this position might expose him to students, professors, and dignitaries of the University and the town, which could be beneficial to the congregation."

"I agree completely. Because of Master Brewster's past visit to Leyden with Secretary Davison, he was a known entity to Secretary van Hout when the congregation sought to remove there. This connection with the city secretary surely aided the group in receiving official permission to settle there. I learned that the good secretary passed on last December in Leyden. Had I been there, I would have attended the funeral. His influence on the people of the city and the University is immeasurable; a more dignified, respectable man, I know but a few."

"Perhaps the godly Master Robinson could be counted amongst

that gifted group," offered Master Brewer.

"You do speak so highly of Pastor Robinson," said Mistress Brewer, looking over at her husband. "I have hopes of meeting him, and worshipping with your congregation," continued Mistress Brewer, as she directed her last words toward Master Carver.

"What are your thoughts, Master Brewer, about making the Continent your home, and possibly even Leyden?" inquired his friend.

Thomas smiled and took his wife's soft hand in his. "I cannot say with certainty what the next years hold for us. If the Lord grants this unborn child life in this world, I expect we will reside here at the estate until the child is at least a year or two in age. But as I speak these words, I realize that even if bestowed the child's health, my father might well remove my right to remain here."

Master Carver responded with a look of confusion. "Explain this to me, for I cannot understand how this could be the case."

"My father does not share our interpretation of the Scriptures, and therefore cannot see the darkness of the indiscretions residing within the Church of England. Instead, he sees our actions and efforts as a kind of war against the church and King James, which to him is blasphemous. He cannot understand why I choose to place resources outside the realm of Fuller's Earth, in his mind diluting our profits. He does not know the extent of my involvement in the book trade and how I support publishing of unapproved works. My father's health has been deteriorating, so the time he has left in this world is likely not long. That he is frustrated with my various endeavors is clear. I would not be surprised if on the reading of my father's will, I am partially or even entirely excluded," explained Master Brewer.

John listened intently. "Did you know that the type we delivered to Giles Thorp is being used to print a five-hundred-page book entitled *Justification of Separation*, written by Master Robinson?"

"I had not heard about Pastor Robinson's most recent work, but am pleased to learn the type from Printer Okes is being put to good use. Of course I will purchase a copy when it becomes available," responded Thomas.

"As will I," stated Master Carver. "The book is a response to Richard Bernard's attack on separating from the Church of England. As you would expect, the actual title is much longer than that, but that is the main part of it. The printing should take place this year. Regarding your efforts, how far have you extended yourself here in England with publishing or distributing books?"

"My involvement here with publishing and distributing books is not so great. I have only funded the publishing of a small number of pamphlets and two books. But you talked of our greater purpose, and I believe investing in the production of and distribution of books will have the most far-reaching effects, here and on the mainland. With the printing press, we can spread the word of God in a most unprecedented and unadulterated fashion. It is the key to illumination," said Thomas with a sharp sparkle in his emerald eyes.

"The press is a powerful tool," agreed John, "and with our contacts in London and Holland, we are well positioned to support printing and purchasing publications to distribute. Our trade in raw wool, finished cloth, and Fuller's Earth must continue to be strong in order to pursue such efforts. How is your business faring presently?"

"The rents from the lands here are reliable and provide the majority of the income, with profits from Fuller's Earth not far behind. The lands I manage belong to me and will remain in my possession, regardless of Father's will. And for you, John, by what means are you most profitable?"

"My business is entirely tied to the cloth trade, with a large portion buying and selling raw wool here in England, selling some on the Continent, and providing broadcloth also to be finished on the mainland. I export a considerable amount of finished cloth back here to England. And there is the Fuller's Earth I handle with you. So there is enough income to support publishing efforts, at least for the present time."

"This travel will be interesting then, and working together we have a chance to expand our contacts."

"At the very least we might enjoy each other's company for the next fortnight. And it will be valuable seeing Master Printer Okes, learning about the state of the Stationers' Company."

"I am curious to know if Master Okes has changed his position on unapproved printings. I think it doubtful, although since he allowed his type to venture to the mainland, perhaps he would be open to assisting with the distribution of certain works here."

"That would be a major step. And a dangerous one at that. I am eager to hear what Master Okes has to say about his present publications and the Stationers' Company requirements. I would be shocked if Nicholas would take the risk of distributing banned publications, but we shall see."

The three friends rose in unison, Master Brewer taking his wife's arm as they walked in silence to the main house. There was a basin of warm water ready for washing their hands and face before the meal. After taking their seats, Master Brewer led the trio in prayer, their eyes and hands turned up toward the heavens. "Thank you, Lord, for this day, for leading Master Carver to us, and for the chance to partake in this glorious food together. We are grateful for your guidance and direction. Amen."

The supper they enjoyed that evening was finer than what most in the country would have for their larger midday meal of dinner. Served on silver plates alongside silver spoons, the friends enjoyed roasted quail and duck, accompanied by boiled salad greens. The men consumed more than they intended in bread and beer, reflecting on the past and musing about their travels to come. John savored the moment, to be with one of his dearest friends and his new bride. He thought of Marie, and what he would have given to have her by his side. God has his plan, and the path is set from birth. Master Carver embraced that truth, regardless of the pain he endured.

They talked more, laughed, and sang psalms together. They enjoyed the remnants of quince pie, a favorite of Anna's.

"Do they have quince in Holland?" queried Mistress Brewer. "If we did decide to move to Leyden, I would need to know what I would be missing from England!"

Both men laughed.

Her husband responded, "You might ponder instead all the things you will be gaining. Most importantly, you will be released from the darkness of the Church of England and into the light of Pastor Robinson, and his congregation. As far as the quince, the markets in Leyden will have anything and everything your heart might desire. There are apples, quince, figs, olives, apricots… and the cheese. Where do I begin with that?"

"Thomas is right. The cheese is wondrous good. Vendors come from all parts of Holland to sell their cheese."

"I do remember Father telling me that dairy cows are important to the Dutch economy. What else do the Leyden markets offer?" inquired Anna with wide eyes.

"The people of Leyden will tell you that what the city has to offer in the weekly markets rivals what most towns offer two or three times per year. There is meat flesh available daily, save for the Sabbath of course, and cloth sold on Tuesdays and Fridays. There is fresh fish at the Wednesday and Saturday markets, although many complain of the high prices."

Master Carver paused. "Should I go on, Mistress?"

"Yes, Master Carver, please do, as it is of great interest to me, and since we might venture over, I care to learn more about this place."

"Well, the list goes on, from corn to peat to pottery. There are secondhand clothes and other items sold a block from my house, on Saturdays."

Master Carver hesitated before he continued. "I must be honest with you, Mistress, what you will miss are not things, but people. I realize that you are a distance from your family already, with them being in London while you reside here in Maidstone. The North Sea, of course, makes visiting much more complicated, but not impossible," said Master Carver with a smile. "I am sitting here before you, so of course it is possible."

"And if the Lord allows, John, soon you will be in the company of your family when we travel north," continued Master Brewer.

"Just so, my dear friend. I promised Master Robinson I would also see about the state of his family. I have some letters to hand over as well."

Of the three candles that had been burning, only two remained lit. "I fear the hour is later than we might expect. My love, you must be ready for your sleep," suggested Master Brewer, extending his hand to his pregnant wife. "John, take this remaining bit of light up with you to your quarters," he offered as he picked up the pewter candlestick.

Since the friends had taken their supper in the private dining room of the Brewers, only Master Carver had to walk the long hallway and climb the stairs to his quarters above.

"I am grateful for the meal, and above all, your company. May God grant us a peaceful night. I bid you both a pleasant sleep and shall see you in the light of the morning. God by you."

"And God by you, John. Be certain to ask Richard for anything you require. It is important that you rest well so that you will be ready for our travels through London and north," said Thomas with a wide smile.

Walking by the light of the candle, John Carver encountered Richard in the hallway, waiting to aid the Brewers' guest. Together they returned to his room, so Richard could help remove his ruff and untie the points connecting the doublet to his breeches.

"May God grant you a restful night, Richard. I will see you on the morrow."

"I wish you a peaceful rest, Master Carver. Please do not hesitate to interrupt my sleep, should you need anything, anything at all," insisted the young servant, who doffed his hat and bowed before departing the room.

Master Carver readied himself for sleep by removing his hat, shoes, stockings, and suit of clothes. After washing his hands and face, he said his day's final prayer and climbed into bed. The mattress filled with feathers soothed his tired body, and he sighed in appreciation of the comfort the bed offered. His head rested on one of eight pillows supported by two long bolsters. He had counted them earlier and realized he had never slept in a bed with so many pillows. He thought of his late wife, and how much she would have enjoyed the luxury of this place.

The candle burned so low it smothered itself in melted tallow. The small fire had been covered earlier, so very little heat could be offered from the hearth. Layers of linen and wool on the bed provided more than enough warmth for the exhausted traveler. He closed his eyes, falling asleep almost instantly, dreaming of the journey that lay ahead.

Two days later the men departed the Brewer Estate, planning to be away for weeks if not months. In the case of Master Carver, he might remain in the northern part of the country indefinitely, depending on the needs of his family. Ultimately he planned on returning to Leyden, but his voyage back to Holland was not pressing.

Their first stop brought them to London and the family of Mistress Brewer. They found Master Offley to be away in Istanbul, so after sharing with Mistress Offley the blessed news of a grandchild, the men remained just one night before continuing on to see Printer Okes at the sign of The Rose.

All three of the Okes children jumped up and down at the sight of their visitors, especially pleased to see their cousin, Master Brewer.

"What a welcome surprise," exclaimed Printer Okes. "I never would have expected to have Master Carver standing here in my shop. What brings you back to England?"

"I believe there is often good and bad news associated with the decision to make a long journey. The bad, or sad part, is that I have lost my wife, and two sons before her. She died last summer, not from childbirth, but from the loss of the child. She died from a broken heart. I questioned if that was possible, and now that I have witnessed it, I know it to be true. The good, is that I was able to locate Master Brewer with ease. I sought him out to coordinate efforts for supporting the separated congregation in Leyden, and to see what we can do together in the way of publishing."

Nicholas nodded as he listened, with eyebrows slightly raised, hoping the men would not ask him for something that would conflict with his commitment to the Stationers' Company.

Sensing this, Master Brewer spoke to allay his concerns. "We are here not to ask anything of you, Nicholas, that would jeopardize your position. The type is more than enough. In fact, you likely already know that it is in the hands of Printer Thorp in Amsterdam. He is publishing a work of Pastor Robinson's entitled *Justification of Separation*. Mayhaps some copies will make their way to London," suggested Master Brewer.

"I would be surprised if they did not. Many of my fellow printers distribute banned works and manage evading fines or reprimand. It would seem the same inspectors make all the 'surprise' searches of those shops and inventories. I am sure their silence comes with a good deal of coin. For me, the risks alone are too great. Making a living as a printer is difficult enough without giving the Stationers' Company reason to suspend printing rights, remove an apprentice, or worse. One of my fellow printers ended up in the Fleet Prison for selling books sent here after the Cologne book fair last spring. The books ended up at his doorstep without any trace of their path or publisher. It is extremely tempting to sell something that has cost you nothing to create, especially if it carries a message you believe in."

His apprentice, John Reynoldes, listened intently, remaining quiet with respect, as an apprentice should. He secretly wanted Master Okes to take more risks in this way, but it was not his reputation or family at stake.

"I understand your position, Master Okes," replied Master Carver. "We are grateful for the type you parted with. As we have told you, it is already being put to use by Giles Thorp. And when we allowed him to borrow it, it was clear he had much experience in using discretion when printing something that might cause a stir over here. We did not come here to ask anything of you that would put you at risk with the Stationers' Company. We were passing through London on our way up the Great North Road and wanted to see you and your family. Master Brewer has some happy news to deliver."

"Indeed I do, and I will get right to the point. Praise God, Mistress Brewer is with child."

"Oh, Cousin, that is wondrous news," exclaimed Mistress Okes as she crossed the room to embrace Thomas.

"I expect she is back in Maidstone in the comfort of your estate then? I recall she isn't very fond of London, regardless of her pregnant state."

"You are correct on both accounts," said Master Brewer with a smile. "She does fear the plague, and although she would prefer to be with me, you know how unpleasant traveling can be."

"Yes, of course." Although for Rose Okes, she never did mind the bumpy rides, late nights, or other unexpected inconveniences of traveling with the Queen. She rather enjoyed the adventure, and now that she was settled with a family, she missed it. But she never uttered a word of those thoughts. She was content with her life. She loved Nicholas. Her children were growing up quickly, and she smiled at them as their six bright eyes stayed locked on Masters Brewer and Carver.

As if mesmerized, young Rose Okes spoke first. "Mother, might I speak?"

Her mother nodded for her to proceed.

"Pray pardon, Master Carver. I am not sure if you remember me. I was much younger the last time you were here."

Everyone in the room laughed a little. It was evident the young girl was nervous to speak to her elder.

"Yes, Rose, I do remember you. You are growing into a lovely young lady," responded Master Carver.

"Thank you kindly, Master. I was wondering about something I think you might know of. My father has told me you have been living in Holland, in a city called Leyden, and that you live near to Master Brewster and his family. Have you seen Jonathan Brewster? Can you tell me how he fares?"

The young girl blushed to such a degree she felt her face burning red. Elizabeth looked across the room, her angry eyes filled with contempt. She thought her younger sister a fool to ask such a question before everyone in the room. Rose didn't notice her sister's reproachful look, and even if she had, she wouldn't have cared. In Rose's mind, her older sister was overly concerned with the opinions of others. Rose took pity on her, believing she lacked thoughts of her own. She was a poppet, following whatever rules society or the King created. Elizabeth was too concerned about Rose's behavior. Rose was not certain if it was in jealousy, for fear of embarrassing the family, or out of genuine care for her. Whatever the reason, she resented it.

Master Carver smiled. "I did see Jonathan last month in Leyden. He and the Brewster family as a whole have settled quite well into the city." As he continued, John turned to Mistress Okes. "I understand you are close with Mistress Brewster. I must tell you, in June of last year, not long after arriving in Leyden, the Brewsters buried an infant son. Praise God the good Mistress Brewster was spared, and is now recovered."

Mistress Okes nodded, grateful to learn of the news, but still felt great pain knowing her friend suffered such a loss.

"And Nicholas, you will be glad to learn that your lessons in printing did not fall on deaf ears. Master Brewster has taken work at a print shop run by an Englishman named Basson. Thomas and his son, Govert, own a shop marked by the sign of The Music Book, just down the alley from where Master Robinson lives. He will be reading and removing errors from titles in Greek and Latin, to be printed for the University of Leyden."

"That is something to celebrate," said Printer Okes with a proud smile. "I always knew William had a passion for books and printing. This should also be an excellent way to become further integrated into the city, and learn what opportunities exist for other members of the congregations."

"Master Brewster will learn more about the printing business there, and publishing. We hope eventually to fund works that will spread the word of God and help others to find their way out of the darkness and into the light," explained Thomas.

Nicholas nodded, but offered no words in response. What Master Brewer was talking about were titles that would not be approved by the Stationers' Company or allowed for distribution in England. He expected they would be banned, in conflict with King James and the Church of England.

"In the meanspace, Master Brewster is obtaining most of his income teaching English to University students, using Latin as the common language between teacher and student. As far as the city itself, Leyden is a pleasant place to live, not only with its tree-lined canals and vibrant markets, but also with the diversity of its population. The streets teem with those fleeing the wrath of the Catholic Spanish, along with University students coming from all corners of the world to study Theology and Medicine, among other things. I am hopeful that, in time, the Brewers will join us there as well," said Master Carver with a wink in the direction of his close friend.

"And what else about Jonathan?" inquired Rose timidly, but with persistence.

Elizabeth sighed loudly in disgust.

"Yes. Yes, young Rose. I apologize for digressing. Jonathan was looking well, and as always shared a promising outlook. He is quickly learning Dutch and discussed the options for work in the cloth trade, mentioning something about ribbon making. I do not know if he has started in that trade already or is looking to. Many in the congregation have found work combing or carding wool, some weaving, others laboring as tailors or hatters. I am sorry to tell you that the children have to work as well, spinning wool and mending stockings and linens."

"When you return to Leyden, would you please pass along my regards to Jonathan?" Rose paused then hurriedly added, "And to Patience and Fear as well?"

"Yes, of course. The Brewsters consider you their dearest of friends and will be most pleased to learn you are well and that they are in your thoughts."

The conversation continued into the night, during and after supper. While the adults continued talking, the children assisted in clearing trenchers, spoons, knives, and cups. Rose poured salt from the salt cellar back into the box by the hearth. Elizabeth and Robert removed the linen napkins and bid their parents and the guests a good night. Assisting her brother as they readied for bed, Elizabeth ensured Robert washed his face and hands before saying bedtime prayers. The eldest and youngest Okes children shared a small room upstairs, while Rose made her bed up the ladder from there, in the loft. Although these quarters afforded less space, it granted Rose much-desired privacy.

The relationship with her sister was fraught with challenges. When they were younger it was more of a standard rivalry, something expected for sisters. Now aged fifteen and twelve years, a sharper, almost hostile edge had developed in Elizabeth. For Rose, her sister alone created the negativity. It was as if her older sister envied her. Rose did have a closer connection with her father, learning and assisting when she could with his work. Mostly this meant running errands, like delivering a folio to a bookbinder, or retrieving supplies. Elizabeth would always be pleased to remind Rose that she was a woman, meant to learn the ways of housewifery and nothing more. Whatever the reason for their disharmony, Rose was tired of pondering why and had abandoned trying to repair a relationship broken by a mysterious source.

While Elizabeth and Robert prepared for bed, Rose sought out their maidservant, Katherine, for some paper and ink. "Yes, Rose, you will find everything you need to write a letter by your father's desk. Have you asked his permission?"

"I have not, but I dare not interrupt him now and want to have the letter ready for Master Carver to take should they leave on the morrow."

Katherine nodded and resumed scrubbing the iron pot. She admired the young girl's spirit but feared it would land her in a world of disappointment, if not heartache. Mistress Okes had that same adventurous nature and had been able to fulfill her cravings for excitement by serving in the Queen's Court. She had adapted to married life and the role of a mother as she should, but Katherine noticed oftentimes her Mistress peered out the front shop windows, and wondered if she longed for any pieces of her old life.

Rose completed her letter in little time. Even though the candle was burning low when she began, she was so swift in putting her thoughts to paper that the candle lasted long enough for her to melt the wax and apply a seal. She impressed only half of her father's seal, leaving space below to carve her initials using a pin from her pocket.

"That did not take you very long. If you leave the letter with me, I will be able to give it to Master Carver discreetly tonight."

"Thank you, Katherine, for helping me. I think about Jonathan often, and did not want to miss the chance to send him something. I will be going up to the loft now for the night. Sleep well."

"And you as well, Rose."

Rose had already bid good night to her parents and their guests, so she made her way to the loft. As she passed by where her sister and brother slept, she could hear their voices but could not make out all the words. "Good night," she whispered as she climbed the ladder.

In her hurry to compose the letter to Jonathan, she had forgotten to wash her face and hands before bedtime. Already up in the loft, she decided it was not that important and removed everything but her smock before climbing under the warmth of her sheets and woolen rug. Safe in her solitude, she smiled as her mind took her to what she imagined the streets of Leyden to look like. What a lovely city it seemed to be, and as long as Jonathan Brewster resided there, she had a reason to want to see it for herself. After saying a prayer, she adjusted her pillows once more before falling asleep.

A level below, the muffled voices continued.

"Do you think Father will move us out of England to this place called Leyden?" asked Robert timidly.

"I think not, Robert. Father is committed to printing within the Stationers' Company, which requires him to stay here. So I would not expect we would move away from London even."

"From what I have heard Master Carver and others say, the Church of England is not good, and remaining in it will lead to terrible things now and after this life. Sister, why is it so wrong, and why do we remain in it?"

"You have big questions for such a little boy. I will try to make sense of it for you, but I do not have all the answers, either. Those that have left this country to move away from the Church of England believe that the national church is not a true church. A true church is a congregation that gathers voluntarily with members making a confession of faith. The King's Church requires people to attend a parish church based on where they live."

"So it is not a choice here?" repeated Robert softly to himself.

"Right. Every person in England goes to an assigned parish church nearest to where they live. And each Sabbath the parishes are directed to read certain parts of the *Service Book* and the *Book of Common Prayer.* The congregation in Leyden would never use such books. They take direction only from Scripture, which means directly from the Bible."

"Is there anything else that is bad?"

"Be careful, Robert, in describing the King's Church as bad. That is considered treason! Rest your mind from such thoughts, and ready yourself for sleep."

Elizabeth wanted to answer her brother's questions, but not even having seven years to him, she was cautious to say too much. In time, she would explain more about those that had separated themselves from the Church of England, and how reminders of the Pope's religion had no place in their church. Over time, she would guide Robert in the ways of the true church. For one, there should be no worshipping of idols or statues. Nor should there be stained-glass windows, wearing of the surplice, kneeling at communion, or making a sign of the cross during baptism. They absolutely would not accept the hierarchy of bishops and archbishops and their power to determine the leaders of parish churches. That sinful structure remained from a time when the country was Catholic, before the birth of the Okes children.

In time, Elizabeth would make it clear to her younger brother that the local church did not decide who served them as their minister, or who taught them as elders. In Leyden, Master Brewster was elected Ruling Elder by the congregation, a position to be held for life. She would tell Robert all about Pastor Robinson, the Leyden group's chosen spiritual leader. From her parents she learned that Pastor Robinson was a gifted preacher, and a man who followed the words of the New Testament in guiding the congregation.

Robert was not quite ready to lay his head to rest. He sat upright in the bed, wide-awake and full of concern.

"Based on what you say, Elizabeth, I fear for our family, as we worship at the parish church within the Church of England. I've heard our cousin call it impure and filled with darkness and the stench of Rome."

"Robert, if we stay in England we must go to the Church of England services. If we fail to do so then we will be pursued and questioned. That could lead to imprisonment, or worse." She lowered her voice even more. "The small group we meet with on Wednesday evenings, in the bowels of the church, that is our true church. That congregation is similar to the church in Leyden. We want reform and purification of the King's Church like those in Leyden, but for many reasons we choose to remain in England. You cannot speak a word to anyone about this. There is a reason Mother and Father call the Wednesday meetings private. It is the same reason Father hides certain works away from the inspector's eyes. Do you understand?"

"I believe so. I will pray that God understands as well. And that the Lord realizes we belong to a true church."

Even without seeing her brother's face, worry shook his voice. It was certainly justified, as she shared his fears. "Let's pray together then, so He will hear us."

They sat in the bedstead, eyes and palms facing up into the darkness of the room, with Elizabeth leading the prayer.

"Forgive us, Lord, for attending the services of the King's Church. It is something we are forced to do. We seek to follow your light through your Word, in a true church led by those elected, those with the gift of prophecy. Hear our confession of faith and know it to be true. Amen."

Robert lay down, humming Psalm 100. It provided comfort, and even more peace when his sister added the words. Together they sang softly, until sleep set in.

CITY of LEYDEN · RESIDENCES

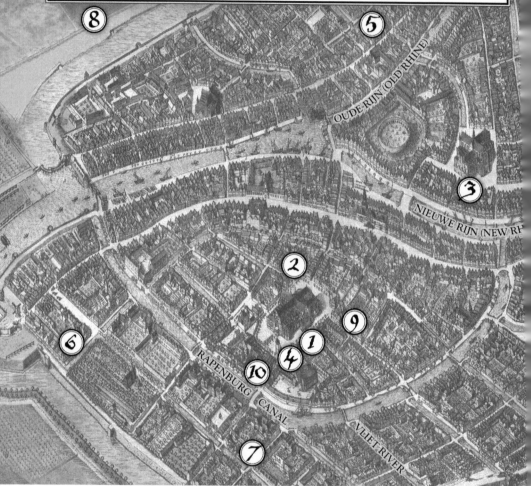

1 The Green Close, Pastor John Robinson
2 William Brewster
3 1st Carver Residence
4 Thomas Brewer
5 William Bradford
6 William Jepson
7 Robert Cushman
8 Philippe de Lanoy
9 2nd Carver Residence
10 G. Basson (Print Shop)

All residences confirmed by primary sources except for those of John Carver, which are both plausible locations.

ADAPTED MAP OF LEYDEN BY PIETER BAST, 1600, LEIDEN MUNICIPAL ARCHIVES, THE NETHERLANDS

Having his congregation familiar to him and in close proximity was a necessary component in leading his flock. Pastor Robinson began renting the Green Close (#1 on the map) in 1609, when the group arrived in Leyden. Not long after, the property was purchased, which included a main house, and thirteen small surrounding homes. It was here that the congregation worshipped, until they were forced into an official public space, in 1619.

Chapter Eleven

John Robinson's Congregation
and the Green Close

A year later, April 1611
Leyden, the Netherlands

"If I had thought I would be put to hard labor, I would have delayed my arrival from Amsterdam," quipped Master Brewer as he helped William Bradford load a wooden chest into the cart outside.

"I do apologize, Master Brewer. Your coming was a surprise to me, as was Master Carver's decision in giving up the lease on this home. I would have asked Jonathan or another from the congregation to assist with the removal of my belongings had I known the rental agreement was to be ended," explained William. "I briefly considered taking over the rental myself, but securing University students as tenants can be unpredictable. My intention is to pursue citizenship and then purchase a home. I will stay with the Brewster family in the meanspace."

"Yes, Master Brewster informed me your business in weaving is progressing for you. What type of cloth is it?"

"It is serge weaving principally, but I also weave fustian. Once I become a citizen I can enter the guild, and after that I want to purchase a home with space for at least one loom."

"I am impressed with your advancement in such a short period of time. For a man of twenty-one years, you are doing well for yourself, in a new trade and foreign city no less," commended Master Brewer.

Bradford nodded with pride as he responded, "I am blessed having Pastor Robinson and Master Brewster guiding me. Being part of the congregation encourages me to work so I might assist others in need. Many of the children are working from dawn to dusk, as I am sure you know. It is out of necessity that many of us have taken up trades in which we lack experience, and trades related to cloth are the most common here. Most are weavers now, and some call themselves drapers. Jonathan Brewster is making ribbon, while many are combing or carding wool. Some, like William Jepson, the carpenter, or Isaac Allerton, the tailor from London, have been able to retain their trades. Roger Wilson, a baker in England, has told me he will start weaving instead. There are some brewers as well. Whatever can be done to keep us from starving, and an honest trade in the eyes of God, is something we will pursue."

"Yes, to adapt is necessary, and finding honest work essential," agreed Master Brewer. "I have been in Amsterdam, where I spent time with the printer Giles Thorp, learning about his trade. He also spoke of those in the Ancient Brethren, and it is not a very different story there, although the congregation is triple the size and still contending with conflict. It was very wise to detach and move to Leyden. I have hope my trade in Fuller's Earth will benefit the congregation here. Other goods I have been trading include saltpeter, used in making gunpowder, and an exotic material used in making vibrant red dye, called cochineal. I am considering moving my wife and daughter to Leyden, one reason being that my father intends to disinherit me. His days on this earth are numbered, and in truth, I expect him to be gone by the time I return. His disagreement with my position on the false ways of the King's Church has led to his severing ties with me."

"Will you retain any of the estate lands and claim to Fuller's Earth if he does disinherit you?"

"Yes, there are parts of the land that I own already, so I will continue to receive rents, and rights to the Fuller's Earth. We also have the support of my wife's family. Her father, Master Offley, oversees trade in the Levant Company, so he is no stranger to the merchant opportunities outside England."

"Master Brewer, your presence in our congregation here would be a blessing. Have you spoken with Pastor Robinson about making a confession of faith?"

"I have. I have. I want to make my confession and covenant alongside my wife. That piece is important to me, that together, we make this critical union with Christ."

William nodded in understanding. "Of course. I would expect that. As far as our time in Leyden, I believe we will be residing here for many years at least, if not indefinitely. Pastor Robinson and some others from the congregation have initiated the process to purchase the Green Close. And Master Brewster is advising those who have the means to become citizens, especially those in trades with guilds. Some, like myself, intend to purchase homes as opposed to renting. The city affords opportunities in the cloth trades, and an increasing need for carpenters and stone carvers as the population grows. I expect some from the congregation, like Pastor Robinson and Master Brewster, might enroll in the University. This city is rich with people from other parts, our congregation being one of many seeking a haven. I don't expect it will be an easy or prosperous life here, but we can meet and worship as we like."

"I agree with you on all accounts. I do wonder what will transpire as we near the end of the truce with Spain. It is never advisable to remain in a country under siege, especially if threatened by a merciless Catholic Spain."

William nodded again. The truce would end in a decade, which to William was certainly real, but seemed a century removed. Both men continued loading William's possessions into the cart.

"I have yet to pack the bed linens. And there are books and candlesticks belonging to me on the table by the hearth. I have to place cups, trenchers, spoons, a mortar and pestle, and spices within that chest, before it is ready to be loaded. The majority of unpacked items, including the chairs and table, belong to the owner of the house. Who did you say this cart belonged to?"

"It belongs to Roger Symonson, the mason. He and one of his day laborers will be over while there is still light to move your things to the house of Master Brewster."

"Master Brewer, are you staying with Master Brewster as well, or with Master Robinson, or elsewhere?"

"With Master Robinson, at the Green Close. There is some room directly with him, at the main house. The twelve surrounding one-room houses are all occupied, as you would expect."

"Yes, they are completely filled, as I inquired about that myself when I learned of the need to move from Master Carver's place. I mentioned that Pastor Robinson is taking steps to purchase the Green Close and the houses around the courtyard. The formal agreement was started in January of this year, and the details should be completed within the week."

"Yes, I did learn of that decision. Pastor Robinson, his sister-in-love Jane White, and the Jepson and Wood families will own the property jointly, as I understand it. It is clear that your congregation intends to remain here for some time, as we discussed."

"How soon would you consider moving your family here to Leyden?" asked William as he folded the linens and pillowbeers.

"I expect it will take considerable time to get my estate in order, even if Father should disown me. I have lands that belong to me outright and contracts in Fuller's Earth that will require looking after. So I will have to appoint someone for that purpose. Depending on Master Carver's whereabouts in England, I might be able to rely on him, should he not be returning to Leyden himself. I do intend to obtain official permission in leaving the country, so as not to arouse any suspicion with the authorities. Most importantly, we have a daughter newly born, and I should think my Mistress would not want to be moving before her second year of life."

"Praise God. I trust your wife and daughter are well, since you have journeyed here."

"Yes, thanks be to God that little Mercy and her mother have been well from the start, and I can only pray that the Lord continues to keep them so. It should be in their best interest that they reside at our family estate in Maidstone, as opposed to London, where the Offley family is living."

William closed the lid of the last trunk to be loaded. As the men hoisted it onto the cart, Roger Symonson and another man from the congregation turned the corner of the Torensteeg, both slightly out of breath.

"I do apologize, Master Brewer, for our tardiness," said Roger as he and his companion removed their hats, bowing deeply.

"Recover yourselves. I am grateful for your assistance, as you have labored a full day already."

"As you would expect, Master Brewer, our congregation seeks to aid one another whenever possible. It is our good fortune that William's possessions are not so many that we require a horse for moving the cart. I think, William, if you help us, we should have enough strength to move your things to the home of Master Brewster."

"Most certainly," said William as he laid his coat across the loaded wooden chests, while turning up the sleeves of his doublet and shirt.

Thomas Brewer walked ahead of the cart, ensuring a clear path along the route. It took the greatest effort to move up and across the bridge spanning the Nieuwe Rhine, then up a slight incline onto the Breestraat. After passing the Town Hall, the route remained fairly level.

Master Brewer approached the door to the Brewster home as a University student was exiting. The men acknowledged one another without words, nodding with respect in passing. Master Brewster was still by the door, so there was no need to knock, as he was expecting them anyway.

"Good afternoon, Thomas. I appreciate you accompanying William in moving his things here. There is ample room in the loft. Enough for you if you require a place to stay," said Master Brewster.

"You are too kind. I do appreciate the offer, but I will remain at the house of Pastor Robinson during my time in Leyden."

"Very well then. Would you at least stay for some supper? It should not take long to unload the cart, with all the able hands present. I will fetch Jonathan as well."

Young William walked forward, slightly out of breath as he doffed his hat and bowed to Master Brewster.

"Good day, William. It pleases me greatly that you will be staying with us. Mistress Brewster and the children are happy as well. Would you and Roger… and is that James with him? Ask them if they wouldn't mind bringing the cart around the corner, to the other entrance of the house. There is more space there to maneuver and unload."

"Yes, of course. Thank you again for allowing me to remain with you. I am most grateful, and you can trust I will make this only temporary, as I would not want to be a burden to you."

"Impossible, my son, for you to be trouble in any way. You know you are a part of this family. You have told me before you are saving for citizenship, and to purchase a house. However long this takes will be as God wants. Your time with us is but a gift. Let me call to Jonathan and make quick work of this. The staircase to the loft is steep and narrow, so that will be a challenge. If need be, we can empty your chest before carrying it up, as that might be the only way to get it where it needs to go. Once your things are moved, it would gladden our hearts if you would all stay for supper. Mistress Brewster is cooking a quail pottage."

"There is nothing I would enjoy more than remaining in your company for supper," responded Master Brewer. "I shall inform Mistress Robinson of my intentions so they are not waiting for me there. I will return in a moment's time."

"I do apologize, Master Brewster. James and I have a cartful of bricks to transport before the day is over. We left our job so we might help William, but need to return to our work."

"I am grateful for your assistance and apologize for taking time away from your work."

"That is not necessary. It pleases me to be of use to a member of our congregation," said Roger as the two men turned to start unloading William's possessions.

With Jonathan's help, they had the cart unloaded into the loft in less than half of an hour. William was relieved that the task of removing his things to his newest residence was complete. Roger and James hurried off to the work waiting for them, passing Master Brewer as he returned to the Brewster home for supper.

"I am sorry, William, that you had to move your things once more, but in truth, it warms my heart having you with us," said Mistress Brewster as she embraced the young man.

"It does feel as if I am returning home, and I am most grateful to be here. Can I be of use in preparing for supper?" inquired William.

"Would it trouble you to fetch two gallons of beer for us?" asked Mistress Brewster as she reached into her woolen pocket for coin. "Take this in case they question your request to add it to our account. They won't be familiar with you and might refuse to add the amount to Master Brewster, his bill."

"I can accompany William," offered Jonathan. "The distance is not great, but two gallons can become heavy quickly. This way, there won't be any trouble with adding the cost to our account."

"Thank you, Jonathan. Off you go then. I should have supper ready within the hour."

Patience busied herself laying the board. The linen tablecloth had been spread across the vibrant Turkey carpet by her mother moments before, leaving her to fetch napkins, trenchers, and spoons. She sought out more drinking cups, and in standing on the tips of her toes, pulled down two from the cupboard top. She chose a pewter cup for Master Brewer and a black three-handled cup for William. Her family had their cups on the table already. Patience and Fear would sit to the side of the table on a bench, their trenchers and shared cup atop a linen-covered barrel.

Then she filled the salt cellar and placed a long loaf of wheaten bread on the table. Once they returned with the beer, her mother would fill the pewter tuit can for the table. With Master Brewer as their guest, Mistress Brewster decided to make a quail pottage with the relics from dinner. She added barley and parsnips, salt, peppercorn, sage, thyme, lovage, and marjoram. At the last moment she decided to add the dried yellow-orange leaves of calendula, adding warmth to the pottage.

"Patience, take that pot of water and bring it to a boil. I would like to make hasty pudding as well. The wheat flour is in the sack within the cupboard. Fetch that once you hang the pot in the hearth, and then put some butter in the small green dish. You can use some of the butter for the hasty pudding, and what remains can go on the table."

"Yes, Mother," answered Patience, with Fear on her heels. "Fear, hand me the lid for the pot, please."

The little lass nearly ran to get the wooden cover for her older sister, savoring the chance to be of use.

"Fear, you are so good at helping. Would you put more peppercorn to the mortar and pestle and make a powder of it for me?"

The little girl nodded with big eyes and the widest of smiles.

"Patience, fetch the mortar and pestle for Fear. It is too high and heavy for her to reach."

"Yes, of course, Mother," answered Patience as she turned away from the hearth, reaching for the iron mortar and pestle on the shelf above her head.

It was unusual, having guests for supper. Typically, anyone outside the family would be invited for dinner instead. But the circumstances were unusual, with William moving into the house, and Master Brewer traveling from England.

After everyone washed their hands and faces, they took their places around the table. Masters Brewster and Brewer sat across from one another, in the middle of the longer sides of the table. Mistress Brewster was to be seated next to her husband, with William and Jonathan directly across from one another. The lasses made their places on a bench to the side of the table.

Patience and Fear sat with wide eyes and ears, their presence detected by sight only. For certain, the Brewster children knew their place and wouldn't think of speaking unless spoken to or granted permission. Jonathan, having eighteen years to him, was blossoming into an industrious young man, and was allowed to engage in the conversation.

"I understand you are working in the ribbon trade. Are you weaving the ribbon or reselling it?" inquired Master Brewer.

"At the moment I am doing both. I am weaving myself with a

hand-loom so I can understand all the ways of the business. In order to master the trade, I believe you need to know it through experience, from beginning to end. The work can be tedious and at times difficult, depending on the pattern. Since I have begun weaving the ribbon myself, I have a much better appreciation for its value and selling it.

"I am also working on techniques producing garter ribbon and a type of decorative braid known as burgundian, used in the latest fashions. These are kinds that you cannot make with the ribbon-mills. I trust you have learned of the ribbon-mills that can produce twelve ribbons at once, all with one turn of a crank. The city of Leyden has granted protection to this mill monopoly until 1617. You cannot manage these ribbon-mills solely with child labor, as with the hand-looms."

"You are wise to approach the trade this way. Do you have children employed in your service? Do you have a plan as to how you want to develop the business?"

"I do have three children from the congregation making ribbon for me. Until the expiration of the ribbon-mill monopoly, I will make the more complicated types of ribbon and braid that the mills cannot produce. Like William, I would like to purchase citizenship. Eventually, I want to increase the business so that I am overseeing many ribbon weavers, mayhaps a roomful of them. If I am able to produce substantial amounts, I could even distribute the ribbon back in England."

"I trust you and your father will keep me apprised of your progress. If you do continue down this path, I might be able to assist you in some way, especially with distribution in England."

"Yes, Master Brewer. I appreciate your interest," said Jonathan, glowing with pride.

"How are the others in the congregation faring?" asked Master Brewer.

"Most in our congregation have found occupations or trades to pursue. There are merchants, brewers, masons, carpenters, tailors, hat makers, carders, combers, weavers, spinsters, and bakers, to name some of the ways our people are surviving here. As you would expect, some are faring better than others," said Master Brewster.

Master Brewer nodded as he listened. "Master Robinson appears

connected with the University of Leyden. I understand he is well regarded amongst the professors of Theology. Do you think he will enroll
in the University?"

"You are correct, in that his godly gifts are widely known and well
regarded. It would not surprise me if he did enroll, but I think in time.
He is dedicated presently to leading the flock in the ways of God, and
offering direction with housing and finding work. You will be worshipping with us on the morrow, will you not?"

"I will, and am very much looking forward to it. I was telling William I am considering leaving England to make my home here with
you, in Leyden. It is a matter of determining whether it is the right
direction for Mistress Brewer and our daughter, Mercy. I expect worshipping with Pastor Robinson will be enlightening in many ways. I
will not make my confession of faith or covenant with the congregation until my wife is by my side. I believe it is something we should do
together, making this union with Christ."

Master Brewster nodded firmly in agreement.

"It will take some time to get my business in England in order. I
will also apply for an official permit of travel, for doing business in the
Netherlands. I do not want my departure to be riddled with suspicion
or the cause of scrutiny here in Leyden."

The scent of quail pottage overtook the conversation as Mistress
Brewster moved to serve her husband. He smiled at her, but held his
hand up and gestured for Master Brewer to receive his pottage first.
The hasty pudding steamed in its bowl, prompting Jonathan to stand
and portion that out as he waited for the quail.

"I am able to do that, Brother," offered Patience, who was eager to
be doing anything other than sitting idle on the bench.

"As long as you are careful. The bowl is heavy and the
hasty pudding hot."

Patience proceeded to hold the bowl with all her strength, offering
hasty pudding as if it were a bowl heaping with grains of gold.

Before placing their napkins, Master Brewster led a prayer, with
Master Brewer providing the ending with words of thanks. Mistress

Brewster prayed standing by her husband's side, as she was not yet ready to sit. As any good housewife would, Mary wanted to be certain her guest and family had everything they required for supper.

William sliced the wheaten bread, offering a piece first to Master Brewster, then Master Brewer. After that, each person cut away at the long loaf for themselves, save for the girls. Mistress Brewster cut pieces for her daughters.

"Do you think, Master Brewster, that you will continue renting, or do you intend to purchase a home in Leyden?" inquired Thomas.

"My expectation is that I will continue to rent this house. The location is favorable, not only to that of Master Robinson and the Green Close, but to the University and the markets. I prefer this location and also the size of the house. It affords me the opportunity to take in William, and mayhaps more if need be. Master van Thorenvliet is not only a fair man to rent from, but has aided us in additional ways in settling in the town."

"That makes a great deal of sense. Regarding citizenship, there would not be a need for that, seeing that your work, chiefly teaching English to University students, does not benefit from being part of a guild," commented Master Brewer.

"Precisely. And longer term, I am considering pursuing a role in either publishing or printing, or both. And in either of those cases, there is no guild in place," responded Master Brewster.

"I would expect there are a number of printers and presses in the city, serving the needs of the University, along with the general population."

"Yes, there are quite a few. Some only have one press, while others are running multiple presses at different locations. I think I have mentioned them before, but the Bassons have a shop at the end of the alley where our pastor lives. It is marked by the sign of The Music Book, and a father and son from England run the place. I have been hired by them to find errors before printing, but have also translated one publication from Greek to English."

"Yes, yes. Master Carver did mention that to me more than a year ago, when he visited my estate in England. That is an excellent opportunity for you to be so closely connected to the trade. What are your impressions of the Basson family and of printing as an occupation?"

"I do respect the Bassons a great deal. They were living at one time in Cologne, in the German States. Then they moved their home and shop here to Leyden, to capture the growing needs of the University and city. I think being English, they would be inclined to aid in our efforts, but as far as their religious inclinations, they are not aligned with ours. At best they tolerate our decision of separation from the King, his Church."

"Regarding printing as an occupation, it comes with significant costs, especially if you are running your own press. I was astonished at the amount of inventory in the Bassons' shop, sitting on the shelves and in the back storeroom in the form of unbound books. I suppose Printer Okes carries the same burden in his shops in London. I understand the publisher pays for some of the initial cost of producing the books."

"Indeed. The key role of the publisher is to invest in the creation of the book. I know the printer and publisher come to terms regarding the quantity of books printed and how much is paid at the time of printing, with the remainder collected once the books are sold," responded Master Brewer.

"At least here in the Netherlands the printers are free from inspections and restrictions. There is no body approving what can be printed, unlike the situation in England within the Stationers' Company," added Master Brewster.

Patience and Fear began clearing the trenchers and spoons while Mistress Brewster filled the brass basin with warm water from the kettle. As she scraped the soap with her knife, the shavings fell like snow onto the water, melting in its warmth.

"Fear, can you reach the clean rags hanging from the line?" asked her mother.

She clutched the miniature red clay pan in her left hand, leaving her right hand free to bring the rags to her mother. The little pan, one that would make *panekoeken* if it were larger, was a coveted gift from her father, something he found on the Nieuwe Street, where secondhand items were sold. With this size she could play with her poppet, pretending she was a housewife. Now she required both hands be ready to help her mother, so she carefully slipped the clay valuable into the safety of her linen pocket.

"I can. Here they are. Would you like me to dry things once you rinse them?"

"Please do," responded her mother with an approving smile. "Patience, add turf to the fire, please."

She picked a brick from the basket, placing it carefully on the burning pile within the hearth. Not liking where it had fallen, Patience reached for the iron tongs and moved the piece to a better place.

"Mother, I would like to add one as well," stated Fear, not even having five years to her.

"You can do so only with Patience by your side. There is no hurry to be working in the hearth, and you may only do so with assistance. Do you understand?"

"Yes, Mother. I will never work around the hearth alone," responded Fear earnestly.

After Fear placed a piece of turf under Patience's watchful eye, the girls filled another brass basin with warm water and laid out clean linen for the household and guest to wash their hands and face after supper.

"Let us pause in our tasks and complete our supper with prayer," said Master Brewster, sitting with his palms and gaze upward.

"We thank you for the love of our friends, and for the food you have provided. We are blessed to take in William, who is like a son to us, and have in our midst Master Brewer. On the morrow, as we worship together, we will experience the ministry of John Robinson, surrounded by the love of the covenanted members of our church. May the reading of Scripture and prophecy show us the light, and move Master Brewer to return here with his family. Let us repent and ask that God forgive us for any known or unknown offenses. May God watch over us. Amen."

"Amen," recited the others.

"Thank you kindly for the company and the supper. A place I would rather be, I know not. The only way this could have been better is if Mistress Brewer and our daughter, Mercy, were here to meet you and worship with Pastor Robinson. But in time, I believe it should be so."

"Indeed. As in all things, it will be as God decides. Take this lantern along with you. Your walk back to the home of Pastor Robinson is but a few steps, but you are not so familiar with the city, and with darkness setting in it is best to see where you are and with whom you share the street."

"As you wish, Master Brewster. God by you all. I shall see you on the morrow."

Once Master Brewer departed, the home operated as it normally did, with the exception of William spending time unpacking his things. Many of the household items the Brewsters already possessed, but he did add two trenchers and pewter spoons to their inventory. He also set out his candlestick and oil lamp, both made of green glazed pottery. Lastly, he brought to Mistress Brewster three different drinking cups, two of pottery and one of pewter. Then with Jonathan's assistance he laid out his mattress, pillows, sheets, and woolen blanket.

"Did you ever suspect you would be moving your things this many times in less than five years?" asked Jonathan as they readied the bedding.

"To be honest, I didn't really know what to expect when we left Scrooby. For a time it seemed we would not even get out of England. Now, being settled in Leyden, it is only a slight inconvenience having to move across the Rhine from one house to another."

"Praise God, you are right. I will leave you to your sleep. Anon, William."

The Brewster household fell into slumber, the day having been filled with cooking and cleaning and time enjoyed with friends. Heat from the hearth crept into the room, but the fire cover contained the danger of wayward sparks. There would be no cooking on the Sabbath, something Mistress Brewster planned for each week. If the weather stayed pleasant enough, there would be no need to burn peat on the morrow, either. Buried in a nest of warm ash were a dozen eggs, roasting in readiness to break the fast.

Hours later, rays of morning light landed in the courtyard of Pastor Robinson's Green Close, illuminating the space for Sabbath worship. Warmer weather beckoned herbs and trees to spring from their slumber, showing signs of life in vibrant green shades. As Master Brewer looked out the window, he thought it so picturesque he envisioned his wife walking through the grass, holding Mercy in her arms while looking up at him, a most loving smile on her face.

"It is a comforting scene, is it not?" commented Pastor Robinson. "That I have members of my congregation living in homes surrounding my own is a blessing," he continued as he gestured to the twelve small houses serving as the perimeter of the courtyard.

"I could not think of a better arrangement," replied Master Brewer. "It affords an opportunity to develop an even closer connection with your members. I know you believe it necessary for all covenanted members to be known amongst each other in the congregation."

"It is true. And that the congregation should never increase in size to where there are members unknown to me and to each other. Then the church becomes a false church, like in the Church of England, where attendance at a parish is dictated by geography rather than a covenant with Christ. Many ministers in England have links still to Rome, as does the organization of archbishops and bishops. The parish itself has very little say in electing ministers, elders, and deacons, and as far as the power of excommunication, that too is held by the ecclesiastical courts. King James demands us to conform. To read from the *Book of Common Prayer*, a book conceived from man instead of Scripture, and not the words transcribed by the Apostles, the last penmen of the Holy Ghost. We are not to use the help of any book, beads, crucifixes, or the like, to teach, or provoke us, but only the help of the Spirit of adoption and prayer, working in our hearts effectually, and teaching us both what and how to pray as we ought.

"You understand, Master Brewer, that I could speak passionately for hours, explaining and justifying a separation from the Church of

England. But the irony is, that you are standing here before me because you are not a person that suffers from a lack of faith and understanding."

"Just so, Master Robinson. As far as continuing on with your reasons for worshipping here in Leyden, I have in my possession your book, *A Justification of Separation from the Church of England*. In fact, I purchased five copies from Printer Thorp that will accompany me back to England. I can assure you one copy will end up in the hands of Master Carver, who is presently in the part of England near to Sturton le Steeple, where your family and that of your wife resides. I believe he has some business connected to the lands inherited by the sons of Master Alexander White, the father of your wife."

Pastor Robinson nodded. Master Brewster had informed him of Master Carver's whereabouts and proximity to both his and his wife's families. The pastor was hopeful to have knowledge of how they fared, but would have to wait patiently for a letter or traveler's word.

"Would it be a bother to give you a letter to carry back with you to England? My wife has written a letter in hopes of it being delivered to her sister Catherine, Catherine White. Mistress Robinson knows her sister is also of a mind to separate from the King's Church, and is looking to come here to Leyden and join our church."

"Of course I can take it back with me to England, and will make a most earnest effort to put the letter in the hands of your sister-in-love. Master Carver has been traveling for business to that area, but I do expect him to return to my estate, mayhaps even before my own arrival there. He is likely to return north before the autumn months and can deliver it then. The other possibility would be for me to leave the letter with Printer Okes in London, who in turn could ask Hugh Mercer of the King's Post to carry it."

"In whatever way it is least burdensome and most likely to deliver to Catherine. If she does decide to venture here to Holland, would you consider accompanying her across?"

Master Brewer waited a moment before answering. "I think if Catherine cares to remove to Leyden, Master Carver would be better to aid her in her travels. I say that because she will have to leave quietly, without a pass for ports. I will be obtaining permission for reasons of business, and taking my family."

"I understand. I expect Master Carver would be agreeable, and having many trustworthy contacts, he should be able to leave England unnoticed."

Master Brewer nodded in agreement and continued, "Upon my return to Leyden with my wife and daughter, my hope is for us to make the covenant together. That is my desire, but Mistress Brewer will have to come to the decision to join on her own. She will need to feel the love in her heart and see the light and truth revealed by the reading and opening of the Bible. There are a number of laymen in your group with the gift of teaching and prophecy. I do not believe Anna has experienced anything like this."

"There is great beauty when a man and woman follow God's plan in joining together in marriage, then uniting with Christ in covenanting into the church. Our gathered church is a place where God's love is revealed. We are a company of faithful and holy people, with their seed, called by the Word of God into public covenant with Christ and amongst themselves, for mutual fellowship in the use of all the means of God's glory and their salvation.

"It will be a blessing to have your family join us on the Sabbath, whenever that might be. I understand you have lands to manage and other business to tend to before leaving England. And you said you will apply formally for permission to leave the country for the reason of doing business in the Netherlands?"

"Just so. When I return, I care not to arouse any suspicions surrounding my departure from England. The last thing I would want to do is draw attention to your congregation here."

As the two men entered the space of worship, church members bustled around them, carrying benches into the sun-drenched courtyard. Many living nearby brought benches from their homes outside of the Green Close. Jonathan Brewster and William Bradford walked in and placed one bench on the side where the men were sitting, and the other on the side of the women and children.

A number of the younger unmarried women would remain inside Master Robinson's house minding the small children, expecting to be relieved of this duty in the afternoon so that they might hear the explanation of the Scripture read that morning. Sometimes, the older children would take on the task of watching the younger ones in the afternoon time of worship.

As Master Brewer watched the members funnel into the courtyard, he noticed a strong bond between the people, a connection borne out of their belief in God and His direction spoken in Scripture, and explained by their gifted pastor, Master Robinson. They hugged, kissed, and laughed in gathering for their coveted Sabbath worship. After working all the days before and after the Sabbath, the people greeted one another with genuine care and happiness in their togetherness. It was clear that for many, they had sacrificed a great deal in leaving England in order to keep their church in this foreign city.

Just then, Master and Mistress Brewster made their way into the courtyard, with Patience and Fear following closely behind. Mary and the children took their places on the side for the women and children, across from where the men were sitting.

"Master Brewer, please find your place next to me," Master Brewster said and gestured. "Jonathan has carried a bench over for us."

"Of course, Master Brewster. It would be an honour. Am I correct in understanding your role as Ruling Elder to be an elected position and one that you will serve for life?"

"It is true. I have been elected by the members and am expected to assist our pastor in keeping order to the church. If any disruption with a member or members should arise, I aid in resolving conflict. Also, I have experience in teaching and in prophecy, when we connect the meaning of Scripture to our present lives. It is an enormous responsibility that God has called me into, and I pray daily I can serve Him and our people justly."

"A more gifted and godly man, I know not. There is a reason you were elected to such a position. You have knowledge of many languages, read hundreds of books, and spent some years at University. You served under Secretary Davison in the Court of Queen Elizabeth, and managed a stop of the Royal Post and manor grounds for the Archbishop of York. Such experiences in life are uncommon and invaluable. Also, you led many in your church safely out of England to Amsterdam, and had the foresight to remove here to Leyden. Above all, you are a gracious and humble servant to God and man alike."

"You are too generous in your words, Master Brewer. It is my great fortune to be a part of this plan with Master Robinson. We started in Leyden with one hundred in our congregation and now in just two years' time have added more than fifty to our group. We do not wish our numbers to grow so large that we find one another unfamiliar. I fear that is what led to disorder within the Ancient Brethren, when–" Master Brewster halted his words at the sight of Master Robinson looking upwards with his palms also up, readying himself to start the Sabbath service with prayer.

And so the pastor began. "May God show his mercy in all our aberrations, and discover them unto us more and more; keep us in, and lead us into his truth: giving us to be faithful in that which we have received, whether it be less or more; and preserving us against all those scandals, wherewith the whole world is filled. Amen."

The congregation followed the prayer singing the 128th Psalm of David. Master Brewer learned from Printer Thorp in Amsterdam that in the coming year, he would print a psalm book translated directly from Hebrew by Henry Ainsworth. If such a version did become available, Thomas anticipated that psalms derived directly from Hebrew would be preferred by this church.

Then Master Robinson began to read from the New Testament, on this day from the book of Matthew. He started at the thirteenth book, reading through the eighteenth. He first covered the parable of the wheat and the tares, and then reviewed a fundamental principle of their gathered church, the importance of telling it unto the church. This concept allowed unresolved conflicts or issues with a member to be revealed to and resolved by the church as a whole.

Master Brewster rose from his bench and joined Pastor Robinson.

This next part of the service would be for teaching, provided chiefly by their Elder. Their gifted teacher reviewed parts of the six books in Matthew in greater detail, ensuring that the members understood the meaning of the words as written in the Geneva Bible. For Master Brewer, it took only a few moments to see and hear why this man was so respected and revered. He had expected Master Brewster to have skill in teaching, as he made his living teaching English to University students. But here, as he stood before the congregation, any person of any education or gender could see, hear, and feel the gifts bestowed by God upon this man, and how with an outpouring of love, he shared them.

He spoke in a soft but strong voice, so that all could hear but not be overpowered. Master Brewster was not so unlike Master Robinson, except the former had not been degreed in Theology and ordained, and thus could not administer the sacraments of communion or baptism. His teaching lasted for more than an hour, after which the group sang another psalm, this time Psalm 23.

Then Pastor Robinson continued with his sermon, his words revolving around last book of Matthew he had read earlier, that eighteenth book. He illuminated the principle of "telling it unto the church", or sharing a transgression openly among the congregation. Trouble that could not be resolved privately should be shared with the church leaders. If those steps failed, the conflict should be brought to the attention of the congregation as a whole, and dealt with, with input from the church. In contrast, the Church of England handled a serious issue with a member by turning to the longstanding hierarchy of bishop and archbishops, and the ecclesiastical courts. Decisions regarding excommunication were also handled in this way. For Master Robinson and his congregation, a core component of the church was the possibility to discuss issues openly. For some, this reason alone was enough to pursue separation from the church of King James.

As Master Robinson finished this part of the worship, Masters Brewster and Fuller readied the bread and wine for Holy Communion. Pastor Robinson delivered the sacrament, which nearly all partook of. Those too feeble in body, their leader sought out, so that no one desiring would be forgotten.

Another psalm was chosen, this time the 108th. As the last words were sung, Pastor Robinson broke into prayer, finishing with a motion of his hands, dismissing the group for the taking of their dinner. Many members departed the area of worship in conversation or song, with some quiet in contemplation. For the majority, dinner had been prepared the day before, so after the meal, in just over an hour's time, they would return to their pastor for the remainder of the service.

Patience, Fear, and Mistress Brewster left the courtyard ahead of the men, walking home to lay the board and ready the food for dinner. In the short walk back, Fear reached for her mother's hand, while Patience kept pace just slightly behind her mother.

"Mother, may I ask you something?" inquired Patience.

"Of course. What is it?" responded her mother as they continued home, rounding the alley by the northeast end of the Pieterskerk.

"The Scripture from the book of Matthew that Master Robinson read this morning, in particular the parable speaking of the wheat and the tares— I am not certain if I understand its meaning. Does it warn us that there will always be sinners within our church, and that God asks we keep them among us, until the time of final judgment? Does it mean there are wrongdoers in our congregation, tares among the wheat, that Master Robinson and Father must let grow alongside us?" questioned Patience with fear in her eyes.

Mistress Brewster stopped walking and turned back to respond. "Patience, the parable speaks of the field to mean the world in total, and not a single congregation. Regarding the tares, they are not people overtly evil in nature. It might be someone presenting as faithful and true, who turns dark in a silent, hypocritical way. The parable reminds us it is not our place to rid the field of tares, for in doing so, much of the wheat would be ripped out and ruined. The tares will be collected in the end and burned, with the wheat gathered and kept within the shelter of the barn."

She continued, speaking to both of her daughters. "God's plan has brought our church together, and we are blessed that our members appear good, like wheat in the field. If tares do exist or rise up, the skill of our pastor, your father, and the other leaders, will curb the growth of such weeds, so the need for pulling not exist at all."

The girls both nodded, but only Patience grasped the meaning of what her mother had to say.

"It pleases me that you are thinking about the meaning of Scripture, and that you trust in my explanation. The afternoon will be dedicated to opening the Scripture further, which should aid in your understanding. If any questions remain, speak with your father. Come now. We should not tarry any longer. I want to have dinner ready when the men arrive home."

After the midday meal, the flock of Master Robinson again left their homes for the courtyard of the Green Close. By the time the bell in the alley sounded twice, the last of the members filtering in found their places on the benches. Those that entered last were greeted by the beautiful sound of the 27th psalm pervading the air. Patience Brewster sang with joy, as this was her favorite psalm. Singing alongside her mother, she looked up at her, filled with love and contentment.

Pastor Robinson came before them in prayer, after which he gestured for Master Cushman to come forward. "Let us open our minds and hearts to the light of the Scripture. I implore you to search the Scriptures, *Scrutamini Scriptura,* remaining open to the meaning and the truth. We are blessed to have on this day Master Cushman, who feels compelled to teach us further, and guide us in connecting the words of Matthew to our lives."

Master Cushman, whom Master Brewer did not know very well, walked as if weighed down. But as he turned to face the congregation, he appeared changed, filled with spirit, in readiness to release his words. His words rang out in a heartfelt prayer of thanks to God, to be sound in mind and body, and able to stand before them. After that, he endeavored to prophesy, making certain the members understood the meaning of the Scripture read earlier, talking on the verses regarding what should be done if transgressed by another. At first, one should go directly to the person and seek out a solution. Should this not suffice, those able to offer guidance and direction should be invoked as witnesses. If the trespasser still refuses to hear, then it should be told unto the church. Pastor Robinson stood by listening to his words, so should anything be obscure, to clarify it; if doubtful, to clear it; if unsound, to refuse it.

When Master Cushman finished speaking, Master Fuller rose to address the congregation. Also possessing the gift of prophecy, he spoke, but not for as long as Master Cushman. Because the Sunday afternoon organ recital had begun at the Pieterskerk, the sound of belting pipes infiltrated the courtyard. In conjunction with the noise of children playing in the churchyard across the alley, the cacophony forced Deacon Fuller to raise his voice to an uncomfortable level. Having to talk at a volume that felt like shouting, he stopped speaking sooner than planned. The disturbances were a reminder of the importance of keeping the Sabbath as imposed by Christ on His churches. Keeping the Sabbath properly was a serious acknowledgement of their covenant. He followed with a prayer, then requested members spare what they could for the collection box being passed around. The majority had very little to give; those faring better put coins in the box. Master Brewer would make his contribution privately, directly to Master Robinson.

Pastor Robinson closed the Sabbath services with a final prayer, his words shaped from spontaneity as opposed to reciting a written text. As he did every week, he reminded the church to repent each day, perhaps even more if necessary, as the time of death was near but the hour never known. Many were moved to tears at the day's experience. Master Brewer scanned the benches with soft eyes, feeling love for those around him, even those he did not yet know. The group combined their voices into the sweetest sound, singing the Ainsworth translation of Psalm 20 with a passion and beauty unknown to him.

As the people sang, he closed his eyes, absorbing the peaceful melody, allowing it to seep deep into his soul.

BIBLIOTHECAE LUGDUNO-BATAVAE CUM PULPITIS ET ARCIS VERA IXNOGRAPHIA,
CLAES JANSZ. VISSCHER (II), 1612, MUNICIPAL ARCHIVES, LEIDEN, THE NETHERLANDS

The University of Leyden library, housed in the Beguinage Chapel, was originally a Catholic church. Students and professors were drawn to Leyden to study theology, medicine, history, law, among other disciplines. Pastor Robinson and Master Brewer both enrolled in the University, where Robinson debated publicly in a famous exchange with one of the leading Theology professors. Robinson's congregation as a whole had a higher than average rate of literacy.

Look closely at the image, and you can see the names of the subjects and the chains that locked the books to their shelves, as they were quite valuable. Because of the University, there was a steady demand for printed materials, which meant printers and binders were also a necessity.

Chapter Twelve

The Printers

More than three years later…
August 1614, London
Master Printer Okes's Sign of The Rose

Master Printer Okes would not let it be known, but his heart sank as the discussion continued deep into the night. They sat in the back room, in the company of the press, his apprentice John Reynoldes listening to Masters Brewer and Carver as if they were revealing the secrets of alchemy. Only Benjamin Grendon, due to complete his eight-year apprentice term with Master Okes at the end of 1616, chose not to attend the meeting. His objective was to join the Stationers' Company and possibly remain working with Master Okes.

The younger apprentice was Edward Winslow, a man not signed on to him but to Master Printer John Beale, who unfortunately could not guide the young man from his prison cell. It was not the first time Beale had been cited by the Stationers' Company. Master Okes agreed to take on apprentice Winslow for the duration of his Master's jail sentence, expected to be a year's time. Edward arrived loaded with aptitude and was pleasant enough in his manner. He and John Reynoldes worked well together from the start, gaining Master Okes productivity and the possibility of signing on Winslow, should Beale break more Stationer Company rules.

Edward Winslow was sitting on the edge of the bench, the light of the fire revealing to Master Okes the excitement in the eyes of the young apprentice. John Reynoldes listened intently, but in a calmer, more contemplative way.

"What we require to begin the venture of publishing books are skilled hands to set the type. Then we will utilize the press of an established Leyden printer, such as Govert Basson, who is situated very close to the home of Master Brewster. Depending on the arrangement with the press owner, you might be operating their press, or they might insist on operating it. Master Brewster's home is large enough to accommodate both of you, as well as the type, ornaments and equipment needed for setting the pages," explained Master Brewer.

"The practice of printing is an admirable art, one to which some ascribe as much importance as that of preaching. It is a great gift of God, acting as an instrument in spreading the word of the Gospel. Do either of you have any interest in participating in this effort?" asked Master Carver.

"What books do you intend to publish, and what do you plan to do with them? Furthermore, what is your desired timing?" asked John, glancing at Master Okes as if looking for forgiveness for posing the question. He would miss his longtime apprentice, but come April of the next year, John's service would be complete, and Master Okes did not expect him to remain at his shops.

"As far as the type of books, they will be theological in nature, most not of a sort that would be permitted to be published here in England. We intend to sell them in Leyden and other parts of Europe, and possibly here, if we can find a safe channel of distribution. I expect some will appeal to a broad population desiring purification within the King's Church. Some will be reprints, and not only in English, but in Latin in some cases. We will consider printing in Dutch as well. Our hope is for economic success with the more known and popular works, so that we might print new tracts speaking against the bishops and the need for separation. Our purpose is to illuminate the truth that religion be based only on the Word of God and His direction derived from Scripture. Regarding timing, I realize your apprenticeship ends the beginning of April of next year. If you could come across to Leyden by the end of 1615 or early in 1616, we could start publishing books within two years from now. I believe Master Brewster would be aligned with that timing."

"Yes, I believe so," agreed Master Carver.

"Next month I will be applying for permission to travel to Flushing in the Netherlands for the purpose of business," explained Master Brewer. "I expect I will receive the pass for ports as requested, and make my way to Leyden by this year's end. I will stay with Master Robinson until the rents begin anew in May. Then I will rent a house only two doors from the pastor's home, in the direction of the Rapenburg. There could be a chance to purchase this place, should I desire to do so. Regardless, I will be well settled in Leyden before your arrival, as will Master Carver, who will be living around the corner on the Nieuwsteeg, with his wife Catherine. If you decide to come to Leyden, you will be staying with Master Brewster, who is also very near to the Pieterskerk."

"There would be room for one of you with Mistress Carver and me. As Master Brewer explained, I will be but a stone's throw from both the houses of Masters Brewster and Robinson."

"Has word of your marriage reached your pastor in Leyden?" asked Master Okes. "I can only imagine the happiness within the congregation in learning you have joined in marriage with the sister of Mistress Robinson."

"This is a beautiful story of how the path laid out by God is planned already, and what a perfect union you have made with Mistress Carver. I still remember more than three years ago, when Pastor Robinson asked me to bring the letter from his wife to her sister, back to England. And then his request to deliver his sister-in-love, Catherine, to Leyden." Master Brewer laughed out loud. "For some reason I immediately suggested that Master Carver might be able to deliver the letter. I went on to say he would be best to accompany her to Leyden as well," recounted Master Brewer with a smile. "I never would have dreamed they would someday be married. It truly is God, His plan."

"I concur completely, my good friend," responded Master Carver. "In truth, it does surprise me that I did not begin courting Catherine sooner. How long do you think we have been doing business with the White family?"

"Really, as long as I can remember. I recall visiting Master White as a young boy in accompanying my father on his business dealings. This was before the death of Master White, I think in 1595," remarked Master Brewer, his voice trailing off.

"Before the turn of the century, I would say. Doing business with the Whites is one of the chiefest of reasons in traveling north. I believe the family of Alexander White to be one of the wealthiest in England, with the vastness of land ownership rivaled by few."

When Master Carver visited the White estate the year after Marie's death, he was in such a fog he did not take notice of Catherine. It was not until two years after that, in the spring of 1612, when he delivered the letter from Leyden that he took notice of her. Catherine had endless questions about Leyden, from the journey there to the nature of the city and life within the congregation of Pastor Robinson, her brother-in-love. The combination of the contents of that letter, along with the responses of Master Carver, had Catherine ready to leave England straight away.

Not long after, the couple began courting, confirming God's plan. Catherine desired to make covenant with Pastor Robinson's congregation in Leyden right away, since for years she read and studied the Geneva Bible, and knew the light of God's word. For her, removing to Leyden meant far more than reuniting with her sister.

When he had left Leyden, Master Carver was unsure of the timing of his return there. Once Catherine entered his life, that uncertainty vanished. It was as if she were waiting for him to arrive so they could make their union in marriage, and then remove to Leyden to make covenant with Master Robinson's congregation.

"Regarding the word of our marriage reaching Leyden, I did send a letter in the fall of last year to Master Robinson, indicating Catherine and I intended to wed before the year's end. Whether or not he received my written word is unknown. Mayhaps he has learned of our union by word of mouth. If not, I can only imagine the look of surprise on Mistress Robinson's face, to see her sister before her in Leyden and married to me."

Master Carver continued, "As far as this business of publishing and printing, I do want to be clear that this labor is something between Masters Brewer and Brewster, and not me directly. I will support the effort as I can, but if you men intend to come to Leyden, you will be working for them and not me. That being said, you are welcome to lodge with me and Mistress Carver as long as desired."

"I have interest in this venture, or at least in learning more about it," interjected Edward. "It is difficult for me to say with certainty that I will leave England, not knowing what the future holds with Master Printer Beale. Should he be released within the year and my apprenticeship continue without further interruption, I might finish out my contract."

Master Okes spoke next. "Edward, you realize if you leave England within the next two or three years, that would require breaking your contract with Master Beale. That is a serious decision, and will likely come into question should you pursue another contract or trade."

"I have to be truthful, Master Okes. In my mind, my contract with Master Beale has been compromised with his condemnation of binding me to a scrivener. I have been blessed by your kindness, in taking me in as your own apprentice. Working with you and John has been a privilege. Without question, my Master is a capable and extremely productive printer, which is why I agreed to sign on with him. Just before the signing of my contract, he printed a fascinating book relating Robert Hartcourt's voyage to Guiana. At the very beginning of my apprenticeship, I had a role in setting the type for an edition of John Dod and Robert Cleaver's work on the subject of Communion. That was before he sent me to work with the scrivener."

Edward paused momentarily, carefully choosing his next words. "Should Master Beale continue breaking the rules of the Stationers' Company, I will have no choice but to apprentice elsewhere, or pursue this opportunity in Leyden. I would not know what to expect living in the Netherlands, but playing a part in publishing religious works that would be banned here is truly God's work. Also, I understand that Master Robinson is a charismatic leader and respected among the Theology professors at the University of Leyden, which also intrigues me. I am curious to experience a Sabbath service with his congregation."

"I too wonder about this pastor, and how the service differs from that of the Church of England. There must be something special about this man for people to risk their lives in leaving the church and England," added John Reynoldes.

Printer Okes continued to listen, almost in disbelief. It wasn't that he expected John to stay on with him, and really, Edward was not legally connected to him by contract, but now two very capable men could be putting their skills to use outside of England and the Stationers' Company. He was torn– a Master Printer dedicated to the Stationers' Company and the King, all while contrarily taking a risk in worshiping secretly within an underground reformed church. Outside of sending the type over to the mainland with Master Carver years ago, he had not connected that risk of non-conformance directly to his livelihood. He wondered if some day he would be asked to have a hand in distributing or selling the books produced in Leyden by Master Brewster. The thought of that caused him a great deal of anxiety. He calmed himself by recognizing if the request did arise, it would be years from then.

"Master Okes, do you have anything to impart or counsel to provide?" asked Master Brewer.

"I think you should do what your heart tells you, and what you believe God wants. Neither of you have a wife or children to look after." As he made this comment, his eyes fell directly on Edward Winslow, who had taken a liking to his daughter, Elizabeth. Whether there was a future between them was unknown, but should he leave for Leyden, it would make it unlikely. "If you venture to Leyden and print books that would be banned in England, and are somehow connected to them, understand that makes a return to the Stationers' Company virtually impossible. You will most certainly forfeit your chance to become a Master Printer here."

Both young printers sat quietly, shifting their gaze from the dwindling flames to the concerned faces of the men around them.

"When would you want a decision?" asked John.

"Ideally by the end of the year, for if you choose to remain here, we will seek out others for assistance in setting the type in Leyden. If you choose to work with us, I will cover the cost of your travel and can assist in the transportation arrangements if necessary," explained Master Brewer.

"I do appreciate that most generous offer. I fear I am stepping out of bounds, but would you consider paying the passage for the woman I intend to marry? Her name is Prudence Grendon, and we have been courting for more than a year. She is the sister to another apprentice of Master Okes, Benjamin Grendon."

"I can promise to cover her expenses should your plan to marry remain intact. And what about you, Edward? Do you also have a woman you desire to wed that you want accompanying you to Leyden?" quipped Master Brewer.

As he was only a year into his apprenticeship, all in the room thought the idea of this quite amusing. Everyone but Edward and Master Okes, to a degree. Nicholas and Edward had never spoken of it formally, but he had seen on numerous occasions the way the young apprentice looked at his daughter. Edward and Elizabeth were both nineteen years of age, and in the Master Printer's mind, too young to be courting seriously, especially with Edward in the initial phase of his contract.

With Nicholas troubled by this more than a month ago, Rose Okes gently reminded her husband of their own start. He was an apprentice when they met, and she serving as a maid to Queen Elizabeth, courting for years before marriage. The initial meeting produced an intense and immediate connection, and maybe, his wife offered, it was the same for their daughter and Edward.

As Master Okes looked across at the young man, he could see a bit of himself in him. The ambition and love of books, and learning the craft that could impact the minds of so many, drove Edward as it had Nicholas as a young man. His family was of good standing, even better than his own, with his father successful as a merchant and the means to send Edward to the King's School of Worcester Cathedral. Even though it would not be Edward's intention, what Nicholas did not want was his daughter to be hurt. What were the odds that this man would be in a position to support her and a family? And what were the chances that should he move to Leyden, his heart would remain committed to her?

Of his two daughters, he feared more for Elizabeth than he did young Rose. Elizabeth was more conservative. Some might describe her as tentative, to the point of being vulnerable. Rose, on the other hand, had an adventurous spirit, needing more than ordinary experiences to make her come to life. That too made her father uneasy, but strangely, he worried less about Rose. If the budding relationship between Elizabeth and Edward was real and he left London, Nicholas expected Elizabeth would be absolutely devastated.

After the awkward silence, Edward cleared his throat and, while looking at Master Okes, admitted there was a young woman he would want to bring over to Leyden. "Master Okes, if you were not aware already, I want now to make it known that I have been spending time with your daughter, Elizabeth. I apologize if this comes as a surprise to you. Due to our age and my newness to the trade, I myself did not recognize it formally as courting. Otherwise, I would have come to you directly. But now, with the prospect of moving to Leyden in the service of Masters Brewer and Brewster, it is something I should discuss with you, and Elizabeth, of course."

"I do appreciate your honesty, Edward. This is something we can talk of further when afforded more privacy, but thank you for raising the issue."

"Rest assured, son, you have time in which to make this decision. At least another five or six months, and from then a year or more until the actual move," explained Master Brewer. "If you make the move and have not yet married, I will pay also for your future wife to cross the North Sea either with you, or at a later date. In fact, if you were to marry Elizabeth Okes, I would bring over her entire family to celebrate your wedding day," said Master Brewer with a smile, as he nodded in respect to Master Okes.

The flames fluttered rapidly, the flickering a warning they would soon expire. Master Carver stood first, with the others following. "Think of this discussion as a spark glowing orange, captured within the folds of blackened, charred cloth, growing bigger with each breath. Masters Brewer and Brewster will have everything in place for you should you decide to ignite and spread this fire of the printed word."

The five men paused to give thanks and offer a prayer before retiring for the night. Barely visible to one another, Master Okes led the short prayer. In his mind, he was grateful for the talk to be over, and thought maybe the two young printers would lose interest over time.

Aided by familiarity, John felt in the darkness for the handle of the iron peel, stifling the stubborn coals with a pile of ash. His mind raced with fragments from the conversation, along with visions of how he imagined Leyden to be. Extinguishing a candle with a stiff exhalation, he carried out the other with the group following, leaving the press alone in the dark. Or so they thought. Tucked in the corner, crouched behind a stack of unbound books, hid Elizabeth Okes.

Her presence there was unintentional. She had ventured into the press room after supper, seeking out the board of Nine Men's Morris to play with Robert. Not finding the game in the vicinity of the press, she wandered into the depths of the storage space, searching around piles of books and folios for the carved wooden board and stone pieces. Without success, a frustrated Elizabeth turned to leave and was startled by the gathering of the men in the press room. She realized quickly by the size of the fire that they intended to stay for at least an hour's time. Her heart racing, she struggled in deciding whether to make herself known and leave, or stay hidden and be a passive participant. In a way, Master Brewer made the choice for her, as he spoke almost immediately about the need for the assistance of trained printers in Leyden. She shuddered at the sound of the words, straining her eyes through the darkness to see Edward's reaction.

Her body stayed still, you could say in a state of shock. Maybe she had not even realized the depth of her feelings for the young apprentice until being faced with the idea that he would leave London for Leyden. From the start, he was contracted under Master Beale, and would not be staying with her father for more than a year. But she expected he would return to Master Beale once he was released from prison, and would be but a walk away. As she listened, it became clear he had serious interest.

She adjusted her coif, releasing the knot and tying it a bit tighter, needing something to do with her nervous hands. Smoothing her apron repeatedly, overcome with anxiety, she realized she might vomit or faint. Edward was the first man who had evoked any feelings in her. Before him, she feared she lacked the ability of caring for or desiring a man. Before him, she had felt nothing.

Trembling with the fear of desertion, she crouched in a position of self-protection, like a gargoyle atop a pillar in a Roman piazza. As the excitement built amongst the men, tears rolled down her face. The tears pooled in her velvet gray eyes, spilling over like the edges of a lake after a heavy rain. He was going to leave her; she sensed it, without him saying the words.

In time he did reveal his thoughts, and when he did speak of her, speaking of his feelings to her father, she nearly toppled over. She had no idea that he thought enough of her to consider her in his plans for the future. His blue eyes glistened in the light of the fire as he spoke, and to Elizabeth, he appeared like a cherub carved by the hand of God. Her eyes traced his profile, enjoying the picture, especially as her gaze drifted from his nose down to his chin. As she did that she imagined her lips passing gently from his, following the thin trail of soft brown hair down his chin. That thought quelled her apprehension, curving her lips into a smile. She loved this man, without being certain of what love was.

Elizabeth had gone from sitting to standing, watching intently as the conversation came to a close. Master Carver stood first, with her father offering a closing prayer. John Reynoldes smoldered the last of the flames in the hearth and blew out one of the two candles, ushering in the hour for sleeping. Captured by the blackness of night, Elizabeth stood frozen in the darkness. Across the room, there was nothing to be seen within the hearth save for the glow of transient embers, accompanied by the lingering smell of smoke. She continued to stand, as if in a trance, working to decipher the night's conversation. Placing on the scales both fear and hope, Elizabeth watched as the sides moved up and down, eventually stopping in an equal, balanced place.

She moved slowly, carefully making her way out of the storage space and into the room with the press. Walking past the press, she unconsciously reached out, passing her hand along one of the oak beams, seeking comfort in its familiarity and power. The press had been there before her, and would be there long after. That consistency and reliability consoled her in this night of uncertainty. With that in mind, she climbed the steps and lay quietly upon the mattress where her brother slept soundly. She prayed for at least a farthing of an hour before removing her girdle, apron, waistcoat, petticoat, bodies, and coif, down to her smock and stockings. After untying her garters, she decided to leave her stockings on for sleeping. Sliding down the feather-filled mattress and under the sheet, she wrapped her arm around her brother, needing the comfort and warmth of a human connection.

Closing her eyes and beckoning the peace of sleep, she was uncertain whether the voice she heard was real or imagined.

"Elizabeth, Elizabeth, are you awake?" whispered Edward intently.

She shot upright in the bed. "Yes, Edward, I am here. I am awake. What is it?"

"Praise God you are not already sleeping. I will not be long, as I do not want to awaken Robert. Please, come away from him so I can speak with you." She climbed carefully out of the bed, replacing her coif quickly and covering her shoulders with a blanket, before making her way to Edward's voice. In walking she stepped on one of Robert's clay marbles, the surprise and pain of it nearly dropping her to the floor. She grunted in discomfort but recovered quickly, without disrupting her brother's sleep.

As she neared Edward, he reached out in the darkness for her hands, grasping them as if saving her from a raging blaze.

"Elizabeth, I want you to know that I care deeply for you." He spoke with authenticity and urgency. "I need you to know that I love you. I met tonight with Masters Brewer and Carver, and we spoke of printing books in Leyden, in the Netherlands. Depending on what happens with Master Printer Beale, I might consider traveling to Leyden and aiding their efforts. I realize it is unlikely, but in the event this occurs, if we are still in contact, would you consider joining me, or traveling with me there?"

Without any words, she found him in the dark and gently kissed his forehead while tracing her finger along the tract of soft brown hair running down his chin. Moving her hands on either side of his face, she kissed his mouth so naturally and filled with love, leaving him without any doubt that she would. With that exchange, they stifled any insecurity and uncertainty that might have existed. Elizabeth smiled as she clung to him. As frightening as it had been to hear the conversation and feel the fear of abandonment, it precipitated the revelation that Edward shared in her hopes for a future together. They held each other, exchanging comfort and love, pleading with time to stand still.

ACADEMY BUILDING REBUILT IN 1617, CREATOR UNKNOWN,
LEIDEN MUNICIPAL ARCHIVES, THE NETHERLANDS

The University of Leyden Academy Building, (Academiegebouw) and the Botanical Gardens to the right. Situated on the Rapenburg canal, the University was incorporated in 1575, turning one of the oldest buildings in Leyden (and former convent), into the primary academic building. The University was granted by William of Orange to the people of Leyden, who survived the Spanish siege of their city, which ended in 1574.

The University of Leyden Botanical Gardens (Hortus botanicus), started by botanist Carolus Clusius in the 1590s, was regarded as one of the finest medical/ teaching gardens in the world. His extensive network and international channels delivered specimens from all corners of the planet. In addition to students and professors, the public enjoyed strolling through the rows of unique plants and herbs.

Chapter Thirteen

1615

July 1615, Leyden
December 1615, London

July 1615, Leyden, Knowing the Fair City

It took only a handful of days before printer John Reynoldes decided he preferred Leyden to London. With landmarks like the Pieterskerk, the Burcht, and Hooglandsekerk, he was able to navigate the city without difficulty. In truth, his work did not require him to move about the city much. When he did venture out of the home of Master Brewster, it was to carry out an errand nearby related to printing, or explore the city for his own pleasure. Eventually, Master Brewster would request he travel to Amsterdam and retrieve type and ornaments from Printer Thorp there. The more intensive work would begin with the arrival of Edward Winslow, who was expected to terminate his apprenticeship in London and make his way to Leyden and join their effort.

John thought often of his Master Printer, Nicholas Okes, wondering how he fared. Serving as an apprentice for eight years, their relationship was built on respect for the trade and one another. At the end of his apprenticeship in April, John had considered staying on a number of months to aid with the work in the shop, but feared that months might turn into years. Another apprentice, Benjamin Grendon, who would eventually become John's brother-in-love, intended to stay on as a journeyman printer. Benjamin's apprenticeship was to end in December of 1616, and prior to that, a young man named Andrewe Driver was to begin his contract.

So with that in mind, John convinced himself that he was not abandoning Master Okes, but instead embarking on a spiritual mission supporting God's plan. Their parting was professional and amicable, as one might expect, but the day John Reynoldes left for Leyden, the light in the eyes of Master Okes dimmed a little. Watching his apprentice leave his shop was not the issue. What troubled him were the thoughts of what might lie ahead. Soon, Edward Winslow would leave for Leyden, which meant eventually his daughter Elizabeth would follow to marry him. His mind would wander farther. Mayhaps his wife, his daughter Rose, and son Robert, would travel to Leyden for the wedding, and then what if his younger children would want to remain there? For John Reynoldes, there was no way he could have known Master Okes was plagued by such thoughts.

In the meanspace, John enjoyed strolling the botanical gardens of the University, dreaming of the day he could walk there with Prudence. He imagined it would not be overly long before Edward would accompany her in the journey from London. Prudence had never been away from England, and even if she had, John did not want her traveling alone. Completing his apprenticeship with Master Okes on the third of April, he had pleaded with her to leave with him at the end of that month. Her mother having fallen ill, Prudence could not leave her side, as much as she wanted to be with John.

On this day, being Wednesday, and a market day, he walked up and down both sides of the Oude and Nieuwe Rhine, getting a sense of what was available, and where. In particular, he favored the cheese he could purchase at the kaas, or cheese market. Never before had he tasted cheese like this, so rich and with so much variety and flavor. There was young and old cheese, wheels from Gouda, of course many from Leyden, with some containing cumin. Later in the month, he had learned there would be a fair dedicated to cheese. When Prudence did arrive, he would take her on her first market day to where the kaas was sold. He wanted to be certain of her comfort in this foreign place. Being in another country had its challenges, especially a city drawing a third of its people from all corners of the world. Some were there seeking work in the cloth trades, or requiring religious sanctuary, or both. Many came to attend the University of Leyden, studying Theology, Law, or Medicine, among other subjects.

Master Brewer himself had enrolled in the University in February, not long after his arrival to Leyden. John had often heard him speak the praises of the place, from the quality of the professors, to that of the other students. Access to the University library was also something Master Brewer cherished, with its close proximity to his home. He lived only two doors away from Master Robinson, in the direction of the Rapenburg. Sharing a property line with the homes of Masters Brewer and Robinson, the former Catholic chapel of the Beguinage served as a University building, including the library and a room for practicing fencing, along with an Anatomy Theatre. Of those in the congregation of Master Robinson, Master Brewer was the only member enrolled in the University. Of course, as in England, to enroll one must be learned in Latin and Greek, and not many in the church had that knowledge. Exceptions would be Masters Brewster, Carver, and Robinson, and John had understood that Master Robinson would also enroll before the summer's end.

John reached into his wool pocket for groots to pay for cheese he could lunch on as he walked through the market. He had a small inheritance from his late father and was being paid a weekly stipend from Master Brewer, with lodging offered at no cost by Master Brewster. The stipend would increase once the actual setting of pages and printing began. John was eager for Edward to arrive and the work to begin. With John's apprenticeship complete, he yearned to be the lead printer of a publication. Master Brewster reminded him that without an actual press, there would be times when only the pages would be set and the printing be done elsewhere. Still, John remained hopeful he would have the chance to operate a press owned by another, and pondered that as he savored his cheese. He turned and began making his way north and east, in the direction of his favorite baker.

"John, pray pardon," called out a voice behind him.

John turned, showing a look of surprise. It was not often he encountered a familiar face when walking through the markets.

"Good day, John. I am pleased to see you are finding your way around the city and have discovered the marvelous cheese. I have just received a letter from London indicating that Edward Winslow will terminate his apprenticeship by the end of October, with plans to depart London in the first months of next year. He confirmed he is to accompany your betrothed, Prudence, here to Leyden. Sadly, I must inform you of the passing of her mother, though she suffers no more, and is in God's keeping."

John nodded, grateful to know that Prudence would be with him soon, and that she no longer had to watch her mother deteriorate in sickness.

"As promised last year, when we met in the home of Master Okes in London, I will pay for the passage of Prudence Grendon and her belongings. Master Carver has agreed to her lodging with him and Mistress Carver, in the home he is renting in the Nieuwesteeg."

"Excellent good, Master Brewer. I am grateful for your generosity in getting her across, and am pleased that she will be so near to me, staying with the Carvers."

"That is the beauty of this city. Even though the walls and population expand, it is simple to walk from one end to another in little time. Fortunately, for our church, we are mostly concentrated near one another. I also favor the closeness to the University buildings. That reminds me, regarding the convenience of being close to people and places– the print shop of Govert Basson, where Master Brewster has worked in the past, at the corner of the Kloksteeg... it is looking as if Printer Basson will print our initial publication. We have not yet worked out the details, and as we do, I will keep you informed."

Master Brewer detected a look of disappointment in his young printer. "I know, John, you want to be printing as well as setting the type and ornaments. I think in time we can work out this arrangement, whether it be at the shop of Printer Basson, or with another printer. In truth, I am doubtful our work with Basson will run very deep, seeing that our religious views are conflicting. On the other hand, Printer

Thorp in Amsterdam could use the aid of trained hands. I know Master Brewster has indicated you must go there to retrieve our set of fonts. Since there are months before Edward is to arrive, I would like you to spend some time working with Printer Thorp in Amsterdam. He has already confirmed that there is room enough to lodge with him on a temporary basis.

"You will benefit on a number of levels working with Printer Thorp, as he connects directly the commitment of printing to the church covenant. In Amsterdam, he aids Henry Ainsworth, following him after the split in the Ancient Brethren. Master Thorp is greatly respected, as he will not print words conflicting with his own convictions. He is a godly man, with many spiritual gifts, serving as a deacon since 1612, and newly elected as church elder.

"Presently, he is working with Master Ainsworth to print his Bible commentaries, leaving little time for anything else. This project could take a number of years, after which he spoke of printing a French translation of Ainsworth's *La Communion des Saincts,* with the aid of Jean de Lecluse, an experienced translator and church member," elaborated Master Brewer.

"Was it not just a year ago in the shop of Giles Thorp where his inventory was raided and confiscated?" inquired John in a concerned tone. "Mayhaps if I am connected to Master Thorp, it could bring undesirable attention to our endeavors in Leyden?"

"Your concern is valid, but bear in mind it is no secret that Master Thorp is the printer for those who have separated. Much of what he puts out from his presses is done so anonymously, especially the more controversial tracts, so outside of cracks in fonts and ornaments, the source of a book maintains its air of secrecy. Rest assured he is a gifted and discreet man, and I expect you will both gain greatly in working together. This experience in Amsterdam will keep you productive and sharp, as I expect the work on our own publications will not begin until the middle of next year, the first book being published either late 1616 or even the start of 1617."

"I am here to provide my printing skill in whatever form you believe serves God best. My training being complete, I am capable of running a press. If at the start it is best that I work in the shop of Master Thorp in Amsterdam, I am glad to aid there. Should it be necessary that in Leyden I set pages as opposed to manning a press, I will accept that. When I left London and the Stationers' Company, I did so understanding that I might be most useful in proofreading and setting type. I am here to help spread the word of God with my knowledge of printing, understanding that you and Master Brewster should guide me accordingly."

John meant every word he uttered, there being a measure of pride working with proven men of the trade, like Printers Thorp and Basson. Even so, he was hopeful a situation would arise in which he could be running the press. In time, if it was in God's plan, it would be so. In the meantime, he enjoyed the cheese and the beauty of the city, wondering how Amsterdam would compare.

December 1615, London– At the Sign of The Rose

Young Rose tried everything possible to keep her hands from shaking, but it was as if her body were no longer under her control. Royal Post carrier Hugh Mercer had stopped in earlier, staying long enough to promise his return later that day. Since then, she could do nothing but wait.

Her feelings for the carrier of the King's Post had a history that extended for months, even more than a year if she thought back long enough. It wasn't until the last months that she recognized reciprocation of those feelings. At first Rose was surprised, as she expected a man like that, always on the move, meeting people in different inns and places, would hardly take notice of her.

But during a visit two months before, which was not planned, as they never were, something happened that was different. During that visit he shared a very vague rumor with Master Okes, as opposed to delivering a letter or word of importance, and spent the remainder of his time taking some food and drink and talking with young Rose. It was then that she realized she was not alone in her feelings.

Even though that excited her, making her feel good on many levels, her desire increased to a level of distraction. She found very quickly that it was not easy to love someone who was largely absent and unpredictable in his return. She longed each and every day for him to gallop up to the shop door and knock with urgency to come inside and see her. She found herself glancing continuously out the shop windows, envisioning his arrival, only to be disappointed by the reality of his absence.

On this cold December morning, Rose heard the click of a horse's hooves on cobblestones. As Hugh Mercer dismounted, her dream came to life, with Rose doing everything she could to hide her heightened emotions as he entered. He never did detect the magnitude of her feelings, as he was busy hiding his own.

Rose felt dizzy as the blood rushed from her head and through her body. She wasn't sure if it was a pleasurable experience, or something undesirable. Either way, it wasn't in her control, which in principle bothered her. All the time spent thinking about when she would see him again, and what they would talk about– the pressure of making the most of what little time they shared was something that plagued her. And for the most part, she blamed herself for letting him have such a grip on her.

Rose discarded those thoughts as Hugh Mercer entered the print shop. She acted surprised to see him, even though in her mind, he was constantly present.

"Good day. What brings you to our shop?" asked Rose in a quiet, unremarkable voice. "Should I call my father for you?"

Hugh Mercer stood silently, seeking words that refused to surface. His thoughts raced wildly, and he really did not know what to say. On this stop he actually had books and a letter from Master Brewer to deliver, but as he dismounted his horse, he gasped, realizing he had forgotten the bag containing these items. He would have to return to Hampton Court for the bag. He cursed himself silently for making such a foolish blunder. His mistake would cost him most of the day, losing an opportunity to visit with Rose.

He thought about her much of the time he rode his long and tiresome routes, trying desperately to remember all the details of her features– the shape of her face, the color of her hair and eyes. Often, he placed her by his side, envisioning her smile and how she responded to his presence and conversation.

One of the reasons he stopped that day at the sign of The Rose was to help define his feelings about the printer's daughter. He knew he had feelings that went beyond friendship, and that frightened him, as he was courting another woman in his home village of Sturton le Steeple, not far from Scrooby Manor. He was thirty years of age, courting a woman with twenty-five years, who assumed their next step to be marriage. It was not an arranged situation but close enough, as both families expected the two to marry. To be truthful, he held the same assumption, and cared deeply for this woman, easily imagining a future with her. Why then, was he unable to get Rose Okes out of his head? He needed to understand his feelings and desires, hoping to reconcile them and move on with his life.

Rose's desire for the post carrier began before his. Maybe he sensed her interest, but for more than a year, since she was sixteen, she often thought about him, wondering when he would stop in next. Wondering if she would ever be alone with him, and what it would be like should she ever have the chance. Her visions of him did not consume her, but were enough to enter her mind many times in a day, and the daydreams progressed the more times she saw him and the older she became.

Now, nearly eighteen, her longing for Hugh Mercer was nearly unbearable. She was attracted to everything about him. His appearance, his smell, how he spoke and moved–all of his ways appealed to her. She loved his hair color, which was a light brown with streaks of the color straw, and how its length lay beyond his collar. The depth of his ocean-blue eyes lured her in, while his boyish smile beckoned her closer. He was taller than most men, and had the most perfectly chiseled chin, as if carved by the hand of Michaelangelo. And even though he wasn't fond of his uniform, she liked it, because she thought it made him look official and important. He likely would have laughed at that notion.

During some of his past visits, her heart had raced so wildly that sweat escaped her skin. She wanted to be even closer, physically connected if she had her way. This was her first experience of feeling a burning, pulsing sensation inside her. When she was much younger she adored Jonathan Brewster, but this was different. She tried to talk to her older sister about this, but Elizabeth was disgusted and annoyed, and refused to speak of it. Maybe she had never experienced it herself and was concerned about that, considering she was courting the apprentice printer Edward Winslow.

Rose contemplated speaking with her mother about her feelings, but hesitated as she might put a stop to the contact altogether. But then Rose remembered her mother's path with her father, and how they met by chance and defied the odds of being together, standing in different stations of society, among other obstacles.

She decided on the most debilitating path possible. She kept all of her feelings to herself, and collectively, they swallowed her whole. Some days were better than others, when she was overridden with studies, chores, and errands, and had no time to dwell. But most days were not like that, and she spent hours in the shop, maybe leaving to take some books over to the sellers at St. Paul's churchyard, or to the binder's place. But even then she was scanning the public spaces for Hugh Mercer, the man she could never quite force completely from her thoughts.

As if in a dream, there he stood before her, speechless and almost awkward, but in her eyes, flawless. They gazed back at each other without words, as if frozen by the magic between them.

"Y-Yes, I am here to see Printer Okes, please," stammered Hugh as his eyes shifted nervously off to one side. As Rose turned to find her father, Hugh Mercer shook his head in disgust at his clumsiness. What was he going to say to Printer Okes? He fidgeted as he stood, rifling through his brain for the tidbits of rumors circulating through the court and countryside.

"Good day, Master Okes. So sorry to disturb you. I haven't much to share today. And I just realized I departed the palace in such a hurry I left behind my other leather satchel, the one holding the two books and letter that Master Brewer sent over from Leyden for you. I will have to make my way back to Hampton Court and retrieve that for you before I return north."

This was no trouble for Printer Okes, as he did not have to make the return journey, but even he noticed how uncharacteristically scattered in mind and body the post carrier appeared. "Yes, Hugh, whatever your time affords in terms of getting those books to me. I do not want to impact your route or other obligations."

"No, not at all. I have a day in London to do as I wish." As he spoke those words, he inadvertently glanced over at Rose, who interpreted his words as suited her, making her blush. She realized that her fantasy world could be colliding with the real one, and she cared not to stop it. The post carrier hurried out the door, nearly stumbling as he turned back, promising his return later that day.

His forgetfulness cost him most of the day. Instead of a well-deserved day of rest, he was back on his horse, racing back to Hampton Court, fighting the cold and wind. He was so angry with himself for forgetting the books, he ground his teeth as he chastised himself for his carelessness. Both he and his horse needed the rest, and above all, he desired to spend the day with Rose.

Eventually, he made his return, as the day neared its end. He would not have time to return to the palace to sleep, so he carried his belongings, planning to spend the night at an inn near the sign of The Rose. He would have no other choice.

Rose had an exceedingly productive day, riding high on the excitement of Hugh Mercer's promised return. Usually she spent her days dreaming of his presence, and on this day he was actually returning to her father's shop. She spoke to herself throughout the day, warning that he might not spend any time with her at all, that by the time he made his return from Hampton Court, it would be close to dark. Even as she recognized the depth of her vulnerability, Rose imagined a magical encounter that spanned hours as opposed to minutes.

Finally, the moment arrived when she heard the sound of the hooves against the cobblestones, and moments later Hugh Mercer knocking at the door. Rose stood frozen, eyes wide and filled with a mixture of excitement and fear.

He entered breathing with effort, carrying the leather satchel he had forgotten, along with his belongings. His rosy cheeks revealed the frigid temperature, and upon entering he made his way over to the hearth. As he held his hands in front of the fire, he caught Rose watching him out of the corner of his eye. He was almost certain she had feelings, that if not matched his, came close. His face filled with even more color, and not from the closeness to the fire.

"Would you care for a cup of beer?" asked Rose as she broke from her statuesque state. Hugh turned with a smile and nodded. He took a seat on the edge of the bench near the fire and continued to rub his hands together, contemplating what he would say to Rose in the little time he would have there. For the moment, they were the only ones occupying the room. Elizabeth was out running errands, and her mother, brother, and Katherine were upstairs. Her father was busy working the press in the back room. It might have been the first time such a luxury had presented itself. And surprisingly, the carrier found the courage to turn to her and share some of the thoughts he had locked up for the past month.

She stood before him, stunned as he spoke of his feelings for her.

"Rose, I am not sure how to say this, but I think of you often as I travel each day. It is almost as if I cannot get you out of my mind, even when I try. For me, what is troubling is that I am courting a woman from my birthplace, in Sturton le Steeple, and…"

As he continued to speak, Rose's heart struggled to beat. She didn't hear the rest of his words, as she was too busy digesting the idea that Hugh Mercer was not really an option. Even though he had just finished telling her that she occupied his thoughts, he followed that with the worst possible reality– that he was committed to someone else, and unavailable.

Or was he? If he was so taken with the woman he was courting, why was he sitting before her, revealing his thoughts and feelings? Rose continued to listen, the entire time vacillating between shutting him out and leaving the door open. Deep in her soul she believed she belonged with this man. To be fair to herself, she needed to take the risk of finding the answer.

Her instincts pushed her to this decision, but not without hesitation. A little voice warned her not to go down this road. But she could not stop. She had been down the road so many times in her mind that she desired to see how this was to unfold. God's plan would happen as it should.

"So I am sorry, Rose, if this is confusing to you. I am confused myself, about why I am sitting here telling you my feelings, when I am obligated to another. In a way, I was hoping you could assure me of how silly this was, and send me on my way," he said with a nervous laugh.

"I too am sorry for doing anything to jeopardize this commitment you have already. But in truth, I have held you in my thoughts for so many months that you can actually mark the time in years. My heart has leaped each and every time you have walked through the door, so mayhaps you detected that, and that is why you are exploring your feelings. For me, it is clear. I have imagined myself with you many, many times. I have dreamed of the day that we would sit here talking before the fire, alone."

That was all the invitation the post carrier needed. He moved along the bench so that their legs touched, then reached up and brushed her cheek with the back of his hand, finding her chin, and drawing it towards him. He kissed her mouth lightly at first, and she responded in kind, until they were comfortable enough to unleash their passion. She wrapped her hands around the base of his neck, playing with the hair she had admired for so many months, smiling to herself as she did it.

Her dream was unfolding, and in this moment she told herself to enjoy it, and not to feel badly, or worry about what would happen in the days and weeks ahead. The couple made the most of their time alone, hugging, kissing, and caressing one another, knowing this might be their only chance.

Then a noise at the shop entrance startled Rose enough to make her pull away, and a moment later, Elizabeth entered, shivering and out of breath.

"I don't think it could get any colder out there," said Elizabeth as she shuffled over to the warmth of the hearth. She hadn't even noticed Hugh Mercer, so when she looked up to see him on the bench next to her sister, she stopped, piercing him with the most quizzical look. In shifting her eyes to her blushing sister, she realized she had interrupted more than just sitting and talking. She frowned at Rose and rushed off in disgust to find her father.

"What do you think she will say to your father? I pray to the good Lord she does not impart her opinion on what was shared between us as she walked in. She did seem quite bothered by my presence," he said with a concerned look on his face.

"I am not worried. Elizabeth has more bark than bite. I expect she will not utter a word."

Printer Okes entered the main front room and smiled at Hugh Mercer. "You have made it back, I see. So much for a day of rest. You have been on your horse all day, just like any other. I take it you remembered the books this time?"

"Yes, of course, the books sent from Master Brewer– they are here in my satchel." He rose awkwardly from the bench and unlatched the leather bag, removing the two books sent from Leyden. One was Henry Ainsworth's translation from Hebrew of the Psalms of David and the other written by Master Robinson on the justification of separation.

"Ah yes, I was expecting something like this. Is there an accompanying letter or anything else?"

"Right, yes, the letter." He fumbled deeper in the bag and located Master Brewer's letter addressed to Master Okes and handed it to the printer.

"Are you feeling well?" asked Printer Okes. "You seem unlike yourself today."

"Yes, thanks be to God, I am feeling well enough," responded the post carrier as he cleared his throat and smoothed down a crease in his uniform.

"Would you like to take your evening meal with us? I can imagine you have not yet eaten and are hardly eager to return to the frozen streets."

"Thank you, Master Okes. It would be my great pleasure to remain here for supper. Is there anything I can fetch your maids in preparation?"

"No, my good man, we have plenty. We should be ready to eat within the hour. Please, have Katherine bring you whatever you need to make your stay comfortable. In fact, you should probably consider staying the night, as it is already dark, and it will be a treacherous journey back to Hampton Court or an inn farther north. Just east of here, about two blocks, you will find a place called The Brass Bell that will stable your horse. Tell them you are staying with me if they claim they are full. Go now, if you would like to remain here for the night."

"Yes, Master Okes, I will go at once. I am grateful for your offer to stay with you, as I am exhausted from my unexpected travels today. I will stable Mercury straight away. Thank you again for your hospitality." And off he went, motivated to stable his horse and spend the night in the home of the young woman he desired.

Rose Okes remained on the bench, exuberant, not sure if what was happening was actually real. This was evolving into something beyond her dreams. She sprang up and went to see if she could assist the maids in preparing supper or Hugh Mercer's sleeping area. Katherine requested Rose gather materials to start a fire in the back room, where currently her father's inventory lay. With great enthusiasm she collected tinder and a small kettle of stone coal, all while envisioning the scene hours from then, after slipping into the carrier's quarters.

Elizabeth spent the evening meal with eyes darting between her sister and Hugh Mercer, attempting to intercept looks or evidence of something she already knew existed. Rose wondered why it bothered her so much. Perhaps she worried about what Edward would be doing once he was away from London, living in Leyden. Her older sister had been so unpleasant to her of late that she couldn't be bothered about it. All Rose cared about now was indulging in fusing her fantasy with reality. She had spent far too many hours daydreaming about this man, and here was her chance to experience what, until now, only her imagination dared to offer.

Rose could barely suppress her excitement during the meal, and in one instance, nearly choked on the beef in her pottage. She pretended like she was laughing to cover her carelessness, but her sister knew what was happening and glared with contempt.

To make matters worse, her mother began asking carrier Mercer about the woman he was courting. Rose cringed at the questions and did her best to drown out the sound of his replies. That was a painful piece of his life she cared to know nothing about.

Other than Elizabeth, no one else at the table had an inkling of the magic between the post carrier and Rose. It was an unlikely match, considering they saw each other so infrequently, and their gap in age spanned more than a decade. The age difference itself was not a huge barrier, but it was known that he had been seriously courting someone for many months, and typically, that status was enough to stifle interest elsewhere.

Rose knew that a future with this man was improbable, if not impossible. The problem for her, and for Hugh Mercer, was that the feelings could not be changed or controlled. There were days when she wished more than anything she could extinguish her thoughts and the deep desire she held in her heart for him. As draining as this could be, this was her life, with logic failing to pull her out of what seemed like a bottomless, soul-sucking hole.

On this night, she did not care about logic, or all the hours she spent in the past wondering about his whereabouts, or fantasizing about being alone with him. On this night she would live it, and as she looked over at him with wild eyes, she promised herself she would not regret a thing.

As he soaked his bread with the last bit of pottage, he caught a glimpse of her eyes as they flashed away. Without feeling hungry, he

continued eating, swallowing the food but not tasting much of anything. Excited but nervous, he wondered how far she wanted this to go.
He worried if they were caught, that Master Okes would be furious and
refuse his return there. As he pondered that idea he realized that would
not happen, as his favors of delivering information were indispensable.
He would be allowed to visit the shop by providing letters, shrouded in
a heavy cloud of shame.

The evening meal seemed to go on forever, and then Katherine
returned with jumbles, extending the mealtime further. Hugh smiled
and accepted the knotted cookie graciously, in spite of his lack of ap-
petite. What he hungered for was Rose, and now that the opportunity
lay before him, his body was alive and ready. The last thing he wanted
to do was spend his time eating, and he expected Rose was thinking the
same way, as she did not take any of the sugary treats. Even that made
Elizabeth suspicious, as jumbles were one of Rose's favorites.

Rose ignored Elizabeth's glare as she stood, turning away from the
table to help Katherine with the scullery from supper and readying the
house for the night. Hugh did his best to keep his eyes on the table,
even though he wanted to watch Rose every moment he could.

With the table cleared and main area tidied, the house quieted in anticipation of the sleeping hours. Robert took his Bible and
sat on a stool by the fire as Katherine heated the water for washing
before bedtime.

"Please excuse me. I wish to check on my horse before removing
to my sleeping quarters. I won't be long." After bundling up, the post
carrier burst out into the icy night air.

"Rose, please see that his sleeping area is comfortable for when he
returns," instructed her mother.

"Yes, of course. Katherine and I brought out a clean mattress cover
and ticking. We wiped down the bedstead before setting the bedding
inside, and left a clean chamberpot at the base of it. I readied the hearth
for a fire as well."

"Very good. Does he have fresh linens and warm water to wash?"

"I will bring those in now, Mistress," assured Katherine as she turned to the fire to check the warmth of the heating water.

"Very well then. I see you two have things in order. I am off to bed then, and trust you can handle any of Mister Mercer's further needs."

In the dim light of the dying fire, her mother could not see the redness of Rose's cheeks.

"Yes, we will make sure he is taken care of," said Rose in the quietest of voices. She was not ashamed, but worried that her opportunity would be compromised.

Katherine acted oblivious, but had detected months the interest Rose had in Hugh Mercer, months before. The maid did not judge. It was not her place to, and what was so wrong with Rose experiencing the purity and ecstasy of passion and love? In truth though, nearly all would say that in the eyes of God, to engage in this activity before marriage was a most sinful act. If Master and Mistress Okes were to learn of this, the consequences would be severe and long lasting, her reputation marred for life. Katherine's other fear was that the young woman would be left with a broken heart. In spite of this, she would do everything that night to aid in making the young girl's dreams come true.

Sitting by the fire, Robert read the final words of a verse in the book of John, then carefully closed the Bible. He did not have the slightest notion of what was to happen between his sister and Hugh Mercer. Yawning as he stood, he placed the Bible in the center of the table and bid them good night with barely enough strength to make his way up to his sleeping quarters a staircase above.

"Are you not coming to sleep?" asked Elizabeth in an accusatory way.

"Oh, pray pardon, Elizabeth, I did ask Rose to aid me in the scullery," interjected Katherine.

Elizabeth looked at them, trying to determine if they were working together to achieve a sordid end, that of her sister engaging with this postal carrier. She really wasn't sure of anything, whether they were working in concert, or if there was truly anything of substance between her sister and Hugh Mercer. Maybe she was just sick with worry that she would be betrayed by the man she loved. Edward Winslow, who in October ended his apprenticeship with Master Beale, would be leaving for Leyden in a matter of months. Elizabeth stood stuck in a trance, gazing through the fire's glowing embers, her view blurred by tears.

"Elizabeth, are you well?" asked Katherine as she gently touched the arm of the young woman.

"Yes. Yes, of course. Surely my sister can help you. I need to be heading to bed. Mayhaps it was the jumbles on such a full belly of pottage that has sapped the strength from me. Whatever it is, my mind is foggy and body sluggish, so I had best ready myself for sleeping. Good night, Katherine." She turned abruptly to face her sister. "Be wise in your choices this night." And with that, she turned and climbed the stairs.

Rose was glad to see her go. She was tired of Elizabeth's nasty looks and judgmental, probing stares. Never before had Rose possessed feelings like this for a man. And even though she understood her desired path was not wise, and mayhaps shameful in the eyes of God, she refused to ignore this opportunity. Furthermore, if this was not truly in God's plan, then it should not unfold this way.

For months she had struggled with this torturous problem, when one day she realized that her thoughts and feelings existed for a reason. Even if her future did not lie with Hugh Mercer, why not know one of the greatest gifts of humankind? The prospect of love, and caring so deeply for another, that the importance of self is stripped away. Rose felt connected to this man on every meaningful level of life, from her heart to her soul, and everything in between.

That he was courting another woman ripped her apart. She was no fool. Falling in love with a man many years older, who was committed to someone else, was not her plan. As her parents had explained, her path on Earth had been set forth by God, and could not be changed. She was validating her desires with this logic, while allowing herself to hold fast to the belief that she was not a bad person and that she should not be punished for her feelings.

"I think we have everything tidied up, Rose. Do you want to check in with Hugh and see to it that he has everything he needs?" asked Katherine with a most subtle wink.

Rose blushed a little, realizing that even Katherine knew her intentions. For once though, someone was on her side. She appreciated this and was so relieved to have an ally.

"Yes, Katherine, I will see to it that he is most satisfied with his stay here," said Rose with a bit of a nervous giggle. "I believe he is still out checking on his horse. I will make sure everything is in its place. The bedstead is clean and ready, and I will take back this basket of stone coal and this kettle of warm water to keep by the hearth. I have the clean linens as well."

"Be mindful of the fire, as you will have one burning past the curfew. May God grant you a good night, Rose." The maidservant then looked around to make sure no one else was looking and gave Rose a quick embrace. Katherine left the main living space with genuine care for Rose, praying that this time spent with Hugh Mercer would result in happy memories and not ongoing pain and frustration with his absence.

Printer Okes, who had stepped out after supper to speak with a printer a few doors down, bounded back to find his home surprisingly empty. The cat was the only one present to greet his owner, and rubbed lovingly against his stockings. Master Okes assumed everyone, including Hugh Mercer, had taken to their beds, so he locked the main door and retired to his own bedstead.

Luckily for the post carrier, Rose crept into the main room and decided to wait for him there, in case the house had been locked up for the night by her father. She heard a quiet knock, then the rattle of a locked door refusing to open. Rose hurried to open the door before Hugh knocked louder and stirred the house. This was her opportunity to be alone with him, and she would have done anything to protect that time.

"Oh, good evening, Rose. Thank you for being here to let me in. I was fearful for a moment that I would be locked out and would have to share a stall with my horse," he said with a nervous laugh.

"That does not sound so desirable. I think I would be much better company than Mercury."

"Are you implying that you would like to spend some time with me in my quarters, or am I presuming too much?"

"No, you have understood me perfectly. I have spent many hours dreaming that this day would come, and here it is. It is almost unbelievable we are here together, and alone."

He smiled at her tenderly as he reached across for her hand, squeezing it gently. "Should we go together to my quarters and start a fire?"

Rose never answered. She kept her hand in his, and they carefully crossed the floorboards, intent on keeping the house asleep. This time was sacred, and they would have done anything to preserve it.

The tinder, in the form of frayed rope and charred cloth, sat patiently, waiting to be lit. Still holding his hand, she pushed the other inside her knitted wool pocket, seeking out flint and steel. Taking them from her without words, he reluctantly released her hand to start the fire. He removed a bit of blackened cloth from the pile and crouched in front of the hearth, not caring not to spend overmuch time with the fire. Wanting to place his attention on Rose, he struck the flint against the steel with the greatest precision, producing a spark on the first attempt. Cradling the glowing spark in the folds of the black cloth, he blew carefully, the burning orange spreading like lava down a mountain. Placing it at the base of the rope and cloth, he put his face near to the cloth and blew with strong, long breaths, until smoke transitioned to flames.

Rose sat on a stool adjacent to the hearth, putting order to the peel, the bellows, and basket of stone coal. She had to do something to calm her nerves, as she had never been alone with any man before. And with Hugh Mercer, so many deep feelings were connected to him that poor Rose was overcome with a suffocating pressure.

Hugh sensed this. It was not that he was overly experienced himself, but certainly, with thirty years to him, more so than Rose. "Come, Rose, sit next to me," said Hugh as he patted the space next to him.

She placed herself beside him, on top of one of the many wooden trunks sitting in the storage area of the printer's home.

For what seemed like more than a minute, he looked at her, watching her eyes look back at him. Really, it was only for a few seconds, but with the intensity so high, time stood still. If only that could really happen, to remain in a place, with the person of your dreams, as long as you wanted. But then Rose thought, would it be so special if it could go on forever?

His lips on hers brought her back to the moment, and very quickly she adapted to his actions, kissing him back so naturally even she thought she had done this before. In a way she had, in all the hours she imagined this very scene unfolding. He directed the next steps, but by no means was she a bystander. She cherished every touch from his hands, and equally the feeling of his body in response to her. Every aspect of this experience was new to her, and she loved it.

There were very few words between them. Mostly there were smiles, with each one looking to the other for cues and clues. They never discussed their plan, or how far they would take things, or what would happen next.

She rose from the trunk to face him. The fire glowed behind him, making him appear as if were from another world, and to her, he was. She adjusted her petticoat so she could sit herself directly on him, her legs wrapped around his thighs. He held her close, the two embracing, when she leaned back and created enough space to kiss his mouth. The passion flowed like a hot spring. Every part of her burned for him, and as they kissed he started unhooking her waistcoat, as she fumbled with the buttons of his doublet.

Their kisses ranged from soft and delicate, to deep and primal. He pulled off her waistcoat while she continued to struggle with his uniform's buttons. Nearly frantic to rid himself of his clothing, he quickly undid the bottom buttons, dropping the doublet to the floor. At the same time, she untied her bodies, loosening the string and pulling them over her head.

Loosening his breeches so he could remove his linen shirt, he revealed his chest and defined muscles. Rose looked at his chest and abdomen with wide eyes, reaching out to feel the ridges in his skin. All of his riding produced a strong and solid body that she hadn't imagined under his uniform.

Those muscles worked to lift up Rose as he stood, and with her arms wrapped around his neck and legs around his waist, he walked them both over to the bedstead, placing her down gently as he kissed her mouth. She lay back calmly as he loosened her petticoat from around her hips, bringing it down her legs and off completely. Swiftly he removed her shoes, garters and stockings, and helped her up to stand in front of him. Realizing he would be lifting off her linen smock, she raised her arms, allowing him to pull it up and off of her. She removed her coif, keeping her hair braided and bound by the hair tape in case of the need for a quick departure.

Even though this was her first experience of this kind, she was surprisingly calm now. It all seemed so natural and comfortable. With her standing before him, completely unclothed, he kissed her passionately, but so gently that she needed to pull him closer. She wanted even more of him, so she explored his mouth, seeking to brush his tongue with hers. This surprised him at first, but he complied happily, smiling as he responded to her request.

He lifted her back on top of the bedstead so she could rest comfortably on the mattress while he removed his breeches. The light from the fire was not intense, but bright enough to reveal shadows and silhouettes. The lack of light was not an issue, for their senses of touch, taste and smell gave them all they needed to enjoy each other.

He stood to the side of the bedstead, gazing at her, tracing his fingers down and across her body. He explored with respect and the most genuine interest in knowing her. He watched his hands as they carefully carved a path to her most intimate place, committing the beauty to memory. She loved watching him, his eyes following his hands like Da Vinci shaping marble.

She gasped as he kissed her breast, and then made his way down her body with his mouth, brushing her abdomen with his lips. It was like nothing she had known. Sheer intensity and vulnerability all wrapped into one, and with him, she was more than ready to receive it. She opened her legs for him, wanting him to go deeper, and sensing this, he complied. Her response to him was pure and clear in wanting more of him, causing him to react in kind, like a magnet to her motion.

He climbed into the bed without breaking contact with her, using his mouth in exploring her chest, with his hands stroking the inside of her legs. In all the hours she fantasized about him, never for an instant did she imagine this. This more than surpassed any of her ideas, and she closed her eyes to enhance the feeling.

At the same time she reached down to feel him, not knowing what to expect. He moved his mouth up towards hers, as she moved her hand down his body. Instinctively, she was drawn to the hardness of him, yearning to feel that more than with her hand. She shifted her hips so that he could become part of her, uniting them as one.

Both their bodies trembled as he brought himself above and in line with her, so that with just a slight movement he was inside her. As she raised her hips, arching her back to feel him as deeply as their bodies would allow, he bent down to kiss her neck. Never before had he felt this sensation. And even though this was Rose's first experience, somehow she knew this was exceptional. There was nothing awkward about what was happening. Her love for this man had built for so many months that it should culminate in this ecstasy.

He could tell as he moved that she was in love with him. No woman would open herself up so completely without being committed on other levels. As gratifying as that was, it did concern him. What would he do? To some degree, he belonged to another woman. But perhaps Rose was the woman he was destined to be with and marry. He pleaded with his brain to stop the inquisition and allow him to enjoy the time rather than contaminate it with difficult questions.

There was nothing more real or human than this. He kissed her cheek, then her neck, moving more quickly, adding to the passion. He was getting closer and closer to climax, and she could sense the heightened activity. Even though she was not feeling exactly the same thing, she could appreciate what was happening. He moved faster, and even faster yet, until he pushed himself into her one more time, deeper than the last, holding his breath as he absorbed the magnitude of the moment. He shuddered twice more, then placed his hands on either side of her face. He kissed her forehead before he exhaled, smiling while looking into her loving eyes.

Living a life on the road meant Hugh Mercer had contact with all walks of life. Over his years, he had learned many things about a variety of subjects. In particular, within the walls of the taverns and inns, most men found themselves on the subject of women. So even though he didn't have much personal experience, he learned indirectly. He heard from countless men what women desired. He always listened intently, intrigued at the ways to unlock the mysteries of a woman.

With that knowledge, as his breathing relaxed to a more regular pace, he traced the outline of Rose's chin with his index finger, locking his eyes on hers. Then with the softest of kisses, he brushed his lips against hers before moving his mouth down her neck. Never breaking contact with her skin, he kissed her breasts, then moved down the center of her abdomen. She arched her back and relaxed her hips, anticipating he would continue to move down her body. His lips moved down onto her most sacred spot, making them both gasp.

This was something he had never done before, and he was shocked to find it so pleasing. Stroking his hair, she looked down, trying to get a sense of what might happen next. With one hand on her abdomen, he put the other near to his mouth, slowly moving a finger within her. Rose closed her eyes, her body tingling and trembling in this most heavenly rapture. Intoxicated by her reaction and the feeling of her on his tongue, Hugh Mercer found himself more aroused now than he had been a few minutes before. His body reacted, and moments later, he moved up and entered her again.

He moved slowly, then gently rolled her on top of him. She laughed nervously, but enjoyed looking down at him, feeling a sense of control. She leaned down and kissed his mouth, pulling back with a smile. Still inside her, he drove his hips upward. At the same time, she pushed down, wanting every bit of him. The feeling was indescribable, surpassing anything she ever could have imagined, and as her body quivered, she could feel the intensity build. It felt so good, but at the same time, Rose felt as if she was losing some control. This foreign sensation was a little frightening, so she found herself in a mild panic when she felt a hotness escaping her.

He looked up at her with the widest of eyes, realizing he was experiencing what he had heard only a handful of men talk about. He closed his eyes and placed his hands near their place of connection, rubbing the warm fluid into his flesh. Rose sat back and moved her hips so there was one final surge, and then collapsed forward onto his chest. He stroked her hair while she regained her breath.

As she raised her head to face him, he kissed her mouth tenderly. It was as if God had created her to complete him. She moved off of him and nestled her head between his chin and shoulder, resting her cheek on his chest. There was no other place in the world she would rather be, her arm draped across his body. He looked down at her and kissed the top of her head, wrapping his arm around her, thinking he would stop time if he could.

They fell into a peaceful sleep, each dreaming of the other, entwined in their slumber. The fire was no more than a few stubborn embers when they came to consciousness. Rose sat up with a start, trying to gauge the time of night, knowing she had to make her way to her sleeping quarters undetected. They dressed quickly, without words. They had so much they wanted to say that with such little time, they decided to say nothing at all. The avalanche of emotion stifled her words, her head spinning as she searched for his eyes in the darkness. Maybe his gaze would soothe her panic and answer all the questions she wanted to ask about the next time, and their future. But as hard as she tried, she couldn't find his eyes. She felt his hand grab hers, turning her to face him. Placing his hands on either side of her face, he lifted her mouth to his. With a passionate, love-filled kiss, he silenced her concerns.

"Will you be all right?"

"Yes, as long as no one detects me coming from your quarters. I want you to know how special this night was for me. Hugh, I have thought about this happening, many times actually, long before tonight. I will miss you. May God grant you a safe journey north."

And with that, she left hurriedly, afraid of what he would, or even worse, would not say.

He sat there in a daze as she faded into the darkness. There were things he wanted to say, and she had vanished before he had a chance. He thought he might go after her, but knew better than to risk waking anyone. Perhaps he would see her in the morning. Even then, it would be unlikely they would have a chance to speak privately. He lay in his bed, looking up in a trance. There was no way he could fall asleep now. But he must try, as he couldn't retrieve his horse yet, and would require rest to function in his travels that day. He closed his eyes and thought of Rose, recalling what had just transpired, replaying it with great pleasure. As he thought about her, his consciousness slipped away, allowing him to fall deep into a fantastic dream.

Hugh awoke before the rest of the household. He found himself covered in sweat and jumped out of the bedstead. Stumbling towards the hearth, he reached into the kettle for water to splash on his face and rinse his hands. Hurriedly, he buttoned his uniform and tidied up the bedstead before making his way through the Okes' main room and out the front door. He caught a glimpse of Katherine out of the corner of his eye.

"Good day, Katherine. I must be off to an early start," he said without looking up at her. "Do tell Rose I bade her farewell. And thank you."

"Yes, of course. Safe travels."

When Rose awakened, she was not sure if she hoped Hugh Mercer would be there or not. On some level she wanted to leave things as they were the night before, safely in a realm of fantasy. On the other hand, she craved for more. So she dressed quickly and made her way into the main room, her heart racing. As soon as she saw Katherine, she knew he was gone.

"Hugh Mercer has left. He bade you farewell."

Rose nodded as her heart continued racing. He was gone. She had no idea when he would return, or what their future held. She stood frozen, paralyzed by the uncertainty of it all. What she did possess, that no one could take from her, were the feelings and images from the night before. Those memories she owned, and would cherish forever.

The home and main printing location for Master Printer Nicholas Okes, the sign of The Rose represents the importance of the creation and distribution of books in the period. The press and the people who operated them impacted how people learned and affected religious beliefs, potentially altering culture and the direction of society. And that is precisely why the Stationers Company in London and printers elsewhere in the world had rules to follow, with their government keeping a continuous eye on them and their work. Printing and the press facilitate the principal connection between the characters, keeping the link between London and Leyden strong throughout the book.

Chapter Fourteen

1616

February 1616, London

The shop at the sign of The Rose teemed with emotions. Master and Mistress Okes wore brave smiles as their daughter, Elizabeth, agonized over the departure of Edward Winslow. She either stood or sat next to him the entire time, watching and soaking in every last image of the man she loved.

Across the room, apprentice Benjamin Grendon helped his jubilant sister, Prudence, prepare for her journey to the Netherlands to reunite with her betrothed, printer John Reynoldes. "I expect you have packed all that you need, and done so carefully?" inquired Benjamin of his sister.

"Of course, Benjamin. In the chest I have all of my wardrobe and bed linens, with personal items buried within. Before her passing, Mother gave me a ring that will travel safely in my pocket," said Prudence as she patted the wool pocket hidden beneath her brown apron. "John sent a letter explaining I will stay with Master and Mistress Carver, with a bed and household necessities available for my use. Their generosity is wondrous good, and even more pleasing is that it is very close to where my John is staying, with the Brewster family."

"From what I know of Leyden, the city is manageable to navigate, with landmarks throughout. Even with the recent expansion of the city walls, you can walk from one end to the other if need be," added Master Okes. "You will find people from all over the world living in Leyden, some attending the University, others seeking a haven for matters of religion, or both. In any case, when you are not able to be with John, you will spend much of your time with Mistress Carver and other members of that congregation."

Rose and young Robert remained present, but invisible as they looked down from the top part of the staircase. Rose watched her sister suffer Edward's exit, knowing that peace would not return to Elizabeth until either she joined him in Leyden or he returned to London. Rose was plagued similarly, by her love for Hugh Mercer. She never knew when she might see him again, and in reality, there was no commitment between them. Even worse, he might by now be the husband to another woman. At least her sister was properly courting Edward, and the intention on both sides was to continue the relationship, in spite of the great distance between them.

Their mother was filled with empathy, able to relate to the pain of being separated from the man you loved, not knowing when you would meet again. That was often the case with her and Nicholas while she served in the court of the Queen. She looked over at Elizabeth with understanding, knowing that her oldest daughter would soon be overcome with emptiness. She had no idea that her younger daughter was also stricken with grief from the absence of the man she yearned for. No one other than Rose knew the depth of her void in longing for Hugh Mercer, and obsessing over his absence. Even Katherine, who was aware of their rendezvous only months before, could not detect the endless cavity of sadness that devoured the girl. Rose hid it well, as it nipped the edges of her soul.

Elizabeth tried to make the most of her last moments with Edward, but already she was dreading his departure. He took her trembling hands in his, to calm her and reassure her of his love and commitment to her. He too was devastated to be separated by a sea, but he expected to send for her once his life there was stable and he could afford to marry her. He was driven by the challenge of printing books that could alter the minds of men in the ways of God.

"When will you send for me?" asked Elizabeth in a shaking voice, afraid to look up.

"I can promise it will not be more than two years," responded Edward earnestly. "By then we should be publishing books, and depending on their nature and in what quantities, I am hopeful I will have the coin to send for you. Master Brewer has promised to pay for your passage, but even so, I care to bear that responsibility. What is for certain is that you will not travel alone. In fact, I will come back to London if need be. Mayhaps your family will come for the wedding and accompany you?" suggested Edward with a smile aimed at Master and Mistress Okes.

"Mayhaps you will travel back to London and get married here," suggested Printer Okes. He laughed to cover the awkward silence, but his wife knew his words bore a hint of resentment. Her husband did not verbalize his frustrations, but she knew it troubled him that John Reynoldes was now contributing to the production of books in Holland instead of England. How could it be that a young man he trained for near unto a decade would choose to print books out of the country, thereby diluting the efforts of the English printers? So many books came into England from the Netherlands bearing a false title page, hiding its true origin from the buyer. Of all the books printed in the world, half of them were born of Dutch presses. Regulatory laws existed, but were rarely enforced. Many of the Bibles being sold in England were actually printed in the Netherlands, high in quality, and at half the price.

Now Master Okes looked on as his daughter suffered in the wake of Edward's decision to leave the printing trade in London for the work in Leyden. As much as he understood the pious purpose of the work to be done with Masters Brewster and Brewer, Edward's skilled English hands were leaving the Stationers' Company and his daughter. If the young couple were to endure their time apart and be married, Elizabeth could be departing herself for Leyden before long.

Edward recognized Master Okes's irritation. He guessed the Master Printer harboured resentment over the loss of John Reynoldes to the presses in Holland. And now, he had to watch as another Englishman of the trade left the country, with his own daughter likely to follow.

"Master Okes, this is a difficult time for us all. This venture in Leyden affords me opportunity in a variety of ways. I expect I will earn enough to support Elizabeth and a family, should God grace us with children. Regarding the nature of what is to be printed, are we not serving God by putting into print the truth of His ways? Like ministers who preach and pray in the name of God, we as printers serve Him by spreading the word by publishing and printing. You would do the same here in London if you were not shackled by the King and his rules imposed upon the Stationers' Company. As to what we print in Leyden, it is a real possibility I could be back in London to coordinate the distribution of these books, which I trust you want no part of."

"You are most correct in that assumption. I have dedicated my life to this trade, and living here, I must abide by the rules of the Stationers' Company and those of King James. I fault you not for printing words that might illuminate the hearts and minds of many in the ways of God. Surely, you can comprehend my perspective. I have lost a competent printer in John Reynoldes, and suffer in watching my daughter pained by your departure. I think it is difficult for every one of us in some way. Do not misconstrue my mood as one of anger, targeted at you. I am disappointed in this turn of events, as a father and a printer."

Silence commanded the room. Edward fixed his eyes on Elizabeth, and for more than a moment, he wondered if he was making a mistake. She looked back at him but couldn't keep her eyes on his, for she was ashamed of her weakness and afraid he might see the depth of her vulnerability. As much as she wanted him to stay in London with her, she knew it was in God's plan for him to work in Leyden.

The scene playing out below made Robert uncomfortable. From what he could understand, only Prudence truly wanted to make the journey to Leyden. She was overjoyed at the prospect of reuniting with Printer Reynoldes. He looked at Rose and thought he saw a tear roll down her cheek. Even she was overcome with sadness. A linen pouch of clay marbles accompanied him on the step, serving as a means to calm him. He plunged his fingers in repeatedly, letting the pressure of the hardened, glazed clay balls soothe his uneasiness. As he held onto one of the larger green marbles, the rest of the sack fell forward, allowing the smaller brown ones to escape loudly down the stairs.

The marbles made a noisy descent, like hail hitting the roof. With the silence shattered, Prudence secured her trunk, confident everything was in place after checking the contents for the tenth time. She had nothing else to do while the others clutched to the final moments before their departure.

"Should I load the trunk?" asked Benjamin, looking to do anything other than stay in the shop. Prudence looked over at Edward before answering, and reluctantly, he produced a painful nod. Elizabeth felt as if she would be sick at any moment, so she rose up and threw her arms around Edward, clinging to him as if they were aboard a sinking ship and only his arms were keeping her from plunging to a frigid, watery grave. Then to everyone's surprise, including her, she turned without words and scrambled up the steps. Her abrupt exit was made worse by the marbles, forcing her to avoid them and then step around her siblings at the top of the staircase. As much as she tried to muffle her sobbing in the folds of her apron, the woeful cries traveled back down the stairs, piercing Edward like a dagger to the heart.

As Rose went after her sister, the group below expedited their leaving. There was no need to prolong the suffering.

Edward embraced the Okeses then bowed and doffed his hat before making his final exit. "I am a man of my word, Master Okes, and I will send for Elizabeth, if not come back myself," assured Edward.

"I doubt not your promise, Edward. Safe travels to you and Prudence. May God keep you well. Please send our love to Masters Brewster and Carver. And to John, John Reynoldes," requested Master Okes.

"Also to my cousin, Master Brewer," interjected Mistress Okes. "Please send him and his family our love."

"Of course, Mistress. I will write once I arrive in Leyden and tell you of my travels and experience in settling there. I am hopeful we have regular channels of correspondence through the trade of Master Brewer, with letters exchanged here safely through the hands of Hugh Mercer."

After embracing Mistress Okes with a strength that conveyed the value of his promise, he looked up the stairwell, straining to catch a final glimpse of Elizabeth. Sadly, all he saw was a frantic Rose rushing back to the top of the steps after hearing someone utter Hugh Mercer's name.

Finally, Prudence and Edward departed, and at the sound of Master Okes locking the door, Elizabeth unleashed the most horrific moan. One would have thought she was just informed of Edward's death. Rose tried for more than an hour to calm her sister and at least ready her for bed. Elizabeth's state of despair was so great that she refused even to remove her apron. Rose was able to take her shoes from her feet, placing them under the bed by the chamber pot. Rose moved the grey wool hat from the bed linens onto an iron hook above the bedstead. Elizabeth took to the position of a fetus, curled inward to self-soothe and protect. Rose sat at the edge of the bed and with a delicate hand removed her sister's coif. She sobbed for hours with Rose by her side, at times stroking her hair. Eventually her sadness turned to sleep, and only then did Rose leave her, grateful for Elizabeth to escape into the freeing, kinder realm of the unconscious.

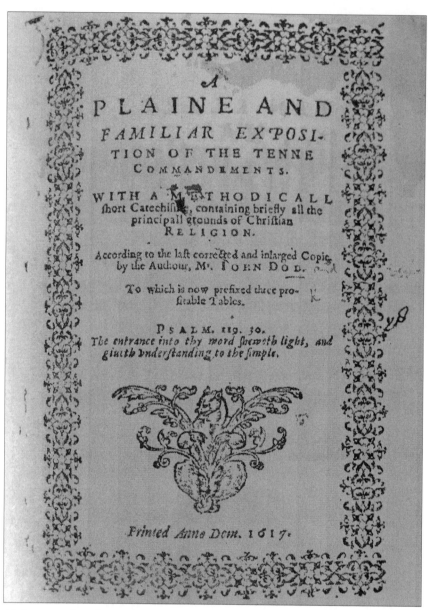

A

PLAINE AND
FAMILIAR EXPOSI-
TION OF THE TENNE
COMMANDEMENTS.

WITH A METHODICALL
short Catechisme, containing briefly all the
principall grounds of Christian
RELIGION.

According to the last corrected and inlarged Copie,
by the Authour, Mr. IOHN DOD.

To which is now prefixed three profitable Tables.

PSALM. 119. 30.
The entrance into thy word sheweth light, and
giueth vnderstanding to the simple,

Printed Anno Dom. 1617.

Title page of Dod and Cleaver, A Plain and Familiar Exposition of the Ten Commandments, *a reprint, 1617. This book published by Brewster-Brewer was likely one of the better-selling books, as there were many editions. Unlike some of the other books published in 1617 by Brewster, this title page does not indicate the publisher or where to find it (In Vico Chorali/ In Choir Alley), which is where Brewster lived, adjacent to the Pieterskerk. Notice the bear ornament, which can be found in multiple Brewster publications.*

Chapter Fifteen

1617

January 1617, London

Whenever Hugh Mercer traveled to London, he stopped at The Clock Tower, an ordinary sitting directly across from Master Okes's sign of The Rose. He always sought the corner table by the front window, where he could covertly watch for his love, young Rose. Every day since their magical night together, he dreamed of walking across to the sign of The Rose to visit with her and hold her in his arms. The reality was very different, for when his duties for the King's Post brought him to London, he aimed to escape direct interaction. By doing so, he would not have to reveal the painful truth of having wed another woman.

He was miserable with his life, and this decision. He had gone through with what was expected of him instead of what he truly wanted-ed. How could he ever adequately explain this to Rose? All she would hear was that he chose another. She would be devastated, and rightly so.

This conflict defined him. He stared out the window at the door to the shop of Printer Okes, longing to see Rose, even from his pitiful place of hiding. The sad truth was that if he saw her leave the shop, it was then he would cross the street and deliver the letter to Master Okes. He was a coward. Or was he? He loved Rose and would never hurt her with intention. How could he possibly speak of his marriage without destroying her? But he imagined it would be far worse if she were to learn of his marriage from someone other than him.

As he drank his beer he gazed across the street, mesmerized by the front entrance of Printer Okes's shop. His eyes widened as the door opened, presenting Elizabeth and young Robert. He looked past them to try to see Rose, without success. Perhaps she was not even there. He hung his head, holding it just off the table, his forehead in his hands. There was no resolution that kept all involved intact. Should he leave his wife, an innocent woman would be shamed. His reputation would be ruined, for that matter, and possibly be disinherited. In that case, he would be free to be with Rose, but what were the chances she would even want to be with him?

Just a few feet away, within the walls of the sign of The Rose, Rose sat writing a letter. She had pondered for the last months how she could communicate with Hugh Mercer, since each time he delivered a letter, she was away from home. The first two times this happened, she was maddened by the unfortunate coincidence. When it occurred a third and fourth time, she realized the timing had to be intentional. Other deliveries he made to Master Okes's stall outside of St. Paul's Cathedral, at the sign of The Black Bear. How could more than a year have passed without them even seeing one another? She did not expect to repeat the night they shared, but reconnecting with conversation seemed reasonable.

To think that the man she loved avoided her with intention was something she could not bear. She was so confused. The night they had shared together was absolutely beautiful. So why would he not return to her? Two answers plagued her. The one that filled her with horror was that he had married the woman he had been courting. The other idea, almost equally debilitating, was that he had lost his love for her. In either case, her life did not include him. She longed for him in every way. She yearned for his conversation, his gaze upon her, his hands lovingly caressing the curves of her body. The list was endless, and tragically Rose fell asleep, awoke, and struggled through her days missing a man that might never return.

She could not have known that Hugh Mercer sat but a few yards away in The Clock Tower as she poured her heart into the ink lettering the paper. With this letter she could pose all of her questions and make known her feelings. He would stop in eventually, somehow knowing when she would be absent from her father's shop. She feared a number of outcomes, from never receiving a response, to receiving a reply riddled with rejection. Doing nothing was not an option for her. She needed to take this risk to preserve her sanity and offer the chance to move on with her life.

Only Katherine knew the extent of her suffering now, and almost daily she listened to Rose torture herself over this man. In the kindest way she could, she would ask her why she wanted a man that had made himself invisible. Poor Rose could not let herself believe his feelings had changed from that night they shared together. Hope overshadowed her suffering and insecurities. Something deep within her would not allow her to give up on Hugh Mercer.

She wrote the letter fairly quickly, considering the depth of the contents. This was not so surprising, considering how much time she spent thinking of the post carrier. She had been composing this letter in her head over the last twelve months, so when it was time to put the ink onto paper, it flowed easily. She melted the magenta wax and sealed it not with her father's stamp, but by carving her initials and the almost-imperceptible shape of a heart. Satisfied, she carefully placed it in her woolen pocket and, donning her winter coat, mittens, muffler, and hat, set off for the stalls near St. Paul's Cathedral.

She decided to take the letter to the sign of The Black Bear, where the newest apprentice, Andrewe Driver, would be. Although she had not known him for very long, he seemed trustworthy and reliable. She could be certain he would give the letter to Hugh Mercer should he stop there. The post carrier had left letters there the last two times he had something to deliver, so she assumed he would continue that pattern.

"Do you care for more beer?" asked the woman working the ordinary.

"One more, please," replied Hugh Mercer, as he put his coins on the table, taking his eyes off of the door at the sign of The Rose for only a moment during that exchange. He drank without tasting anything. Ever since his wedding, he lived like a ghost, existing like a shadow of his old self. He rarely if ever looked forward to anything. Traveling the roads of England offered him some escape, but while he was in London his thoughts of Rose overwhelmed him to the point of dysfunction.

Quickly draining his cup, he gathered his leather bag and put on his heavy gray wool winter coat. After slinging his bag across his shoulder, he replaced his wool head and hand coverings, and with one more careful look across the street, decided to venture to the sign of The Black Bear, near to St. Paul's. There was a good chance Rose was inside the sign of The Rose, and he did not have the courage to face her.

In the time it took him to order his last beer, Rose had left her father's shop and made her way down Foster Lane, south towards St. Paul's Church. After only a few paces she was swept up in the current of the crowd, masked as one of many in a sea of people traveling in the same direction.

Moments later, Hugh Mercer left the ordinary and took to the streets. He, too, joined the throng. With longer legs and a faster pace, he overtook Rose without even knowing it. Together, but separately, they walked with urgency to the same place. He arrived near the shop only moments before Rose, still not realizing her proximity. If he had known she was only paces behind, he would have vanished.

She saw the sign of The Black Bear and was looking forward to handing the letter to Andrewe. It was a relief of sorts, to have recorded her feelings on paper and know that before long, Hugh Mercer would read those words. She made her way past a handful of people and around one very tall man before she saw him. Like a statue she stood completely still, frozen in disbelief. If she reached out she could touch him, the man that invaded her mind every minute of every day. Without thinking, she did just that. She reached out, tugging gently on his coat. Assuming it was a pickpocket, he grabbed at her hand as he wrenched his body around to face her.

The look on his face was something she would never forget. His face transformed from ecstatic, to fearful, to sad, then defeated, all in a matter of seconds. He let go of her hand, embarrassed to have taken it with such force.

"It is you, Rose. I am sorry for taking your hand in that fashion. I thought you were a pickpocket." He laughed nervously as his voice trailed off, his eyes averting hers.

She said nothing. She was stuck in the moment. Tears welled in her eyes, and she could see he was trembling. He took her hand again, this time gently, leading her away from the crowd. They found some respite by a tree, at the edge of the stalls.

Before she could ask him any questions, he spoke again.

"Rose, I am sorry. It has not been fair, my absence. You see, I have been tormented by this, by us. Not a day has gone by without you in my thoughts. You must know that."

"And for me, my days are filled with thoughts of you. With the beautiful memories we made, and dreams of our future. If you think of me often, why then do you avoid me when you visit London?" Her courage started surfacing. "How do you explain delivering letters to my father only at times when I was not there? It was as if you were somewhere nearby, watching, waiting for me to leave… and then you avoided the sign of The Rose altogether by delivering the letters here to the sign of The Black Bear."

He looked back at her in silence, not because he wanted to see her pain, but because he knew it might be the last time he could look at her so closely. Her eyes were the most magnificent in the world. Deep green like emeralds, their beauty unmatched, but what he cherished most was how she looked at him. She looked at him with acceptance and love, in a way that brought him comfort and peace. It was so easy to be around her, the way God had intended. He had no choice but to tell her of his marriage, and then it would all be over.

He went to take both of her hands in his, but she was busy pulling something from her pocket.

"Rose, I wanted nothing more than to see you, talk to you, hold you in my arms. To take care of you. I've missed you desperately, but…"

"But what?" It was very pleasing to hear his words, but she feared something devastating was coming next.

"I made a terrible mistake. I went through with what was expected of me instead of pursuing my real love. I married Sarah, the woman I was courting back home. In truth, you are the love of my life, Rose Okes."

Although they were surrounded by hundreds of people generating noise and visual distraction, Rose heard and saw nothing. It was as if the words uttered by Hugh Mercer insulated her from the crowd, but not in a protective or pleasant way. She was stunned, hurt, and angered, all at once. This man that she loved, that she thought God meant her to make union with, had chosen another woman, then stood before her professing his love. How many hours had she spent thinking about him, wondering of his whereabouts, dreaming of their future together? She respected and believed in him, and he betrayed her. Worse than that, she had given herself to him, and trusted he would return. More than a year since that night, she had wasted endless time dreaming unknowingly of a married man. She had left herself so vulnerable to him, and as they stood there, surrounded by strangers, Rose's face showed the pain of someone taking a knife in the gut. In her mind it was worse than that, for she imagined him carefully cleaning the steel blade before plunging it into her flesh.

She had the letter in her hands. A page filled with carefully crafted words, revealing her emotion and hopes of more than a year, forced by Hugh Mercer's absence to be written instead of spoken. A letter that she realized he did not deserve and she could not deliver. He had wronged her. He had disrespected her. He looked down at the letter in her hands, reaching out for it timidly.

"Never. Never will you know the words written on this paper."

She broke apart the wax seal, exposing the words inside. By now, tears were rolling down her cheeks. She wasn't even certain if they were tears of sadness or anger. Likely they were a mixture, and as they dropped on the paper, the ink bled, turning the words into rivulets of meaningless streaks. She tore the letter in half, returning one part to her pocket, and ripping the other into pieces. He winced as if in physical pain, with no way to save the shredded letter from drowning in the puddle at their feet. He dropped to his knees as if being shot from behind by a musket, attempting to catch the pieces, to salvage anything he could, because he expected she would refuse to speak with him again. He picked up a part of the wax seal and held it in his hand as if it possessed great value.

Still on his knees, he looked up at her, his eyes begging for forgiveness.

"Hugh Mercer, I loved you long before the night we shared together, and I have loved you since then. The last year I spent hoping and praying for your return. But as each day passed, my fear of your abandonment grew, especially when it seemed you were purposely avoiding the sign of The Rose. Still, I believed our love so special that someday, we would be together."

"Rose, while we are both living, there is a chance. I would never wish harm to come…"

"Stop. Just stop. I waited patiently all these months to see you and hear your words, and now I have heard enough. Please, come off of your knees so I can bid you farewell."

He rose slowly, desperate to extend their time together. To his surprise, she drew herself closer, wrapping her arms around his neck, gently stroking the hair at the back of his head. She closed her eyes while kissing the side of his neck, then his cheek, inhaling his scent. They locked eyes as she stood on the tips of her toes to kiss his forehead, then his mouth, tenderly.

"There is no question you should have offered the truth once you were married. You owed me that honesty. It will take years for me to heal, and for complete forgiveness. When there is great love, it comes with the chance for terrible pain. It is the risk we take to love. I do not regret our time together, and this might surprise you, but a part of me will always love you."

Like the night they had spent together when they parted ways, he cupped her chin in his hands and lifted her mouth to his. "I want to remember your face, and how you make me feel when I look into your eyes, until the day I am gone from this earth." He continued to look at her, working so hard to burn the image into his mind. He knew it would be his last chance to touch her, to kiss her, to look at her mesmerizing green eyes like this. He kissed her one more time, and as he did, tears slid down their cheeks, colliding on their lips.

"Rose, I am so sorry. I never meant to…"

She put her finger to his lips to stop his words. "God has His plan, and so it is that we are to go on with our lives, our paths separate. Mayhaps they will cross again. Until then, I will pray to the Lord to find peace and forgiveness. Safe travels, Hugh Mercer."

And with that, she turned and left, refusing him an opportunity for any last words. She didn't want to look back either, and if she had, she would have seen him on his knees, fishing bits of torn parchment from the muddy puddle.

September 1617
A letter from Edward Winslow in Leyden to Elizabeth Okes in London

The 3oth Day of August, 1617

Dearest Elizabeth,

I write with regret for the time you have been forced to endure in waiting for this letter. Its delay is nothing more than circumstance, my love. You must know that I am thinking of you most minutes in the day and often dreaming of you at night. I have written at least three letters since the last one you received, but discarded them as I had little confidence in getting them to you. The correspondence channels we have been using, associated with the business of Master Brewer, have changed and are not as regular. It is only because of Master Carver and his travels to London that I have a reliable means of conveying this communication to you.

Living here in Leyden is nothing short of exhilarating, save for your absence. There are so many things I want to show you and share with you. You will see the congregation of Pastor Robinson is a close-knit and loving group, one that I would like to join. I will wait for you, as my hope is that we make covenant and a confession of faith together. You will have to see the light and make that decision for yourself, once you are here and have the chance to hear the preaching of Pastor Robinson, along with the teaching of Master Brewster and the gift of prophecy of others.

Do not fear, my love. Master Carver will be escorting you to me when he returns from his discussions in London. I expect he will be departing sometime in late October or early November, after conferring with the members of His Majesty's Council for Virginia about the prospect of a merchant venture. He has carried with him a letter defining the church of Master Robinson by a list of seven points, or articles. It is meant to clarify the nature of his congregation so that the investors in London, and ultimately King James himself, would understand the group not as a threat but a means of expanding his name and kingdom.

What has led Masters Carver and Cushman to London is the result of much consideration on the part of Pastor Robinson, along with Masters Brewster, Carver, and Fuller. After much discourse, they concluded that for sundry weighty and solid reasons, the group seeks the possibility of removing to some other place. I do not want to write overmuch in this letter, for Master Carver can inform you himself, but the congregation of Master Robinson is pursuing opportunities to better their economic prospects by removing from Leyden. Many in the congregation are suffering, as are their children, under the burden of their labors. Master Robinson believes many more from England would come to join us if the conditions were more tolerable. So the hope is to make arrangements that will allow for a better life, perhaps even the chance to own land, while of course keeping the congregation intact.

The discussions, I imagine, will take a number of months, if not years, from what I have heard. I do know there is threat of war here when the Twelve Years' Truce ends in 1621, and also, Master Brewster has some concerns about how the reform of the Dutch National Church might impact our group.

Mayhaps you are wondering now if the congregation is to remove, and we become part of that group, would we be moving as well, and to where. Do not worry, Elizabeth. God will show us His plan. First, you must join me here in Leyden, so we might unite in marriage. I am living now with Master Brewster, in his garret where we set the pages for the books we are having printed. John Reynoldes and I are busy sun up to sun down setting type, or carting pages to a press in Leyden. Already this year we have published four books, with at least another four intended to be completed by the year's end.

I believe Master Carver has carried with him more than one copy of each of the initial four. You and your family might have interest in the reprint written by William Ames, Ad responsum Nic. Grevinchovii rescriptio conracta. There is another, this one printed for the first time, by Thomas Cartwright. The title reads Commentarii, Succincti & Dilucidi in Proverbia Salomonis. These books Master Brewster declares himself as the publisher, and where the book can be purchased, identifying his location as In Vico Chorali, in Choir Alley. The home he is renting lies adjacent to the choir alley of the Pieterskerk.

As we continue our work I believe the plan is to reprint some works that are familiar to those seeking reform, that will stir not so much controversy. We have already printed in English one fitting that description, by Dod and Cleaver. Your father might even have interest in distributing that one.

When I listen to Masters Brewster and Brewer discuss future efforts, it is clear that their hope is for the more conventional works to sell in large numbers in order to support the efforts in publishing new, and more daring ideas. In those books when we set the pages, we will mix the type to mask their origin, and of course not mention where or by whom the book is published. From what I have heard Master Brewer say, we will be fortunate to remain unnoticed and unmolested.

John Reynoldes and I do as we are told, although we are allowed to offer suggestions. I am enjoying the challenge of the pace of it, and believe we are doing God's work in spreading his Word. The press is a powerful weapon against the atrocities of the bishops, and I am more than satisfied to use my skill and knowledge in wielding such a formidable tool. John is quite content as well, in his work and his life here.

He is a member now of Master Robinson, his congregation, and less than a fortnight ago, married Prudence Grendon. We did celebrate at the home of Master Robinson, and how I missed you terribly the entire time, even in light of the happy occasion.

Since their marriage, John and Prudence have moved to one of the small homes enclosing the courtyard of Master Robinson. Mayhaps that will be an option for us as well, but presently, all the other homes of that sort are occupied, as there are only a dozen. It could be that we remain with the Brewster family, who of course you know very well already. There are two other options that have already been offered to us. The first is to stay with your cousin, Master Brewer. If you have not already heard, he purchased a home in June of this year from Master Jean de Lalaing, just two doors down from Master Robinson, in the direction of the Rapenburg. The house is known as the Groenehuis, or Green House. The other option would be to stay with Master and Mistress Carver, who are living on the Nieuwesteeg near the south end of the Pieterskerk, very close to Masters Brewer and Brewster.

It is with sadness that I must tell you the Brewers have buried a child on this very day. The child was born with his life already taken, and him well settled in the arms of the Lord. Mistress Brewer appears well enough in body, and I imagine will suffer otherwise for some time. Mercy Brewer fares well, having now seven years to her.

In nearing the end of this letter, I desire to share more uplifting news. Tell your sister that Jonathan Brewster has made inquiry about your family, and in particular, her. When I mentioned I was sending for you, and that we were to be married next year, he asked with the widest of smiles if "any of the Okes family would be in attendance." Then he was trying to recall the age of your sister, and I confirmed she had nineteen years to her.

Jonathan has done fairly well for himself here. In fact, he would be well suited to Rose, from what I know of her. Of course, I said nothing about your concerns regarding what has transpired between Rose and Hugh Mercer of the King's Post, as we know not what the truth is there.

At the end of June, Jonathan became a citizen of Leyden, with

Master Isaack de Syde and Jan Sebastiansz. van Hout as witnesses. He has grown his ribbon business to a rather respectable level, so much so that there is discussion of Jonathan and Master Brewer entering into a formal business arrangement later this year. He is producing so much ribbon he has started exporting product to England. The advantage of this is that we have a means of hiding the books amidst some of these shipments.

I believe you know as much as I now. The city is fair, Elizabeth, with beautiful tree-lined canals, and churches that appear to touch the sky. The University is impressive, bringing to the city gifted minds from all over this world, and supporting the most amazing botanical garden. How I dream of walking through the rows with you. In the winter, when the canals freeze, it seems as if the entire town appears somewhere on the ice. What a scene it is!

Trust yourself with Master Carver in escorting you to me. Ready your things, my love, for in a short time, you will be on the water, destined for me. I dream of this day, now and until our moment of reunification occurs.

With all my love,
Edward

Leyden, August 30
Anno: 1617

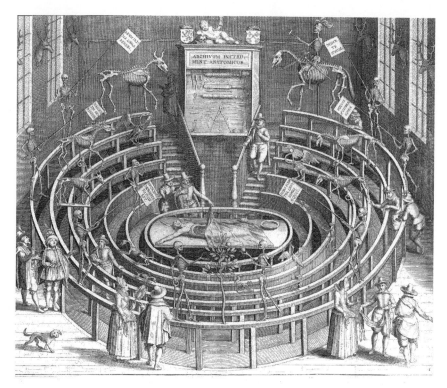

VERA ANATOMIAE LUGDUNO-BATAVAE CUM SCELETIS ET RELIQUIS QUAE IBI EXTANT DELINEATIO,
1644, CLAES JANSZ VISSCHER II, LEIDEN MUNICIPAL ARCHIVES, THE NETHERLANDS

The University of Leyden, Anatomy Theater, located in the former Beguinage Chapel, along with the University Library. The Anatomy Theater was the stage for human dissections, which occurred in the winter months (to avoid the stench in the hot summer). The general public could attend with a ticket, in addition to University of Leyden students and staff.

Chapter Sixteen

1618

London to Leyden
February 1618, London, at the Sign of The Rose

Rose looked out the shop windows as she did every morning. And every morning she scolded herself for continuing this routine. She could not help herself; it was a habit that had started years before, the practice of looking out for Hugh Mercer, hoping one morning he would walk by and peer through the blurry glass into her emerald eyes. She often wondered what she would do if he did walk by, or if she saw him by happenstance in the crowded London streets. She had no idea what she would do or say. More than a year removed from their last words, her thoughts and feelings for him remained.

"There is no need to pity me," she would remind Katherine. "There is much for me to do, especially with Elizabeth having gone to Leyden. How long has it been since she left with Master Carver? Has it been more than two months already?"

"Just so. They departed in the first part of November of last year," responded Katherine. "That is when you began spending much more time at the sign of The Black Bear, and ferrying goods to and fro the main shop here. I know your father values your efforts."

Of course Rose wanted to aid her father, but more than that, she required as much distraction as life would offer. From the time she had walked away from Hugh Mercer, she ventured from anger to sorrow, back to resentment then sadness, and finally a year later was on a path to forgiveness. Even in light of all of the pain throughout this progression, deep down, her love for him persisted. Maybe that was why she offered to make many trips to The Black Bear, so there would be more of a chance to see him again.

Rose was grateful to have Katherine to confide in, someone who would not judge, or feel compelled to parent as her mother would.

"Do you still feel any anger towards him?" she had asked Rose the week before.

"I do not. I felt peace once I accepted that a life with him is not a choice of his or mine, and that a marriage is dictated by God. It removed the anger and pain of rejection, and the blame I wanted to place on him. I am ashamed to have submitted to the selfish power of human desire rather than take comfort in what is clearly the Lord's plan. Of course I believe in His path, but what I cannot overcome is the feeling of missing Hugh, and longing still to be close to him."

Katherine listened with care and concern. She recognized Rose was progressing in her healing, and was hopeful that the motivation for Rose visiting The Black Bear had to do with the apprentice, Andrewe Driver.

"You know, Rose, he is a good-hearted young man, and he would do anything for you."

"I would not disagree, but I look to him more as a brother than anything else. As honourable as he is, and as much as I trust him, a number of years must pass before he is to become a husband and father. He is still early in his contract as an apprentice, with more than six years remaining. I care for him, but not as a wife should."

Every now and then Katherine would revive this topic, and every time Rose would answer in the same fashion. Katherine would have done just about anything to help her get beyond Hugh Mercer.

Fortunately for Rose, her days in London were few, as she readied her things for Leyden. It was really her mother, with her father's permission of course, who decided they would make the journey to celebrate Elizabeth's marriage to Edward Winslow, determining it an opportunity for her children to experience another part of the world. As a former maid to the Queen, Rose was accustomed to traveling. She longed to travel outside London, and Master Okes had arranged for his wife and children to venture over to Leyden with another printer, Sabine Staresmore.

Goodman Staresmore had traveled from the Netherlands, involved in the distribution of books not legal in England, as well as delivering letters written by Masters Robinson and Brewster, intended for Sir John Wolstenhome. The letters were written in response to the communication Sir Edwin Sandys had sent after the London visit of Masters Carver and Cushman the previous fall. The hope of Masters Robinson and Brewster was to clarify their position on religion, likening their views and practices to that of the French Reformed Church, indicating only small differences. Ideally, King James would be willing to overlook those details, and offer his blessing and formal approval in their settlement of the New World.

"Master Okes, I expect to be returning to Leyden by the midst of March at the latest. I have delivered the letters to Sir Wolstenhome already, and have remaining some business about the books brought over from the Low Countries. The ribbon made by Jonathan Brewster is packed into... let us call them, specially made barrels. In each one there is a space for other things. I will not trouble you with those details, as I understand you want no connection with those forbidden works. If, for any reason, your position changes, please make it known to me. Should you need to find me, I will be staying at the home of Master Printer Walter Burre. You know him well, I am sure, with him owning The Crane, the stall adjacent to The Black Bear."

"Yes, of course. Master Burre is a good man, although I do worry if his choices might lead him to prison, or worse. Do send him my regards." After clearing his throat, he continued, "I am grateful for your willingness to escort my family over to Leyden. I expect Master Carver will be venturing back to London this summer, or the fall at the latest, at which time Mistress Okes, Rose, and Robert can make their journey with him back to London. In the meanspace, we shall await your return here, in a fortnight or so."

"Just so, Master Okes. I shall be back before long for your family.

Do trust I will convey them safely to Leyden. Fare thee well," said Printer Staresmore as he doffed his hat, bowing slightly before making his exit from the sign of The Rose.

March 1618, at the Sign of The Rose

The Okes family, save for Master Okes, prepared for the journey. For Robert and Rose, the idea of traveling filled them with wonderment. Leaving by the middle, even late March would ensure their arrival well before the midst of April, as even in the fiercest winds and waters, the journey should not last longer than a fortnight. With fair winds, the trip would take a matter of days.

Before her departure to the Netherlands, Elizabeth had spoken of recording their intentions of marriage with the Leyden city clerk at the beginning of April. The banns were posted at the Town Hall for the three weeks following. After the third reading, the couple usually completed the marriage process within a matter of days, followed by a celebration of some measure.

During one of his visits to the sign of The Rose, Master Brewer had described the Town Hall in Leyden, with the magnificence of the stone-carved white façade facing the Breestraat. Rose tried to picture it as he spoke of the stone bannisters and angels perched along the rail, ready to see it with her own eyes. She was eager to do a number of things. First was to flee from London, and feeling haunted by the prospect of Hugh Mercer. In Leyden, there would be no chance of seeing him, which resolved the conflict of both wishing for and fearing their reconnection.

Leyden could be a new start for her. In a letter to her sister, Edward Winslow had mentioned Jonathan Brewster, and his inquiry of her visiting Leyden. He had now five and twenty years to him, and had become a citizen and a competent man of business in the ribbon trade. His success had been enough to earn a partnership with Master Brewer three months before, which she knew was quite an accomplishment.

Could it be that God's plan intended for her to make a life with Jonathan? Of course, only time would reveal His Providence, but the idea of it did stir her thoughts.

Rose was looking through the wooden chest that held her and Robert's things. Of course, it was mostly clothing that the trunk contained, but there were other things, like a comb and a small mirror inside. Her mother had cautioned her about taking too many belongings, like bedding, which the household they would be staying in would have already. Rose expected they would stay in the home of Master Brewer, who would be certain to afford them whatever they might need.

Robert peered into the chest and sorted through his clothes again, making sure he had all he required.

"I am certain we have checked enough times, Sister," said Robert with a smile. "What we have forgotten we can do without, or obtain in Leyden. Cousin Brewer has said that you can find anything in the world in the markets of Leyden. Besides, we should be gone from here no more than a number of months. I know Father wants us back not long after the wedding so I can begin my apprenticeship with Master Robertson, the mason living nearby in Whitechapel."

"Robert, quiet for a moment," whispered Rose as she put her finger to her lips. "Do you hear the voices below? Could it be Printer Staresmore has come for us now?"

"Mayhaps so," said Robert quietly as he closed the trunk. "I shall go down and see."

Something in Rose told her it was not Printer Staresmore. Her stomach ached so severely she fell to her knees.

"Sister, are you alright? Why are you on the floor? Are you ill?" asked Robert, nearly out of breath.

Rose ignored the question altogether. "Tell me, Robert. From whom are the voices coming? Who is here?"

He hesitated. Robert did not know the nature of the history, but he was aware of some connection between his sister and the post carrier. He had no choice. He had to tell her.

"It is Goodman Mercer, of the King's Post."

Even before he answered, she knew somehow. As he finished his words, a tear had already made its way down her cheek. She could not live with herself if she stayed in her chamber, like a coward. This was her chance. All the hours... no, days, spent wondering about Hugh Mercer and how he fared, had amounted to this opportunity.

Without responding to Robert she rose quickly, smoothed her waistcoat and petticoat, and straightened her coif while making her way to the front of the shop. She decided to pause, standing quietly in the back room, concealed by the shadow of the press. Her father's words rounded the corner and reached where she stood.

"I cannot believe he has been jailed," responded Master Okes. "I saw him so recently, at the end of February. He had already delivered the letters to Sir Wolstenhome, and mentioned he would be sending his own letter back to Masters Robinson and Brewster, reporting on the state of things."

"Sadly, it is true. He was worshipping with others who have separated from the King's Church, in a private home. Authorities raided the gathering, and although Printer Staresmore escaped, his whereabouts were later made known by Francis Blackwell, in exchange for Blackwell's own release. The letters Printer Staresmore wrote, I have with me. There is one addressed to you. His hope was that you could send the other letters on to Leyden with your family. He seemed to think Goodman Masterson, who was with him the night of the raid but not found by the authorities, might be traveling back to Leyden this month," explained Goodman Mercer.

"I can only hope Goodman Masterson shows himself soon and cares to make a speedy return to Leyden. Otherwise, there will be no purpose for my family to travel to Leyden if the wedding has passed. Regarding the traitor Blackwell, that truly sickens me. It is an irony that he calls himself a leader, with his propensity for betrayal. It is someone with a false and selfish character who stains the reputation of others that have separated. I would dare not follow someone like Blackwell across the street, no less across the sea to the New World. I know he has approached persons of good rank and quality about settling in

Virginia, and I cannot imagine anything worthwhile coming from him or his venture. Regarding Printer Staresmore, do you have any idea how long he will be imprisoned?"

"I know not. He is writing letters to anyone who might aid in his release. He also penned these letters needing to find their way to Leyden. Do you think Mistress Okes will agree to carrying those communications across with her? Or she could put them to Goodman Masterson if he journeys with your family over to Leyden."

Goodman Mercer paused. "Will Mistress Okes be bringing Robert to Leyden?"

"Robert and me," said Rose in the calmest tone, as she walked from the shadows and into the light.

Hugh Mercer said nothing. Words came from no one. Hugh and Rose stood staring at each other for what seemed a farthing of an hour. Master Okes looked back and forth, their gazes unbroken. Regardless of what this was about, he was far behind in his work with much to be done on the press.

"Do you have anything more, Goodman Mercer? I apologize, but I must get back to the press. Printing rights to two large publications for Cambridge University are forthcoming, and I must finish up this book I am printing now. If my work were not so demanding, I would care to escort my family to Leyden myself, and be there for my Elizabeth's wedding."

"Understood. I will be on my way, Master Okes. I am hopeful that Goodman Masterson or someone else from the church in Leyden will arrive in time so your family might be accompanied over. Until our next meeting, I bid you farewell."

"Fare thee well, Goodman Mercer. Take care in your travels."

And with that, he returned to the press, his absence permitting a continuation of the conversation should his daughter desire. Katherine had been there all along preparing dinner, minding a hen simmering amidst sage, thyme, and marjoram, with a neighboring pot boiling with turnip, onion, and skirrets. With Katherine there his daughter was not alone. Besides, she was soon to have one and twenty years to her, and could manage such things.

"Rose, will you walk outside with me, as I ready my horse?"

She realized then that the post carrier was trembling, with tears in his eyes. Could it be that he, too, was still conflicted and tormented? For a moment, she hoped he was, but that thought vanished quickly. If her love for him was genuine, she would not want him to suffer. They walked out to the street, his back to her as he adjusted his satchels and readied his horse for the next ride.

"How have you been faring, Rose?"

As he waited for her to respond, she could see the pain in his eyes. Behind the pain, she could see the love he still held for her.

She was not sure how she should answer. She wanted him to be happy with his life, with his wife. If she told him how she felt, it could make him question his decision. But then all that happened did so according to the Lord. With that in mind, she told Hugh Mercer the truth.

"I miss you every hour of every day. Mayhaps it is even every minute of every day. I respect your commitment, and believe whatever happens, it is in God, His plan. I get through each day with the strength the Lord provides, and I have come to accept your absence. As you know, we are readying to travel to Leyden for the wedding of my sister, Elizabeth, and I am hopeful that this adventure will prove a blessing for me."

"You must know that I want only for you to have a long life filled with happiness, even if it must be without me. As far as missing you, it is as you described. It is the same for me. No matter how many miles I travel or days that pass, you are in my thoughts. I try to push them out, but it is not to be. My conscience is tortured by this, as I have a wife I am to be guiding. These thoughts are a measure of betrayal, which I repent each day. Perhaps it is because of me, then, that a month ago God delivered our child without life, looking like a monster."

Rose did not have a chance to respond before her mother approached the shop, walking with a man not familiar to her.

"Good day, Mother. Is all well?" asked Rose as she curtsied to her mother and the man with her.

"Good day, Goodman Mercer. Yes, Rose, all is as it should be. Praise God, Goodman Masterson of the Leyden Church found me at the sign of The Black Bear. He will be able to travel with us to Leyden, seeing that Printer Staresmore is still confined in a jail cell. We will be leaving within a fortnight."

Goodman Masterson nodded in agreement as he looked over at Hugh and Rose. Goodman Mercer had already removed his hat and bowed.

"Are you a printer also?" asked Rose.

"No, presently I would call myself a wool comber. Many of us living in Leyden have work in some part of the cloth trade, whether it be combing or weaving. I come from Sandwich and have made the trip from England to Holland many times before.

"Will we find your father inside?" inquired Goodman Masterson.

"Yes, he is busy at the press. He will be most pleased to meet you. There was concern that our journey to Leyden would not be, or we would have to travel alone."

"Did your father think I could not get over to Leyden safely without an escort?" asked Mistress Okes with a raised eyebrow, followed with a smile. "I have more experience traveling than most men, and furthermore, we will be leaving the country legally, with our pass for ports."

Rose had no desire to comment further. She was caught up in her world with Hugh Mercer. She cared not if anyone accompanied them in their travels. In fact, at that moment it did not matter to her if she made the trip at all. If she had a choice, time would stop then, so she could stay forever with him.

"Rose, come now. Come inside at once. What are you doing out here in the street, anyway? If you care to leave the house, remember your hat, please." Her mother gestured for her to come inside with an annoyed look on her face.

Rose did not have a choice in the matter. What was she to say? That she needed to finish her conversation with Hugh Mercer, a married man and the love of her life?

"Safe travels to you, Rose. I hope you find what you are looking for in Leyden. I will see you again. I must believe that. The thought of never seeing you again is more than I can bear." He attempted to smile, but between the drying tears and the sun in his face, his misery was not to be disguised.

She said nothing. The last time they had parted ways, she walked away, refusing to look back. On this day she stood still, facing the direction of his departure, watching him and his horse as they neared an intersection. In the wake of his leaving, she realized her search for clarity was clouded now by more confusion. During the last year she had sought forgiveness, and an end to her suffering, and now she feared it might never end.

She did something she had not done before. She ran after him. She did it without thinking. She reached up to hold her hat in place, realizing in feeling her coif that her hat sat waiting on her bed. Her decision to wear two petticoats that morning was weighing her down, but she kept running, stepping in snow and nearly slipping on ice, crying out after him, "Hugh, Hugh, stop! Please stop." She cared not about who was looking at her and what they might say.

By now, he had made his turn. She hoped he would have noticed her as he made a turn to the right, but it was not meant to be. Rose's lungs burned taking in the icy air, and as he vanished from her view, she bent over with her head in her hands, not knowing whether to cry or scream. She would have done anything to have those last moments back. And she would have given just about anything to have the horrid feeling gripping her removed at once.

"Oh, La. Rose! Rose, have you gone mad? What is the meaning of you running down the street like this, shouting after Goodman Mercer?" The concerned mother questioned her daughter with a combination of frustration and disappointment, grabbing her by the arm as they returned to the sign of The Rose. This was a married man she was chasing after. What was behind this rash action?

"Please, forgive me, Mother. I know not what I was thinking. I took leave of my senses, and I am sorry for it," said Rose with tears ready to fall, and a heart so heavy she wanted to collapse right there, onto the street. With the aid of her mother, the two Roses returned to the print shop.

At the same time, Hugh Mercer slowed his horse. For all the time he spent thinking about Rose and what he might say to her, he couldn't leave without saying more. Mayhaps she was standing outside still, having watched him go. He turned his horse around so quickly they nearly spun into the ground. Managing to keep their balance, he dug his heels in to reach her before she was gone. His heart pounded at the thought of her presence, and as they rode back to the sign of The Rose, his hopes were high Rose would be in his sights when he rounded the corner.

His cloudy exhalation nearly blocked the view of Mistress Okes nudging her daughter through the print shop door. He slumped down into the saddle as he watched their backs. Looking up once more, his eyes widened. But it was Mistress Okes, and not her daughter, looking back at him. She said nothing. Her look was not of anger, and not of sadness. If anything, it was a look of fear. Her eyes pierced him so intensely he shuddered, her head shaking as if to say, "No Hugh Mercer, not my daughter, and most certainly, not now."

April 1618, Leyden

By the time they arrived in Leyden, it was a Wednesday, the fourth day of April. The winds could not have been any fairer, making the journey smooth and without incident.

"I do not understand all the trouble people speak of in traveling by ship. We did not get sick, not even once," declared Robert with pride.

Mistress Okes laughed aloud. "We were accompanied by more than Goodman Masterson on this journey. Good fortune in the form of fair and gentle winds brought us comfortably into Amsterdam. Now we have only to make our way to Leyden. Mind you, an easier journey you will likely not experience again. You might expect traveling on a ship is a simple thing, but think on having to travel on a ship for months instead of days. Imagine sailing the Atlantic through violent storms, encountering ruthless pirates, while attempting to reach the New World. You realize people like us, not just sailors or explorers, are embarking on such ventures?"

Rose said nothing, but was thinking about what Master Carver had mentioned the last time he was in their London shop. The congregation of Pastor Robinson was looking to remove from Leyden, more than likely to the New World. She did not know if Edward and her sister would join that congregation, and if they did, would they be on a ship crossing the ocean? What about Jonathan Brewster? His father was an elder in that church, so she expected the entire Brewster family would stay together.

Stop, Rose. Stop these thoughts from plaguing you, she admonished herself. She believed that everything was dictated by God's plan, so worrying about what might or might not happen was foolish, if not sinful. At least she was not fixated on Hugh Mercer for once. The trip was a most necessary distraction. For certain, it was a relief to have her mind on something else.

Together with Goodman Masterson, they continued their journey on to Leyden. This was the portion where Mistress Okes was most grateful for his aid. He spoke some Dutch and had made the trip from Amsterdam to Leyden many times before. It was something she could have struggled with, mayhaps putting herself and her children in danger. She smiled at Rose and Robert as they boarded the boat bringing them down the Amstel to the Rokin, and eventually to the craft that would take them to Leyden.

Since the journey from England to Amsterdam was without inconvenience, Rose and Robert expected that getting to Leyden would be the same, if not simpler. Fortunately, they were correct in their thinking, and just hours later their eyes absorbed the tallest peaks of Leyden in the distance.

"It is beautiful, is it not?" remarked Rose to her brother.

He watched the city creep closer, his eyes wider than she had ever seen them. He wondered how long it would take to find their sister, or their cousin, Master Brewer. The city looked large enough. Robert did remember Master Carver speaking of the place, describing it as manageable in walking and finding your way, with the landmarks of churches and other town buildings.

"Do you think Elizabeth will be there when we arrive?" asked Rose.

"I think it unlikely she will be there to see us disembark, but I understand the home of Master Brewer, where she is staying, is close to the canal," responded Mistress Okes.

"There is the possibility she will be standing there, waiting," said Goodman Masterson. "This trip from Amsterdam is a scheduled journey, so she might take a walk near to the steps on the Rapenburg each day. It is not an impossibility, especially since she knows you are coming for the wedding."

Rose was encouraged by this and positioned herself closer to the rail. She wondered now how Elizabeth was faring in this place, and whether she and Edward had already joined the congregation of Master Robinson. As soon as the vessel made the turn from the Vliet onto the Rapenburg, Rose recognized her sister standing at the top of the steps where they aimed to disembark.

As complicated as their relationship could be at times, Rose's heart warmed at the sight of her older sister. She thought her brave to be living in this foreign city, about to be married to a man who might think it best to take them across an ocean to a New World.

As soon as Elizabeth saw them, she began jumping up and down. It was so unlike her to do so, and Rose could only assume that all of this change brought with it a measure of loneliness and desperation, allowing some of her hardness to soften.

Rose mirrored her actions and waved with excitement. "Hallo, Sister! Hallo!" Mistress Okes smiled and put her arms around the two children beside her, content that in moments she would be reunited with the third. The only part of the family missing was Nicholas. She imagined her husband hard at work on the press and sent love to him through prayer.

Rose was the first to disembark, running up the steps into the arms of her sister. The two sisters held on longer than they ever had before.

Robert was not far behind, and although younger, at fifteen years of age, he was much taller and wrapped his arms around them both.

When Elizabeth broke away from her siblings to greet her mother, she held on to her as though if she let go, her mother would disappear. They continued to hug and kiss as their belongings were carried up the steps and loaded onto carts. Their destination was not far, nearly in eye-shot in fact. Goodman Masterson spoke to the men with the carts, instructing them to bring the chests to the Groenehuis, on the Kloksteeg. The men nodded and were on their way to the home of Master Brewer.

Now happily reunited, the Okes family followed the carts along the Rapenburg, making a turn to the right down the Kloksteeg towards the home of Master Brewer. As they made the turn, all save Elizabeth looked up in awe at the sight of the city's oldest church. They would have a regular view of the north and west sides of this magnificent structure from their lodgings within the Groenehuis, but only a person lacking sight would not stop and marvel at the beauty of the old church.

"That is the Pieterskerk, where those of the national Dutch Reformed Church worship. The other large church used by the Dutch Reformed is the Hooglandsekerk, not more than a few minutes' walk from here. Both are remarkable in their size and appearance, but Pastor Robinson and his congregation do not worship there. For now, the group meets at the Green Close, just two doors away from Cousin Brewer. The congregation has grown now to nearly three hundred, and there is talk of the city allowing use of the former Beguinage Chapel, near to where you disembarked."

Mistress Okes noticed the sparkle in her daughter's eye when she spoke of Pastor Robinson and his congregation.

"Elizabeth, have you joined the congregation here, the one you speak of?" asked her mother.

"Not yet, but Edward and I intend to, once we are betrothed, and make the confession of faith as a married couple. I imagine you will attend the services of this church as well. There is also the chance to worship with the other English congregation here, that of the English

Reformed Church led by Hugh Goodyear. Pastor Goodyear lives in the home of Master Brewer, so you will come to know him before long."

Goodman Masterson walked ahead and provided the cart drivers further instructions as he knocked on the door of the Groenehuis. Gertie Savore, the servant of Master Brewer, opened the door and showed a wide smile upon seeing that Elizabeth's family had arrived.

"Welcome! Welcome to Leyden. Please come inside at once. I expect Master Brewer to be returning soon, as it is getting close to dinner time. He is nearby, I believe at the home of Master Brewster. And Mistress Brewer is not far either, I think at the yarn market with Mercy. She mentioned also they might be browsing the free fair as well, the first one of the year. It is mostly of leather and hides, but there are vendors from many parts selling their goods. I believe it to be ending today, so you should visit after dinner if you have interest."

She then quickly turned to the men pushing the carts, motioning for them to enter, and explaining in Dutch where to deliver the chests. The Okes family had two chests, one being larger than the other, and Goodman Masterson had one, which would be brought to his home in the north and east corner of the city.

Rose's heart picked up its pace when she heard the Brewster name. She expected that Jonathan was not far away either, and she was eager to see him again, curious to know how she would feel when her eyes settled on him. How would it compare to the emotions that stirred in the presence of Hugh Mercer?

The men struggled to get the smaller trunk up the narrow staircases to the home's third level. They returned with red, sweaty faces. Speaking rapidly in Dutch to Gertie, they pointed to the hoist hook at the top of the house. Goodman Masterson intervened, and after more discussion with the men, they placed the larger trunk inside the Groenehuis, in the front room where Master Brewer conducted his business. Then they were off to drop the final chest at the home of Goodman Masterson before returning to the river in search of more work.

"Do not have any concern about getting the chest up to your quarters," assured Gertie. "Master Brewer will hire men to hoist it up, and we can bring it in through the window."

"Certainly. It is no trouble for me to remove what I need until the chest makes its way up," responded Mistress Okes.

"Very well. Please come in and get settled. There is warm water and clean linen for washing. I know how exhausting and uncomfortable travel can be. I have journeyed between Leyden and England a number of times myself," said Gertie with empathy.

The Okes family shuffled into their cousin's home and, after taking what they needed from the larger chest, climbed the two circular staircases to the third level of the Groenehuis. Gertie followed them with a brass basin of warm water and left them to wash and refresh themselves after their long journey.

They had at least washed their faces and hands before hearing a number of voices swirling below. None of the voices, save for that of Master Brewer, were recognizable. There were the sounds of a woman and a young girl. Mayhaps this was Mistress Brewer and their daughter, Mercy. There was the voice of another man, mayhaps Pastor Goodyear. Rose stood there listening, and there was something familiar about the voice. Could it be Jonathan? She was eager to see him again, after a decade removed from their last encounter. Imagine, she had only eleven years to her when they saw each other last. They had played Shut the Box when the Brewster family sought refuge with them. Even though Rose never won a single game, Jonathan had given her his turn, something she had not forgotten. He would have five and twenty years to him now, and she was more than ready to cast her gaze upon him.

"Cousin, are you up there?" shouted Master Brewer with excitement.

"Yes, Thomas. Robert, Elizabeth, and Rose are all up here. We are all here, save for Nicholas," answered Mistress Okes.

"Please, come down as soon as you are ready. My wife and daughter are here, as well as Jonathan Brewster, whom you remember, I am sure."

Elizabeth nudged Rose at the mention of Jonathan's name. "He has been asking about you. He is most handsome, and now a citizen, doing quite well in the ribbon trade. Most importantly, he is committed to no one, and while you are here, you have the chance to see him, daily if you like," added Elizabeth while raising an eyebrow. Rose winced at the comment, as it was clear she was referring to Hugh Mercer, and all his complexity.

For certain Rose wanted to see him, and decided to change her coif and waistcoat before revealing herself to Jonathan. Part of her wanted nothing more than to be overcome with emotion upon seeing him again, and another part of her thought it impossible to love someone other than Hugh Mercer. The voice of their servant Katherine trickled through her mind. "I understand you love him, but he is married now, and you must move on. Trust in God's plan."

Their mother was the first to walk down to the ground floor, her cousin rushing to hug and kiss her.

"Please, Rose," said Master Brewer as he turned to his family, "meet my wife, Anna, and our daughter, Mercy."

The women curtsied to one another, then embraced.

"I am most pleased to meet you, Mistress Brewer. I have heard much about you and your family, and thanks be to God we are safely in Leyden and blessed to be staying with you. Thank you for keeping us here in your home, so we might be a part of the wedding celebration of Elizabeth and Edward."

"Of course, Mistress. We are honoured to have you here. Mercy has been eagerly awaiting the arrival of her other cousins," said Mistress Brewer as she smiled at her daughter.

Mercy clutched her poppet in one hand and removed her hat with the other, curtsying to Mistress Okes.

"You are quite a beautiful girl, Mercy. How many years do you have now?" asked Mistress Okes, smiling at her young cousin.

Mercy looked up at her mother to be certain she had permission to answer, and once her mother had nodded, she answered in a soft voice.

"Thank you kindly, Mistress Okes. I have eight years to me."

Just then, Robert and Elizabeth reached the ground level, with Robert running to his cousin.

"How is it that you've become a young man already?" asked Master Brewer as he embraced Robert, now with fifteen years to him.

"I have grown a fair bit, haven't I? I am nearly as tall as you, Jonathan. The last time I saw you, Jonathan, which I do recall, I had only five years to me."

"I remember that time as well. You were quite unhappy with the outcome of Shut the Box, but took it well enough, especially with so few years to you."

"You are looking very well indeed," commented Mistress Okes. "Your parents must be proud of your accomplishments, now a citizen and growing your ribbon business so successfully that you entered a partnership with Master Brewer."

Jonathan nodded as he recovered from bowing to Mistress Okes, replacing his hat.

"My parents are pleased that you are visiting for the wedding. Mother has been anticipating your arrival for weeks, and has much to share and show you. Fear and Patience have been speaking of you often, and I just realized you will be meeting Love and Wrestling for the first time! You must come to our home once you have recovered from your journey."

"I think I will visit shortly after our dinner. How I miss your family, especially your mother."

Mistress Okes noticed Jonathan's gaze was no longer meeting hers, but looking past her with wide eyes.

"Rose," whispered Jonathan so softly it was barely audible. The house fell silent as Rose walked into the room, everyone watching and waiting for her reaction.

"Master Brewer, dinner will be ready in less than a farthing of an hour!" shouted Gertie from the kitchen, a step up and farther back than the area they were occupying. With the silence disrupted, the room returned to its boisterous chaos, and eyes shifted away from Jonathan and Rose. His blue eyes sparkled, remaining locked on her, as they would in target practice on the militia range. As he walked towards her to greet her properly, he could see her cheeks were a crimson color. Could it be that she was shaking as well?

"The dinner is ready. Please come and sit," called Gertie, wiping the sweat off her forehead with the forearm of her smock. The kitchen area was large enough to accommodate a long table, and only Mercy and Robert had to sit off to the side, at a smaller, round table.

Mistress Okes watched her daughter out of the corner of her eye as they made their way to the table for dinner. Even she could not read her daughter easily. Clearly, the sight of Jonathan Brewster evoked feelings of some sort, but she was not certain of what kind.

Scents of the dinner flooded the space, the aroma of fish pottage overtaking the air. Gertie had used lovage and fennel, along with onions and garlic, and all Rose could smell was the fennel, of which she was not fond. Before sitting down she knew she could not tolerate eating then. She put one hand on her stomach, and with the color of her face a pale green, she politely excused herself from the kitchen.

"I do apologize, but I am overcome with an unsettledness in my stomach. My belly is so wobbly, I care not to eat a thing. Mayhaps it is the effects of the journey, but I fear I must return to my bedstead."

Jonathan stood up awkwardly as Rose turned to go, concerned for her well-being, and disappointed by her departure. He expected her state was of a temporary nature, and discarded thoughts linking her sickness to her feelings towards him.

"Rose," called out Gertie, "I will be up shortly with some mint leaves and warm water. I might also have a few pieces of candied ginger."

"Thank you kindly, Gertie. I will bring it up to her," said Mistress Okes, wanting to talk to her daughter alone and understand the true source of her unrest.

Mistress Brewer stood as well, making her way over to Mistress Okes. "Mayhaps she is due to start her monthly courses? Should I have Gertie fetch additional linens and warm water?"

"I am most grateful Mistress, for that offer, but I think this is an accumulation of things brought on by the journey. The other piece to this is that when Rose was very young, mayhaps with only four years to her, she became extremely ill after eating a fish pottage. The experience was so severe that she has not eaten fish pottage since, so I imagine this history plays the biggest part in her feeling ill."

As she explained this, she looked out of the corner of her eye at Jonathan. His blue eyes danced with life as he spoke with Master Brewer, and with five and twenty years to him, Rose could see the young man had so much to offer her daughter. His success in the ribbon trade was clear, and that he was a citizen was no small thing either. She and her husband, Nicholas, had known Master Brewster more than thirty years. Since he came from such a respectable family, Mistress Okes had hoped this union was in God's plan.

Young Rose did not realize it, but her mother had an inkling about her past with Hugh Mercer. She was not aware of the night in the back storeroom, but it was clear her daughter had some connection to the post carrier, even if it was in the form of hope.

As she made her way up the final staircase with the infusion of mint leaves and candied ginger, she could hear the gentle sobs that the down-filled pillows failed to stifle. "What is it, Rose? Are you feeling that badly?"

"Not in my stomach, Mother. I hurt in my heart, and in my head. I held so much promise in the idea that I would arrive here and meet Jonathan again, and that I would feel so strongly that there would be no question of God's plan. I have no averse feelings, but the intensity I expected is lacking."

"Rose, more often than not, when people meet and eventually become betrothed, that excitement is short-lived, if ever felt, even from the beginning. I think in rare cases it is there from the start, and does not fade. If this extreme feeling is something you have known before, ask yourself, was it something that could be sustained?"

When her mother phrased it in those terms, she felt foolish. She felt silly, but still, she had no interest in eating fish pottage. Instead, she chose to rest in her bedstead with the candied ginger and mint infusion to drink. She would eat something at supper, at least some bread and beer, and as she thought more about it, she remembered talk of cheese and all its glory.

Mayhaps a bit of sleep would cure her concerns. She closed her eyes, and within minutes slipped into a dream, surfacing on the deck of a ship, but to where was unclear. Surrounded by strangers, with sailors yelling and swearing, she was told to get below decks. As she made her way down to that dark, dank unpleasant place, a man's muffled voice called out to her. So she went towards it, reaching out in the blackness, determined to know its source. Feeling for him, she grabbed on to a shoulder, and as he turned to face her, she awoke, never knowing who was calling to her.

It was close to supper now, with Rose having slept more than three hours. She woke sweating and confused as to her whereabouts. It took her a number of seconds before she recalled she was in Leyden, in the home of her cousin. She sat up in the bed, her waistcoat wrinkled and coif askew. With her vision blurred, she did not notice her sister sitting at the edge of the bed.

"How now, Rose. How are you feeling?" asked Elizabeth with concern.

"I am feeling well enough. Hungry, in fact. Is it time for supper, or have I slept so long it is time to break the fast?"

Elizabeth laughed a little. "Time for supper. Also, Jonathan has left, if that matters to you. How was it seeing him?"

"Oh, where to begin with Jonathan. He has many favorable qualities, and I have thought him handsome for as long as I can remember, and still do. His skill in business appears to be more than adequate. It is just that I thought I would feel something more when I saw him."

Elizabeth did not have much compassion for her younger sister. She never said much while she was still in London, but she thought Rose a complete fool for wasting even a second on Hugh Mercer.

"So am I to assume that you were expecting, or at least hoping to feel what you feel for Hugh Mercer? Why would you want to feel that? The endless hours of wondering and waiting when you might see him again, hoping he would stop by with a letter or a word? Have you not realized he has mistreated you all of these years? Sister, I would think it would be the last thing you would want for yourself. Jonathan provides consistency, decency, and respect for you. You can start a life together, instead of being the hidden piece in the twisted life of Hugh Mercer.

I know you believe God has His plan, so trust in it. Seeing Jonathan and not having feelings like those you have for the post carrier is likely a blessing. Love comes in many forms, and you might find that the intensity you seek will come in time, as you grow to know and care for each other. That is how it worked for Edward and me, and we are to be married before the month's end. And happily, I might add."

Rose drank the remains of the mint infusion, savoring the liquid even in its cooled state. *The potter did lovely work with this cup,* she thought, admiring the combination of mustard and brown colors. As her sister rambled on, Rose distracted herself by tracing the flower pattern carved into the cup, her finger following the curves in a most soothing fashion. Even though she appreciated the concern, neither Elizabeth nor her mother could understand her feelings, so she wished for them to leave her to herself.

"Sister, I think I will rest here as opposed to coming down for supper. I have grown tired and have discomfort again in my belly. If you could bring me a cup of beer and candied ginger, I would be most grateful. I will choose sleep over supper, and pray that come morning I feel refreshed and can begin anew. Remember I am here for you, to celebrate your wedding, not to find a bridegroom of my own."

The sisters hugged, but neither one felt any better.

"You will find true love, Rose. God will not fail you in that way. Just keep your heart and mind open, and it will…"

"Please, Elizabeth, let me sleep. We can talk more of this if we must, in the morning. God by you and good night."

And with that, Rose turned her back to Elizabeth, wanting to do nothing more than sleep.

April 27, 1618, The Wedding Day

Her mother stood behind her, setting the crown of flowers on top of her daughter's head, her hair flowing freely. Rose was by her side, brushing Elizabeth's long hair, which was brown like chestnuts, glowing in the light shooting through the top front window. The three women were filled with the joy that weddings brought, and as they readied the bride, they merrily sang "Go to Joan Glover". "Go to Elizabeth and tell her I love her, and at the mid of the moon, I will come to her…"

"I think we should add more calendula to the wreath," announced Mistress Okes, disrupting the song.

"I agree," said Rose while Elizabeth sat silently, watching her reflection in the mirror. She looked a bit nervous, but more than anything, appeared rested and content. Her gown was absolutely beautiful, a rich green, dark like a forest of pines. Master Allerton, one of the congregation's tailors, had made it, and Edward had presented the dress as a gift. For certain, the people they passed in the short walk to the Town Hall would recognize they were going before the city magistrates.

The Brewer home was bustling below them in preparation for the bride-ale later that day. Master Brewer had offered to host the celebration at his home instead of using an inn or ordinary, with Mistress Brewer hiring additional help to ready the food and drink. With the Green Close of Master Robinson only two houses away, all expected music and dancing to spill over into the courtyard as the night progressed.

The activity in the Brewer home was reaching its peak as the Okeses descended to the ground floor, ready to depart for the Town Hall. They would walk the short distance to the home of Master Brewster, where the Allertons and Jonathan awaited their arrival, having agreed to serve as witnesses before the magistrates.

Elizabeth strolled down the Kloksteeg like a queen, her eyes and hair glistening, and her gown and crown revealing to the world she was to be married that day. Her family encircled her, also in their best clothes, with Mistress Okes walking proudly ahead, Rose and Elizabeth following, and Robert at the back of their train.

As they passed the home of Pastor Robinson, Mistress Robinson noticed them from the front room and came rushing out to hug Elizabeth and greet the rest of the Okes family.

"Oh, Elizabeth, how beautiful you are in your green gown. Master Allerton made it perfectly, just lovely it is. I won't keep you, I know you must be anxious to reach Edward. We will see you soon for the festivities. God bye you, Elizabeth."

"God by you, Mistress Robinson. We will see you soon, as a married couple!" exclaimed Elizabeth as she curtsied.

After passing the south side of the Pieterskerk, they arrived at the home of the Brewsters moments later, where the Allertons, Jonathan, and Edward were waiting outside.

"Edward insisted we wait out of doors so that we were ready for you," announced Master Allerton as he removed his hat and bowed to Mistress Okes.

Since they had arrived in Leyden, Mistress Okes and her family had chosen to worship with the congregation of Pastor Robinson. She did spend one Sabbath in the company of Master Goodyear's English Reformed congregation. She found this church more than acceptable, more to her liking than her parish church back in London, but still, she preferred to hear the sermons of Pastor Robinson.

Love, Wrestling, Patience, and Fear Brewster spilled onto the alley to watch Edward and Elizabeth set off for the Town Hall. With their witnesses and the Okeses following, they walked the short distance to the Town Hall, just down the alley and turning right onto the Breestraat. William and Mary Brewster stayed within their home, not wanting to disturb or delay the couple. Mary intended to venture over to the Brewer home, to lend the use of her large colander and see if she could aid in the preparations.

The couple to be married walked ahead, almost as if they were unaware of their family and friends behind them. Elizabeth was beaming but nervous enough to remain silent in their walk.

"Elizabeth Okes, you are the most beautiful woman in all the world," declared Edward, nearly breathless.

Her cheeks were on fire from the comment, and she smiled bashfully but did not reply. She was unsure as to why she said nothing, because she thought the same of him, that he had to be the most handsome man in the world. He looked majestic in his finest suit of clothes, the blend of wool dyed with woad in the deepest blue. The silver buttons were a recent addition, replacing pewter ones he could use elsewhere.

She was grateful to God for bringing them together, believing Edward's manner a combination of all things good. Blessed with impressive intellect, his personality was gentle but not meek. He would be a good husband, providing and teaching in the ways of serving God as a married couple, and in time mayhaps, as a father.

When they reached the Breestraat, they had to first approach the guard at the gate of the barricaded area. Weeks before, due to dissension among factions in the Dutch Reformed Church, the area surrounding the Town Hall had to be protected from riots and protests. Comprised of pickets and heavy timbers, the enclosure would not deter their marriage, but did mark the instability within the Dutch Reformed Church. After Jonathan explained their purpose for being there, as he was the most fluent in Dutch, the group was allowed to enter. Edward took Elizabeth's hand and together they ascended the stone steps on the left, twenty-four in total. They passed a stone-carved cherub leaning comfortably on an hourglass. Always, there were reminders that this life was fleeting. Still, she smiled. She was marrying the man she loved. Their witnesses followed close behind, and together, they entered and proceeded to the office of the magistrates.

There was a couple already there, so they had to wait. This was not a problem, especially for Jonathan, who could spend the minutes visiting with Rose. In the last three weeks, they'd had occasions to be together, such as after Sabbath worship. The past Tuesday, the Okes family were guests for dinner, and following the meal Jonathan and Rose played chess and draughts.

For Rose, she had no choice but to be guarded. She was still in a state of recovery from Hugh Mercer, and the last thing she wanted was to be paralyzed by love. In truth, part of her wanted to find everything wrong with Jonathan, so she would not be tempted to take any risks. He, on the other hand, yearned to feel more, not perceiving any of this as a threat. He thought Rose beautiful and clever, and wanted to know her in every way possible. Oftentimes, he dreamed of spending days on end with her. So many places in Leyden he wanted to show her, like the botanical gardens of the University, and in the wintertime, ice skating on the canals. Also in the winter, he thought she might have interest in viewing the Anatomy Theatre, in the University building just behind the house of Master Brewer. His blue eyes fixed on her, he wondered what she was thinking, and if she too had thoughts of him at that moment.

"Jonathan, pray pardon, they are ready for us," said Edward as he turned him gently by the shoulder.

"Of course, yes, the magistrates," responded Jonathan, a little embarrassed by his distraction.

"Come in, please. Stand before us," commanded the magistrate. "Let us begin. State your names. Let me check the records. Yes, the banns have been read three times, in the last three weeks. We may complete the betrothal then."

"Appearing in the presence of the magistrates of the city of Leyden, Edward Winslow, on the one hand, and Elizabeth Okes, on the other, have come and, as they declared by hand and mouth, freely and without pressure from anyone, have made promises of engagement and marriage to each other, that nothing, whether love or suffering or anything else, would cause them to desist from their faithfulness to each other in marriage as legal man and wife, to live with each other in all unity, affection, and love according to the ordinances of God and according to His holy word, all with the help and approval of God without whose gracious assistance we can accomplish nothing, not even the least thing. Done before the aforesaid magistrates on April 27, 1618. All this so long as the present marriage has not been dissolved by death, in witness of which they have invoked and called upon the Almighty God, praying that He will bless them with His Holy Spirit, accompany and fill their marriage with his grace and favors. Thus done before the aforesaid magistrates in Leyden."

As the magistrate stated the oath, Edward and Elizabeth held hands and stood at an angle that allowed them to look at both the magistrates and each other. Elizabeth trembled with excitement. She was married now, and a housewife. Edward turned towards her and embraced her, kissing her on the mouth and then on the cheek. The witnesses gathered around them, as no one else was waiting for the magistrates, joining in with hugs and kisses and words of congratulation.

"Shall we make our way back to the home of Master Brewer?" offered Mistress Okes.

In unison, the married couple started off and everyone else followed, making their way back to the Kloksteeg and the Groenehuis.

People walking by the home could tell something out of the ordinary was happening. Many hired hands were working in both kitchens, and men were busy hanging a large tapestry near the main table. A maidservant was straightening the Turkey carpet after beating and brushing it, bringing the red and blue colors back to life. At the courtyard of the Green Close, John Coprario of Pastor Robinson's congregation could be heard practicing on the lute.

Robert ran ahead to alert the household that the married couple was close by. Buzzing with activity and excitement, the preparations continued in a final fury. Master Brewer stood at the main entrance of his home, welcoming the Winslows with open arms.

"God bless you, Edward and Elizabeth. Come now, let us celebrate your union. We have an assortment of food and drink that would rival any feast in the courts of the King."

"It is true," said Mistress Brewer, with Mercy by her side.

"Pray pardon, Mother. Might I speak and tell Elizabeth and Edward what we have prepared for the feast?"

"Yes, Mercy, although it might be difficult to remember everything."

"There are many choices of meat flesh, such as roast lamb in warm butter, roasted ribs with cloves and rosemary, farced chicken, mutton with sauce, flounder, mussels, and oysters," described young Mercy as she counted on her fingers. "We have eel and savory pies, and Father says the crust is the lightest and flakiest he has ever tasted!"

"We used all the herbs and spices I have ever heard of, and probably more. Let me think. There was salt, peppercorn, mustard, cinnamon, nutmeg, ginger, rosemary, thyme, marjoram, basil, dried calendula flowers, sage, parsley, fennel, and I know I must be forgetting something. Mother made certain we offered plenty of boiled salad greens and root herbs. I helped to make a cabbage pottage, and an onion pottage with spinach as well. There are spice cakes and loaves of rye, half-pound rolls of white manchet bread, along with different cheeses, and a variety of sweet things, some I have never seen before. What I favor most are the almond tarts, but we have lemon pasty, *olie-koecken*, dried pears, raisin cookies, and quince pie, which are all toothsome," finished Mercy, nearly out of breath.

"Well done, Mercy. That is a most impressive list, and we are grateful to God and your family for providing it. It truly is a glorious feast your family has offered. Have you heard the music playing?" asked Edward as he bent down to Mercy's level.

She shook her head from side to side. "You might ask your parents if you can walk over to the Green Close, where John Coprario is in the courtyard practicing the lute, and there is a small pipe organ as well," said Edward, still clutching Elizabeth's hand. Then he turned to Master Brewer. "That you would host our celebration at your home is more than generous. How I prefer to be here rather than an inn or ordinary."

"Yes, Cousin, this is more than I could have dreamed of. The spice cakes look so perfect they should be captured in a painting," added Elizabeth.

"Excellent good," said Master Brewer. "It pleases me that you are content. We can expect many from the congregation to celebrate with us, at least for some of the evening. If the numbers are so great we cannot remain inside, we can venture into the courtyard of Master Robinson."

At that moment, Master and Mistress Robinson entered with arms open, ready to embrace the newly wed couple.

"It warms my heart to see you joined in marriage. The Lord has selected you, one for the other, so you might support each other in your faithful journey."

"Just so, Pastor Robinson, and it will not be long before together we join your church, making covenant in a marriage with Christ," responded Edward. As he said this he turned to Elizabeth, as she nodded in agreement.

Mistress Okes heard the exchange of words and recognized that Elizabeth's path would keep her from returning to London. With Edward involved in the printing operation of her cousin and Master Brewster, he was taking a risk, printing books forbidden in England. Aside from that, what she feared far more was the talk of removal from Leyden, and possibly going to the New World.

Rose gazed over at her youngest daughter, who was talking to Patience Brewster, when she noticed Jonathan across the room. He was attentive to and respectful of her daughter, and clearly capable of becoming a loving husband and father, but he too could be venturing away from Leyden. Then she saw Robert talking to William Jepson and Roger Symonson, the first having experience as a carpenter, and the other as a mason. Robert was due to begin his apprenticeship in masonry once they returned to London. Mistress Okes could not help but wonder if God's plan would take all three children away from her.

"Mother, what is it? You are looking lost and sad. Are you thinking about Father again?" asked Rose.

"Yes. Yes, I was thinking of how much he wanted to be here, and how happy he would be to see Elizabeth on this day. I do not think that smile has left her face since we finished with the magistrates, do you?"

It was then that Mistress Brewster entered the room, the friends embracing as if they had not seen each other in years.

"What a luxury it is to see you so often. How long will you stay in Leyden now that Elizabeth has wed?"

"I am not certain, really. I did promise Nicholas that I would try to return to London with someone from your congregation. It sounds as if the talks with the merchants in London have gone quiet, so I know not when Master Carver plans to return there. I cannot say I care to go in haste, but I do miss Nicholas, and Robert will start an apprenticeship once we get back."

"What of Rose? Is there any chance she would stay longer?"

"Are *you* asking, or is the question coming from Jonathan?"

"I am asking, but I imagine my son would take great interest in the answer."

"We expected to return all together after the wedding, but we both know that God has His plan."

"Just so, Mistress. We will wait and see what He has in store for–"

"Family, friends, and members of the church, please gather closer to me," requested Master Brewer in a loud voice. "I welcome you to our home, so we might celebrate the marriage of Edward Winslow to my cousin, Elizabeth Okes, now Elizabeth Winslow. May their union be blessed, lasting for many years and growing stronger with time. You must expect obstacles, but with love, faith, and forgiveness, the Lord will lead you through. Now raise your cups, and let us rejoice."

There were additional words spoken by Master Brewster, followed by a prayer led by Master Carver. It was after his prayer that Jonathan approached Edward and Elizabeth, and from his pocket pulled the two halves of a shilling, handing one half to each. Edward put his arm around Elizabeth and whispered something in her ear, making her blush. Then they both carefully put their half-coins safely in their pockets.

After the meal, the group migrated to the Green Close, where the eating, drinking, singing, dancing, and game playing continued for hours. The men measured their strength playing pitch the bar, while others hit the shuttlecock with wooden battledores. Some of the children blew bubbles from the shells of oysters filled with soapy water. Other used stems of broken clay pipes to blow the bubbles, with friends awaiting the descent of floating globes, caring to catch them safely on pillows.

They received gifts, such as a scummer, a beautiful brass colander with a flower pattern stamped in, the largest pipkin Elizabeth had ever seen, and a wooden foot stove, among other necessary things.

Of the gifts, she favored a book the most. She valued it for the content, but also the connection to her husband. The book was entitled *The English Housewife,* printed by Master John Beale, the type set by Edward himself. For Edward, he too cherished a book received, but in his case it was *The New Herbal,* the edition published in 1595. The author, Rembert Dodoens, was a professor of botany at the Uni-

versity of Leyden, and the information revealed the invaluable useful-
ness of plants.

The day and night were magical. Music played on a little longer, but
with the beer running dry, the end of the celebration was near. Mistress
Okes was grateful for many things that night, namely to see her daughter happy. The purpose of the visit was served, and now she had to see
to her return to London, with Robert and Rose. She feared the longer
she stayed, the greater the chance of one or both wanting to remain
behind. That, she knew, was something Nicholas would not accept.

September 1618

What Mistress Okes feared did occur, at least partially. She remained
in Leyden nearly four months after the wedding, then returned home
in late August, and with only Robert. It was not as if Rose stayed
against her mother's wishes, but still, it would be difficult to justify
to Master Okes. Since the time of the wedding in April, many things
occurred to make Rose want to remain in Leyden, and her mother
allowed that choice.

After the wedding, Robert began talking nonsense about remaining in Leyden, desiring to pursue masonry there, or possibly learn the
trade of pipe making, with the growing interest in tobacco. Mistress
Okes would hear none of this, and fortunately, come August, Master
Carver departed for London to reconvene with members of the Council for Virginia, and accompanied them home.

Regarding Rose, the most significant reason for her to stay in Leyden was that the Brewer family required her aid. Mistress Brewer was
with child, and the pregnancy brought with it serious difficulties, forcing her to remain in the bedstead since the middle of August. That
Master Brewer could afford to hire help was not a question, but it was
better for Rose to be there caring for Mercy, as opposed to a paid hand.

The other reason Rose cared to remain in Leyden was that her feelings for Jonathan had shifted. Mayhaps it was due to his change in

behavior towards her. Not long after the wedding, he had decided he would not put so much effort into things. It was not that he no longer cared, or did not desire her, but he was tired of offering so much, only to receive a marginal response. Whether it was conscious or not, no one would ever know, but Rose's feelings began to grow. Now she thought of him outside of times when he was present, and wondered when she would see him next. Elizabeth noticed the difference and asked if she had ceased her thoughts of Hugh Mercer. Rose laughed aloud at that question.

"Elizabeth, I am glad for your sake that you cannot understand my experience with Hugh Mercer. No matter how much time has passed or what happens in my life going forward, Hugh Mercer will always have a place in my thoughts and heart, no matter how small or infrequent. Regarding Jonathan Brewster, I do feel for him more, and in a more serious way."

"It pleases me, Rose, to hear that. Jonathan is a good man, from a family that our parents approve of. And if you do choose to stay in Leyden, we would remain together here, and beyond, should we remove."

That was so, but in truth, the principal reason Rose stayed was for her cousin, and Mistress Brewer and Mercy. While she was still in Leyden, she would see Jonathan as often as she could.

On this day, they arranged their meeting in the Pieterskerk churchyard, near to the bell tower, just opposite her cousin's home. It was a convenient option to meet outside there, as opposed to Jonathan entering the home and the two of them having to answer questions about where they were going and when they might be back.

Rose paced a little, trying to calm her nerves. Each time she reached the window and peered out onto the square, she was anxious as to whether she would see him or not, wondering what she would do if he did not follow through on his commitment to meet her. But she kept reminding herself that this was quite unlikely, given that Jonathan was a man of his word and reliable, and those were two of the many reasons that she cared to meet him.

She stood in the window, looking across the yard towards the old prison building. Jonathan had explained that on the other side of this brick building there was a place called the Gravensteen, where criminals were executed. She was glad that she had not witnessed any herself, seeing that her cousin's home was so near to it. She did admire the grand Pieterskerk, constructed with red and white stones, hexagonal ends, and mysterious little red doors halfway up, along with castle-like turrets. Even though Master Robinson's congregation did not worship there, she felt comforted in its presence, regardless of her lack of connection with the religious happenings on the inside.

"Oh dear, there he is," Rose whispered to herself. In all of her pacing, she had lost track of the time. She rushed down the circular wooden staircase and out across the alley, into the churchyard.

Rose blushed upon meeting his gaze, and at that moment his blue eyes shone a little brighter.

"Good day, Rose. It pleases me greatly to have you standing before me, looking as lovely as ever. I was hoping you might like to take a walk through the *Hortus Academicus* over at the University. Have you been to the botanical gardens before?" asked Jonathan.

"I would very much enjoy that, as I have only viewed them from afar," said Rose.

Jonathan bent his arm so that Rose could latch on to him. His suit of clothes matched the color of the leaves changing orange in the autumn air, with his light-blue stockings matching the sky where puffy clouds parted. Rose adored him in this suit, smiling lovingly in his direction. Together, they walked to the end of the Kloksteeg, past the printing shop of Govert Basson, then across the bridge and over the Rapenburg, to the site of the Academy Building.

"The entrance to the gardens is just to the right of the Academiegebouw, through the arch," remarked Jonathan as he gestured that way.

"This place is magnificent," said Rose as she marveled at the long brick structure. The University Building had seven segments and a pair of arched windows stacked one atop the other. She favored how the top row of windows was longer than those below. Connected to the building on the right was what looked to Rose like half of a bricked house and a span of gate continuing on to another structure constructed of brick. Past the arched gate lay the gardens.

"Was this building made for the University?" asked Rose.

"No, it was at its beginning a convent for nuns of the Catholic Church. The University began in fifteen hundred, five and seventy, after surviving the siege of the Spanish. William of Orange awarded the city with the University, and I think it the most perfect symbol of fortitude and a place to nurture growth and mankind. The garden itself was created by Professor Clusius. Likely, you have heard of him, but he no longer walks the Earth."

"I have heard Master Brewer mention his name before, in speaking with Master Leighton. You know Master Leighton, who lives also with us and studies Medicine at the University?"

"Yes, of course. I have spoken with him on numerous occasions. He is quite knowledgeable, and in his studies, spends much time in these very gardens we are about to explore.

"I have been here many times, and as you might expect there is order and meaning behind the arrangement of things. You can see the space is divided in four quarters, with each of those quarters having a total of sixteen rows of plants. If you were to be a bird with a view from above, you would see clearly the pattern of the quadrants on the lower left and upper right, with the rows running vertically, in four sections of four. There are paths that cross both vertically and horizontally within each subset of rows."

"Yes, I see now that in the top left and lower right quarters the rows run horizontally. So let me figure that. There are four quadrants, each with four sets of four rows. Six and ten rows, four times... totals four and sixty rows to the botanical gardens. And look there, in the lower left area. There are four rows enclosed by a fence. That is curious. I wonder why that is."

"Well, let's have a look over there," said Jonathan as they turned to the left. "I can read the names in Latin and make some sense of them, but I am not certain why they are enclosed like this. I will have to remember to ask Master Leighton," remarked Jonathan.

They continued to stroll the gardens, arms entwined. Rose favored the varieties of her namesake the most. The rose was known to loose the belly, as well as gladden the heart and head. Her mother and Katherine favored to use rose water in baking, as did most good housewives. There were white, pink, and purple ones to discover, and they walked the space, seeking them out.

"I recognize a number of these herbs. Look. Are those called tomatoes... or apples of love? And over there, that of course is tansy, next to those white roses. Tansy is quite good at keeping insects and other unwanted pests away, but a woman with child should be mindful of it."

Jonathan nodded firmly in agreement. "Look, there are houseleeks. Their juice is wondrous good should you burn your skin. Here is lovage, one herb you will find in all Dutch gardens."

"Yes, I should think so. I also favor to use lovage in pottages, and just yester morrow we dropped the juice of it in Mercy's ear, for she complained of pain," said Rose. "Look. There is mint on the corner, with rosemary and sage beyond, and fennel. Sage is one of my favorite herbs, for cooking and medicine. Anytime I have the rheum, it is the first thing I do– roll up a leaf of sage and put it straight up my nose. It is excellent good cut in small pieces and baked with salt, and used to whiten the teeth. Now, fennel... fennel I do not favor at all. Do you?"

"In small amounts, I should say."

"What are those very tall stalks over there?" asked Rose, pointing to a crop planted along the perimeter of the gardens.

"It is a corn called maize, I believe. There is tobacco here, too, we should have a look for," suggested Jonathan.

Without much warning, as could happen in Leyden with the winds rolling in off the North Sea, a cloud moved over the garden, releasing a wall of rain.

"Here, let us take cover under the cupola," suggested Jonathan, reaching for her hand before running for shelter.

Sitting in the middle of the gardens, the little structure was beautifully carved, with lions adorning the four archways. It was quite a romantic place to be trapped, so Rose welcomed the rain. She looked down, and at their feet were stones placed in the pattern of a sun. She was admiring that when she felt Jonathan's hands reach for her chin. Gently, he lifted her face up to his and kissed her softly. She closed her eyes, feeling warmth rush through her body.

The skies cleared, but they chose to linger under the cover of the cupola. He kissed her once more on the cheek, taking her hand so they could resume their tour of the garden. As she perused each row of the garden, she was astounded by the variety of plants, their origin, height, and the properties they possessed. Some were growing close to the ground with broad leaves. Others looked like small trees, and still many had flowers, several with leaves looking more like fronds. It was the diversity, and the chance to see varieties from all corners of the world, that impressed her the most.

She noticed also the different visitors to the garden, and smiled at the other courting couple walking the rows. All the other people sharing the space were men, some writing in books, some talking in pairs, and others meandering alone. One man stayed at the rail of the four fenced rows, never moving from that place.

"I wonder what that man is pondering. He has not moved from his position on the rail in the time we have been here," commented Rose.

"One never knows with this place. He could be contemplating a concoction that will cure fever or purge phlegm. That is the beauty of it, that at this University there is so much knowledge– from Botany to Medicine, to Theology and Philosophy, and beyond. The painters here and across the Low Countries are brilliant as well. That is one of the reasons I enjoy being in Leyden, to be surrounded by learned men, in the heart of discovery. Oftentimes, I will venture over to the sign of The Music Book– you know, the shop of Govert Basson? There he has books on alchemy, and many times you will find men willing to discuss it.

"In talking of books, there is one just published by my father and Master Brewer that you must bring back to your father, Master Okes. It is one written by Master Robinson, called *The People's Plea, The Exercise of Prophesie.* I would take only one copy, and hide it well, deep within your trunk. You do not want to be answering questions about it."

"I understand. I know my father will want the copy, but as you know he intends to stay within the Stationers' Company, and the efforts of my cousin and your father can be dangerous to him."

"I agree, Rose, and of course respect your father and his choices." As he said this, he reached for Rose's hand. "I respect your family, and I respect you." He bent down and kissed her cheek softly.

"Jonathan, I am confused when you talk of Leyden and how much you favor being here. I know you are doing better than most with your ribbon business. Why then, would you remove from here with the others? Why not stay in Leyden?"

"In truth, I am still considering remaining here. We are lacking an agreement with the Council for Virginia, and time passes. Some will still discuss about where to remove to, although in the minds of Master Robinson and my father, they are decided on the New World and the northern part of the Virginia territory. There are good reasons to leave, to be sure. The Twelve Years' Truce will be ending soon, in sixteen hundred one and twenty. To fear the Catholic Spanish is a wise thing. It was not long ago this city was nearly destroyed by them. The drums of war beating should be heard and heeded.

"You might have noticed since your arrival here that the tensions have heightened within the Dutch Reformed Church. The power of two factions, the Remonstrants, or Arminians, and the Contra Remonstrants, has been shifting this year, and the Arminians will be ousted completely, I think. There might be some violence associated with this change, and I pray we are unaffected.

"Another reason to leave is that for many in our congregation, they are suffering in poverty, barely getting by. For most families the children have to work, and they are aging quickly, as are the adults. Some of the children are running off to become soldiers and sailors, or marrying into Dutch families. We are English and favor to keep our ways intact. Our pastor will often say that many of those who both write and preach now against our church, if they were in a place where they might have liberty and live comfortably, they would join us."

"When do you think you will leave then?" asked Rose with trepidation.

"It will all depend on the work Masters Carver and Cushman do in London, in negotiating with the merchants. There has been some indecision and lack of unity within that group, so we must take care to have a stable agreement and plan. A venture over to the New World is dangerous enough."

Rose said nothing, as there was nothing really to say. She decided it best they cherish the moment and continue admiring the gardens, as opposed to fearing the unknown.

October 1618

Mistress Brewer had been bedridden since August, and it was not yet the beginning of October when labor ensued. Sadly, a healthy child was not produced by her tireless efforts. Anna Brewer gave birth to a son on the second day of October, and even before the end of that day, his life had expired. A terrible twist to this was that on October third, the city celebrated its independence, the anniversary of the relief from the Spanish in the century before. Rose watched helplessly as her cousin's wife lay ill in body and tortured in mind, while Master Brewer buried the boy across the alley in the Pieterskerk.

The month worsened for the Brewers, with Mistress Brewer becoming sicker, and then dying on the twentieth of October. Then, Master Brewer fell ill himself. The sickness did not keep him from walking, and by the grace of God he remained sound in mind. To recover, he moved temporarily out of the Groenehuis to a place around the corner, on the Nieuwesteeg. It was there he drew up a second will.

Now that his wife was gone, he declared John Carver executor of his estate, save for a select few legacies, including two hundred guilders to the deacons of the congregation to which he belonged, the one led by Master Robinson. One hundred guilders were to go to John Carver, twenty guilders to Gertie Savore, and forty guilders to his present servant. The rest of the estate and the care of Mercy Brewer were to be managed by his close friend, John Carver. If Master Carver were to die, he was to be succeeded as guardian by William Jepson.

After the age of thirteen, Mercy was to receive two hundred fifty guilders annually. If Mercy died before she was twelve or before she had a will, Master Brewer divided his estate up into many parts, with some going to family in England, and some going to Master Carver and Master Brewster. Much of the rest was to be split among the English congregations in Leyden, those of Masters Robinson and Goodyear, and in Amsterdam, to the church led by Master Ainsworth. Masters Robinson and Ainsworth would also receive parts of a portion directly. Half a portion was to go to deposed preachers of Master Carver's choice, and one of the final quarters, to purchase all the books that Master Carver could get ahold of in this land or elsewhere, that had been published against the bishops and forbidden by them.

With the physical condition of Master Brewer unimproved, Mercy and Rose moved in with the Carvers. Mistress Carver was more than welcoming, living alone while Master Carver was handling the negotiations in London. Edward and Elizabeth had lived there briefly as well, after they were married in April, but had since taken a place of their own in the close of Master Robinson.

Being with Mistress Carver was a comfort to young Mercy, having lost her mother, and even to Rose, with her mother back in London. Rose believed she was meant to stay longer in Leyden, not only to help with the care of Mercy, but also to share more experiences with Jonathan. She was growing to love him, and found now her heart would skip at the sight, and even the thought of him. Unlike Hugh Mercer, in which the intensity was strong from the beginning, with Jonathan it was developing. As scared as she was to fall farther into this, it felt safe enough to explore.

November 1618

Jonathan wanted to share and show Rose as much as possible, knowing that at any time she might return to England. Thanks be to God Master Brewer was nearly recovered, and with his health restored, her journey back to London before the year's end was likely. That being probable, Jonathan looked for opportunities to show Rose special places in Leyden. He learned from his father that the Anatomy Theatre of the University planned a dissection in the coming weeks. Since the presentations occurred only in winter, and sporadically at that, Jonathan pursued tickets for the event. He was fortunate in that a student of Medicine, Alexander Leighton, was living at the home of Master Brewer. Through him, he was able to obtain the tickets.

The following day, Jonathan knocked on the door of Master Carver's home with great excitement. Rose had seen him approaching, so she raced to the door before the servant could answer.

"Good day, Rose. I have two tickets to view the presentation at the Anatomy Theatre for next week, and I would care to have your company in attending."

"Of course, it would please me to join you," responded Rose. Her sincerity was evident, for she could not think of a place that she would not go with him. To be around him was all she wanted, so even though viewing a cadaver's dissection lacked desirability, being with Jonathan most certainly did.

The day could not come fast enough for her, and finally the time arrived for her to ready herself for Jonathan and the Anatomy Theatre. She combed her chestnut hair and carefully secured her coif, covering it with a black wool hat. Jonathan had gifted her a golden silk ribbon, and she wore it proudly around her hat. She dressed in one of her favorite petticoats, one colored a deep violet with a band of dark blue at the bottom. Her knitted waistcoat matched the petticoat perfectly, and over that she buttoned her deep-ocean-blue waistcoat. After checking that her violet stockings were smooth and the garters tight, she gave her shoes a coating of mink oil. Since the theatre sat very near to Master

Carver's home, she elected to leave her coat behind, knowing they had but a short walk down the Kloksteeg and around the corner on the Rapenburg before they were inside the building. Rose expected the crowd would keep the space warm enough.

Jonathan wanted to sit as close as possible to the display table, but upon showing their tickets at the entrance and looking up at the audience, it was clear their options were limited. As they entered the amphitheatre and accessed the circular rows of seating and standing areas, Jonathan could see right away by the dress of the other observers that they were either students of Medicine, doctors, or wealthy individuals who could afford the time to be there.

Since the place was packed with people in each of the seven wooden rows and their accompanying railings, Jonathan gestured for Rose to ascend the narrow aisle to the highest level of the viewing area, their only choice being to jostle amongst the already-large group populating the top railing.

"Here, Rose, there is room here. Come closer to the edge so you can see better," said Jonathan as he guided her against the wooden ledge. His attentiveness never went unnoticed, being a welcome departure from her brief pockets of hurried time with Hugh Mercer.

When she glanced to the right, a large skeleton of what looked to be a cow with small horns peered down at her. "Jonathan, look. There is an owl and monkey riding that cow!" exclaimed Rose, trying to suppress her laughter.

"Yes, the monkey appears to be the right proportion to ride that calf. As strange as it looks, it works, does it not?"

Rose nodded in agreement and proceeded to gaze about the theatre in wonderment. She appreciated the uniqueness of such a place, and observed the different types of people who shared the same curiosity, feeling slightly intimidated by their obvious wealth and status. Excitement filled the air, and with the theatre packed to its capacity, the people hushed as Doctor Paaw made his way to the table where the sheet-covered body lay.

There was no chance of mistaking Doctor Paaw, standing before the observers in his bright-white coat, taking command of the room. In addition to the cadaver, she could see a brass pan and sponge, and what looked to be a knife. She stood on the tips of her toes while holding the railing, straining to see what else was on the table. She could see a large book adjacent to the body, and possibly a second knife. Her eyes followed the right arm of the specimen down to the hand, which appeared to be grabbing the edge of the table. Rose blinked two or three times before shaking the idea that any life remained in this man.

A number of the spectators were looking upwards and all around, and as she did the same, she realized there were skeletons interposed amongst the crowd. The combination of life and death in the space was eerie, yet intriguing. The skeletons were not only human. There were monkeys, deer, goats, birds, and squirrels. Directly across from where they were standing and a bit to the right was the skeleton of a horse, with a human skeleton sitting atop, a pickax in one hand and the other holding the reins. With a hat topping his skull and a sword strapped to his left hip, he looked as if he might ride off at any moment.

Jonathan gestured to the scene directly in front of them, where the iron shafts secured to the rail held up two human skeletons, one holding a shovel, and one holding an apple. They were facing one another, and in betwixt stood an apple tree, with the serpent winding up the trunk. Just beyond the skeleton representing Adam, she noticed words on a banner, written in Latin. The banner was held by a different skeleton, this one off to the left.

"Jonathan, what does that say on that flag over there?" asked Rose, gesturing to the left.

"It says 'The Beginning of Dying Is Birth,'" translated Jonathan.

As she contemplated the meaning of the words, she felt someone tugging her petticoat. The someone had four legs, making her smile, relieved it was a playful dog as opposed to a playful man. She bent down to pet his soft grey fur, not realizing the man next to her, an assistant to the doctor, was carrying the flayed flesh of another unfortunate prisoner. He moved away quickly when he saw the dog's interest, wanting to remove any temptation for the dog to sink his teeth into this prized item of display. Rose looked over in disbelief, staring at the body of skin, intact in one large piece, as its keeper made his way through the audience.

The dissection had begun, so the crowd ceased their talking in order to hear the words of Doctor Paaw. Rose continued to scan the theatre, at times bringing her attention back to the doctor and the organs he was extracting from the body. She looked beyond and above the demonstration table, where a massive case displaying the dissection tools hung. Atop that cabinet lay a stone-carved angel, its right hand resting on top of a skull, the left hand holding an hourglass. The angel smiled down at the audience, a gentle reminder of life's fleeting nature.

Rose was surprised by her interest in the demonstration. She had never been to a lecture of any sort, and now she was seeing and hearing about the contents of the human body. To view organs, such as the liver and kidneys, was fascinating to her. To see in such raw fashion what God had created was incredibly meaningful, and that Jonathan would bring her there impressed her. She did respect his interest in varied subjects, including alchemy, which some in his congregation did not view favorably. While she watched Doctor Paaw extract pieces from the dead prisoner, it was impossible to escape the idea of her own mortality and its inevitability. She turned to look at Jonathan, thinking he might be the man God intended for her. In time, he noticed her eyes upon him and returned a loving look, as if he knew her thoughts and agreed.

WINTER LANDSCAPE WITH SKATERS, C. 1608, HENDRICK AVERCAMP,
RIJKSMUSEUM, AMSTERDAM, THE NETHERLANDS

Jonathan Brewster and Rose Okes skating on the canal (cover image).
Avercamp's paintings are some of the most iconic Dutch works from the 17th century.
His ability to capture all layers of society in one space is unmatched, making his
work unmistakable. It is a luxury to be able to view in one setting, the elite of
society, in their silk and gold thread, standing beside a beggar or peasant. Scholars
of wardrobe look to Avercamp and his stunning examples for evidence of style, color,
and culture—it is the perfect photograph from 400 years ago.

Chapter Seventeen

1619

January 1619, Leyden

Thomas Brewer sat at his desk and decided to light another candle. He was thinking about his printing venture, and how the changing political landscape in the Netherlands was making his efforts increasingly risky. The Synod of Dort convened in November of the last year, which most expected would result in replacing one religious faction with another within the Dutch Reformed Church.

In addition, in December of 1618, the States General issued an edict demanding stricter controls on publishing. England was putting pressure on the Dutch government to pursue and punish publishers printing seditious or scandalous books, libels, songs, or news. Also, the names of authors and printers, place of printing, and names of the translators were required, with printers retaining a copy of each item printed, and another being sent to designated officials. Master Brewer had concern that his publication efforts might be severely impacted, if not shut down altogether, depending on how seriously the edict was enforced.

After losing two children and his wife within a span of fourteen months, he wanted to do everything to keep Mercy safe, even if it meant having Rose take her back to London. Although that might be the most prudent plan, he wasn't quite ready to separate from his daughter, so Master Brewer requested that Rose stay with Mercy a bit longer in Leyden.

"Rose, I understand your parents are eager for your return, so you should be traveling back to London before the middle of this year, at the very latest. Master Cushman will be going there before May, as he is wanting to get the business underway with the Council for Virginia, or at least attempt to. He or Master Carver will accompany you, and depending on the state of things, I will likely have you bring Mercy across as well."

As her relationship with Jonathan progressed, the news of staying longer was pleasing to her. Each week they would do something new together. A week before, they walked through the markets and then by the castle of the city, the Burcht. The more time she spent with Jonathan, the less time she spent wondering about Hugh Mercer or reflecting on their past. She was so grateful for that change, it made her value Jonathan even more.

On this winter day, he was bringing her to the canal for skating. Rose had taken Mercy before, but not having skates of her own, she walked while Mercy skated. Jonathan promised he would bring a pair of skates that Patience and Fear used. When dressing that morning she decided to wear her black *bouwen* with blue silk sleeves, and a white petticoat with stripes of blue silk at the bottom. There would be all manner of people on the ice with them, from penniless peasants to the wealthiest in the city. Rose enjoyed that aspect in addition to the prospect of skating.

The ice was peppered with people, and as Jonathan bent on one knee to tie her skates, she found it difficult to stay balanced. One skate was on and tied, and the other he still had to lace the leather. She noticed a well-dressed couple to her right, sitting on their sled. Mayhaps they had taken a ride earlier. The woman seemed disinterested in the man, or possibly upset. It was difficult to tell. Rose was more intrigued by the massive red plume erupting from the man's hat. She thought to herself that Jonathan would never wear something like that, even if he could afford it. She looked down at him as he worked so diligently. She favored the color of his doublet, that of ground mustard, and his dark-brown breeches. His dagger he had moved out of his way, to the back of his girdle. Jonathan dressed in a practical way and always looked orderly and tidy, not unlike his father.

While he finished tying the skates, she looked up to see a boy running across the ice, grasping a stick. It was not clear whether he was chasing a top, or something imaginary. In any case, he was clearly enjoying himself, and it made her wonder about children of her own, and whether God would bless her with any. Jonathan was finished now, and looked up at her with love in his boyish blue eyes.

"How do the *schaatsen* feel to you?" asked Jonathan, proudly using the Dutch word for skate, and smiling as he looked up at her.

"The skates are on well enough, and not too tight. I think we should try them," responded Rose.

As they set off on the ice together, she wished she had a muff with her, as she saw so many couples sharing. That way they could stay connected by grasping hands within the muff, enjoying the skating to the fullest in remaining linked by flesh.

To the left of them, four well-dressed men skated past in a single train, holding each other at the waist. Jonathan and Rose slowed themselves to prevent colliding, then made their way past a man dressed elegantly in a yellow suit with an enormous plume to match. Rose decided it had to be the largest plume on the entire canal, even larger than the red one she was admiring earlier.

"Jonathan, does your mother own a *huyk*?" asked Rose as she gestured to their right, in the direction of a couple holding hands. It looked as if the woman was holding the man upright as he struggled on his skates.

"She does not, although she does favor them. They are so useful in the colder months, serving as both a cloak and head covering. I have heard many women make use of it during long, cold Sabbath services, hiding their closed eyes. Goodwife Priest, of Master Robinson, his congregation, had one made by her husband, Degory. I dare not imagine her falling asleep listening to a sermon of Master Robinson, but the huyk is also useful in keeping a young child near and warm. Why do you ask? Do you favor them?"

"I do. Mayhaps I can ask Master Brewer about having one made before we leave. It is something my mother and I could share, and since there are members of the congregation in that trade, we would be offered a fair price."

"True enough," replied Jonathan as they skated on, near a young man who had fallen with his head first, and at such a speed his hat landed two feet in front.

Jonathan turned around and asked in Dutch if he needed any help. With an embarrassed look, he shook his head no, so they skated on.

"I think the game *kolf* looks interesting," commented Jonathan as he turned around and pointed to four men playing behind them, by the frozen shallop.

"Have you not played it then?" asked Rose.

"A group of men let me have a swing once, but I've never played an actual game. There is a version in which you aim the ball at a target and try to reach it with the fewest hits, and then there is the game where you see who can hit it the farthest. The time I took a swing it was the game of distance, and I hit it so imperfectly the ball flew more to the side than forward. I was completely embarrassed."

A small brown-and-white dog ran across the ice in front of them, causing them both to wobble. Just as they recovered from that, a white horse decorated in all its finery, boasting a blue-and-pink plume, came near to them on their left. The majestic beast pulled a large red sled, driven by the man who had rented them both for the afternoon. His wife and daughter, facing forward, had the better views as they glided along the canal, while the driver's mother sat opposite, enjoying the sight of her joyful grandchild the most.

"Did you see how the tail of that horse is braided? The ribbon looks to be trimmed with gold, and look how bright the red appears," commented Jonathan.

"Yes, it is a feast for the eyes, skating on this icy stage. Have a look at the group behind you, at how majestically they are dressed. I would guess the value of the silks they are wearing amount to more than most on this ice will earn in a lifetime. I am curious to see if they offer any coins to that beggar walking by."

"What a contrast it is, the beggar looking ghostly white, almost inhuman, with tattered rags for clothes, approaching some of the wealthiest souls on the canal. It reminds me of the paintings filled with candles, an hourglass, or a skull, warning how life and all things material are fleeting."

"Of course the reminders of that reality, that our time in this world is brief, and that death escapes no one are never far, are they? Those wealthy people, dressed in all their finery, will turn to dust, just as the beggar will."

"Just like what is left of that cow carcass over there," said Jonathan as he pointed past the men playing kolf. Under a large tree with branches populated by crows instead of leaves, a dog and crows shared a meal.

"Do you think you will be saved, and after this life live on in God's Kingdom?" asked Rose.

"We are of the same mind, Rose, believing that our paths are predetermined, from before birth even. Whether we are selected for eternal life, and saved by Him, this truth will not be known until the transition of this world to the next. My father teaches that we must live as God instructs through Scripture, hoping to be saved, but not expecting it."

Rose's response was interrupted by the ball from the kolf game rolling into the blade of her skate. The momentum was enough for the ball to ricochet off her skate and shoot into the freshly cut icehole of a fisherman. At first he looked annoyed, but since he was able to remove it easily, he tossed it back to the men with a grin.

"I think we might be invisible on this canal," said Rose with a laugh.

"Do you think we should skate on and try to find some panekoeken?"

"That is a most wondrous idea."

Weaving their way around the wooden sides of a frozen bridge, they aimed for a tent in the distance. It wasn't long before they were upon it, enjoying their pancakes.

"I will miss you, Jonathan, when it is time for me to go back to London."

"And I will miss you. The separation does not have to be permanent, you know. Our church continues to work on plans for removal from here. We have not given up hope."

"But your removal will not be to London. That is for certain. What are you implying? That I could join you in your venture?"

"I-I d-do not know what I am asking or saying," stammered Jonathan. He had gotten ahead of himself. He was not ready to ask Rose to marry him, but if he was removing to somewhere like the New World, he would have to.

"Let us enjoy the day and not speak of such weighty things. There is no actual plan in place for your removal, and for now, I am here in Leyden, not London," said Rose, alleviating the awkwardness.

Jonathan smiled, grateful for her words. Without adding any of his own, he took her arm gently, and the two resumed skating.

March 1619, Leyden

"Will you consider going back to London, and mayhaps aid Cushman in his efforts with the Council for Virginia?" inquired Master Brewer of his closest friend, John Carver.

Master Carver had no desire to return to London, as it was very clear the Council for Virginia was in such dissension that nothing would get accomplished.

"My good friend, I believe you really desire for me to escort Rose and Mercy to London. That is the truth, I am certain, which I well understand," responded Master Carver. "I am willing to do it chiefly because Master Cushman is going to be traveling with Master Brewster. With the authorities hunting William, I think it best Mercy be distanced from that."

"That is reason enough, is it not?" agreed Master Brewer. "The English Ambassador Carleton, who resides in The Hague, is determined to find Master Brewster and question him, if not imprison him. I've learned there is great pressure from the English government on this subject, as King James is absolutely outraged by the publication, *De*

Regime Ecclesiae Scoticanae. Not surprisingly, he has taken great personal offense, and has charged his Secretary, Robert Naunton, with apprehending the printer responsible. Carleton pursued other printers elsewhere in Holland and has concluded it is our friend, Master Brewster," said Master Brewer with a look that indicated it was true.

"I can imagine you might have concern for yourself, as the publisher. Enough said then. I will plan to depart for London by the first of May with Mercy and Rose. Is that timing acceptable?"

"The timing is excellent good, John. In the meanspace, I will make Rose aware. Considering her courtship with Jonathan, she might have some trouble with the news."

May 1619, Leyden on to London

Both Rose and Jonathan agreed that their parting should not be cause for sadness, expecting it would be but a temporary state. He promised to write her letters, and she agreed to reciprocate. When they said farewell that day, they did so with the comfort that there would be a reunification, and fairly soon.

Elizabeth was devastated when she heard her sister was to return to London. She had been gaining hope that Jonathan would ask her to marry him and Rose would stay in Leyden. Then she expected Rose would also join the congregation of Master Robinson and remove from Leyden along with the Brewster family. Elizabeth understood she and Edward would join the venture, wherever the destination might be.

The separation of father from daughter was far more tragic. Mercy had nine years to her now, but after recently losing her mother and nearly her father the previous fall, she did not want to move away from him. In truth, it was the last thing he wanted, but the levels of instability, intolerance, and violence were increasing in the city. Just days before, an older member of Master Robinson's congregation was stoned and nearly killed by boys mistaking him for an Arminian, the group likely to be ousted from the Dutch Reformed Church. Each day it seemed more prudent to remove.

At the beginning of May, not long after the departure of Master Carver, Rose, and Mercy, the Synod of Dort ended, with the Arminians declared heretics and deprived of their ministry. This was very much expected, but even so, protests and riots ensued.

The pressure to have financial backing and a plan for removal was increasing, not only due to the political and religious changes within the Netherlands, but also due to the Twelve Years' Truce expiring in less than two years. Some in the congregation, like William Bradford, had already sold their homes, or were preparing to.

Also at the beginning of May, Robert Cushman sent a letter back to Leyden, confirming the dysfunction of the Council for Virginia and noting that Master Brewster had fallen ill in London, and that he was unsure of his whereabouts. He also mentioned that news of Francis Blackwell's venture to the New World had made its way to London, describing the journey as an utter failure. The ship had reportedly lost its way, running out of fresh water before reaching land. The Master of Ship, some of the sailors, and Blackwell himself had lost their lives, leaving only fifty of one hundred eighty alive. Incredibly, merchants overall were undaunted, and thought it a chance to learn from the errors rather than abandon that means of turning a profit.

By this time, Master Carver had safely delivered Rose and Mercy to London. What a celebration there was upon their arrival, for each day that dawned Mistress Okes held hope for Rose's return. It was pleasing to have Mercy join them as well, although Mistress Okes mourned the loss of Mistress Brewer, and prayed for her cousin, Thomas, in Leyden.

Master Carver stayed as well, for a week's time. "Do you have any idea where Master Brewster might be?"

"He stopped here briefly, staying only two nights," explained Master Okes. "This was in the latter part of April. When he awoke after the second night he described feeling ill, with aches to him, insisting that he cared to go elsewhere, mayhaps north, for he feared a cough or worse might be coming on. Where he went, I know not."

"I wonder if Hugh Mercer has heard anything. Has he been by

lately? Is he still a regular source of information and able to carry letters for you?" inquired Master Carver.

Mistress Okes wondered if her daughter could hear the conversation, since she was in the back room with Mercy.

"He does. He comes by even more often now," answered Master Okes. He turned to the back room and lowered his voice. "He lost his wife after childbirth, with the child dying as well. Since then, he stays away from his home in the North, and has been in London much more."

Master Carver did not know much about Hugh Mercer, but he was aware that young Rose had been quite fond of him at one time.

Rose Okes did hear the conversation, and without realizing it, had sat down on the three-legged stool near her. She felt numb and isolated, as if she were no longer in the back room of her father's shop. How could he have not sought her out, or even left a letter, and told her this himself? How ironic, not to mention frustrating, that this professional messenger failed miserably at communication. There were so many questions she wanted answers to. Where was Hugh Mercer now? If she were to see him, what would she say, now that she and Jonathan were courting?

"Rose. Rose, please answer. Does this stitch look right to you? Rose? Why won't you answer me?" pleaded Mercy, who was getting frightened. She tugged on Rose's petticoat to get her attention.

"Oh dear, I do apologize, Mercy. I am all right. I was just lost in thought, that is all. Your stitch is perfect. Would you like me to show you a chain stitch?"

"Yes, I would like that very much," answered Mercy, beaming at the compliment. She took her poppet off the bedstead, propping her against the sewing basket. "And Sarah would like to learn too," said Mercy with satisfaction, as she smoothed the poppet's petticoat.

July 1619, Leyden

In the midst of July, another edict was passed by the States General that was cause for concern. The law was aimed at stifling the regrouping of Arminian congregations, the faction just overthrown. It prohibited separate religious meetings, as well as money collections, contracts, or agreements made in such gatherings. It was unclear how this might impact Master Robinson's congregation, but for certain there was fear amongst the members that they would be suppressed.

Back in London, all was quiet with the effort to secure investors and a patent that would define their removal to the New World. Master Carver tended to some of his personal business dealings and departed for Leyden. He would have desired to return to his congregation with better news, as it was clear the number of reasons were increasing to remove. His good friend, Master Brewster, was being sought after for his involvement in printing certain publications. Now the English government was considering him the printer of a highly inflammatory work entitled *The Perth Assembly*. There were other titles that the ambassador possessed more certainty in their connection to Master Brewster, such as *De Vera Religione*, a first-time publication printed in the past year. The latest works printed by Masters Brewster and Brewer were never before printed and strong in their views for reform. Some were extreme, penned by authors separated from the English Church.

There was no question that the printing activities conceived of by Masters Brewer and Brewster had caught the attention of King James himself. The English officials were under great pressure to locate Master Brewster, and as of July, he was not to be found. Ambassador Carleton went so far as to make a trip to Leyden to track him down personally, without success.

September 1619, Leyden

"I fear I have little time," warned Master Brewster as he entered the house abruptly, labored in his breathing.

Love and Wrestling looked at one another with confused and frightened faces. Their father had been away much of the year, and shortly after his return from England, he was detained in Leyden's city prison cell.

Mary was relieved to see her husband but realized it would be only temporary.

"I prayed many times a day for your release, and readied a trunk in case you had to depart again in haste. How is it that you were set free?"

"Let us say there was some confusion regarding my identity, mayhaps that our friend Jan Orlers created, allowing me to slip away. He suggested I consider going east to the next village, called Leiderdorp, where Leyden jurisdiction cannot reach. At least it is closer than London," said Master Brewster with a sigh.

"As you think best, Husband. Whatever it must be so that you are not imprisoned, or worse. I will manage here, with the children. Master Robinson and the others will come to my aid if necessary. I will wait then to hear from you by letter or passing word. Does the same hold true for Master Brewer? Has he been released as well?"

"He has not. As he is a student of the University, there is a different protocol in these cases. He has additional legal privileges, and certainly cannot be forced to go as a prisoner to England. I am not so worried about Master Brewer, as he has the skill to manage his affairs."

"You had best be off then. It should be better to go in the cover of the night. Do you want Jonathan to accompany you?"

"I think not. It is better if I am alone in case trouble finds me. Children, come. Come together so we can gather in prayer."

Patience and Fear joined them, with Love and Wrestling drawing closer. Jonathan was at the home of Master Carver.

The family stood in a circle, with their eyes and palms facing upwards.

"Lord, guide us as you do, and in my absence keep my family in your protection. We, as always, follow your path, and do so with unfeigned faith and love. Amen."

He turned and embraced Mary, and then each child.

"You will be in my thoughts each and every day I am without you. Follow the direction of your mother, as she carries out His plan, as I would if I were here. It may be months, mayhaps even next year before we see one another again."

The younger boys gasped in disbelief.

Their father continued, "It is better we meet in time, rather than I be shackled in prison, or worse, even, that we never meet again. I love you all and will see you before long. Have faith, and may God keep you well."

And with that, he vanished from his home, making his way east to the little village of Leiderdorp.

November 1619, Leyden

"I promised that you would not find a press," said Master Brewer, shaking his head.

Even so, all of the type, ornaments, and papers taken from the garret of Master Brewster served as evidence. Two University professors had been appointed to examine the texts, one of the two being Professor Polyander, a close friend of Master Robinson. He would have been quite familiar with one of the books, the one he had written the introduction for.

King James was furious, and his secretary and ambassador needed Thomas Brewer to answer his questions. Although the Dutch officials did not care to offend the King of England, they would not abandon their own rules, and offered that Master Brewer go for questioning only if the expenses on both ends of the trip were paid by the English Crown. The other requirement was that Master Brewer not be treated like a prisoner or bothered as such, and returned to Leyden once the questioning was complete.

At the end of November, Thomas Brewer and an escort ventured south to Rotterdam, accompanied by Master Robinson and three others from the congregation. From there, Thomas and his official companion made their way to England, after visiting some friends in Vlissingen, eventually arriving in London in December. King James had the man he wanted, and the questioning ensued.

December 1619, London

Hugh Mercer had tried so many times to gather his courage and face Rose, but failed. He had gone back to waiting in the ordinary across the street, to watch her come and go. Fearing rejection above all, he wasted so many chances to speak to her that it was sinful.

Robert Okes had told him about Jonathan Brewster, and how by the time he and his mother had left Leyden, Rose and Jonathan were considered a courting couple. Robert reported this casually, as if he did not know of the past between his sister and the carrier of the King's Post. He wanted his sister to be happy and treated properly, and was hoping this news would encourage Hugh Mercer to move on and away from Rose.

When he heard the stories from Robert, he winced as if being struck by an object. It hurt him so deeply to think of her with someone else, loving another. He knew he had only himself to blame. Look how he had hurt her by marrying another woman. What was worse were all the times he vanished, creating enormous gaps in time between their meetings. He realized Rose might not know of his wife's passing, and regretted not telling her as soon as she returned to London. As he sat there, in agony, plagued by his poor decisions, he prayed to be granted another chance with her.

For the past three months, he had chosen to do something completely against post carrier etiquette. Not only did he open the letters and read them, but he burned them after.

"I cannot believe I am capable of this," uttered Hugh Mercer to himself as he set the paper on fire. It was not simply paper, either. A letter written by Jonathan Brewster to Rose Okes, likely the fourth or fifth that reached the flames instead of her. It was even worse than that. The letters being sent from her over to Jonathan in Leyden were also intercepted, read, and destroyed.

He decided the next letters he would not read, but throw directly into the fire. At least they were getting fewer, likely the decrease in frequency a result of the discouragement of receiving nothing in return.

If he was not riding for the King's Post, Hugh Mercer found himself at inns and ordinaries, drinking away most of the coin he earned.

"I do not understand it, Hugh," said John, one of the other carriers. "Why do you not speak to her? If it is as you say, that what you have is something special, would she not want to see you?"

"Aye, but now I have done some terrible things that I think cannot be forgiven."

He could not reveal his reading and burning of the letters, for fear that John might impart the information to others in the Post. Something like that could end his life's work.

"We repent to the Lord often, and He forgives. We all make errors. If she loves you, she will understand, and she will forgive you. That is what love is."

There was truth in that, to be certain. If ever he was going to have a chance with Rose again, he had to see her and reveal his feelings, and tell her of the fate of the letters. But not yet. He was not ready. He finished his cup of beer and returned to his horse, then rode fast and far up the Great North Road.

PAINTING BY ADAM WILLAERTS, DATED 1620, POSSIBLY REPRESENTING THE PILGRIMS' DEPARTURE
FROM DELFSHAVEN. ROSE-MARIE AND EIJK DE MOL VAN OTTERLOO COLLECTION.
PHOTOGRAPH COURTESY OF HABOLDT & CO., AMSTERDAM

The majority of Robinson's congregation stayed behind in Leyden, including Pastor Robinson himself. It was discussed and decided that wherever the majority of the group resided was where Robinson would remain. Brewster, as the Ruling Elder, was expected to provide spiritual leadership in the New World, until Robinson and the others could join them. Many traveled to Delfshaven to bid farewell to their fellow congregation members, family and friends, knowing that for most, it would be their last time together. The Speedwell, *one-third the size of the cargo ship* Mayflower, *was hired to remain in the New World, for the purpose of fishing and trading along the coast.*

Chapter Eighteen

1620

January 1620, London

Katherine was steadfast in her belief that the letters had been written and sent but never delivered.

"Rose, I met Jonathan, and know his family. There is no question that he carried out his promise of writing letters to you. Do you not think it odd that your father still receives letters from Leyden, but there are none for you?

We know that Hugh Mercer is now without a wife, but he makes himself scarce. He has taken up his old ways of delivering letters only to The Black Bear, avoiding here altogether."

"What are you saying? That he is intercepting the letters? Do you think he would do such a thing?"

"Love is strange, Rose. And so people do strange things. If Hugh Mercer no longer had feelings for you, he would stop in at the sign of The Rose. But instead, he has vanished. He was here often when you were in Leyden. It is clear to me this has everything to do with Hugh Mercer."

Rose was not certain how she felt about this. Part of her was angry, and part of her could understand those actions. She decided that since it was likely Hugh would continue avoiding her, she would write a letter to him and bring it to The Black Bear, leaving it with apprentice Driver.

The letter was not hostile in sentiment, or accusatory even, but stated a request to meet. She asked him directly to stop into the sign of The Rose during his next trip to London.

She waited, and waited still longer, and when nearly a month had passed, she gave up hope of receiving a visit or any response at all.

"Good day, Rose," said a voice behind her.

She had just left the sign of The Rose to visit the baker, and there he stood. It was almost as if he was waiting and watching for her to leave the shop. Knowing Hugh Mercer, he had been across the street at the ordinary.

Recognizing it was him before she turned to look, she closed her eyes and took a deep breath, bracing herself. This would take all of her courage, and to complicate things, she was uncertain how she would feel upon seeing him.

When she faced him, he said nothing. He stood there, uttering not a sound, but with tears in his eyes.

"I burned them, Rose. I read the letters and then destroyed them."

"Both his to me and mine in return?"

"Yes, all of them. I am so sorry. I know what you are likely thinking. That if I truly loved you, I would want you to be happy. That I am a monster for committing such a weak and disgraceful act. That I should have come to you, as soon as you returned from Leyden and told you my child and wife had died. I should have, and I will likely regret that for the rest of my days. I am no monster, and I do love you. But I was weak, and I lacked the courage to face you for fear you loved another. I was so overcome with the thought of your rejection, I took leave of my senses."

She said nothing for the longest time. He thought she might remain silent and walk away for the last time. She chose not to walk away, but still, she said nothing.

Then he saw the tears in her eyes, and finally, she spoke. "I can tell you, Hugh Mercer, that I am surprised. Surprised that when I laid eyes on you moments ago, that I felt something other than anger, or nothing at all. I often wondered what I would feel if I did see you again. Mayhaps it is the love of God inside me that can take anger and pain and turn it into something good, because when I look at you, I know there is still love for you."

He started to respond, but she interrupted.

"I expect I will love you in some way until the life has gone out of me, but I struggle to understand your fear of me. I know you call it a threat of rejection, but how did you think we would have a chance together if you disappeared?"

"I learned that you were together with Jonathan Brewster, formally courting. All I could expect was rejection. As I am sure you were told by now, I lost another child, and my wife shortly after. I haven't been right in the mind for months. Regardless, there is no excuse for taking your letters and burning them."

"I think you mentioned you read them also?"

"I did."

"I cannot understand how I love such a coward. You could have brought me the letters and talked to me. Told me your wife was gone and that you were free to be with me. Regarding Jonathan, you read the letters. You know that we have grown to love one another. I think it is possible to love more than one person in this life. My feelings for Jonathan were built upon, beginning many years ago in Scrooby and developing over the months in Leyden. It took time and trust, and it was safe. He was there, and he did not run away."

"He was there because he could be there. As a post carrier I am required to be away, and once I had married Sarah, there was no chance for us."

"Right, because you married Sarah. I did not choose to fall in love with you, Hugh Mercer, but you chose to marry her, and we are now standing here talking only because she is in God's hands. There is a man in Leyden who must think I have turned on him, not responding to his letters as I promised."

"Why are you talking to me then?"

Rose was quiet. "I am talking to you because I deserve to know some things. I am tired of being left to wait and wonder, and then either see you by happenstance or write a letter begging you to communicate with me. If you loved me, you would want to take care of me, no matter what the risk to yourself. And regarding Jonathan, I do love him, but he is in Leyden and looking to remove elsewhere. If I stay committed to him, he will expect me to follow, as any good woman would do. What concerns me is that if I loved him like a wife should, would I not follow him earnestly to the ends of the Earth, no matter where that might be?

While visiting Leyden, whenever the subject of removal would arise, it would trouble me, as I cannot fathom venturing to the New World. I cannot even imagine the perils of the crossing itself. I have heard stories of murderous savages and disease, and to me it sounds like traveling to the pits of hell."

"So are you saying you would not go if he asks you?"

"No, I am saying that at this time, it is not a comfortable thought, but not an impossibility either. I believe firmly that our paths are set, no matter what we want or think. God has His plan, and He will reveal it."

"So what shall we do going forward, between us?"

"As a start, you will take this letter through its channels, without opening it or burning it. That will be a step in earning trust. You can also stop in as you normally would. I am not asking you to come and visit me each time you are in London or exchange letters, but carry on in a regular way as opposed to hiding."

"Fair enough," said Hugh Mercer, relieved she was allowing him any place in her life.

They parted ways with no further words, and for the first time, Rose left his company feeling well enough.

February 1620, Leyden

With the Council for Virginia floundering and failing to deliver any sort of proposal for removal, Master Robinson's group was willing to listen to any reasonable plan. A very compelling opportunity arose on the second of February, coming from Dutch merchants of the New Netherlands Company. After speaking at length with Master Robinson, who promised that more than four hundred English families from England and Leyden would be willing to settle in New Netherland under this agreement, the Company approached the States General proposing the following venture. They presented the opportunity to their government as stated here.

"Now it is the case that a certain English minister is living at Leyden, well versed in the Dutch language, however, who would be well inclined to move his residence there, assuring the applicants that he knows a means to obtain more than four hundred families both from these lands and from England, if they would be protected and preserved in those same lands from all violence from other potentates, but the authority and under the protection of your Princely Excellency and their High Mightiness the Lords States General, to plant there the true, pure Christian religion, and to instruct the wild Indians of those same lands in the true teaching and to bring them to belief in Christ."

The Dutch investors felt the pressure to move quickly, believing King James intended to settle at the mouth of the Hudson himself, a place where the Dutch had a fishing settlement since 1609. With the proposal they requested for their protection a Dutch warship be stationed there.

April 1620, Leyden

After more than two months and consultation with Prince Maurits, the States General determined the acceptance of this venture would be a breach of the Twelve Years' Truce, which was still in effect. They wanted not to offend Spain, France, or England.

With that plan dashed, God brought before them yet another opportunity. This time, an English businessman named Thomas Weston turned up in Leyden, having ties to merchant Edward Pickering of Master Robinson's congregation. Weston came promising financial support and the means to provide transport to the New World. He spoke with Master Robinson at length, assuring him of his commitment and support from many contacts in London. In their discussions, specific terms were drawn up regarding the cost of investment, the duration of the venture, and what would be owed and gained by whom at the end of seven years. At the same time came word of a plentiful fishing territory in the more northern part of the Virginia territory, called New England. This area was known to be rich with fish, and a place that could yield substantial profit.

The prospect seemed hopeful, and the plans progressed. The development of the venture was not without its confusion, as some investors waffled and pulled out, preferring Guyana to the New World. Others desired to place their money in the more southern parts of Virginia. Fortunately, some additional support did come from Amsterdam, from an Ancient Brethren member named John Beauchamp.

With this plan appearing likely to proceed, some of the Leyden congregation sold their houses, with no intention of changing their direction. They were relying on their agents, Masters Carver and Cushman, now in London confirming conditions and receiving the money for provisions.

With word that plans were being put forth to leave for Virginia, Master Brewster quietly returned from Leiderdorp before leaving Leyden again, this time for London. The stop was exceedingly brief, but time enough to put his business in order and speak with his family about the next steps.

"Jonathan will lead you from here when it is time. I have spoken already to Master van Thorenvliet about the rent, and he is allowing me to pay the amount owed through July. If you are not departed by then, I fear failure will be our only course, going so late into that country. You will have direction also from Master Robinson, should you require it. I expect the boys to travel well enough, and Fear and Patience, well, they have gone through the other moves and proved strong."

"Of course, Husband. We will manage here, and hope the same for you in London. Where will you stay?"

"My idea at the moment is to stay with Master Okes, but only if he is truly agreeable. There is inherent conflict in my presence there, seeing as the English government would take me for questioning on account of some of the works I printed here, and Master Okes being a member of the Stationers' Company. I know it concerns him, to be connected to this."

"I trust you can judge such things and will move elsewhere if necessary. Do you know the whereabouts of Master Carver or Master Cushman?"

"I know not, but it should not take me long to know their location. Master Okes has many good sources of information, such as Hugh Mercer, and others."

"At least when I see you next we will stay together, in our journey to the New World. No matter what happens, we will be in each other's company for whatever God has in store."

"It is true. This last year has tested my strength in being away, and in hiding no less. I am grateful for the prospect of having us all together again, regardless of the place. Lest I forget, please handle the packing of as many of my books as is possible in the journey. I think for us the cost will be in getting them to Delfshaven, and from there and beyond, the passage should be part of the venture. I will take one chest with me now, and whatever books you and Jonathan deem less necessary to bring, please sell or give those to Master Robinson."

"Of course, William, and if I require advice on what is most important, I can ask Master Robinson. I will not disappoint you with my decisions."

"I would think not. Now, I should be away. I suspect the girls are with Mistress Carver presently."

Mistress Brewster nodded.

"It is good of them to provide her company in Master Carver's absence. He has been away overmuch the last year, like me."

"Yes, and Jonathan is tending to some business with the ribbon, getting ready to send a larger shipment back to England."

What that meant was books published by Masters Brewster and Brewer would be hidden within those barrels.

"I see. Excellent good, then. I believe I have everything I need. I will seek out someone to bring these chests to the canal. There should be a boat leaving within the hour traveling southward. Stay strong, Mary, and have faith the Lord will guide you. And remember, this is just the beginning. Now we are relatively safe here in Leyden. Should we go as planned, before long we will be facing angry seas and dangers unknown.

Take comfort in the Lord and His plan. I shall see you in Southampton. God by you, my love."

May 1620, London

It was the purest irony, that Hugh Mercer was charged with delivering letters to Rose written by Jonathan Brewster. The post carrier needed to atone for his transgressions, and he knew that if there was any chance for a future with Rose, he must follow through on his promises. In a strange twist, it allowed him the time to see her and visit.

"Here you are, Rose. As promised, I have delivered your letter unread and intact."

"Very good, Hugh Mercer. You have done your job well," jested Rose.

She read the letter with careful attention, knowing from Master Brewster, who had been in hiding in the Okeses' home for the last weeks, that Merchant Adventurers in London led by Thomas Weston were funding the venture. She was eager to read on, and learn whether Jonathan was going to ask her to marry him and join him in the voyage. As she read, her eyes saw the words she had been dreading. He was asking her to join him in the voyage, but there was no mention of betrothal. This was confusing to her. How could he expect her to get on a ship and spend days if not months in dank terror, without commitment? It was nearly insulting.

Hugh Mercer waited for Rose to finish reading. It was quite awkward, knowing that the woman you loved was reading a letter from a man who loved her. It hurt further, knowing she had strong feelings for Jonathan as well. He had no choice but to be patient and wait.

He glanced over at Rose and sensed some agitation. She said nothing, but stood up abruptly and went over to the hearth to stir a pottage of cabbage. Peppercorns waited in the mortar to be pounded, and Rose did just that. She ground them finer than necessary, striking the iron mortar so intensely that Hugh was forced to cover his ears. Then with the pestle she pushed mountains of pepper into the pot, oblivious to the quantity she was adding.

Certainly, she cared for Jonathan, but she trembled at the thought of boarding a ship destined for the New World. She feared storms and pirates, not to mention the stories of brutal savages on the other side. All of this, and Jonathan could not bear to pen the word betrothal, wife, or marriage?

"Hugh, would you like to walk to the Tower Bridge?" asked Rose, already knowing the answer.

The two departed the sign of The Rose as if they were a couple. In Hugh Mercer's mind he would remain patient, keeping his jealousy contained. In time, Rose would be his, as it should be. For Hugh Mercer, he could only pray that was in God's plan.

June 1620

There were many putting ink to paper in the first days of June. Robert Cushman was caught in the middle, with the Weston Adventurers demanding changes to the terms drawn up earlier in Leyden. Cushman had little negotiating power, with the investors threatening abandonment should the changes not be accepted. Master Cushman knew of many in Leyden who had sold their homes, readying their estates for removal. The prospect of immediate hardships outweighed the potential long-term ill effects of the alterations. In his mind, there was no chance to ignore the requests. Master Carver was in Southampton already and not present to impart his views.

The decision to acquiesce catalyzed a terrible reaction from Master Robinson and others in Leyden, and Master Carver in Southampton. Not a soul could understand the reasoning behind agreeing to such changes. That decision brought much frustration and discontent. Those things being altered that were deemed most significant to those aiming to settle were first, that after seven years, all profits, land, and dwellings built would all be divided amongst the adventurers and the planters. Originally, the terms indicated those settling would retain the land and homes built. The other deviance from the original plan was that no longer would those settling have two days to work for their own gain. They would keep the Sabbath, but all other days they would toil jointly for themselves and the good of the company.

Letters rifled over the North Sea, being sent from Master Cushman to Leyden, and from the leading men at Leyden to Cushman, the letters likely crossing paths over the water. Master Robinson at the same time sent word in early June to Master Carver, and within the borders of England, Cushman wrote still another letter to his fellow agent Master Carver.

Those letters coming from Master Cushman held a common theme, in that he had no choice but to agree to the changes, or else the Merchant Adventurers, including Thomas Weston, would rescind their investments and obligation in the matter. Furthermore, Cushman explained his efforts were constant and diligent, and that those in Leyden who had chosen him as their agent, now peppered him unfairly with doubt and accusations of negligence.

There was tension and confusion regarding the path forward. Ships had not yet been hired for the crossing, and money for provisions was in multiple hands. Master Carver stayed in Southampton, as did Christopher Martin, one of the men coming directly from England, as well as Master Cushman, now in Kent. The adventurers feared money would be wasted with the lack of coordination of purchasing.

In Leyden, the request to hire a ship there was met with confusion. They did not have the funds to do so, so ultimately, the ship was hired in England and sent across to the port of Delfshaven, just south of Leyden. A ship of sixty tons, she was called the *Speedwell,* and sailed over to Delfshaven under command of Master Reynoldes. A fine ship, she was intended to stay in the New World for fishing, for the northern part of the Virginia territory was said to be overrun with fish. All that was needed to be done by those in Leyden was to procure the salt and nets. Spirits were lifted with the arrival of the *Speedwell,* although disdain for the alteration to the terms remained.

At the home of Master Okes, Master Brewster sat in the back room, sorting through and unfolding the unbound pages that were hidden in his son's ribbon shipment from Leyden. The merchant channels forged by Masters Brewer and Carver were invaluable, as were certain customs agents. Master Brewster worked quickly to organize the pages and ready them to be sent to a binder. He wanted to get this evidence out of the shop of Master Okes before agents of the Stationers' Company made any unannounced inspections. Master Okes put a great value on his longtime friendship with Master Brewster, as did Master Brewster, and he cared not to abuse it. He understood and respected Master Okes's apprehension in being connected with works that were illegal in both content and place of origin.

With the shipment there was another letter from Jonathan Brewster to Rose. Master Brewster sought her out, knowing she would be pleased to receive it. He entered the main room, but she was not there. He found Katherine by the hearth, adjusting the pot to a lower place on the trammel.

"Pray pardon, do you know where I might find Rose?"

"Good day, Master Brewster. I believe she went to deliver some books to The Black Bear. She should be returning any time."

The door opened as Katherine finished speaking, with Rose and Hugh Mercer entering together.

"Good day, Master Brewster," greeted the couple.

To be certain, it was a bit awkward, but Master Brewster was not one to speculate or judge.

"Are there any letters for me?" asked Hugh. "I ran into Rose at The Black Bear, and thought it best to escort her back and see if there was any correspondence to retrieve. Do you have anything for me, Master Brewster?"

"Thank you, Goodman Mercer. I do have a letter for my son, and one for Master Robinson. Before I fetch them, lest I forget, this letter is for you, Rose, from Jonathan. I will retrieve the letters, and I nearly forgot— there is a package as well for you, Rose." He handed her the letter as his eyes fell on Hugh Mercer.

Rose felt a bit uncomfortable, but in truth, she was running an errand to The Black Bear when she met Hugh Mercer. Whether he was waiting there, hoping she would stop in, was not her doing.

Master Brewster offered Rose the package and handed over his letters destined for Leyden to Goodman Mercer, thanking the post carrier for his efforts.

"No trouble at all, Master Brewster. Anything I can do to aid Master Okes and his family, I will do, at all costs."

As he said this, he glanced quickly in Rose's direction. The meaning was not lost on Master Brewster.

"I do understand. That is very good of you. We all do what we think best and right, and God decides. Thank you again, Goodman Mercer. I must return to my work in the back room. Safe travels to you, and God by you."

"And God by you, Master Brewster," said Hugh while removing his hat and bowing.

Rose curtsied at the same time, but said nothing.

She clutched the letter written by Jonathan, not knowing if she should read it immediately, or wait for a private moment. She decided instead to open the packaged item, which was covered in oilcloth. Methodically, she removed Jonathan's wax seal and untied the knots also covered in wax. Next was the oilcloth, followed by the clean sacking beneath, all of which she opened carefully, caring not to damage the contents. Reaching inside, feeling before looking, her fingers brushed against the soft wool, telling her it was likely something for her to wear.

As she freed the huyk from its packaging, the folded pleats fell open, allowing Rose to admire the richly dyed black garment. Jonathan had remembered from the day they went skating that she desired a huyk, one that she intended to share with her mother. The beautiful black head covering was typically Dutch, and would be a unique sight as she walked the London streets. So pleasing it was to her she cared to seek out her mother and Katherine straight away, but then she noticed the tormented look on Hugh Mercer's face.

He looked at her but offered no words. She realized he cared not about the huyk, but was curious about the contents of the letter. Each day, he dreaded a letter that would reach London for Rose, requesting her commitment for marriage, which would equate to removal to the New World. Not only would he lose her as his wife, but he would likely never see her again.

"Rose, before you read that letter, I need to tell you... and ask you something." He was suddenly trembling, but strong in his conviction.

"I love you more than words can convey. I am happy when I am with you and lost in your absence. I come to life in your presence, and am the person I want to be when we are together. When we connected years ago, it was not the time for us to be together, at least not as a married couple. God's plan took me north, back to Sarah. But God keep her, she is gone, and now I am here before you, asking for you to become one with me, to be my wife."

He stepped forward, and the couple embraced, for regardless of her answer to the question of betrothal, she would never reject him as a friend. She felt connected to Hugh Mercer at her core, and expected that would never change.

"Hugh, I believe all those beautiful words you just spoke. I feel them for you as well. When you are not here in London, I miss you so terribly, my heart aches. It is as if I am lacking something, like I am being pulled apart. I have felt this way for years, and for years, I have been trying to overcome it. You did marry another, which absolutely destroyed me. You waited to tell me of that truth, and then once I had returned to London, you did not seek me out but instead stole my letters, read their words, and added them to the fire. You can see, then, why I have some trepidation in turning my back on Jonathan, to be with you."

He winced at the words, but on some level, they were no surprise. He could only hope that he had more time, and that the letter she held did not ask the same question, of betrothal.

"Will you read the letter then, and at least tell me if he offers you the same commitment?"

She nodded as she peeled back the wax seal. As she unfolded the pages, she walked towards the hearth, her back to Hugh Mercer. Her eyes absorbed the ink rapidly as she read in silence.

Letter from Jonathan Brewster to Rose Okes
June 12, 1620

To my sweetest Rose,

In spite of some difficulties in the details of the plans to remove, we are readying for departure out of Leyden. I am not certain of the number that will be going from the congregation of Master Robinson, but my family in its entirety will go, as will Master Allerton and his family, Goodman and Goodwife Bradford, Mistress Carver, and sundry others. Some, like Goodman Bradford, will leave their young children behind and send for them accordingly.

I should think there will be at least sixty of us going on the first crossing, with others to follow once we have planted with success. Of course, our pastor, Master Robinson, promises to join us in time, with the others. For now he must stay with the majority of the group, and my father will serve in guiding those who remove, and leading the services on the Sabbath.

There will be two ships crossing together. The smaller of the two ships, called the *Speedwell*, will take us from the Netherlands, leaving out of Delfshaven. The plan as I understand it, will be to meet the larger ship, I believe her name to be *Mayflower*, at Southampton. The *Mayflower* will start out of London and make her way down to meet us, and this should be happening as early as next month.

So, my love, what I would like to ask of you, is to be very careful when you seek out the ship, as I am told there are a number of ships called *Mayflower*. You are looking for the *Mayflower* with a Master of Ship named Christopher Jones.

I only wish I could see your beautiful green eyes at this moment. How they are probably wider than ever at the realization that, yes, I am asking you to journey with me in this life, as my wife.

If you are like me now, you have a smile so wide that it fills your face. Rose, I do want to be with you, now and always. I can only pray that you want the same. Regarding our congregation, it will be my father leading the church in the New World, and you will be able to join our community, but only if you find it in your heart. That is not something anyone can choose for you. But you can choose me, and whether you will join me in this venture.

You can attempt to send a written response, but it might not find its way to me before I leave Leyden. I can accept waiting until I reach Southampton, but in truth, I will hold my breath, not knowing whether you will be there waiting to join me.

We both understand that whatever happens, we follow God, His Providence, and must accept that as truth. In the meanspace, know that my heart aches for you, and that I miss you deeply. Even if you decide not to marry me, mayhaps you can travel to Southampton still, to bid me farewell.

One last point, before I close. Some of the men in the congregation have mentioned your brother, Robert, and wondered if he would have interest in joining our group. I realize he has recently begun his apprenticeship in masonry, but if you can pass along to him to consider venturing to the New World, where his skills could build shelter and protection, I would be indebted. I know Robert would have stayed in Leyden if your mother had allowed it, so let it be known to him that we were asking for him. You can also convey to him that since he has seventeen years to him, he would be granted a full share, worth ten pounds sterling. You would also have a share, giving us two shares as a married couple. The expectation is that after seven years, these shares will equate to land ownership. Your sister and Edward will for certain be aboard the *Speedwell,* as we put in to Southampton.

I fear I have written more than necessary, and will close here. Please ask my father about a package I sent, for in that, there is something special for you. I hope to see you in less than a month's time. May God keep you well and strong.

In faith and love, yours always,

Jonathan

Leyden, June 12
Anno: 1620

While Rose read the letter, Hugh Mercer paced by the front window. The irony of that action, one that Rose normally undertook, in waiting and thinking about him, was not lost on her. The smallest part of her enjoyed his suffering, for all the hours he made her wait.

"Is it what I am fearing then, that he wants you to be his wife and join him in crossing the Atlantic to the New World?"

"Just so. It is what you feared from the start, and why you burned the letters."

Silence dominated the room, and again, part of Rose enjoyed his agony. But she loved him and would spare him additional suffering.

"I do not know, Hugh, what to do. There is a piece of me that believes I should choose nothing, not you or him. That I should find my own way for some time. I have to be honest– the idea of crossing the sea does not appeal to me in the least. But I do love Jonathan. And that I love you should come as no surprise. If you expect me to have a decision for you at this moment, I do not. I play no games, I assure you. This is something I must think on, and I will seek counsel from Katherine and my mother. Most importantly, I will pray, asking the Lord to reveal His plan."

He sat now on the bench, with his head in his hands. He was in absolute misery. He would have given anything to have an answer at that moment, even taken a knife in the gut. He tortured himself with memories of all the things he did wrong, all the days he spent in the ordinary, waiting for Rose to leave so he could deliver letters in her absence. He wished he could have turned back the hands of time. He did not deserve her, and as he replayed the history, he was ready to plunge himself into the Thames.

"Hugh, I know you are desperate to know my decision, but I am truthful in saying I know not the direction I will take. Take your leave and get some rest. There is nothing you can do. There is nothing anyone can do."

He had no choice but to leave. To demand to stay would be foolish. He felt numb and sick all at once. He stood and went to the main door.

"I will be back on the morrow, and the next day, until you make your choice. If I receive an assignment that takes me away from London, then I will race back to you at my first chance."

"All right. Then try to rest, and I will see you on the morrow. Take comfort in knowing that God will guide us."

He walked over to her with tears escaping his eyes. He had given up on hiding his vulnerability. The idea of her committing to another while he was free to be with her brought with it excruciating pain. He took her in his arms and held her close, content to feel her sink into him.

They heard steps on the floorboards and released their hold.

"I will be going now, Rose. Until the morrow, then. Sleep well, my love. I will be praying for us tonight. I do love you, Rose. I have always, and always will."

She said nothing but walked back towards him, kissing him gently on the cheek. That reassurance had to be enough, leaving him no option but to return the next day.

July 1620, London

Master Okes paced in front of the hearth, his steps filled with frustration. He ran his fingers through his hair repeatedly, muttering things to himself. His wife watched him with concern. She knew that her husband had kept many things to himself over the years. He stayed committed to the Stationers' Company, while some of his family and friends who separated from the Church of England made choices that endangered his livelihood. He had done his best to maintain a balance between his own desire for reform of the church and upholding the rules of the Stationers' Company.

Nicholas had certainly done things over the years that the Company could have fined him for, or worse. He thought of the type he had sent over with Master Carver, which was used first by Giles Thorp in Amsterdam and then by Masters Brewer and Brewster to publish works against the bishops. The type had since been confiscated in Leyden, and

Master Brewer himself brought to London for questioning. Currently, Nicholas was allowing Master Brewster a place of hiding, with unbound pages of prohibited books delivered to his secret guest in the back room.

In addition, his daughter Elizabeth had married Edward Winslow, joined Master Robinson's congregation, and was part of the small company removing from Leyden to the New World. His daughter Rose was considering a union with Jonathan Brewster, which would mean she, too, would cross the Atlantic.

"My limits have been reached. For years, I have allowed our family and friends to operate as they desired and thought necessary for their faith. Straining my moral boundaries, I kept quiet, suffering my discontent with many decisions. With our children, at least we expected to have Rose and Robert here in London."

Printer Okes turned around to face his wife, startling her with a reddened face filled with rage. Without realizing it, she backed up a step.

"And now, I am so angry I can hardly speak when you tell me that Robert is considering joining this venture to the New World. I realize he is ambitious and brave, and I am certain he could aid in building, but this voyage would be taking all of our children. You have read the stories of the attempts of others. At best, you can expect only half to survive, especially if you are part of the first group. They will arrive to an unknown place, not knowing who or what they will encounter, and for certain have no shelter save for the ship. Already, it is July, and the group from Leyden has yet to arrive and meet the others. Only God knows when they will actually depart on the crossing. I fear it is late in the year, and their chances increased to meet with terrible storms and a cold season on the other side."

He had calmed a bit as he spoke, and Mistress Okes approached him, putting her arms around him. As the two embraced, Nicholas rested his chin on his wife's shoulder, then buried his face in her sage-colored linen waistcoat.

"I just never thought it would come to this, Rose. It is possible that all three of our children will leave us, and to be honest, I have no intention of following them. The prospect of acres of land does not interest me. We will remain here in London, and I will continue printing as long as God gives me the strength to do so. I held on to the dream that Robert and I would build a home of stone someday, but that vision appears shattered. Rose, I will tell you the Lord has blessed us in our marriage, and I am grateful for our love and your loyalty as my wife, the constant over these years."

"Nicholas, I will always be by your side, and I also recognize the strength of our union. As far as our children joining this risky venture, I am in agreement with you. Elizabeth is surely to be on one ship. Mayhaps there is a way to keep Rose and Robert in London. With Rose, I care not to intervene in her decision to marry Jonathan. I know that she herself is uncertain, as she speaks of her deep feelings that linger for Hugh Mercer. There are certainly complications with both men, for different reasons. As far as Robert is concerned, he has only seven and ten years to him, and we could forbid him from going."

"I have thought that as well, that we could stop him from going due to his age, and that he is in the midst of his apprenticeship. As parents, we have never had to intervene like this. In reality, even with our rejection, he could still leave."

"True, but I believe if Robert understands our concerns, he might reconsider. It was difficult enough to have Elizabeth leave to marry Edward in Leyden, but at least Leyden is a civilized place. To have all of our children on these ships, I agree, the thought is unbearable. We could lose them all. We must do something– at the very least prevent Robert from joining. Rose will have to decide herself, and mayhaps she will choose neither man. That would probably be the most prudent path."

He hadn't meant to hear their words, and the conversation had progressed too far for him to reveal himself. Apprentice Andrewe Driver had been working in the back room setting type when he caught the words of the discussion. He had great respect for Printer Okes and knew that in many cases, the choices of others caused his Master great turmoil and risk within the Stationers' Company. This man he admired had endured enough, and it angered him that now he might lose all of his children in this one venture. He resumed his work, pondering ways to extricate his Master from this mess.

July 1620, Leyden

Those electing to partake in the merchant venture packed the most necessary items, certainly near unto their entire wardrobe, linens, and bedding. The plantation would not be producing their own cloth or making clothes, shoes, or hats, so those items would be most valuable. Things like Turkey carpets, cups and dishes made of pottery, brass kettles and iron pots– all of those things had to make the journey. There was some talk of a blacksmith joining the group in London, but he would be used for repairing things and making nails, as opposed to making an abundance of new items.

Mistress Brewster prepared to pack the brass bed warmer, iron tongs, mortar and pestle, and roasting skewers. After a visit to the apothecary, Fear and Patience busied themselves packing dried seeds of various herbs, such as lovage, calendula, sage, thyme, and fennel. They took also seeds of spinach, endive, peas, and cowcumber. There were many more herbs to take, some being seeds of root herbs like turnip and skirrets, which they stowed in canvas sacks.

"Girls, be sure to take seeds of southernwood and wormwood. You know those are necessary for ridding pests, and worms in the belly in the case of wormwood. It is uncertain what we will find in the way of herbs in the new place."

Each family brought along what they favored most, and also those things necessary for balancing the humours. A person prone to melancholy might take with them the seeds of pot marigold and borrage, whereas, if phlegmatic, one would want hot and dry things, such as pepper, sage, mustard, and radish. If choleric in nature, then the seeds of cold things like cowcumber, salad, and lettuces should be brought. Those that were sanguine would care not to drink as much wine and keep to moderation.

The Brewster girls packed seeds of mullein, aloe, roses, and cloves of garlic. They filled the last sacks with spices like cinnamon, nutmeg, ginger, mustard seeds, and of course, salt and peppercorns.

"Mother, what about wheat and barley? Should each family be packing the seed of English corn as well?"

"We should pack a sack of each, but I expect this is something the company will be providing. Whether these corns will take to the soil and the weather of our new place, only God knows," explained Mistress Brewster.

The youngest Brewsters, Love and Wrestling, were more concerned about their game boards and balls, and both agreed they should carry a sack of clay marbles.

"I think we should bring a board of Nine Men's Morris and some pieces. And ball and cup for certain. That will not take up so much space, and I know we will use them during the voyage."

"Well enough. I will take two whipping tops for us, and the leather balls," decided Wrestling.

"What do you think about nine pin? Do you think Mother will allow us to bring them?" inquired Wrestling of his brother, Love.

"Perhaps leave them behind. We can always fashion those in the new place. Also, I am imagining we will have all the space we could ever want, to run and play, and wander about."

"In truth, that is how I imagine it as well, land and trees as far as the eye can see. Traveling on the ship will be another matter entirely. Even if we don't have access to all of our games, we can always amuse ourselves with games of word and wit."

"And there are always songs to sing," added Love. And so he began to sing one of his favorites, "The old dog, the jolly old dog, as he lay in his den-a. Huffa, tro-le-lo, as he lay in his den, Buffa, tro-le-lo, as he lay in his den-a."

Their mother was not paying any attention to their exchange, being overly busy packing for the family.

"I think this stool I will leave behind with Goodman Reynoldes. We can fashion something crude like this once we are settled. We will take the main table, and those two carved cupboards. The cupboards we can load with trenchers, spoons, cups, pitchers, candlesticks, oil lamps, bowls, and anything else that will fit. This blue-and-yellow plate with the green fish painted in its center, for certain I will bring this. Then of course we have the four chests filled with books. I think Master Jepson was arranging to have our things brought to the canal on the morrow, after breaking the fast," mentioned Mary Brewster to her daughters.

"Mother, I think we should take this pipkin, and this smaller kettle," suggested Fear.

"And I think we need at least one more basket. This broom for certain we will need," offered Patience.

"Girls, I do not disagree, but we are limited in space. We have to bring the books, though I worry I have not chosen the right ones or enough of them. We already have a larger kettle with another nested within, and a larger pipkin packed. We will have to rely on our good neighbors and borrow what we cannot bring. I have spoken at length with Mistress Carver, and she is bringing two kettles and more baskets than we have packed. The hearth will require firedogs and a trammel, so each family will likely be bringing those things. We have packed cloth and yarn for mending, along with the sewing baskets."

"Mother, that mirror belongs to you. We should take that along."

"That, I can agree to, as I imagine something like that will be difficult to replace in the New World. Please, pack the mirror next to the comb and brush."

"What about things like candles and oil of olive, vinegar, and soap? And sugar and butter?"

"Pack all of those things, as once we get across the ocean, they will all have to be resupplied from England. Wrap the case bottles in linen, or find a wooden case box, as we cannot afford to have them break."

Mary addressed her four youngest children. "I want each one of you to put a change of clothing, along with two shirts or smocks, into that trunk over there. That will be the trunk we keep close to us during the voyage. Everything else will likely be put into the hold, with limited access, if any at all. I am not certain, either, if we will remain on the ship we are taking from Delfshaven, or whether we will be on the larger ship. What is the name of the ship taking us to Southampton? I cannot remember her name."

"It is the *Speedwell*. With her name, you wonder if the large ship will keep pace with her," exclaimed Love with wide eyes.

"I understand the larger ship, called the *Mayflower*, is three times the size of the ship here, so the *Speedwell* might have to work even harder in the rough, high seas. She will be a useful size in the New World, for fishing and mayhaps trading along the coast," responded his mother.

"Do you think we will be tossed about in terrible storms?" asked Wrestling.

"Anything is possible, but trust in the Lord, that He will keep us safe regardless of what we encounter, whether it be on

sea or once we land," assured Mary.

Both Love and Wrestling nodded. Although it saddened them to be leaving their pastor and the majority of the congregation in Leyden, they were eager to see their father again. That alone made it easier to leave the only city they had known.

With most things packed, Mary looked around her home, feeling empty herself. This home they had rented for more than eleven years was starting to look abandoned, although some things that belonged to the owners, the van Thorenvliets, would stay, such as the bed curtains in the main room.

She knew she would never return, and although she believed removal necessary, she shuddered at the thought of the journey ahead, and how little they would have in the way of conveniences. One thought that brought great happiness to her was that of reuniting with her husband. The last year had been difficult as she managed with his absence.

Items not packed would be bartered, sold, or given to a member of the congregation. It was fairly simple for Elizabeth Winslow, not long ago coming from London. She fit everything into her trunk without having to make any decisions about leaving something behind. She cared for Leyden well enough, but was intrigued by the idea of venturing to the New World. Edward was certain this was the best chance for them. This opportunity to own land, and worship as they wanted, could not compare to staying in Leyden, especially with the printing operation dissolved. There were many more from England who would have left the King's Church and joined them in Leyden, if the economic prospects were better. Also, the possibility for war to resume was very real, with the Spanish a vicious enemy.

July 21, 1620, Leyden

On this Tuesday, the twenty-first of July, Master Robinson gathered his congregation prior to their brethren's departure to Delfshaven. Their minister called a solemn day of Humiliation, a day dedicated to fervent prayer and fasting. They met in the Green Close, with Master Robinson reading from Ezra, comparing that text to their present situation. Joining in the purest prayer and song, they sang the 107th psalm, sung in the sweetest, most glorious unison:

"Such as in ships or brittle barques, unto the seas descend."

Those expert in music, like John Coprario, played instruments, making notes sounding like rain falling from heaven.

Master Robinson and his family, along with many of the others staying behind in Leyden, desired to accompany those departing to Delfshaven. The trip was not very far, but far enough that they would go and stay the night, saving their last farewell for the morrow.

Some left their fair city of Leyden just as they had arrived, now walking down the steps on the Rapenburg and departing by way of the Vliet River. On this day, they traveled south towards Delft and on to Delfshaven.

For Elizabeth, the departure was not as sorrowful as for some, who had lived in the city for more than a decade. And worse than that, some were saying farewell to people they would likely never see again. For Goodman Bradford and his wife Dorothy, they had to endure the daymare of leaving behind their young son, John. The decision was of the worst kind, lacking any reasonable option. William had read about previous voyages and realized they were traveling later in the season than they should be. Taking his young son was something he was not willing to do, not with many in the congregation able to care for him, at least until it was safe to send for him. Many more wanted to join them, so young John could come in the second or third crossing. Goodwife Bradford agreed reluctantly, but really, there were no circumstances when a mother could accept leaving her child behind.

The short voyage to Delfshaven delivered them to more friends, those coming from Amsterdam to lend their support and bid farewell. Even though more than sixty would be leaving on the *Speedwell* for Southampton, there were more than two hundred from both Leyden and Amsterdam to honour their embarkation. The small port town supported their needs by allowing the group to stay over the night, affording them the chance to pray and bid farewell on the morrow. Their congregation, family, and friends were grateful to be allowed respite and shelter within the walls of the port's Dutch Reformed church.

Elizabeth was exhausted in every way. Certainly physically, she was glad to stay in one spot for some hours, and emotionally, she was in a strange and unfamiliar place. After she made her bed in the pew of the church, she closed her tired eyes and attempted to rest. Most around her chose friendly entertainment and Christian discourse over sleep. Shifting from one side of her body to another, she awoke from her broken slumber, sensing the movement of her husband.

"Elizabeth, my love, it is time to rise and ready ourselves for our departure to Southampton. It could be that your sister will be there, waiting to join Jonathan."

"Yes, I am more than ready to know if she will be there. I expect she will be there with the rest of my family, at the very least to bid farewell to us, and others in the congregation. My mother is quite fond of Mistress Brewster, and grew to know Mistress Carver when she visited Leyden for our wedding. The difficulty for Jonathan will be that when he sees Rose, he will have hopes that she is there to marry him and accompany him on the journey."

"Only God knows what path she will take. I do hope for your sake she joins our group, so you have your sister alongside you as we build a life in the New World."

"I remember also Jonathan saying that in his last letter to Rose, he mentioned the idea of my brother, Robert, signing on to the venture. I can understand why they would want his strength and skill, but for my parents that could mean all three of their children would vanish. My father would not leave London, and of course my mother will remain with him. I cannot imagine how my parents are feeling at this moment, at the prospect of watching their children sail away."

"With fair weather it will not take us long to reach England, so soon we will have all of these answers. Come. Let us ready our trunks so they can be carted to the shallop. The *Speedwell* is to be departing in less than two hours from now."

They broke the fast with bread, cheese, and beer. Elizabeth ate quickly, barely tasting the cheese she typically enjoyed so much. She looked across the church at her husband, who was busy sharing some last words with fellow printers Giles Thorp and Sabine Staresmore. Elizabeth recalled Goodman Staresmore having been imprisoned in London, due to betrayal by the words of Francis Blackwell. Master Thorp was part of the group traveling from Amsterdam to see them off. They removed their hats and then embraced, expecting they would never see each other again.

The finality of the removal was overwhelming. To calm his flock, Master Robinson read from the Geneva Bible and led them in prayer. They sang again the 107th psalm, the words so relevant they both stung and comforted.

"And they in their distress besought:
he saved them from their sorrows. He them brought
from darkness and death's shade: and broke their bands."

Now many began to cry and wail in the pain of leaving so many people they loved. Worst of all, they were separating from their gifted minister, having to wait patiently for him to join them.

As they walked from the church to the end of the port, many of the local people either walked alongside or looked on from their homes and shops. Those departing went aboard and their friends with them, where truly doleful was the sight of that sad and mournful parting, to see what tears did gush from every eye, and pithy speeches pierced each heart; that sundry of the Dutch strangers that stood on the quay as spectators, could not refrain from tears. Yet in truth it was comfortable and sweet, to see such lively and true expressions of dear and unfeigned love.

Master Robinson and many other friends not leaving on the *Speedwell* boarded her to speak some last words and lead a final prayer. The tide forced the unwanted but inevitable parting, their reverend pastor falling down on his knees, and they all with him, with watery cheeks commended them with the most fervent prayers to the Lord and his blessing. And then with mutual embraces and many tears, they took their leaves of one another, knowing it could be their last.

The winds and weather were fair, in a matter of days delivering them to Southampton quickly and comfortably. After they had weighed anchor, Elizabeth could hear the sailors shouting back and forth to one another, working the ropes and sails. When all was secure, Master Reynoldes allowed them to disembark.

Elizabeth felt an ache in her head and a wobbly belly. Her humours were out of balance not because of the short voyage over water, but because she knew not which of her siblings, if any, would be joining her. She was hopeful Rose would marry Jonathan so that she would have the company of her sister in the New World. It would also mean she would choose Jonathan over Hugh Mercer, which for Elizabeth would have been no choice at all. She resented what the post carrier had put her sister through. She worried though that Robert would join the merchant venture as well, which could result in all three Okes children departing. This, she knew, would devastate her parents.

Many of those traveling on the *Mayflower* were not far away, and when word spread that the *Speedwell* had arrived in Southampton, they hurried back toward the ship. The reunion was joyous at the start, especially that of Master Brewster with his family. Master Carver could not have been happier than when he laid eyes on Mistress Carver, it being many months since he saw her last. In truth, every member of Master Robinson's congregation was grateful to be rejoined, regardless of the tensions associated with the alterations of the agreement.

Master Weston had traveled from London to see them off, and was pleased to have the agents and other congregation members reunited. In spite of the objections to the changes of the terms, the mood was amicable. Master Carver took comfort in having Masters Brewster and Allerton in his midst. He had already done so with Master Brewster, and now he walked with Master Allerton, so he might explain he had nothing to do with the changes in the terms with the Merchant Adventurers.

"I have described to many how I was here in Southampton when Master Cushman agreed to the changes in the conditions, whilst he was in London. I cannot tell you how frustrated I am even now, and many weeks have passed. All of the work leading up to our leaving, the many trips back and forth from Leyden to London, and to have it come to this?" stated Master Carver, who was severely agitated.

Master Allerton did his best to calm his friend. "Clearly, it is by no fault of your own that we find ourselves in this state. It is known in the mind of Master Robinson and everyone else in our congregation that this was the doing of Master Cushman. You do not bear responsibility for agreeing to anything other than what was proposed by Master Weston in Leyden, and furthermore–"

"Pray pardon, but am I hearing what I think I am hearing? More complaints about my lack of skill as your agent? That you all want to place the blame on me for agreeing to changes desired by the investors? I know Master Robinson has instructed you all not to agree to anything, but do you not realize that had I ignored the desires of the investors, that all would have been lost? What would I tell Goodman Bradford, one of the many who had sold their homes already? I did not want to delay things any more than they had been. It is nearly August already, and still we are sitting in Southampton. Do you not see the risk of arriving to the New World in the colder months, without shelter and only our provisions to keep us alive? I was asked to serve as an agent in this work, and I have done so. Only in the eyes of God will I be judged.

Think and say what you will, but I care only how the Lord knows me."

And with that, Master Cushman walked away swiftly, joining the company of Master Weston and Christopher Martin.

Elizabeth sighted her sister and the rest of the family while she waited to board the bark bringing them ashore. Putting her hand to her forehead to block the glare of the sun, she squinted to see if there was any evidence of a trunk or trunks near her brother and sister. It could be, if they were joining the venture, that their things were already loaded aboard the *Mayflower.* That might be unlikely as well, since she would expect all those coming from Leyden would remain on the *Speedwell,* and anyone connected to that congregation would also join the *Speedwell.* She had no information to confirm that, so she would have to remain patient and speak to her family directly.

As she climbed the steps leading to the pier, her mother ran to meet her. By the firmness and duration of her hug, Elizabeth suspected that both of her siblings were planning to leave. She stepped back slightly from her mother to see the tears rolling down her cheeks. Only then did she notice her father, and that he too had tears in his eyes. He looked tired and defeated. He looked miserable.

In contrast, the happiest person on the pier was Jonathan Brewster, just learning that Rose accepted his proposal of betrothal. He picked her up off the ground and swung her around in a circle, her petticoat whirling as they moved. She was pleased as well, but still, there lingered some trepidation about the journey itself. She wanted to be with Jonathan, but she also wanted to stay alive, and prayed to God daily with that hope.

Likely the most devastated of anyone associated with the people and this venture was Hugh Mercer. He sat in an ordinary, at a table with a view overlooking the pier. Why would he torture himself like this? He watched the woman he loved being lifted up and twirled around by the man she selected, the man she desired over him. He watched because he believed he deserved the pain. Mayhaps it was God's plan, but Hugh had made every wrong choice it seemed, and when he tried to correct it, it was simply too late.

"Another beer," grumbled Hugh, who was drunk already.

While he waited for the beer, the Master of the *Speedwell*, John Reynoldes, entered the ordinary. His first mate and pilot wandered in after him, the three of them sitting at a round table to the left of Goodman Mercer.

"So what do you boys think of all this, this journey to the New World? These people are not seafaring people, and you realize we have to remain in that savage place a year beyond our arrival?"

His crew said nothing, knowing that Master Reynoldes was not finished speaking and he did not want their opinions, anyway.

He lowered his voice, leaning into them. "I think this voyage will be our ruin. I cannot break the contract, but I will tell you that I might entertain some creative ways of keeping us in England, and alive."

The other two men nodded in agreement. They saw the danger of this venture, and the disagreement among the merchants and the planters added to the risk.

"Three more beers, over there," said Hugh gruffly, motioning to the table where Master Reynoldes sat. The server delivered the cup with irritation, setting it down so roughly beer overtook the rim. She rolled her eyes at Hugh as opposed to apologizing, and huffed off to fetch more beer.

"What do you want with us?" asked Master Reynoldes with suspicion.

"I want to know what it will take for you to keep your ship, the *Speedwell*, on this side of the Atlantic."

"I have a signed contract. There's really nothing, nothing but God that can stop us," answered Master Reynoldes with a wink.

"Pray pardon, Hugh," came a frantic voice.

Hugh Mercer turned around slowly, annoyed at the disruption of his conversation. Standing before him was Samuell Watson, an apprentice of Master Okes. Out of breath and drenched with sweat, the apprentice looked as if he had run all the way from London.

Hugh shifted away from Master Reynoldes's table subtly, not wanting Samuell to recognize with whom he was speaking.

"What do you want? What are you doing here, anyway?"

"I am seeking out my Master, Master Okes. I need to speak with him right away. Do you know if the ships have left already for the New World?"

"I would think not, as I am the Master of one of them," laughed Reynoldes, so deeply and hard he began coughing uncontrollably.

"When will you depart then?" asked the apprentice nervously. He was apprehensive to know the answer, and was also intimidated by Master Reynoldes.

"Only God knows, lad, since He will produce the winds. We have provisions to load, and it is yet to be determined who is traveling on which ship. I would imagine it would be at least three or four days before we set off. I will be looking her over myself, to be sure the *Speedwell* is ready to battle the high seas." He paused for a moment, then produced a sly smile. "It seems there are a number of people milling about who have great interest in my ship."

"If I may speak, Master Reynoldes, I think you will find a number of people who would go to great lengths to keep your ship anchored here rather than carry certain people to the New World." Samuell trembled as he spoke, glancing over at Hugh Mercer as he finished his words.

Master Reynoldes looked at him with increased interest. "I see. So who would these people be, and to what lengths would they go?" asked the Master, doubtful that this young man had anything of value to offer.

Samuell walked towards Master Reynoldes and whispered something into his ear. Master Reynoldes eyed him still with skepticism, but it was clear he believed there was truth in the young man's words. The Master of the *Speedwell* responded with something so softly that even his crew could not hear. The conversation was brief but effective, and satisfied with the exchange, Samuell turned back to address Mercer.

Hugh had turned his body away, pretending he was looking out the window and disinterested in their words. In reality, he was probably the most determined person to keep the *Speedwell* from crossing. Resting safely at the bottom of his leather bag was all of the money he possessed. He would have severed a limb if he had to, to keep Rose from going. Whether she would still carry out a marriage to Jonathan Brewster was another matter. He decided that if she stayed on this side of the ocean, hope would remain to make her his wife. If she ventured to the New World, the odds favored her demise.

He pondered how he could bribe Master Reynoldes, without Rose finding out. If she learned of his intervention, she would likely discard him forever. As he watched the group on the pier talking, hugging, singing, dancing, and rejoicing in each other's company, he realized that Rose and Jonathan might be assigned to the bigger ship.

He turned abruptly to Master Reynoldes, almost as if in a panic. "Who determines which ship each person will travel upon?"

"For the most part, those coming from Leyden, those connected to that congregation, will remain on my ship. The man most trained in military strategy, Myles Standish, the soldier by profession, is aboard my ship.

"The larger ship has a collection of people from all parts of England. Some are closely related to the Adventurers. Others have been encouraged based on their trade. There is a man named Alden who is known to have skills as a cooper. Others have experience in travel, and for all, the opportunity to own land far outweighs the inherent risk of the venture. Some of these people seek reform of the King's Church, others have no care at all in the way of it."

Master Reynoldes continued. "I understand there will be men selected as governors of each ship. For mine, it will be Master Carver principally, and for the *Mayflower* it will be Christopher Martin, with Cushman as his assistant. In fact, that is Christopher Martin at the table over there." He motioned to the man. "I hear he has a cruel tongue and no loyalty to anyone or anything. Slimy one he is. Just glad he is not aboard my ship."

"I see. That is useful information," responded Hugh Mercer. "Thank you kindly."

"Hugh, pray pardon. I realize you do not know me very well, but we have reason to speak about some business together. You must trust me in this, and must act quickly and quietly," demanded Samuell.

Hugh nodded, so Samuell sat beside him and revealed his plan. "We can stop this ship from making the journey, but it must be done immediately, and not with Master Reynoldes directly. This is what I suggest," said Samuell, his voice now lowered to a whisper. "I understand you cannot be implicated in this, so I can take whatever money you plan to direct to this cause, and I will approach Christopher Martin. Apparently, he is quite open to these sorts of transactions and skilled at managing them without notice. The idea is he would take some of the money for himself, and the rest would go to Master Reynoldes and his crew."

"And you would trust Christopher Martin? Are you some kind of fool?"

"Our options are few, and time is not our ally. I have borrowed a large sum of money from my father. Meanwhile, the other apprentice, Andrewe Driver, is working to sell books sitting idly in our stores, so that I might repay my family. How many pounds can you contribute? Because we will need at least two hundred combined to move forward."

"You understand that this is near to everything I possess. I cannot believe I am entrusting you with it, but you know already I am desperate, and would do anything to keep Rose here. If you fail me in this, I will come after you, looking for every last shilling."

Samuell understood the importance of his efforts, as he was working to keep at least one of Master Okes's children in England. But even so, it was not the same intensity that drove Hugh Mercer, who was about to lose the love of his life. In Samuell's case, he cared not to see his Master Printer suffer, but nothing so personal was at stake. He looked at Hugh with concern. He appeared mad with emotion. That he was intoxicated exacerbated his condition.

"You can trust me, and it might be better that I handle this. As much as I care for Master Okes and his family, I understand it is different for you. You have told me a bit about your history with Rose, and I do empathize with your circumstance. Your logic might be overcome with emotion presently, not to mention the effects of the beer. I cannot imagine what it would feel like to watch the woman you love leave for the New World with another man. What a daymare it must be for you."

Samuell stopped talking when he realized that Hugh was glaring at him.

"Take this money and keep your word." He dug deep into his leather bag, feeling for the linen sack. Grasping the money, silently, he prayed that this was the right decision. He hoped that this would keep the *Speedwell* and Rose from crossing, and that she would never learn of his involvement. The linen sack hovered low between his knees, awaiting its plunge into Samuell's leather bag beneath the table. When Goodman Mercer dropped the money into Samuell's bag, he felt as if he were tossing it off London Bridge, into the churning waters of the Thames. In a matter of moments, all of this money, amounting to a lifetime of work, would be in the hands of Christopher Martin.

"I need to leave this place. Not just this ordinary, but Southampton altogether," said Goodman Mercer. "I do not know how long these ships will sit here, and I cannot bear to watch it unfold. I feel ill to the core, and I know what you are thinking– I have consumed too much beer. You have no idea, Samuell, the pain that overpowers me. All I can tell you is that when you find a woman you love, one that fulfills you in every way, recognize it and do not let go. Hold on to her for as long as you are alive. Do not be a fool like me. I had the woman of my dreams, and now I've lost her. Even if we are successful with this bribe, what are the odds she will return to me?"

He hung his head like a defeated warrior.

"Oh, enough of this. I will bid her farewell and return to London. I can only expect I have lost her, and likely my money too. I wish you all the best, Samuell, and will seek you out in London. You can tell me then all of what you have accomplished here. Before that, I hope the rumours reach me, that the *Speedwell* failed to be seaworthy, and was left behind."

Hugh gathered his things, shifting himself away from the table, so Samuell stood as well.

"Master Reynoldes, I wish you much luck in failure of this venture, and that you do not even make it out of the English Channel."

"Well said, and thank you for the beer," responded Master Reynoldes with a smile, holding up his cup in the gesture of a toast.

Hugh Mercer looked over one last time at Samuell Watson, but his back was turned, as he was gathering his things and preparing his words for Master Martin.

Hugh stumbled onto the street, squinting as he battled the rays from the sun. He looked terrible, and Rose pitied him as she watched him stumble towards her.

"If it does not trouble you, Jonathan, I should bid farewell to Hugh Mercer."

"Of course, my love. Do what you must."

She walked towards him, sickened by the reality that this was the last time she would see him. For years when they parted ways, it ripped her to pieces because she knew how much she would suffer in his absence. But even then she clung to the hope she would see him again, and deep down, she knew she would. On this day, the finality of the farewell tortured her. Her heart racing, every step she took towards him paralyzed her with the fear that she was making a mistake. All the hours and days she dreamed of him, she could hardly believe she would choose anything other than to be with him. They locked eyes, and this time it was her turn to say she was sorry.

"Stop. Please stop, Rose. It is more than I can bear. All of this. I want you to be happy. You know that. In truth, I wanted you to find that happiness with me. I am sorry I made it so difficult for you over the years, and please, never regret your decision. God has His plan, so I can only hope we will be together in the next life."

She wrapped her arms around him, running her fingers through the hair at the base of his neck. "I love you, Hugh Mercer. May God keep you well."

"I love you," he replied as he dove into the green of her eyes. "You are so beautiful and special. In time, I will try to love again. I will try, but no one can and no one will replace you."

He kissed her forehead and hugged her, and she hugged him back, plagued by the terrible irony of that moment. All the years she waited and wondered and yearned for him— and now she was leaving.

"I should go. It pains me to be here any longer. I will bid your family farewell and be on my way to London."

He walked backwards, taking in the view of her, hoping the image would stay forever embedded in his mind.

Early August 1620, Southampton

"Can someone explain why we must take the time to fit the sails of this ship yet again? We are missing fair winds, consuming provisions, and losing valuable time," remarked Master Carver.

"It is what Master Martin demands is necessary," said Master Cushman, shaking his head. "I know not how I will fare with that wretched man, as his assistant on the larger ship."

"It is confusing to me why Master Martin would have any say about the *Speedwell*, seeing that he is not a mariner or even traveling on that ship. Where is Master Reynoldes, anyway?"

"You will likely find him in the ordinary. That is where he prefers to be when he is not on the ship. I would not question Master Martin, either, as he will turn on you with the most vile words and temper."

Master Carver shook his head with disgust. He walked off to find Master Reynoldes, and on his way encountered Master Weston.

"Pray pardon, Master Carver. As I understand it, the ships should be launching within the next day, and still we are lacking in agreement on the changes to the terms."

"With respect, Master Weston, I do not think we will leave in agreement of those changes. All of the men coming from Leyden refuse the alterations, and have been strongly encouraged by Master Robinson to hold firmly to the original plan."

As Masters Brewster and Cushman walked toward them to join the conversation, it was clear that Master Weston was growing agitated.

He started to back away from them before speaking, waving his finger angrily at them and declaring, "You must look to stand on your own legs then. You tell me you need one hundred pounds more for provisions and to clear things at your leaving Southampton. I will disburse not a penny more, and let you shift things on your own."

He turned his back on them and walked away, not intending to speak any more words. After that exchange he left Southampton altogether, and returned to London.

The group was forced to sell off some of their butter, leaving them lacking in supply. There were other things too they wanted more of, such as oil, muskets, swords, and even soles to repair shoes. Their options being few, and the arrangement riddled with disparity, it seemed they were readier to go to dispute than to set forward on a voyage.

By now, being in Southampton for near unto a week, it was determined who would travel on each ship. The *Speedwell* was destined to carry the congregation from Leyden, and anyone connected to them. All of the Okeses' children would be on the smaller ship, with Master Carver elected as a leader of the group, and William Bradford serving as his assistant. On the larger ship, Master Martin would lead the people coming directly from England, having Master Cushman to aid him.

The Okes family had taken lodging at The Two Bells Inn, just around the corner. There was no urgency to return to London. For them, the delay in the departure was welcome. Master Okes's work was managed more than adequately by his two apprentices, Andrewe Driver and Samuell Watson, and Mercy Brewer was in the loving care of their loyal servant Katherine. They cherished the additional time with their children, who, once the anchors were hoisted, would be gone from their lives. There was nothing worse in life than losing a child, and now the Okeses were losing all three, all at once.

Finally, on the fifth of August, the two ships took leave from Southampton. Bound for the Atlantic, they tracked together west through the English Channel. Regardless of the disharmony with the investors, there was an overwhelming feeling of relief with the journey now underway.

"How many days do you think it will take to cross?" asked Rose as she looked around at the undesirable and confined surroundings.

"It will depend on the winds and what storms we encounter. I know that you are aware of the dangers even outside of the weather, such as pirates and the stability of the vessel itself. Have faith in God's plan, and do not trouble yourself with any worrisome thoughts," offered Jonathan. "As far as an approximation, it will likely take us anywhere from fifty to ninety days. I know that is a wide span, but we are on a smaller ship, so it might take a bit longer."

Since they were not yet betrothed, Rose did not make her sleeping quarters with Jonathan. She kept her chest and Robert's betwixt where the Winslows and Brewsters arranged their things. Back in Southampton, there was work done to demarcate areas for families and some of their possessions. Elizabeth called them cabins, but they did not compare to the quarters of the first mate or Master. The spaces did at least offer an attempt at privacy. Along the edge of the ship there were makeshift bedsteads arranged, so that the wool-filled tickings could be off the ground, with mayhaps a chest and chamber pot stored beneath. Cups, trenchers, spoons, and bowls were also close by, being used throughout the day.

Rose strung some cord, tying one end on a nail hammered into a beam by the side of the ship and extending it to a nail on an inner post. Then she attached more cord to that nail and ran it to a nail driven to a beam close to the ship's side, this one being nearer to the stern. She put the metal rings of the bed curtains through the cord, enabling enclosure of their space with the cover of cloth when desired.

They had been moving on the channel for less than two days, and already the unpleasant smells of the journey were weighing on her. She was told she would grow accustomed to them, but in her case, the smells, coupled with darkness, were more than she could bear. She was overcome with the dampness and lack of light; even the motion was not pleasing. Rose looked around, and all she saw was misery. The children were screaming and crying, the women all looked on the verge of tears, and she asked herself silently why she was there.

Two of the Allerton children were sick, adding to the other unpleasant smells on the ship. The dark deal wood creaked with the pressure of the water and wind, and Rose wondered how this small ship would be able to cross the Atlantic.

It was not long before Rose realized there would be little difference in each meal. To break the fast it was bread and beer, and for dinner, likely a pease pottage, mayhaps with salted pork, ship's biscuit, and beer. For supper, they ate something similar to dinner, but in a smaller portion. When they served the food she would go to the opening where the food was lowered, and she could hear the chaos of the crew, shouting to each other in different languages, but chiefly words in Dutch and English trickled down below decks.

Rose prayed many times in a day, seeking strength for the journey. Master Brewster would lead them in prayer before their meals and, of course, on the Sabbath. They were not even beyond the English Channel, and she could not fathom how she would endure a crossing of the Atlantic. She was in the midst of prayer when she heard shouting from the hold.

"Master Reynoldes! Somebody inform Master Reynoldes that the ship is leaking!"

Two sailors scrambled from the stores below and up to the main deck to locate the Master and report the dangerous state of the ship. After those two men went up, three men came firing down to assess the damage. They eventually returned looking panicked and wet.

"She is as leaky as a sieve, she is! I swear this is a different ship than left Delfshaven. She is straining so much that she is close to bursting at the seams and spewing her oakum!" exclaimed one sailor to another.

Before long, word traveled down to them by way of Master Carver that both ships were putting into the port of Dartmouth so that the *Speedwell* could be looked over and repaired. For Rose, the reprieve of the ship's quarters was a fortuitous shift. For Master Carver and the other principal men of the venture, having to stop in Dartmouth to mend the ship was costly in terms of time, provisions, and money spent in repairs.

Every inch of her was looked over, from stem to stern. The findings revealed a number of weaknesses requiring repair and yet another refitting.

"Why is it, Master Martin, that you are so involved with the *Speedwell*, when you have been chosen to manage things on the *Mayflower*?"

"Master Carver, I thought you to be a more astute business man than that. The *Speedwell* crossing and staying in the New World for the purpose of fishing is one of the most significant pieces in achieving success with this plantation. Without a vessel to fish, we will be hard-pressed to turn a profit, even after seven years."

"Yes, you are correct in that, which is why I am wondering why you have been involved at all in giving orders regarding this ship and its care. You have no experience with ships or travel of this nature, yet you stick your nose in where it does not belong. You are doing nothing but a disservice to all of us, especially those crossing on this ship."

"You ignorant knob. You and those connected to you have no place questioning me or my guidance. Gratitude is what you should be expressing, not griping. I have had enough of your accusations and complaints. Are you certain you are well enough to be leading the others aboard *Speedwell*, or do you need me to manage both?" said Master Martin as he squinted at Master Carver with disdain.

Master Carver was so offended he could not look him in the eye when responding. "Do you know how long we will be waiting here in Dartmouth, since it appears you are directing the efforts with the repairs?"

"Mayhaps a week. It could be more. Is it not more important to go with this ship in good condition, even with a delay, than be without her? As I asked before, you are a man of business, are you not?"

Having received enough abuse, Master Carver turned and walked away, shaking his head as he went. He was concerned about the added delay and the consumption of provisions. What troubled him the most was that Master Martin was directing the repairs. He desired to seek out Master Reynoldes to understand the nature of the problems.

"There is not much to discuss. She has some leaks that will be repaired, and then she will be trimmed once more. We will be back in the water as soon as I deem the work sufficient. It is my own life at stake, and that of my crew, so you can bet I have a care as to how the ship is treated. I have nothing else to say about it, Master Carver, and I have to get back to reviewing these charts. Good day to you."

Master Carver had no choice but to be on his way. He cared not to strain the relationship with the Master of the ship. They were not yet out of the Channel, and already there was tension enough. The journey across the Atlantic could take months, and then Master Reynoldes and his crew would stay on in the New World for another year. A productive partnership would be essential, thought Master Carver, as he left the ordinary.

With the repairs complete, and the workmen and Master of Ship in agreement they could proceed without fear or danger, the *Mayflower* and *Speedwell* departed Dartmouth. Hopes being high and the winds fair, good fortune remained elusive. For after they were gone to sea again above one hundred leagues without the Lands' End, the two ships holding company together all this while, Master Reynoldes complained his ship was so leaky that he must bear up or sink at sea.

"Master Jones, we must put back into port at once!" cried out Master Reynoldes, clearly exasperated. "She is as leaky as a sieve, she is. I cannot go any farther. Even with a great deal of pumping, we are just keeping her afloat."

"Aye, there is no choice in the matter. We shall put into Plymouth and review her condition."

But no special leak could be found, and it was judged to be the general weakness of the ship, and that she would not be sufficient for the voyage. Thereby, they were forced to dismiss her.

"I do not understand this. The ship left Delfshaven and traveled across the North Sea with no trouble at all," remarked Master Carver to Master Brewster. "She has been fitted three times since then, and mended further in Dartmouth, and now she is determined unseaworthy. It defies logic, does it not?"

"It would seem odd, this sequence of events. Like you, I was not aboard her from Delfshaven to Southampton, but neither Jonathan nor Mary made mention of any concerns about the ship."

Now there was the task of removing the people, their possessions, and the provisions from the *Speedwell*. As this occurred they began the critical process of determining who would add their number to the *Mayflower*.

The group coming off the *Speedwell* was mixed regarding their intentions. There were some who deemed the many crosses befalling them a clear warning from God that they were not to go. There were others con-

sidered weaker or with the charge of many children, who were thought
least useful and best if they stayed behind. Those on the *Speedwell* not
wishing to continue informed Master Carver and sought out their belongings. There were even some aboard the larger ship electing to stay behind,
and removed themselves. Master Cushman was elected to lead those not
making the crossing, and take them eastward and back to London.

As the group discussed who would take a place on the *Mayflower*,
Jonathan spoke to his parents. "Will we try to remain together as a family, or should I take charge of any or all of my siblings, and make our
way back to London?"

"I am not yet certain. Let us see how things progress. Master and
Mistress Carver, William and Dorothy Bradford, along with Myles
Standish, who is needed to lead any efforts of our defense, intend to continue onward. I know the Allertons will go all together. The Winslows
are getting aboard the *Mayflower* as well," answered Master Brewster.

Rose shifted nervously as she watched Elizabeth and Edward gathering their things. Her sister was definitely moving onto the larger ship.
With all the obstacles before them, Rose believed there were too many
signs pointing to the ruin of the venture. Nothing about it felt right to
her. Still, she kept quiet as the man she was to marry spoke to his father.

"Let me speak with Master Carver and see where and with whom
the numbers lie," decided Master Brewster.

"Rose, let us at least go aboard the *Mayflower*, and see her state below decks," suggested Jonathan.

She took his hand, and together, they were rowed out to ship. Certainly she was much larger than the *Speedwell*, so she seemed inherently
sturdier. The crew was not very fond of any of them as they were not
accustomed to traveling on the sea, and getting in the way of their work.

Jonathan led the way down betwixt the decks, where they would
spend the bulk of the journey. Other than in fair weather, when the
Master might allow them turns above decks, it would be safer for everyone to remain below. The people were packed like herring in a barrel. So
disturbing was the scene that she shuddered to imagine herself added to
this picture. Staring into a sea of people who were mostly unfamiliar did

not sit well either. She had heard some of these strangers were untoward sorts, and cared not to make the crossing in their company.

In the bow of the ship were animals as well, including pigs and chickens. She noticed two dogs, a spaniel and a mastiff. Of course, there were mousers too, as there were on the *Speedwell*, and every ship for that matter. Even though the ship held the sweet smell of wine from her recent merchant work, the smells from the animals were simply terrible, forcing Rose to hold her apron to her nose as they moved on. Jonathan stopped to speak with someone from the congregation, and while she waited, Rose prayed that it be determined for them to stay behind.

She stepped carefully, trying not to disturb anyone or their things. There were many faces aboard she did not recognize. Many on this ship had come from various parts of England, having nothing to do with Master Robinson and his congregation. She was told only some had wishes for more reform or purification of the English church, with the main purpose of the venture being the chance to own land. This was not so different from the group coming from Leyden, but they, too, needed a place that would allow them to worship as they wanted, in addition to offering better economic conditions.

There was some hollering from above, so Jonathan took her hand, and together, they made their way off the ship and back onto the pier. Already, Master Brewster had made the decision for his family, determining who would continue on the *Mayflower* and who would return to London. He gestured for them to come closer, caring to impart his words to his eldest son and future daughter-in-love.

"Son, I need you to take charge of your sisters. Your mother and I will take Love and Wrestling with us, aboard the *Mayflower*. I want you to return to London with Master Cushman, and decide from there whether you go back to Leyden. Use your judgment in determining when to join us. I have great faith in you and know you will look to the Lord in making such decisions," said Master Brewster.

Rose stood there, utterly relieved. She did not have to join the group on the *Mayflower* and cross the ocean. "Thanks be to God," she said to herself, looking upwards.

"Rose, I am making the decision for your father, to keep your brother, Robert, with you. You will all go back with Master Cushman, and your family can decide if Robert will continue on a later ship. I realize Robert is greatly disappointed, but such things are not planned by us."

"I understand, Master Brewster, as will Robert. My parents will be most grateful for your guidance in this," said Rose as she embraced Master Brewster and then Mary, Love and Wrestling.

Some of the others from the congregation made their way over, seeing that there was yet another sad, and likely final parting of company.

"Hey ho, Rose," cried out Elizabeth with sadness, causing Rose to turn around and face her older sister.

"I trust you have learned I will remain behind?"

Elizabeth nodded, not caring to accept that reality. Feeling numb, the sisters hugged with all their strength.

"I will see you in the New World. Pray for our safe passage and the early days of our planting. And I will pray for you to make your way to us, and soon," said Elizabeth to Rose, with tears filling her eyes.

"I will pray as well, Elizabeth. If the seas get rough, remember that you are part of His plan, and He will guide you through, at all costs. Never give up hope in this," insisted Rose as they released their embrace.

The crew of the *Speedwell* helped sort through and separate the possessions of those staying behind. Those going aboard the *Mayflower* had their things loaded, along with as many provisions as they could stow. Of those provisions that could not be put on the *Mayflower*, much was sold to afford passage back to London. The remainder, and whatever was unused upon arriving in London, could be sold to aid those returning to other parts.

Early September 1620, at the Sign of The Black Bear, London

Hugh Mercer sprinted down the Great North Road towards London. He had heard from another carrier that the *Speedwell* had been left behind. The plot had worked! What he didn't know was whether Rose had gotten on the other ship. No matter how many people he asked, a list of people aboard the *Mayflower* was not yet circulating. He knew the fastest way to find out was to return to London, where information traveled like lightning.

He was short of breath upon entering The Black Bear. Samuell rushed over to him, excited to confirm the rumour that the *Speedwell* had failed to make the voyage.

"You know already then, that our bribe paid off?" asked Samuell in a rapid whisper. "I was surprised to hear that Masters Martin and Reynoldes kept to their end of the deal. It was likely to our advantage that Master Reynoldes and his crew had grown opposed to making the crossing and remaining in the New World for the first year. Thanks be to God they did."

"I did hear some things on the road, and was hopeful they were true. You never know with these matters. Has there been anyone from the venture to confirm this directly?"

"Not to my knowledge, but Master Okes had heard from one of the merchant adventurers that this was the case. So you can imagine that he is hopeful one or all of his children remain in this country."

"I will check at some of the other stalls for a passenger list, and if that fails, go down to the Thames and find out more by word of mouth. One would think those not making the voyage might make their way back to Southampton or London," speculated Goodman Mercer.

"That is a logical plan. If you learn nothing more with those efforts, you might make your way directly to the sign of The Rose. Master Okes might have additional news."

Hugh nodded in agreement. "In any case, you can be relieved that your efforts were successful and my money put to good use. I can only pray that Rose did not board the larger ship. We shall find out soon enough. God by you, Samuell."

Early September 1620, London, the River Thames

Those planning to be on either the *Mayflower* or the *Speedwell* who were arriving back in London were for the most part relieved to be there, as opposed to on the open seas. Where everyone would disperse to remained in question as they voyaged back. Rose was eager to see the looks on the faces of her parents, at seeing two of their three children standing before them. Deep down, she was grateful for the *Speedwell's* failing, longing to be back home. It was not that she did not love Jonathan, but sailing to the New World she believed would be their doom, regardless of the promise of land and other freedoms.

As they disembarked and arranged for their things to be carted to the Okeses' sign of The Rose, Rose wondered about Hugh Mercer and whether he had learned of the fate of the *Speedwell*. Even if he had, he would not know whether she was aboard the *Mayflower*. He was likely not even near London, and instead on the farthest part north of the Great North Road, hundreds of miles away.

"Jonathan, are we intending to stay in London, or were you considering a return to Leyden?" asked Rose.

"I think it best that we go back to Leyden and reunite with the congregation there. It will be safer to wait there and hear of the report of the *Mayflower* returning to England, and the state of things, before arranging our own passage. I cannot put us or my sisters in danger by going too soon. Seeing that we are separated from the King's Church, it is not wise for us to remain in London, either," responded Jonathan. "I expect your family will allow us to stay with them while we arrange for passage to Leyden, yes?"

"I would certainly hope so," responded Rose. "I cannot imagine my parents would turn us away."

The surprise and elation that erupted at the sign of The Rose was unmatched. Rose had never seen this in her father before. It was as though a weight had been lifted, with two of his children returning, as if reborn. Rose and Nicholas embraced before turning to their children and welcoming them home with hugs and kisses. Of all the people not making the journey, Robert was one of the few who were entirely disappointed at staying behind. Young and without fear, he was undaunted by the obstacles they faced. Surely he was pleased to see his parents again, but he thought this venture his opportunity for land ownership and wealth. Now he would have to plead with his former Master to reinstate his apprenticeship.

"Master Okes, will it be possible for me and my sisters to remain with you until we find passage to Leyden?" asked Jonathan.

"Yes, Jonathan, you are welcome here until you make your way to Leyden, but please do that expeditiously."

Jonathan looked a bit confused as to why he would say to do so quickly. He would have expected he would appreciate any sort of delay that would keep Rose there longer.

Noticing Jonathan's questioning look, Master Okes felt obligated to clarify his comment. "Jonathan, I realized as I watched my children board the *Speedwell* in Southampton, that I have spent near to all of my life agreeing to things that are not in the best interest for me and my family. I have agreed to keeping many people over the years in my back room, some of whom had separated from the church and were being sought out. Your father, whom I love dearly, is of course a principal example. I have stored illegal books, sent type overseas, and have looked the other way to aid Master Brewer and others in their cause. Although I would like to see more reform within the King's Church, I am part of the Stationers' Company and am expected to abide by their rules and those of King James. Now that I have Rose and Robert back, I am newly committed to protecting my family. You can stay here with Fear and Patience as you make arrangements for Leyden, but please bear in mind what I have said, and do so quickly."

Jonathan understood his position. He cleared his throat and was nervous to hear the answer to the following question, "I respect your direction, but I must know how this impacts my life with Rose. Will you keep her from returning to Leyden and marrying me?"

Rose held her breath as she awaited her father's response.

"I would never interfere with God's plan or keep my daughter from love and happiness, no matter the cost to me. It was difficult at first when I met my own Rose, to be away from her while she was in the court of Queen Elizabeth. But even at that, no one forced us to be apart, and in time, we realized our dream of being together," explained Master Okes as he squeezed his wife's hand.

Jonathan turned to Rose and asked her to step outside so they could speak alone.

"Rose, I will go straight away in search of passage to Leyden, and I pray I am seeking passage for four. Am I correct in that assumption?"

He shuddered at her hesitation.

"Jonathan, I do love you, you must know that. I mind not living in Leyden, but the voyage to the New World frightens me to my core. I fear it is not in God's plan for me to cross the ocean… do you intend to continue with that course, to eventually go there with your family?"

He was nearly choking on his words as he held back his tears. "I did promise my father I would continue with the plan to travel to the New World, finding a path for you and my sisters. In truth, I think it the best opportunity for our congregation, economically and otherwise. But I do not want to lose you, either."

He paused for a moment. "Rose, is your hesitation truly about trepidation of the New World, or more about your decision in marriage? I am wondering now if this is not more about Hugh Mercer. I have never spoken of it, but I understand you have a past with him. Why you would want someone who has played games with your mind and heart, I know not. From what I can tell, I am the opposite of him in that I respect and care for you, and am here for you, always. There is no confusion or surprises. I need to know that you are committed to becoming my wife, and that you desire me and only me as your husband."

Rose looked back at him with the widest, saddest, most gorgeous green eyes, electing to remain silent.

Flustered, Jonathan made his way to the door. "Let me seek out passage for us to Leyden, and when I return, we can converse further. Mayhaps we go to Leyden and let the Lord's plan unfold in time."

They nodded and smiled at one another to lighten the moment, but deep down, they were both shaken and unsure of the outcome.

"Tell my sisters I have gone to seek out a ship that will take us to Leyden. I will be back in time for supper," promised Jonathan. And with that, he kissed her on the cheek and turned for the Thames.

Hugh Mercer learned nothing from the other stalls at St. Paul's churchyard, and sought out his most reliable contacts by the Thames. Not a soul could come up with a list of those aboard the *Mayflower*, or provide names verbally. One man claimed he had heard a list was circulating, but had not seen it and did not know where to find it. Hugh was so frustrated with his failure to obtain this information, he sat down exhausted on the next jetty steps he came upon. He pondered going over to the ordinary by the sign of The Rose, or seeking out Master Okes directly. While he sorted through these thoughts, a man came bounding down the steps so rapidly he accidentally brushed the shoulder of Hugh Mercer. He turned around to apologize as he continued his descent, shocked to see Hugh Mercer sitting there.

Hugh shot upwards as if kicked by his horse, and rushed down the steps after Jonathan.

"I apologize, Hugh, for knocking into you. Pray pardon as well for my briefness, but I need to find a ship destined for the Netherlands."

"No trouble, but please tell me, is Rose also in London? Is she at the sign of The Rose now?"

Jonathan could not bring any words to his lips as he continued standing there, debating what to do. He looked away for a moment to gaze at the Thames, and when he returned to address Hugh Mercer, the post carrier was gone. He had cleared the jetty steps and was running as fast as God would let him to the sign of The Rose.

Jonathan contemplated chasing after him, but for what reason?

Rose was standing in the front room, looking out the main window as she so often did. For years, she would pace back and forth, peering out those windows each morning and other times of the day, hoping to see Hugh Mercer and his horse appear before her. Every so often, this dream would materialize, and then she would wait many agonizing months before seeing him again. The highs and lows had plagued her for years, and just weeks before when she had the chance to be with him, to be his wife, she chose another. She had no idea where he was at this moment, imagining him somewhere up the Great North Road. Thinking of Jonathan, she knew she could not leave for Leyden, only to be dreading their turn to travel to the New World.

She cursed herself at her folly and wondered if she would ever be happy.

As she was about to turn away and seek out Katherine for counsel, she saw a blur of a man pass the front window, then heard frantic pounding on the door.

"Rose! Rose, are you there? Please, Rose, someone, open the door!"

She gasped at the sound of his voice. Closing her eyes, she cherished the moment of realizing he had come for her and that he stood feet away, on the other side of the shop's entrance. Rose exhaled a breath filled with relief, knowing that her days of waiting were over. She ran to the door, her hands trembling so severely she could not work the lock. They were both tugging and pulling on the door frantically, like fools in love. At last, she was able to get the lock to disengage.

"Hugh. I am here. I am here. Allow me to let you in."

As the door opened for him their eyes locked, staring at each other in disbelief.

"How is it that we have been given another chance?" asked Rose in a whisper.

He looked back at her, still saying nothing, allowing her to speak first.

"All the years that have passed, every moment without you, I suffered. I thought a life with Jonathan would bring me stability and happiness. That is why I accepted his offer of marriage."

The last words stung, leaving Hugh uncertain as to the direction of her thoughts. He braced for what was to come next.

"You might know already, some of us are back in London only because the *Speedwell* failed. She took on water not long after we departed Southampton, forcing us back into port at Dartmouth. There was much concern among the leading men about the cost of time and money, not to mention provisions consumed, but I was grateful to be off the ship. Imagine being confined in a dark space filled with terrible smells and the sounds of children moaning and crying, for what could be months? With the repairs made, we put back into the channel, and sooner than the first time, heard shouting from the sailors, that the ship was leaking. She was taking on water so rapidly it was only by the grace of God we made it back to land, this time to Plymouth."

"I imagine you were filled with fear that the *Speedwell* would falter in the crossing. Mayhaps it is a blessing that she struggled in the Channel, letting her flaws be known before taking on the rough waters of the Atlantic," commented Hugh. As he spoke his words, he could only hope he sounded genuinely surprised by the turn of events.

Rose nodded in agreement. "I was frightened, to be sure, and it was there in Plymouth that the men decided the *Speedwell* could not continue. Of the sixty-odd souls, there were some who removed themselves from the venture entirely, and others transferred onto the larger ship. Hugh, I did pray to be kept off that ship. Jonathan and I had gone down between decks to view the conditions, and envision her being three times larger than the *Speedwell*, filled with more than one hundred people and animals. Thanks be to God, Master Brewster did decide for us to stay behind, with Jonathan taking charge of me, Robert, and his sisters."

"He is down at the Thames presently. The only reason I sprinted to your father's shop was because Jonathan bumped into me on the jetty steps. I had been walking the Thames, trying to locate a list of those people traveling on the *Mayflower*, since I heard on the Great North Road that the *Speedwell* stayed behind. He is seeking out passage to Leyden, but of course, you know that already," said Hugh with sadness in his voice.

"I told him I might not go."

Hugh spun his gaze from the floorboards back to Rose, saying nothing, but hope now flooded his face.

"The issue I have is not with Jonathan or Leyden, but with the eventual removal to the New World. Whenever my mind wanders there, I shudder in terror. If it was in God's plan for me to go, I would think on it as nothing more than following my husband, as any good wife should. My inclination to question it bothers me for many reasons."

"Stay in London, Rose. Be with me. I will move here if you want, or we can live in the North. I care not where in the world I land, as long as it is with you."

Rose moved herself closer to him, taking in his scent while looking up into his sky-blue eyes.

"Hugh, I care not to hurt Jonathan, and I know my sister will be shocked at a change in my decision. But I cannot deny the truth, that I want to be with you. For years I have known this, in my mind and my heart. Even through all the pain and suffering we have endured, patience and forgiveness have prevailed. To be your wife would be the most perfect ending to all of my dreams. I believe it to be our path, and what God wants. He wants us to be together in this world, until we are nothing more than shadow and dust."

She gazed up at him, her green eyes gleaming, standing on her toes to reach him. Rose started to speak again, but he gently stopped the words, placing his finger across her lips. With his other hand he lifted her chin towards his mouth, brushing her lips with his. Then with both hands, one on either side, he framed her face, holding her as if she were the most fragile, valuable treasure in all of the world. He kissed her in the purest, most sensual way, leaving no doubt of his love and intentions. They embraced, locking in a perfect balance of tenderness and desire. Rose melted into him, wanting nothing more than more of him. Connected as one, they let love surge, grateful for this peace and the confirmation that it was time for this to last forever. No more words were needed, the choice being already made. It was God, His Providence, who returned them, one to the other, uniting them now, and for all eternity.

The End

1 6 2 0
forever
U S A

MAYFLOWER IN PLYMOUTH HARBOR

This stamp, issued on September 17, 2020, by the United States Postal Service, commemorates the 400th anniversary of the Mayflower voyage and her unplanned arrival in Plymouth Harbor, Massachusetts, USA. The commemorative stamp honors the legacy of the people who made the crossing, and the alliance formed with the first inhabitants, the Wampanoag "people of the dawn."

Artist Greg Harlin illustrated the stamp, using a combination of watercolor, gouache, and acrylics, with some digital refining, to convey a scene of desolate beauty at the end of the harrowing journey to an unfamiliar world. Art director Greg Breeding designed the stamp.

Main Character List

Fact or Fiction

FACT

John Alden
Isaac Allerton and family
Professor Arminius
Archbishop Bancroft
Elizabeth Barker* Not in novel,
    but actual wife of Edward
    Winslow in Leyden
Printer Govert Basson
Printer Thomas Basson
Francis Blackwell
Willam Bradford and family
Anna (Offley) Brewer
Mercy Brewer (daughter
    of Thomas Brewer
    and Anna Offley)

Thomas Brewer
William and Mary Brewster &
    children (Jonathan, Patience,
    Fear, Love, Wrestling)
Lord Burghley
Printer Walter Burre
Ambassador Carleton
Catherine Carver
John Carver
Marie (de Lannoy) Carver
Richard Clyfton
Professor Clusius
Pilot Robert Coppin
John Coprario
Master Cushman and family

Sir William Davison,
  Secretary of State
Robert Dudley, the
  Earl of Leicester
Andrewe Driver (apprentice
  to Nicholas Okes)
Queen Elizabeth l
Samuel Fuller
  (Deacon) and family
Adryaen Gerrits
Hugh Goodyear
Benjamin Grendon
The Hickmans
Jan van Hout
Jan Sebastiansz. van Hout
King James l
William Jepson
Francis Johnson
George Johnson and father
Master of Ship Christopher
  Jones- of the *Mayflower*
Jean de Lalaing
Master Jean de Lecluse
Alexander Leighton
Queen Mary of Scotland
Christopher Martin
Goodman Masterson
Tobias Matthew
Prince Maurits
Secretary Robert Naunton
The Offley family (Robert)

Nicholas Okes** see note
  below, in Fiction
William of Orange
Jan Jansz Orlers- nephew
  of Jan van Hout
Doctor Paaw
Edward Pickering
Professor Polyander
John Reynoldes
Master of Ship Reynoldes-
  of the *Speedwell*
Prudence (Grendon) Reynoldes
John Robinson and family
Sir Edwin Sandys
Gertie Savore
Matthew Slade
John Smyth
Myles Standish
Sabine Staresmore
Daniel Studley
Issack de Syde
Roger Symonson
Master van Thorenvliet
Giles Thorp
Sir Francis Walsingham
Samuell Watson (apprentice
  to Nicholas Okes)
Roger Wilson
Thomas Weston
Sir Wolstenhome
The Wood family

FICTION

Anne (servant to Brewster family)

Rose Brewer, married to
Nicholas, becoming Rose Okes

Master and Mistress
Burton & family

Catherine (servant to
Brewster family)

Daniel Greene

Hendrijcke (servant to John
and Marie Carver)

Goodman Hollis

Samuel Horn (brewer and
neighbor to Master Okes)

John (Post Carrier)

Katherine (servant
to Okes family)

Margaret (servant
to Okes family)

Henry Mercer

Hugh Mercer (son
of Henry Mercer)

Elizabeth Okes* In fact, the first
wife of Edward Winslow was
named Elizabeth Barker

Nicholas Okes** (Actual
Printer documented in
historical records for this
time period, although not
enough facts available about
his life and family to be listed
entirely as 'Fact')

Richard (servant
to Thomas Brewer)

Robert and Catherine Okes
(parents of Nicholas Okes)

Rose Okes, daughter of Rose
and Nicholas Okes

Sarah (Mercer)

Master Printer Thomas Sayer

Master Matthew Sumner
(tribute to Sting- Gordon
Matthew Sumner)

Master Sutton

Warder Thorpe

George Turner

16th/17th Century Glossary

Regarding spelling and capitalization in the seventeenth century, the rules were more flexible. The writer would spell as the word sounded to them, and capitalize as they desired. For example, the city of Leyden is often spelled with a 'y' in the 17th century, while today we use an 'i'.

In the glossary below, I have noted many terms associated with clothing. The value of the average person's wardrobe accounted for about seventy percent of the worth of their possessions. When admiring Avercamp's painting on the cover of this book, notice the differences among the people and what they are wearing, and how this reveals their level of wealth, or lack therof. When packing for the journey to the New World, one's entire wardrobe would be brought, with no regular source of textiles available on the other side.

Aforesaid - *adj.* previously mentioned.

Anew - *adj.* once more; over again, from the beginning.

Battledore and shuttlecock - *n.* a game/sport related to that of modern badminton.

Beggarly - *adj.* poor economic state, poverty stricken.

Betrothal, Betrothed - *n.* an agreement to marry, the person to whom one is engaged.

Betwixt - *adj.* between.

Biblio - *n.* Greek word for book.

Bier - *n.* a movable frame on which a coffin or a corpse is placed before burial or cremation or on which it is carried to the grave.

Bodies - *n.pl.* are the garment worn by women and girls directly over their smock, enclosing 'the body' in the sense of 'the torso'. The minimal version covers the ribcage, with shoulder straps to hold in place; it acts like a modern push-up or sports bra. The more elaborate version has sleeves, sometimes detachable. The bodies are normally stiffened in some way, either lightly (with cord) or more stiffly (with whalebone). They are closed by lacing, mostly in front, but sometimes behind (for small children and for women with enough servants). The name comes from 'a pair of bodies', meaning the two stiffened shapes (front and back).

Breeches - *n.pl.* were the knee-length trousers or pants worn by men. Most breeches were made of wool, varying from thick unlined woolens for laborers to fine shining broadcloth for rich men. Summer breeches might be made of linen, and the very rich would wear silk.

Bugle - *n.* a type of horn. In this case, the instrument used to sound the arrival of the post carrier.

Cager - *N.* actual name of one of the small ships traveling between Amsterdam and Leyden in the 17th century. The pronunciation is something like ka-a-her, with a prolonged *a* and a throat-scraping for the *h*.

Caudle - *n.* a drink (as for invalids) usually of warm ale or wine mixed with bread or gruel, eggs, sugar, and spices.

Cloak - *n.* a loose and sleeveless outer garment, like a cape.

Coif - *n.* a close-fitting cap made of white or naturally-colored linen, sometimes embroidered.

Cutpurse - *n.* a thief.

Damloper - *N.* actual name of one of the small ships traveling between Amsterdam and Leyden in the 17th century.

Daymare - *n.* a horrible or frightening vision experienced during the day.

Doff - *v.* take off or raise (one's hat) as a greeting or token of respect.

Doublet - *n.* In 1620, the doublet is the short jacket worn by men, with its typical waist tabs and the many tiny buttons up the center front. It originated in the Middle Ages as the lined and padded garment worn under plate armor, hence the name ('doublé' = French for 'made with a lining').

Draughts - *n.* draughts or checkers is a group of strategy board games for two players which involve diagonal moves of uniform game pieces and mandatory captures by jumping over opponent pieces.

Farthing - *adj.* one-quarter; as in, a farthing of an hour.

Fortnight - *n.* a period of two weeks.

Fuller's Earth - *n.* any fine-grained, naturally occurring earthy substance that has a substantial ability to adsorb impurities or coloring bodies from fats, grease, or oils. Its name originated with the textile industry, in which textile workers (or fullers) cleaned raw wool by kneading it in a mixture of water and fine earth that adsorbed oil, dirt, and other contaminants from the fibers.

Fustian - *n.* a twilled fabric with a linen or cotton warp and low-quality woolen weft, with a very short nap.

Garret - *n.* a top-floor or attic room, typically small and sometimes with sloped ceilings.

Garter - *n.* the strip of fabric wrapped around the stocking top to keep the stocking up (as elastic was not yet invented). Though wide silk satin ribbons were sometimes used by the rich, garters were typically about an inch wide and either woven as a narrow band, or knitted. They were often embroidered.

Gentry - *n.* people of good social position; the class of people just below the nobility.

Girdle - *n.* a belt.

Goedemorgen - *n.* Good morning, in Dutch.

Goodman/Goodwife - *N.* a term of civility and respect, given to a married man or woman associated with the middle class.

Gout - *n.* a disease in which defective metabolism of uric acid causes arthritis, especially in the smaller bones of the feet, deposition of chalkstones, and episodes of acute pain.

Kolf - *n.* (Dutch word for club); a sport with characteristics of golf and ice hockey.

Libels - *n.* a published false statement that is damaging to a person's reputation.

Master/Mistress - *N.* a term of civility and respect, given to a married man or woman associated with the middle class and higher.

Mayhaps - *adv.* perhaps.

May Pole - *n.* A maypole is a tall wooden pole erected as a part of various European folk festivals, around which a maypole dance often takes place. The festivals may occur on May Day (May 1) or Pentecost (Whitsun), although in some countries it is instead erected at Midsummer.

Minister - *n.* a religious leader; Minister Robinson administered the sacraments of baptism and communion to his separated (from the Church of England) English congregation seeking refuge in Leyden.

Muff - *n.* a tube made of fur or other warm material into which the hands are placed for warmth.

Pall - *n.* a cloth spread over a coffin, hearse, or tomb.

Petticoat - *n.* for 17th century and the group depicted in this novel, a skirt, typically ankle-length and made of wool. Wool is a versatile material, providing warmth in the winter, and cool enough for the summer. It is also water repellant, stain resistant, and does not burn easily, so it is safe in working around the hearth. Petticoats would have been colored- and for our group, colors like red, yellow, blue, green, gray, and brown would have been some of the many options. Pockets were separate items, in the form a flat bag sewn on a tape, hanging around the waist, and accessed through slits in the petticoat.

Pillon saddle - *adv.* sidesaddle is a form of equestrianism that uses a type of saddle which allows a rider (usually female) to sit aside rather than astride an equine.

Pillowbeer - *n.* a pillowcase.

Pipkin - *n.* an earthenware cooking pot used for cooking over indirect heat from coals or a wood fire. They were not held in direct flame which would crack the ceramic.

Poppet - *n.* a doll; also: a term of endearment.

Pottage - *n.* a meal cooked in a pot, which could consist of vegetables, meat, grains, herbs, fruit, and spices. In today's kitchen you might call this a thick soup or stew.

Potentate - *n.* a monarch or ruler, especially an autocratic one.

Recusant - *n.* an individual who refused to attend services of the Church of England.

Salve - *n.* an ointment used to promote healing of the skin or as protection

Sexton - *n.* a person who looks after a church and churchyard, sometimes acting as bell-ringer and formerly as a gravedigger.

Shirt - *n.* a man's undergarment, knee-length and long-sleeved, worn next the skin. It might be made of hemp or unbleached linen for the very poor, but the typical material was white (bleached) linen.

Shroud - *n.* the sheet in which a dead person is wrapped for burial.

Smock - *n.* a woman's undergarment, calf-length or longer and long-sleeved, worn next to the skin. It might be made of hemp or unbleached linen for the very poor, but the typical material was white (bleached) linen.

Spires - *n.* a tall, acutely pointed pyramidal roof or roof-like construction upon a tower, roof, etc. a similar construction forming the upper part of a steeple.

Surplice - *n.* a loose white linen vestment varying from hip-length to calf-length, worn by clergy.

Transept - *n.* (in a cross-shaped church) either of the two parts forming the arms of the cross shape, projecting at right angles from the nave.

Turret - *n.* a small tower on top of a larger tower or at the corner of a building or wall, typically of a castle or church.

Verger - *n.* an official in a church who acts as a caretaker and attendant.

Waistcoat - *n.* A garment for the upper body, worn between the shirt (men) or smock (women) and the outer clothing, for warmth. Early waistcoats are pull-over garments, but by 1620 they were mostly open in front, and closed with ties or hooks. In this book, I use this term in association with female clothing. There were waistcoats for all seasons and all budgets, lined or unlined, made of linen, of mixed fabrics like fustian or linsey-woolsey, of wool or even of silk.

Walloon - *N.* A French-speaking Reformed Protestant, also referred to as a Huguenot.

Yeoman warder - *n.* a prison guard at the Tower of London.

Yoke - *n.* the heavy wooden implement laid across the neck of oxen who pull a cart or plough. Used metaphorically for something oppressive or burdensome.

Suggested Reading

Bangs, Jeremy Dupertuis. *Strangers and Pilgrims, Travellers and Sojourners; Leiden and the Foundations of Plymouth Plantation.* General Society of Mayflower Descendants, 2009.

Bogels, T.S.J.G. *Govert Basson, Printer, Bookseller, Publisher. Leiden 1612-1630.* Nieuwkoop De Graaf Publishers, 1992.

Bradford, William. *Of Plymouth Plantation.* The Franklin Library, 1983.

Cressey, David. *Trumpets from the Tower: English Puritan Printing in The Netherlands, 1600-1640.* Brill, 1993.

Cressey, David. *Birth, Marriage & Death...Ritual, Religion, and the Life Cycle in Tudor and Stuart England.* OUP, 1997.

Harris, J. Rendel. *The Pilgrim Press: A Bibliographical Historical Memorial of the Books Printed at Leyden by the Pilgrim Fathers (Classic Reprint).* Fb&c Limited, 2015.

Kardux, Joke and van de Bilt, Eduard. *Newcomers in an old city, The American Pilgrims in Leiden, 1609-1620.* Uitgeverij Burgersdijk & Niermans, 2001.

Lindley, Phillip. *Gainsborough Old Hall.* G.W. Belton Ltd., 1991.

Markham, Gervase. *The English Housewife.* McGill-Queen's University Press, 1994.

Myers, Robin. *Stationers' Company (London, England). Records of the Worshipful Company of Stationers, 1554-1920.* Chadwyck-Healey, 1985.

Touring the Novel's Path

England

1. Tower of London, London | www.hrp.org.uk
2. Hampton Court Palace | www.hrp.org.uk
3. St. Paul's Cathedral | www.stpauls.co.uk
4. General walk about Fleet Street
5. River cruise down the Thames to Greenwich
6. Scrooby, St. Wilfrid's Church | www.stwilfridschurch.org
7. Walk the old Great North Road and see the remains of Scrooby Manor from a distance
8. Gainsborough Old Hall (a good indication of what Scrooby Manor looked like) | www.gainsborougholdhall.com
9. All Saints' Church, Babworth (where Richard Clyfton preached)
10. St. Helena's Church, Austerfield (birthplace of William Bradford)
11. Bassetlaw Museum | www.bassetlawmuseum.org.uk
12. Boston Guildhall | www.mybostonuk.com/bostonguildhall/museum
13. The Box Museum | www.theboxplymouth.com

The list above highlights the path I took during a research trip in 2009– there are additional places to visit, such as Boston, Dartmouth, and Plymouth, England. With many of the 2020 celebratory events rescheduled for 2021, visit www.mayflower400uk.org for additional touring options.

The Netherlands

Leiden | www.visitleiden.nl | www.leiden400.nl
1. Leiden American Pilgrim Museum | www.leidenamericanpilgrimmuseum.org
2. Weaver's House Museum | www.wevershuis.nl
3. Pieterskerk | www.pieterskerk.com | www.villarameau.nl (magical accommodations!)
4. Hooglandsekerk | www.hooglandsekerk.com
5. Site of the Green Close, modern day Jean Pesijnhofje
6. Town Hall, Stadhuisplein 1
7. De Burcht
8. University of Leiden, Botanical Garden | www.hortusleiden.nl
9. Museum De Lakenhal | www.lakenhal.nl
10. Stroll down the Rapenburg Canal

Amsterdam   Rijksmuseum | www.rijksmuseum.nl

Delfshaven | www.pilgrimfatherschurch.com

USA

Plymouth/Duxbury, Massachusetts | www.plymouth400inc.org
1. Plimoth Patuxet | www.plimoth.org
2. Pilgrim Hall Museum | www.pilgrimhall.org
3. Alden House | www.alden.org
4. Duxbury Rural and Historical Society | www. duxburyhistory.org

www.beforethemayflower.com

About the Author

A Williams College graduate, the author is a former historical interpreter in the seventeenth-century English Village of Plimoth Colony at Plimoth Patuxet (formerly Plimoth Plantation). While she was at Williams, a course in seventeenth-century Dutch art spawned an interest in the Golden Age of Dutch history, ultimately connecting her to the group of English who separated from the King's Church and sought refuge in Leyden, in the Low Countries, from 1609-1620. Only a fraction of that congregation sailed on the *Mayflower*, but their path is remarkable, deserving its own place in history. The author resides in Duxbury, Massachusetts, USA with her husband, twins, and two dogs, Marco and Polo.

A view of the Hooglandsekerk from the hillside by the Burcht, July 2017, Leiden, the Netherlands.

Made in the USA
Middletown, DE
08 November 2022

14275539R00239